# THE YEAR OF LOVING

Traci L. Slatton

parvati
press

**The Year of Loving**

Quotation from "When the Past Is Present" are taken from Richo, David. *When The Past Is Present: Healing the Emotional Wounds That Sabotage Our Relationships.* Boston, MA: Shambhala Publications, 2008. Print. pp.107-108.

Frida Kahlo quotes taken from Herrera, Hayden. *Frida: A Biography of Frida Kahlo.* New York: Harper Perennial, 2002. Print

Cover designed by Brandi Doane McCann www.ebook-coverdesigns.com

Published by Parvati Press, New York, NY www.parvatipress.com

Visit the author website: www.tracilslatton.com

Library of Congress Control Number: 2016916533

Print ISBN: 978-1-942523-06-2
EBook ISBN: 978-1-942523-07-9

"Even staying with our doubt, despondency, and utter vulnerability makes them all legitimate landscapes of our psychic life.

"Our practice is to hold and relate to our feelings as *teachings* about enlightenment. The teachings emerge both from what incites our feelings and from our ways of responding. Sadness teaches us about loss and impermanence. Anger shows us how we react to unfairness. Fear teaches us about how we handle danger and threat. Joy teaches us about how we celebrate life."

Dave Richo, *When the Past Is Present: Healing the Emotional Wounds that Sabotage Our Relationships*

For Jane Ely, with love

The Year of Loving

# CHAPTER ONE

IN THE BEGINNING, THERE was my bohemian poet mom and square attorney dad, who met at a concert and shared only three interests in common: rock and roll, Renaissance art, and me, Sarah Melissa Paige, conceived in the backseat of a Chevy Impala to the strains of Deep Purple.

How do I know this? My Jewish mom never had a clear sense of boundaries. She would say the most outrageous things, not just to me but to anyone, at any time. "Sarah was a vaginal birth and I nursed her until she was eleven months old," she would tell a store clerk, while I winced. It was one of her lovable quirks. That's what my Scotch-Irish/Cherokee dad would say, with a small smile.

I still miss them every day. Their death was one of the great losses of my life. Painter Frida Kahlo, my soul sister because of her mixed heritage and her devotion to art, had remarked, "There were two great accidents in my life. One was the trolley and the other was Diego. Diego was by far the worst." Sometimes I felt that way about the two great catastrophes of my life: my parents' deaths and my marriage to my first husband George Calhoun, the rich WASP with the perpetual sneer of condescension. George would never forgive me for the humiliation of my leaving him for an impecunious artist.

But let's move past George. Let's go to the end of my second marriage, to the realist painter Clifton Perini.

I was in my gallery in Chelsea, working on an article for *American Artist* magazine. I was trying to explain why excellence, beauty, and the artist's skill were more important than the overvalued and empty wasteland of post-modernism. You can see I'm a woman with strong opinions.

Rosa, my assistant, came in from the front room.

"Sarah, you hear the printer?" she asked, pausing to check her makeup in the reflection of a glass frame. She dabbed at her mascara with her pinky. "A fax came in."

"Something from Clif's lawyer. Or George with a snotty note about not being able to reach me via email," I guessed, in an absent tone. "Nothing I want to see." Will Michelangelo's *Doni Tondo* illustrate my point about the supreme rapture of the human form? I smiled at her.

She sparkled back. "Weren't you waiting for something?"

"Alex's meds," I remembered. I pushed back from my desk and hurried over to the printer, where a prescription lay in the out box.

"Want me to run it in?" Rosa asked.

"I'll go," I answered. I had been writing for two hours, and it was a cold, drizzly day with no foot traffic, so no customers to come in and peruse the beautiful representational paintings I sold. April is the cruelest month. So, on the flimsiest of whims, without bothering to shrug on my coat, I headed out into my life.

The pharmacy was located only a block up on Eighth Avenue. I banged into the door with my umbrella. A gust of wind caught me just at that moment and blew the umbrella inside out and I tumbled through the door askew, my umbrella struggling like a trapped animal and my Jimmy Choos sliding out from under me as if I'd skidded on a candy bar wrapper.

'Cartwheel' would be an accurate description. Which explains why my linen skirt was up around my waist like a belt.

"Now that's an entrance," a man said, his deep voice amused. He bent down and offered his hand. I fought my linen skirt down to cover everything that was on display. It's not like I wear shorts over my thongs —which had twisted up inside my lady parts. Leaving everything on display. I groaned. He cleared his throat. "Don't worry, I'm a doctor."

"You're not my doctor," I said, furiously, batting his hand away. I managed to scramble to my knees and yank my skirt to a more appropriate semblance of coverage. What is it about linen? It goes out of its way to be uncooperative. I have a theory that clothing designers have a hidden agenda to torture women. Of course, it served me right for wearing linen in April. I just loved the navy blue, forties' era suit I'd found in a consignment shop on Greenwich Avenue. *Note to self: check out usability standards before purchasing vintage clothes.*

That blasted umbrella was determined to thwart my efforts, so I dropped it and pulled myself up via the shelves of cough suppressants and analgesics.

"Glad that's so," the man murmured.

Was he still ogling me? I didn't answer because I'd managed to sweep the display of Robitussin onto the ground. I bent over to pick them up.

"Ahem," the man said, and his rich voice thickened with the effort not to laugh. I glanced and he was pointing.

At my behind.

The back of my skirt was still bunched up around my waist. I'd stuck my ass in his face.

I grasped my skirt by both sides and jerked downward as hard as I could. The waist button popped off. Luckily the zipper stayed firmly sealed, or everything I have would have been revealed. Again.

The man laughed outright.

I held the skirt closed with one hand while I shook the other index finger accusingly in his face. "Listen, you!" I started, accusingly.

He blinked, bemused and amused. He was tall and toned, with fine, poreless skin, cropped black hair, and the kind of substantial nose that certain men carry off very well indeed.

It struck me how silly I looked. I broke up with laughter.

After a few seconds, he took off his glasses, rubbed the bridge of his nose, and blinked a few times, laughing with me. "It's not often you find a beautiful woman who can laugh at herself."

"Yeah, well, if I couldn't, I'd have been in big trouble a long time ago," I murmured. He had nice dark eyes. There weren't enough crow's feet or the lines of laughter and sadness that reflect the gravity of a life fully lived to put him in his forties. I smiled. "Thanks for the compliment."

For a moment, the most delicious, open softness encompassed us. We smiled at each other a little sheepishly.

Then I remembered why I was there. A new prescription for my younger daughter Alexandra. Maybe this one would be the magic bullet that kept her from shooting herself in the foot. I desperately wanted it to be, and I could only pray that it was, as I'd been praying for the last few years, watching Alex get herself tangled up with one bad decision after another and get herself thrown out of two schools. She was now at Devon Town, the private school of absolute last resort in Manhattan. If she could graduate, she could still attend a decent college.

I shrugged and waved to the hot man who was at least ten years younger than me and I walked back to the pharmacist. I handed him the scrip.

Katsu, the pharmacist, an old Japanese guy who came to every show at my gallery for the free food and drinks, shuffled unblinkingly off to the back as if he'd never seen me before in his life.

I sighed.

"Excuse me, miss." It was the hot man, looking carefully at my left hand, where I wasn't wearing a ring.

I perked up.

The skin stretching across the cheekbones of his angular face deepened in color. He cleared his throat. "Would you like to get a cup of coffee?"

"Sure," said Katsu, who had returned. "Venti half-caf cappuccino, wet and fat-free. Would you get me a scone, too?"

"Not you," the young doctor said.

Katsu shrugged and then looked at me. "I have it in stock. Come back in an hour." He turned back to the doctor. "Hey, doc, just coffee, or will you buy me dinner, too?"

The doctor grimaced and followed me as I walked toward the front of the store. He touched my elbow lightly as I reached for the door. "About that cup of coffee?"

I straightened myself, which was hard to do with one hand, because the other hand was still gripping the waistband of my skirt, to keep it closed. "You don't have to buy me coffee just because I stuck my ass in your face."

He looked embarrassed and I noted again how smooth and silken his skin was. I remembered being 38. From the vantage point of 48, it seemed innocent and hopeful.

He said, "This is not about your ass."

"You don't like my ass?"

He flushed and looked about twelve years old. "Your ass is very nice. That's my professional opinion."

"You think I'm a *professional*?" I demanded, in a tone of outrage.

He flushed a brighter shade of red. "Coffee. Just a cup of coffee."

"You're sweet." I sighed while I smiled. I had baggage older than he was, and I'm not talking about the dinged-up Tumi cases I take to Europe on scouting trips.

"But …"

He had straightened his back and shoulders and was listening hard—the antennae were practically standing straight up atop his head.

"It's flattering, but I don't think so. Thank you anyway."

---

A few minutes later, torn and bedraggled, I stood in the door of my gallery.

Rosa glided over to me. She's of Mexican and Finnish descent, an actress and a dancer with cascades of black hair and striking pale blue eyes. She's fresh and juicy and sassy. I was newly aware of every wrinkle on my face and every dimple on the back of my thigh. With her lissome dancer's body and face still unlined in her late twenties, Rosa was a better fit for Dr. Gorgeous than I could ever be. What the hell was he thinking, asking me out for coffee?

"Why are you staring at me?" Rosa demanded. She narrowed her big vivid eyes at me. "What happened to your skirt?"

"My umbrella," I muttered.

"OK, don't tell me."

"I tripped over my umbrella," I amended, not knowing that was when I woke up in a dark woods in the middle of the journey of my life. There's a flux to the divine comedy of life, the way it empties out, grows full, and then cracks to empty out again, so that fullness can be reborn. I still don't know if my heart can stretch to encompass all the shattering. But, in that moment, I was just thinking that I should have accepted that cup of coffee. I think I would have enjoyed it.

"Strip it off, Mamacita, my sewing kit is in my purse and there's twenty minutes before I leave for my audition." She waggled her fingers at me.

"I'll take it off in the back office," I said. I was still clutching the skirt to keep it closed properly. "I've been naked in public enough for one day. And thank you."

# CHAPTER TWO

AT FIVE O'CLOCK I went home. Alex was out so I changed into my yoga clothes. They were stinky but that just made me feel virtuous: it meant I practiced a lot. I had to work off the red wine and chocolate somehow.

I was en route to my favorite yoga class—not too easy, not too hard, and only an hour long—when my best friend Trudi called.

"Why are you on my mind?" Trudi asked.

I could feel her blonde head pressing into the phone, willing me to tell her why she was thinking of me. Something was up with me; she could feel it in the ether. She knew me too well. Despite that, she still loved me, which was a real plus in her favor. "What do you think of younger men?"

"You're a cougar now? Isn't that the term?" Trudi asked. She's been married for thirty-five years to the same college sweetheart, an American in her hometown of London on his spring break, all those decades ago. I envied her dedication.

And her luck.

After two failed marriages, I could definitively state there was luck involved in marriage. Trudi had married a sweetheart who remained a sweetheart and who didn't suddenly sprout a grinning narcissistic head at every turn. That was a feat I had never accomplished.

My third husband, if I ever went there and I wasn't sure I wanted to, would have "I am not a narcissist" tattooed on his chest.

"Cougar," I said, wrinkling my nose. I picked up the pace so I could make it to class.

"Do men under thirty have anything to say?" Trudi asked.

"Not under thirty!" I snorted. "Anyone under thirty is a match for

Dani." My eldest daughter, the superstar, beautiful and talented, troubled in her own way.

"Has Dani been in contact?"

"The same," I said. Which was to say, not at all. My oldest daughter had decided that I was the diabolical cause of every bump on the road of her perfect life. It was a decision for which her rich father rewarded her with cars and fancy trips.

An on-going heartache. Another one. I just wanted the troubles with my children to resolve so we could have normal, loving, mother-daughter relationships. I was beginning to despair of that.

"I'm going to talk to that girl," Trudi was saying.

"I wouldn't do that, Trudi. She's decided you're almost as bad as me," I warned. Alex had told me that Dani didn't like Trudi anymore; there was no reason for Dani's feelings other than Trudi's closeness to me. I wouldn't have passed it on, but Trudi was strong enough and close enough to me, to handle it.

"Has she now? Isn't that sweet," Trudi's British accent grew more acerbic. "Anyway, you're the one I need to speak to. Where are you right now?"

"Walking to yoga."

"Call you later." She hung up.

*Cougar?* Ick.

But there must have been something in my vibe, because the young guy behind me gave me a smile that looked like a wide, upside-down crescent. I was in downward-facing-dog, peering through my legs at him while he was still in upward-facing-dog. These dogs, sometimes they just didn't synchronize.

It was intriguing; he was cute in a stocky, curly-blond-hair-with-big biceps way.

At first, I wasn't sure that he was aiming his game at me. But he lingered in warrior two to give me an appraising look when I was reversing direction with the rest of the class. Our eyes met. His gleamed and then I was sure.

Two young guys in one day?

Was I suddenly emitting a new kind of pheromone? That could only be trouble. I darted out after class so I wouldn't have to find out.

———⌒———

Trudi was out when I called her back to find out what she wanted to talk to me about, so I phoned a recalcitrant artist in Santa Fe who wanted to price his landscapes at twice what they were worth. I ordered pad thai delivery via computer. Then I was finally curled up in bed, reading a Sotheby's report on my iPad and listening to an *Ancient Aliens* show on TV.

It was nine pm and there was no sign of Alexandra. She alternated each week between her father's place and mine, and it was her week with me. She was supposed to check in immediately after school. She hadn't.

I'd promised to take her to Café Lalo for hot chocolate and a lush dessert, but she'd forgotten those plans.

I texted her but she didn't answer.

Ultimately, I wasn't even sure she'd gone to school that day. The school hadn't called me, but Alex was more than capable of sending them an email from my account to excuse her absence. She'd done it before, several times. That's why I'd shut down that email account.

As if on cue, the phone rang. George's number flashed across the top of the TV screen. I let the machine pick up.

"Sarah, it's irresponsible of you to change your email without leaving a forwarding address," George said, through the tightly clenched jaws of the tightly clenched mouth of the tightly clenched New England Episcopalian. "I can't believe that you insist on acting with such thoughtlessness when I have a regular need to contact you due to our shared parenting responsibilities." He went on and on.

Groucho limped to the side of the bed. Whining, he laid his muzzle near my foot. I helped him onto the mattress and then turned the TV up louder.

"In view of the love and concern each parent has for the child …"

George was quoting a section of our divorce contract. He was an attorney and he'd memorized the contract. I turned up the TV louder and focused on the speculation that ETs had influenced Leonardo da Vinci. It was more interesting than the legalese of my parental obligations, as if I didn't already know them.

Finally, the voice on the machine stopped. Bad as it was, it could have been worse; it could have been George's wife Katherine on the phone. George just wanted to annihilate me. Katherine wanted to prove she was superior to me. That made her a lot more vicious.

What she didn't know was that I had StatCounter recording hits on my gallery website blog. I knew from the IP address that traveled back and forth from Manhattan to Newport, Rhode Island—where the Calhouns had their beach-side compound—that either she or George were on my blog every other day. Perhaps it was her, because even when we were married George had never found me interesting enough to warrant that kind of attention.

I lowered the volume on the television set and went back to the report on my iPad, because while Leonardo's interactions with the Pleiadians were fascinating, Sotheby's sales figures were more pertinent. Not that it was a published report. An artist who felt wronged by Sotheby's sent me all the confidential reports his cousin who worked there could lay hands on.

Hell hath no fury like an artist scorned …

But they're not angry when they leave you. Therein lay my one and only successful manipulation in life: I'd managed to get Clif to think it was his idea to end our marriage. I still couldn't believe I'd pulled it off. I expected that I'd be supporting him for the rest of my life, all for the pleasure of him withholding sex.

Was it bad luck, or had I just been that stupid in my choice of men?

I couldn't blame my childhood, which had been fine, no better and certainly no worse than most. I patted Groucho and focused again on the report. There had to be a way for me to increase sales in my gallery. Because if I didn't I was going out of business.

I was dozing when Alex came in. She stood in my doorway, standing back so I wouldn't catch the stench of pot on her clothes. It wafted in anyway. She weaved a little, and her big blue eyes were glassy and unfocused, drops of Visine still brimming on her lower lids. Her fair hair lay in tangles over her shoulders. Her clothes that I'd washed so carefully were dirty and bedraggled. Her button-fly jeans were misbuttoned. Had she been screwing some boy in the park? Screwing a drug dealer? Alex liked to put one over on the pharmacy.

*Did I want to know?*

"I'm home," she snarled. She turned and stomped back to the kitchen. I sighed and got out of bed. I caught a glimpse of the kitchen wall clock: two o'clock. On a school night.

"Alex, we had plans you may remember. Also, I expect you to answer my texts," I said quietly.

"Mom, quit being such a fucking bitch!" Alex screamed. "This is why Dani and Katherine and even Dani's shrink say you're so toxic, and why

Dani doesn't want anything to do with you!"

"That's right, quote your ridiculous airhead stepmother to me," I snapped back. "Calling me toxic is really going to solve your problems!"

"You're my problem!" She grabbed a box of cookies out of the fridge, turned on her heel, and stalked back to her bedroom. I followed, watching her shoulders sway. She'd once been a ranked swimmer and still had the strong torso and lithe limbs of the athlete she'd been before she'd dropped out of everything to pursue drugs and boys.

I took a breath and struggled to contain myself. "Alexandra, we had plans, and you have to be responsible and let me know that you won't be keeping them. Also, you have school tomorrow. Two o'clock is a weekend curfew—"

"Mom, don't text me when I'm with my friends!" Alex shrieked. "You're such a bitch!" She slammed the door in my face.

*Charming.*

Did anyone know better how to hurt a woman than her daughters?

I went back to bed but even ruminating on how good it felt to be asked out for coffee by a hot young guy didn't help me fall asleep faster.

# CHAPTER THREE

THE NEXT MORNING I called, texted, and emailed Alex's therapist, Dr. Bailey. Yes, it was overkill, but I was in that place. Any parent in their right mind would be after seeing Alex last night.

Bailey got right back to me.

I didn't remember holding a gun to Alex's head to force her out of control but clearly, that's what Dr. Bailey assumed I had done.

I had to acknowledge that Dr. Bailey cared about my daughter. He was always there for her, and he'd spent countless hours on the phone with me. He had been Alex's therapist for the last five years and maybe, if it wasn't for him, she'd be turning tricks and shooting heroin.

But then maybe, despite him, she already was. I'd read about the heroin epidemic and I was terrified that Alex was dabbling in it.

Dr. Bailey just didn't get it about mothers; how we'd do anything to help our kids and still sometimes make mistakes. How sometimes our best wasn't good enough. How we were expected to be perfect icons of unconditional love, yet were helpless in the face of entitled friends and a culture that idolized easy gain, quick fixes, entitlement, and recreational drugs—the lowest common denominator.

How much harder it was to parent a child when their father denied there was a problem and told the kid, "Your mother is crazy and her rules don't apply at my house." How hard it was to get a kid to stop wasting her life on drugs, when the kid heard the dad speak fondly of being wasted in college, and the stepmother spoke openly about smoking dope, presenting herself as a hipster because of it. You'd think an old money, Yankee family would be more interested in propriety but then, George was always one to thumb his nose at his parents. I was sure that was why he'd married me in the first place. There was no better way to yank his parents' chain than to marry a crossbreed half-Jew, half-Baptist, part-Cherokee.

But hip stepmothers weren't required for a smirky, wink-wink at out-of-control drug use. Didn't every movie and TV show have a scene where the protagonist smoked a joint to prove how cool and hip and rebellious the character was? I was no prude, but watching teenagers wreck themselves on drugs made me wish Hollywood could show a tiny bit of inventiveness—not to say responsibility—and come up with some other way to prove that film heroes were fine human beings.

Dr. Bailey and I had our requisite argument about how Alex was doing.

I said, "Her grades are bad. She's doing no extracurricular activities and she's been kicked out of two schools. There are pornographic Facebook pictures of her," I reminded him. High as a kite, Alex had stripped and pole-danced at a party and her friends had documented the event. I took a breath. "She needs to do something other than get high with her friends so that she has a story to tell colleges when she applies."

He said, "Alex has a story to tell. There's no correlation between good grades and success in life …" Etc, etc. He would do anything to avoid admitting that Alex was in a downward spiral, anything to avoid admitting that, if his methods were working, maybe she wouldn't be in that downward spiral.

Then again, Dr. Bailey's bills were paid by George, so what was Bailey going to admit to me?

Finally, I said something he could hear. "Look, Bailey, she's not been responding to the meds. She's still hyper-irritable with those screaming binges."

"Is she under pressure at home?"

Yes, she was under pressure at home. Under pressure to act like a semi-civilized human being who would have to attend college so she could earn a living and support herself in the future. Under pressure not to document her every ruinous move and display it on the internet. But it would do no good to voice that.

Besides, Dr. Bailey didn't live with her. He didn't wait up nights, hoping she'd come back safely and not get mugged or worse out on the streets of New York City. He didn't field calls from school guidance counselors, teachers, and Kate Osborne's mother concerned because "Alex has vomited and passed out in my living room."

He hadn't been there when I went with her to a clinic to get her chlamydia treated. He wasn't going to have to bail her out or accompany her to another clinic when she got pregnant or got hepatitis C or AIDS. He wasn't going to be living with her or supporting her when she couldn't hold a job as an adult. He had no accountability for my daughter's safety or her future.

Dr. Bailey simply saw her once or twice a week for pay for forty minutes at a time, in the artificial laboratory of his office. But in his eyes and in the eyes of the courts, that made him an expert on the person I'd been caring for every second of every hour since she was born.

In his eyes, it gave him the right to undercut my moral authority with my children, and to teach Alex that only her feelings mattered, not anyone else's, and certainly not her mother's.

That was my angry self, and I was speaking directly to her: *I can't fight the system, screwed up as it is.*

But to Bailey I said, "We have the new prescription, but maybe it's time to start over from scratch. Have someone evaluate her for real; a lengthy evaluation by a psychiatrist who specializes in adolescent drug use."

That got his attention.

"She's only been seen a few times by the doctor associated with her outpatient drug rehab treatment."

*I thought the drug rehab helped her. Too bad George didn't; it's another thing he willfully refuses to address, like her promiscuity.*

I said, "You're right. I think the rehab doctor met her for fifteen minutes twice. Maybe it's time for her to get a clinical evaluation by someone who can spend some time with her."

"Let's see how the new meds work. If there's no improvement, we'll see about a new doctor."

Finally, a glimmer of hope. Maybe a new doctor would have a magical prescription for Alex, one that would avert the train wreck of her life.

———

That afternoon a gentleman of substance came into the gallery. I was in the back office staring at the balance sheet from my accountant, willing it to look different. Willing it to say something other than that I needed to sell some paintings quick. As in yesterday.

Five years ago, I came out of my marriage to George with a nest egg that I'd invested in the gallery. I was an art history major in college and I'd worked at galleries and auction houses as well as at the Frick. I thought I'd make a go at selling really beautiful art—not the pricey postmodern silliness that PhDs, tenured art professors, and most galleries tried to convince people was meaningful—and yes, I was with Clif. I wanted to help him sell his masterful paintings.

I fell in love with the genius and married the Peter Pan.

I didn't realize that trying to support Clif's career by showing his paintings, building his website, and writing a catalog of his work would translate into nearly full-time caretaking.

Rosa came in. She wore a knowing smile on her pretty face.

"Sarah, there's a man here. Freshen your lipstick, he wants to talk to *you*." She winked so I reached into my drawer for my Nars Dolce Vita.

Rosa patted my hair down where I'd been combing it up with my fingers while I glared at the balance sheet. She giggled at how some of my hair stood straight up on end, which was quite a feat, considering its length.

Her smile helped me put thoughts of bankruptcy, divorce, and a drug-addled daughter out of mind so I could interface with a potential client.

"Hi, I'm Sarah Paige, can I help you?" I asked cheerfully. A few small, figurative sculptures stood in the middle of the floor and I walked around them toward the man. I extended my hand.

He was in his late sixties, a silver fox; barrel-chested but in good shape beneath his unbuttoned herringbone overcoat. It wasn't rainy but it was cold like February. He straightened and smiled and shook my hand.

Nice blue eyes. A craggy, appealing face with lines that enhanced his natural authority. In a gravelly voice that made me think of 25-year-old scotch he said, "Hi, I'm Carl Hopkins. I heard you speak at that panel on modern classicism at the Salmagundi Club. I was impressed. I came to take a look-see at your gallery."

The salesperson in me took over, and I evaluated him as a potential customer: upscale clothes, wasn't that an Armani coat? Philippe Patek watch. He had taste and he had means. I gave him my biggest smile and calculated what I could sell him. Maybe the matching set of river nymphs on the north wall? They were some of Clif's finest, and I still loved them.

Hopkins burst out laughing. I must have looked perplexed.

"There are dollar signs flashing in your eyes, ka-chink, ka-chink."

"Oh no," I covered my face with my hands and huddled my chin into my chest. "I'm so sorry. Is it that obvious?" I straightened. "I'm so sorry!"

"No offense taken." His eyes were merry. "I gather the recession has had an impact on your gallery."

"Why do you think I speak at those panels? It's not for the good food they're serving."

He seemed about to say something but his face took on a guarded look. He shook his head once, almost imperceptibly. "Why don't you show me the pieces you were planning to try to sell me?"

"Really? You're OK with that?"

He touched my arm in a casual way. "Of course, that's why I'm here. Lead on."

"This way." I steered him toward the pair of river nymphs I had in mind. "Are you a member of the Salmagundi club?"

"Guest of a member," Hopkins said. "I was dating a woman who belonged and took a lot of classes there."

Past tense. He was single and didn't have to justify his purchases to a wife or girlfriend. Better and better.

"We have a beautiful selection of still lifes in right now, but since you attended the panel, I'm going to start with what's really special. Clifton Perini is the foremost practitioner of modern classicism, and these are two of his finest," I said, waving at the paintings.

They were big, oil-on-panels, each one of them forty inches by sixty-two inches. The one on the left had a standing figure: a smiling, red-haired woman. She was cuddling a wolf, and behind her stretched a cityscape that looked like something da Vinci would have painted if he'd seen skyscrapers. The one on the right showed a seated figure: a blonde woman with her face in her hands, a snake draped around her shoulders, and a similar background. They were mesmerizing, well-crafted, anatomically pluperfect, startlingly beautiful, and they alluded to secret passages through which the splendid energies of the cosmos poured into our world —typical Clifton Perini's.

I still admired his mastery even if I was glad to be divorcing him.

"A bit of the painter Odd Nerdrum in them, don't you think? But the mythic dimension is more pronounced," Hopkins murmured. He was taken by them, as was everyone who saw them.

"Impressive," I exclaimed. "You know your stuff!"

He made a funny gesture of acceptance with his eyebrows. "I'll take them."

"What?" I cried.

"Don't you want me to?"

"Yes, but—"

"But now you've changed your mind?" His face, in structure a patrician oval just a little soft in the jawline, wore that merry look again. His blue eyes crinkled in a very appealing way.

"No, of course, I haven't changed my mind." I paused. "But you didn't even ask how much they are."

"I can afford them, Sarah," he said, lowering his voice confidentially and squeezing my arm.

Now I was really torn. I didn't want to take advantage of this attractive, nice man, but I felt compelled to. How could I call myself a gallery owner if I didn't rip him off, at least a little bit? I could feel my business-self warring with my better self. I tried to effect a compromise. "I don't doubt you could afford anything you wanted to buy, but it wouldn't be right if we didn't negotiate at least a little bit."

He laughed outright again. I wasn't trying to be funny but he seemed highly entertained. When the laughter ended, he said, "Here's what we'll do. I'll give you my card. You'll bump up the price to what you think I'll pay, discount it back to what you're actually selling the paintings for, and then you'll send me an email. I'll have the funds wired into your account. You'll bring the paintings over and install them."

"That could work," I said cautiously, not daring to believe my dazzling good luck.

He nodded and took a card out of his coat pocket as if he'd had it ready. "Here's my card. My cell phone number is on the back."

I accepted it and held it with both hands and studied it. "Carl Hopkins, CEO of Hopkins Advantage Funds," I read. "Thank you very much, Mr. Hopkins."

"My pleasure, and call me Carl. They really are gorgeous," he said, looking at me and not at the paintings. I blushed, I couldn't help it. He smiled.

"It will be a pleasure to have them." Only then he did turn back to the paintings.

"I certainly hope so," I said awkwardly. I didn't know whether to hope that he was including me amongst the having or to be offended that he might be.

Moments later he shook my hand goodbye. He paused at the door.

"You'll do the installation, Sarah?"

"If you'd like, I can ask the artist," I offered.

"Isn't he your former husband?"

"It's cordial."

"No. I was planning to offer you a glass of wine when you come to do the installation, and I wouldn't want to waste a great Bordeaux on him." Carl's eyes looked warmly upon my face. Then he was gone.

"He bought the Perini's?" Rosa said, coming to stand beside me.

"Yes," I breathed. We watched through the windows as Hopkins strolled away.

"Does that mean we're not going out of business?" Rosa asked.

"Oh yeah!" I cried, and we held hands and did a wild half-tango, half funky chicken dance around the gallery.

# CHAPTER FOUR

I STOPPED FOR CHOCOLATES at the most upscale and over-priced candy boutique on the Upper West Side. I was going to buy a large box and eat every one of them. I couldn't wait.

Hazelnut, caramel nut noir, cinnamon praline, dark chocolate ganache, yum!

I wanted to celebrate the sale that would, miraculously, keep me in business when so many small galleries were closing. I liked red wine and champagne, but with an out-of-control kid around, I didn't like to have booze in the apartment.

Alex can't differentiate between a glass of wine with dinner and a full-on pot-and-pill-addled night of debauchery. I hated to drink in front of her; I could see the calculation in her eyes as she watched me. It was a set-up so she could call me a hypocrite when I confronted her about her constant drug use. She was always stoned on something, mostly marijuana and painkillers, although I was pretty sure she experimented with cocaine and hallucinogens, too. Whatever her friends were doing. Whatever anyone offered her.

A year ago, I found Alex getting high in her bedroom, blowing dirty gray smoke out her bathroom window. I said, "Alexandra, this is unacceptable."

"Everyone at school does it!" she screamed. "They all have parents who pretend they don't know. Why can't you be like them? Why do you have to be such a bitch?"

The parents in Manhattan private schools—gotta love 'em.

I'd put Alex in an outpatient teen drug rehab program, and she'd been clean for a while. But George refused to pay for the program and we were back in court for the nth time, where he twisted everything, in his George-like way, to make it sound as if I were arranging for her to find all the potheads and juvenile delinquents in the city.

As if she hadn't already found them.

George just never wanted to see what was really going on with Alex. He'd never truly bonded with her. It had all started at her birth. Dani was an adored oldest daughter but then George wanted a son—all of his brothers had sons. When I had Alex, I'd failed to provide one. His disappointment was plainly visible in the photographs from the hospital: George sat limply holding the infant Alexandra, who might as well have been a bag of apples. His face was bored, his gaze lost in space.

Then, years later, I went and left George for a penniless artist. None of his brothers were divorced. No one in the illustrious Calhoun family ever got divorced—until I left George. It set me up for a measure of retributory scorn that I could never have predicted.

Trudi was the one who kept me sane when George blamed me for Alex's problems, because blame solved everything. How convenient for him that I was the identified problem. It gave him complete absolution.

But I was being sarcastic again. I had to take my sarcastic self in hand.

Trudi was my lifeline during the worst of it with George and Alex and Dani. She'd been my lifeline since we met in graduate school. Trudi was a bit older than me, but she'd gone back to finish her master's. We bonded over our losses and a mutual love for the Victoria and Albert Museum in London. I figured she'd be my lifeline until we were little old widowed ladies living together, sharing a dozen cats and comparing broken hips.

I paid for the chocolate and stood by the window while I tore open the cellophane wrapper. Choices, choices … fresh coconut in white and dark chocolate; that was the ticket. I took the piece, held it close to my nose to breathe in the lush goodness, closed my eyes and dropped the rich splendor on my tongue. Everything else vanished. *Oh, God.*

Dimly, in the background, I heard the door open and close as another customer came in. One last swallow. Dreamily I opened my eyes.

"That must have been some piece of chocolate."

It was the young doctor from the pharmacy in Chelsea. He smiled and raised his right eyebrow. "I wasn't sure if you were eating it or making love to it."

"I'm distracting myself. Oh, and celebrating."

"Odd combination. What are you distracting yourself from?"

"Life."

"What are you celebrating?" he asked curiously.

"Life." I grinned ruefully.

"That narrows it down."

"What are you doing on the Upper West Side? Here, have a piece." I thrust the open box at him. "See for yourself. This one is nougat."

He took a piece and chewed it thoughtfully. "I just moved in upstairs."

"Really? What a coincidence! Aren't you lucky? You can come here every day."

"I'll lose my schoolgirl figure."

"Don't do that. It would be like destroying a masterpiece," I assured him. I let my eyes run up and down his long, lean frame appreciatively.

He straightened. Was he sucking in his gut? Hard to tell, but he emitted that feeling. He said, "I'm glad you approve. That feeling is mutual."

I giggled and hoped my front teeth weren't dark and sticky with candy, which they certainly were. "It's not mutual. You got to see my ass. If you took off your pants then it would be mutual."

A bemused expression floated across his face. "I'd be happy to take off my pants for you."

"Great, then I won't have to distract myself!"

He raised his eyebrows, stepped closer to me and looked at my mouth.

"I can think of lots of ways to distract you with my pants off."

"Aren't you the creative one?" I smiled, because he really was gorgeous. I blushed a little. How long had it been since I'd traded quips with such an immensely shaggable man? What did I know about sex? I'd been married with children my whole adult life.

"I like creative men."

He seemed to take a quick breath.

"I'm more of a math and science guy, but why don't you come upstairs and let's see how creative I can be?"

I hadn't held a man in my arms and felt his weight pressing down on my body since Clif moved out six months ago, and he'd stopped dispensing marital affections long before that. I looked him straight in the eye.

"Bring it."

---

He grabbed me by the arm and half-dragged me out of the store. I had a moment of panic wondering what I had gotten myself into.

Next to the chocolate shop was a door that he opened with a key. In the entrance foyer was a small elevator, which he pushed me quickly into as if he were afraid I'd change my mind.

That made two of us.

I opened my mouth to apologize and tell him I'd made a terrible mistake.

He laid his hands gently on either side of my face and kissed me. He kissed me softly, his breath like chocolate and coffee.

I dropped the chocolate box and wrapped my arms around him. He seemed to like that and his mouth opened, so I put my tongue in it. That was not something I ordinarily did with a stranger but it seemed appropriate, under the circumstances.

The elevator door opened and then closed. He slapped his hand backward on the elevator panel so that it opened again.

We got out, tangled and kissing and breathless, bumping into each other in odd places, elbows and knees and hips. My hair caught on the button of his shirt and his hand shook as he untangled the long strands.

We scrambled down the hallway, and then he pushed me up against the wall beside a door. We kissed some more.

He leaned down and kissed my throat and I moaned.

He peeled himself off of me and opened the door with another key on his key ring. He went in first and gently, clasping my hand, led me in after him.

I caught a glimpse of cardboard boxes, bare hardwood floors, and a few scattered pieces of very fine furniture. An antique Biedermeier inlaid walnut table. Four golden birch chairs with carved central emblems and drop-ear backs that stood in a row. I pushed him down on one of the birch chairs and tossed off my coat. I sat on his lap, facing him.

His hands roamed over my back. He peeled off my black Tombolini suit jacket that skimmed in at my waist and matched the black skirt that was now nestled way up my thighs.

I unbuttoned his blue oxford shirt and kissed his smooth, unlined neck with its forgotten fringe of whiskers near his jaw line. He smelled good, like cedar and amber and vetiver and a tiny whiff of male sweat.

He rumbled a little, deep in his throat.

"Do women take their clothes off for you just because of your voice?" I murmured against his cheek.

"What? No, I met my wife in college and we've been together ever since."

He leaned into me to unbutton my silk blouse but I pressed my hand into his chest and held him at bay. He winced. "Ex-wife."

I bent and kissed his mouth.

After a moment, he pushed me back.

"Are you married? You're not, are you? You're not wearing a ring!"

"God no! Divorced. Twice." Almost. Close enough. Why was he asking now when everything south of my navel and north of my knees was tingling with fire?

He brightened and his fingers went back to my blouse.

But I didn't want to get completely naked. I'd born and nursed two babies and all the downward-facing-dogs in the world couldn't erase the evidence of that.

I slid down off his lap so I was kneeling before him. I placed my hands on his crotch and felt his hungry bulge. It felt so good to be wanted!

He quivered as I unzipped his pants, then he stood hastily and swung me up into his arms. He carried me through the living room into a bedroom with more brown boxes and a badly made wrought-iron bed. He laid me on the bed and then covered me with his body as he kissed me. His hands went under my skirt and he yanked down my tights.

"You weren't wearing panty stockings the other day when I saw you in the pharmacy. Just thongs. Purple ones. Purple is my favorite color."

"I really can't go around showing my bare ass to people when I trip and fall, now can I?"

He laughed, got the tights off, and uttered some sort of exclamation as he stroked my thigh.

"Wait." I pushed myself up on one elbow. "Condoms?"

"What? Right. Safe sex." He was panting and he tilted his head, thinking. Then he looked at my mouth, got distracted and kissed me some more.

I kissed him back for a while. We became even more entwined and everything started to swim around me as if I would implode. I was creaming wet like a monsoon, and surely leaving a big spot on his bedspread. It felt so good to be so turned on but I pushed him off to the side. "Condom!" I exclaimed, urgently, as I unbuttoned his shirt.

"Do you have one?"

"God, no, I was expecting chocolate, not sex."

I ran my hands down his chest, which was muscled and taut and furry. I kissed his clavicle and the muscles quivered in his chest, encouraging me.

"Don't guys carry one in their wallets?"

"I stopped carrying a condom in my wallet the day I met Lisa," he said. "We'll have to get creative."

"Isn't that how you lured me up here?"

"Who lured whom? You told me to take my pants off." He ran his hands up along my bare thighs, making me shiver.

"Well, come on, you're gorgeous. Besides, it's only fair. You've already seen my ass."

"A vision that will haunt me forever." He unbuttoned my shirt.

"Look, if there's no glove, there's no love," I said, my voice weighed down with regret.

"I know, I know, I agree," he muttered. "We can do other things." He reared up enough to place his hand between my thighs and then cup my vulva. He looked in my eyes and his pupils were dreamy and black and huge. "Would you please take off your skirt right now?"

I poked my hand down into his unzipped fly and found something big and delectable to wrap my fingers around. I shook my head no. "Really wish you had some protection. Really, really. Can't we figure out something creative? Anything? Please?"

He leaned down and kissed me, his tongue exploring all the way into my throat. His fingers slid inside me, and I pulsed my hips up against him. Even with my skirt rolled up along my stomach, the motion made his erection strain and swell in my hand.

"I know!" He rolled off me. "Plastic baggies."

"What?"

"Won't be a tight fit but it will be something. Might be good enough."

"Good enough? From a medical doctor? What if I have genital Ebola, would a plastic baggy keep your penis from falling off?"

"If you say it that way, I might lose my hard-on." He tilted his head. "That's not a real disease. I've never read about it in a medical journal."

I got on my hands and knees atop him so I could kiss his chest with its long rolling muscles. It was clear that he worked out. I fondled his hard-on through his pants.

His hand was rubbing gently back and forth from my mons pubis to my anus, his fingers flicking in the crannies, and I hadn't felt anything so erotic since I was a fifteen and my boyfriend and I were necking in his garage.

"Maybe a rubber band to hold the baggy on and make it form-fitting? Is it a zip-lock?" My voice was so husky I almost didn't recognize it as mine. "That'll hurt both of us."

"Fold-top. The texture will be odd but it's smooth and you're well lubricated, so it won't hurt you," he said with some satisfaction. "Wait, I'm putting a rubber band around my dick?"

"Only if you want to be inside me," I said in a kind of stricken moan, because his fabulous frolicsome fingers were ensuring that I was good and ready, which I hadn't been for years. Now that I was, it was dazzling and succulent and liquefying, turning all my bones and muscles into the most pliable essence.

He slid out from under me. "Hold that thought!" He sprinted out of the bedroom. Two minutes later, he returned with a yellow box of plastic baggies. He tossed the box onto the bed next to me and threw off his pants and then his briefs. His erection was big and red and hungry; well-proportioned against his long limbs and torso. He was a beautiful man in all his parts.

"Nice," I said appreciatively, ogling him unabashedly. "Maybe we need the gallon size?"

He laughed as he pulled out a baggy and plopped it on. "I haven't slept with anyone since my wife kicked me out, and I never imagined I'd be doing this when I did."

"Me neither," I said. "Rubber band?"

He held up a thin green circle. "There was one around the parsley."

"You're a bachelor with *parsley*?"

"I put parsley in my morning yogurt shake." He was folding the plastic baggy around his erection, trying first one folded arrangement of the pointy ends and then another. He paused. "You know, if either one of us has genital Ebola, this won't really protect the other. You understand that, right?"

"I know, but at least it's something," I said.

"This is cosmetic, not prophylactic," he said. "Should we talk about our sexual history?"

I pushed up on my elbows. "Only if you want to kill the moment."

"Uh oh." He looked down and then at me. "Show me your breasts, OK? Or say something sexy."

I gathered he was going to lose his erection, which was the last thing I wanted, so I rose up on my knees, shrugged off my shirt and bra, and cupped my hands under my breasts. My nipples were hard and pointy and fawn-colored.

"Stroke your nipples a little, will you? Yeah, that's good." His hands trembled as he slid the slender rubber band up to the base of his penis.

"This is the weirdest thing I've ever done," I mumbled. I was touching my nipples with my fingertips, circling around the stiffened tip and pinching them a little.

"You're hot," he said, giving the plastic bag a turn to secure it. He was on me a second later. "Is there any chance you'll take off your skirt?"

"Nope," I said, wrapping my legs around him.

"Tell me if it hurts and I'll stop, OK?" He paused for a second to meet my eyes, and then he slid into me and it felt good all the way up my insides into my throat and down my legs into my toes, bright lines of pleasurable fire illuminating the world and all the universe. I knew I'd come like I hadn't in years, despite the weird cool plastic texture slithering around my insides. He was pumping into me and it must have been just fine for him because he was moaning too.

---

I got up and pulled down my skirt, found my bra and re-hooked it, and then re-buttoned my blouse.

"Stay for dinner?" he asked. "It's so quiet in this apartment. It would be good to have some company." His dark hair was askew and his angular face was soft and relaxed.

"I think not, but thank you." I leaned over and cupped my hands around his face. "That was the most fun I've ever had with a plastic baggie." I kissed him on the lips.

"Two plastic baggies," he said with evident satisfaction.

"I'll never look at a fold-top in the same way." I looked around for my coat and purse. Right, they were in the living room.

"It's good we found the rubber band. Sorry it pulled off. Next time we'll have a better system." He sat up and swung his long legs around off the bed. "Will you take your skirt off next time?"

"Next time?"

"When can I see you again?"

I ran one hand through his dark hair, which had unfolded into an unruly shag. "My life's complicated. Sounds like yours is, too."

"Screw the complications. We were good together. Let's have a real date."

"Why? Reality is overrated." I walked out of his bedroom and retrieved my coat and purse from under the beautiful birch chairs. "Damn, I dropped the chocolates in the elevator. I guess the chocolate is long gone."

"I'll get you more chocolate." He stood behind me, his face vulnerable. "I'll buy condoms."

I stretched up on my toes and kissed him again.

He put his arms around me and cupped my ass. "Why wouldn't you take off your skirt?"

I closed my eyes and leaned into him, breathing him in because he smelled good and felt good and did good things to me and I was never going to see him again. "I've had two children. The youngest one was a C-section. I've got a big scar."

"I have two children," he said. "Mine are two and five. A boy and a girl."

"Mine are older than that. A lot."

"But you're beautiful!" He pressed me more tightly into him. "And I'm a doctor. I've seen scars before."

"You haven't seen my scar."

"It's beautiful like you," he kissed me.

"That's easy for you to say. You're perfect, like a …" I thought for a moment. "Like one of Michelangelo's Ignudi or maybe his David. But more elongated."

He blinked. "Go out with me. I'll buy you the biggest damn box of chocolate in that store and a whole case of condoms."

"You're too young for me."

I pushed him away and walked out of his apartment and back into my life filled with conflict and obligations and crazy, angry daughters and the kind of plastic baggies that were only used for cruciferous vegetables.

# CHAPTER FIVE

IT WAS 6:45 a.m. and I set Alex's shredded wheat on the table. Shockingly, she'd been home in bed last night when I returned, loose-limbed and soft with release and surprised at myself. I hadn't indulged in such wanton behavior since college. Not even in college. Freshman and sophomore year I was too busy studying and too impressed with myself for being at Princeton. I was too scared about being found out not to belong to goof off for even a few seconds. By junior year, George and I were dating, which ended any chance for fun.

But George Calhoun, with his moneyed name all patina-ed over with decorum and his antique trust fund dating back to the War of Independence and his nonchalant Princetonian heritage, had seemed to offer the respectability and belonging for which I was desperate.

The phone rang, and at that hour, it could only be Trudi. I smiled as I picked up the receiver, and wondered what I would tell Trudi about last night. She had sat patiently through all my rants about Clif, who had specialized in slyly putting me down sexually: "You're so funny," he'd smile when I lay next to him in a skimpy nightie and no panties. He'd kiss my forehead and roll over, instantly asleep.

*Jerk.*

It still made me mad.

I said, with more energy than I expected, "Good morning, Trudi!"

"Sarah, there's no easy way to tell you, so I won't coddle you. It seems I have cancer. That's what the preliminary tests show."

I froze.

"My internist is sending me to a specialist."

"You-you have c-cancer?" I stuttered. "What kind?"

"Pancreatic. Possibly stage 3," she said. "The specialist will know more."

"I'm going with you," I said, numbly.

"No, love," she said softly. "I just can't handle your earnest American concern—"

"You've been handling it well enough for the last twenty years, Trudi! I am going to the doctor with you. I insist. You can't stop me."

"You're an arse," she grumbled.

"Yes, and I'm still going with you."

Trudi sighed. "I suppose there's no reasoning with you. I'll call you back later today to tell you when."

I hung up the phone, devastated.

Alex came in and sat quietly at the table. She sipped her orange juice.

"It's Friday, you're supposed to go to your dad's and start his week," I said out of sheer habit. "Pack everything you need. Clothes, books, homework, toiletries." Hastily I went back into the kitchen to get my coffee. I drank it standing at the counter so as not to set Alex off into one of her episodes. Maybe if Alex didn't have to look at my face she wouldn't start screaming and cursing.

I leaned forward, resting my arm and head against the upper cabinet door. I stared down into my cup and thought about Trudi, watching the patter of water on the surface of my coffee, sweetened with stevia powder and diluted with almond milk.

That wasn't water; those were tears.

"Mom, are you OK?" Alex asked from the doorway.

I straightened and wiped my face without turning around. "I'm fine. I've got your new meds. One every morning with food. In a week, one and a half."

"Are you crying?" she asked in that puzzled voice a child uses when confronted with the possibility that her parent might actually be a person and not a robot whose sole existence was caretaking while continuously affirming that the child was absolutely flawless.

"Text me if you need me. I'll come immediately if you need help," I said. I reached into my purse on the counter and got out Alex's pills. "Better pack the bottles to take to dad's."

"Mom, I know I've been terrible," Alex said. She came and stood at my elbow and leaned her head against my shoulder. She was tall like her paternal Yankee relatives, four inches taller than me, so she had to arch her neck down to do it.

I patted her head, her soft fair hair fluffing around my fingers. I remembered when she was a tiny baby, so sweet and tender. We'd had a blissful nursing bond. I ached for her and me.

"I'm sorry, OK? It's just, you know. It all sucks. All the time. I feel bad all the time. Kids are so mean, especially the other girls, especially since I'm the new girl again. I just want to fit in."

"Alexandra, you're a wonderful girl. You don't need their approval."

"But Mom, it's always been so hard, ever since fourth grade when I got boobs that no one else had, and all the boys were staring at me and the other girls were bitches. No one understands. You and dad are always fighting, and Dani, you know I love her to death, but Dani's all about Dani."

"I'm for you."

"I know you are, Mom. You're like the one person who still believes in me. I don't know why you do, but you do. I love you, you know? I wish I didn't keep disappointing you. I wish I could make you proud of me. Don't cry."

"If you want me to be proud of you, stop doing drugs. Start going to class and doing your homework. Stop trying to fit in. High school is the tiniest slice of life. You won't even see any of these people again after college. It won't matter—"

"Mom, quit, God, please!" Alex stiffened. "Jesus Fucking Christ. Sometimes I believe you're as bad as Dani and Katherine say you are. Katherine says kids have to find their own way."

"That's right, quote your hippie stepmother to me," I snapped. "Her airy-fairy delusions about child-rearing are really going to help you get your life on track!"

Alex walked away. "You're such a bitch. You have to ruin everything."

I stared after her as she marched out. I wished I had held my tongue; everything I said about Katherine and George was reported back to them instantly. I pondered telling Alex that her godmother, the closest person to a grandmother on my side since my parents died in a car crash twenty-six years ago, probably had pancreatic cancer, possibly stage three, that might even have metastasized into her lymph nodes.

But Alex was gone, gone to pack and to pretend to go to school while instead skipping out to get high with her friends and to blame her behavior on everyone but herself.

There was no way I could discuss Trudi's illness with Dani, either. Not only because Dani wasn't talking to me but because Dani was always aggrieved—and furious—whenever I was so selfish as to burden her with my troubles.

It hadn't always been thus. Once upon a time, Dani and I were close. We'd had a fiercely loving relationship, a *real* relationship, one where we were free to be our authentic selves. I remembered snuggling her when she crawled into my bed after a nightmare, which she did until she was fifteen-years-old. From the time she was very little, we had long talks about everything: movies, books, television, her friends, school. When she was six or seven, she confided that she had a crush on someone and invited me to guess whom.

"He's a little brown," she offered playfully, by way of a clue. When she eventually identified Will Smith, I was so happy that she chose a man based on his talent, charisma, and looks—and that she was without racial prejudice. I was so proud of her and liked her so much, in addition to loving her. She had reciprocated those feelings. She made it clear that I was important to her, too.

But in the years after I'd left George, it all changed. Dani picked up a very different attitude from her father.

"Your mother shouldn't criticize you or expect you to take care of her," George told the girls, and, "Your mother, who is not like us, shouldn't do X or Y or Z."

He bolstered his argument with culturally approved sound bites like, "She's your mother. If she really cared about you, she'd put your needs ahead of hers." He said such things in front of me with his usual sneer that let the girls know I was the lesser parent.

I sighed and let it go. Then I sat down to research pancreatic cancer on the internet so I could ask intelligent questions when I went with Trudi to the doctor. The first thing I discovered was that it was aggressive. The next thing I saw were last year's mortality numbers: 53,000 new cases of pancreatic cancer and 42,000 deaths from pancreatic cancer. Then I saw that the 5-year survival rate for stage three pancreatic cancer was only three percent.

———

Trudi's husband Robert and I flanked Trudi as we entered Mount Sinai Hospital, each of us holding one of her arms. We were directed to the oncology wing. I could feel my heart hammering in my throat as we walked toward an elevator bank.

"My internist referred me to this oncologist. He's supposed to be great, everyone raves about him. He's a wunderkind fresh from Harvard," Trudi said. "He's put together a clinical trial that has shown some encouraging results. If I qualify for the trial, it might give me some time."

Robert's eyes welled up and he draped his arm around his wife. He was a big-boned mid-western boy, as down-to-earth and salt-of-the-earth as anyone got.

I wasn't even sure they made men like him anymore.

Robert and I huddled into Trudi as she stood at the administrative desk and checked herself in. The nurse gave her a clipboard with a fifty-page long questionnaire, complete with several pages about insurance and confidentiality.

Trudi found a seat and we sat next to her. She pushed her blond hair back behind her ears and stared at the sheaf of papers.

"You want me to fill it out for you?" I offered.

Trudi lifted her blonde head with an expression that was half grimace and half smile.

"I have cancer, not dementia," she said. "I also have a doctoral degree in art history and I am a tenured professor at Barnard College. I can probably fill out a form. But only if I manage to get the tip of the pen to emerge." She clicked the pen. "Brilliant, I'm in business."

She was trying to be humorous. Dutifully, Robert and I grinned. Our grins were anemic; well, they were downright pathetic. I wondered if that was the way it was going to go with Trudi, who was British, and whose parents had passed to her a stiff-upper-lip ethic: she would joke and stay stoic while she withered away and Robert and I fell to pieces.

*I won't fall to pieces on her,* I vowed, watching her concentrate. *I'll be my best self and I'll be there for her.*

After twenty minutes, she rose with her clipboard.

Robert and I stood as one.

Trudi smiled and shook her head. "I'm ninety-eight point seven percent certain that I can walk to the desk myself."

Robert and I sat down. I stared at Trudi's back as she walked away and then caught sight of Robert doing the same. I touched his arm and whispered, "Robert, we're going to have to do better."

Robert nodded.

"We can't be pathetic; she needs us to be stronger than that," I clarified.

Robert nodded again. He squared off his shoulders then nodded again. Message received.

It was twenty minutes later before another nurse bustled down the corridor. She was young and round with a sympathetic moon face, the perfect psychopomp leading us to the doctor who likely held Trudi's life or death in his hands. She gave us a warm smile.

"Mrs. Waterston? Dr. Bauer will see you now."

Her name tag identified her as Nurse Practitioner Janet Finley. She ushered Trudi alongside her.

"You were referred by Dr. Gelder, right? We love Dr. Gelder here. He's the one who brought Dr. Bauer down from Boston. You're going to love Dr. Bauer, he's young but he's a superstar in oncology, and he specializes in pancreatic cancer." She kept up a running patter as she marched us down the corridor to an office with an open door. Finley draped her arm around Trudi and swept her inside the office; Robert and I trailed behind.

I took two steps over the threshold only to see Trudi shaking hands with my hot doctor.

I must have made a sound because everyone in the room turned toward me.

My hot doctor froze.

One moment he was warmly greeting my best friend in the whole world, encompassing her with kindness and optimism, and the next moment he was a painted marble sculpture, without breath or any semblance of movement, his dark eyes locked onto mine.

"You two know each other?" Trudi asked, intrigued.

"No," I said.

"Yes," he exclaimed at the same time.

So I yelped, "Yes," while he said, "No."

"Brilliant," Trudi said with her most British lilt.

"We shared chocolates out of a box," I said finally. "Hazelnut praline."

"Nougat," he said, flushing deeply and looking all of twelve-years-old. He shook himself like a dog drying out after swimming.

"Nice to see you again, Miss …?"

"Sarah Paige." I stretched out my hand and shook his.

"Scott Bauer." He gripped my hand with both of his and smiled a little as if he'd scored a point, which I supposed he had, as our delicious anonymous episode was suddenly anything but anonymous. He turned to Robert and the two men shook hands.

We all stood there for a moment, looking at each other. Then Bauer seemed to wake up. "Janet, would you bring in another chair for Miss Paige? Mr. and Mrs. Waterston, take these seats."

# CHAPTER SIX

THE DOOR TO THE elevator was just about to open into the private landing of a penthouse on Park Avenue. I took a deep breath, touched the wooden crates at my side, then smoothed down my dress. I wore my best upscale, casual black dress, perfect for five o'clock cocktails in an elegant Upper East Side apartment. I had fresh polish on my nails and I looked yet again at my fingers to make sure that wrestling with the crates hadn't damaged the gloss.

Carl Hopkins was the kind of man who appreciated the ladylike sheen bestowed by a good manicure, a black dress, and a light spritz of Chanel Number 5—the classic formula, before the company ruined it by "updating" it with melon or freesia or whatever they'd added in the name of modernity.

"You look very nice, miss," the doorman said shyly. His voice held a Russian accent.

"*Spasibo*," I said with the correct intonation. I'd studied a little Russian when I went through an infatuation with Russian iconography in college.

He perked up and was about to respond when the elevator doors opened into a foyer lit by a crystal chandelier. The foyer had a terra cotta floor, voile wallpaper, and a small round table bearing an orchid. The doorman waved me out and then grasped one wooden crate.

"Sarah, good to see you," Carl said, in that husky voice that reeked of success. He approached me and kissed my cheek lightly. "Sergei, would you bring these into the dining room?"

Sergei bustled ahead of us with the crate.

I stepped backward and reached for the other crate. Carl stopped me.

"Sergei will bring it," he said. He smiled. "I have a couple locations in mind, I thought I'd show you and see what your thoughts are." He put his hand on the back of my arm to guide me through the foyer.

We stepped into a living room that was probably thirty feet by twenty feet, with north and east exposures, herringbone parquet floors, and gorgeous crown molding.

"Stunning!" I tried not to gape.

Carl shrugged a little. "Thank you. I'm content here. When my wife died, I drifted for a while then I settled here. Here's the first location, where the armoire is between these two windows." He led me across a rug so understated that it screamed wealth. We stopped to face the windows where an antique ebony armoire stood between them.

"That's a beautiful piece. Ormolu-mounted, brass-inlaid ebony." I walked to the armoire and studied it up close. "Louis XIV?"

"You do have a good eye," Carl approved. "Yes. My designer wanted a statement piece in this room, and that's it. Early eighteenth century, attributed to Nicolas Sageot."

I ran my fingers along the motif of Hercules and the Nemean lion on the lower part of the doors. "You like figures, then."

"Yes, always," he said. "Since studying the classics at Yale. That was a couple centuries ago, of course." He smiled ruefully while his eyes played quizzically over my face, and I remembered looking at Rosa in all her bright youth and feeling old.

"The great classics have an eternal appeal," I said, smiling and meeting his eyes directly.

His eyebrows quirked. "So what do you think of moving the armoire and placing the paintings here?"

"Well, it's hard to replace a piece like that, even with paintings as beautiful as Clif's," I murmured. "Where would you put the armoire?"

"In that corner, perhaps." He pointed to the Northeast corner, currently occupied by a small table.

I walked around the living room, imagining the armoire moved and Clif's nymphs in its place. "Where else did you have in mind?"

Carl took my elbow and ushered me through a set of glass folding doors into a formal dining room with a pair of north-facing windows. A long, highly polished oval table graced by a pair of silver candelabra occupied the center of the room. Between the windows stood a sideboard. The wall over the sideboard was bare, newly so, by the looks of the painting leaning against one end of the sideboard.

I trotted over and squatted down to look at the painting. A slender woman in her late forties or early fifties with porcelain skin and auburn hair smiled out from a portrait that had been painted by a master hand.

"Painted by Burton Silverman?"

"You're on top of your game. Yes."

I studied the portrait. The lady had narrow, fine features and her blue eyes showed intelligence, kindness, and a hint of sadness.

"Lovely."

"Yes, Nancy was," Carl said, from over my shoulder. "I miss her still but I can move her portrait to my study."

He had taken Nancy down in preparation; he had directed Sergei to bring the paintings there; that was where he wanted Clif's river nymphs. I rose and studied the room. It was a good location, but how much traffic did the formal dining room get? Tentatively wondering if this was really up for negotiation, I asked, "This room is spectacular, of course, but how often do you come in here? I always advise people to hang their paintings where they're going to see them. Art is to be lived with and enjoyed, closely and intimately."

"I see what you mean," he said in a ruminative tone. "I cross through here a few times a day. Occasionally, I hold dinner parties in this room. On Thanksgiving, my daughter and son bring their families over. My daughter and my daughter-in-law cook the meal and we all eat here." His face lit up with pleasure at the family memory.

"That's a wonderful tradition." But it still wasn't going to put the paintings in front of him all that often. I tried another tack. "Mr. Hopkins, you spent a lot of money on these beautiful paintings, isn't there a location where you'll get to see them twenty times a day?"

"I suppose we could move the armoire," he said, looking doubtful. He didn't have to say it aloud, I heard his thoughts: if he'd wanted the paintings in the armoire's spot, he would have already moved it.

Was there a way to maneuver the situation?

"Do you use the living room all the time?" The room was pristine as if no one ever sat in it.

Rather than answering, he took my elbow again and led me through a country kitchen with a southern exposure and into a cozy, wood-paneled library. It was lined with bookshelves and had luxurious wall-to-wall carpeting—the buttery plush kind my toes itched to snuggle—and a custom built-in high-def flat screen television. A corner extension had been turned into a home office, and wooden shutters that matched the panels were folded open. A *New York Times* lay open on the desk.

"I spend most of my time at home in here, when I'm not in my bedroom," he admitted. "But you can see, there's not much wall space."

"Wall space, no, but lots of great books," I said with a lilt. I loved books. It was that love that had gained me admission to Princeton. "Classics, huh? The *Iliad*, the *Odyssey*, and the *Aeneid*?"

"Oh, yes. In Homer and Virgil's original tongues." His eyes sparkled. "You?"

"Art history and comparative literature. So I read Homer and Virgil, too, in translation."

"So long as you read them," Carl said. He and I exchanged a smile.

I turned back to the library and looked around. Almost no wall space. "Bedroom?"

He raised one eyebrow. "It's always nice when a beautiful woman asks to see my bedroom." I must have made some kind of face because, as he re-acquired my elbow, he hurried to add, "I'm not hitting on you, Sarah. I just have to say that. It's obligatory. Reaffirms my manhood."

"I don't want to leave myself open, but does a man as dashing as you need to do that?"

He didn't answer but his step got jauntier. He directed me back into the kitchen and then up a staircase. "These used to be staff rooms up here when the building was first built, but the prior owner turned it into bedrooms."

We arrived at a spacious master bedroom with an eastern exposure and a fireplace with a hand-carved mantel. A door led to an outdoor balcony.

I nearly shrieked, "Don't tell me that fireplace works!"

He chuckled. "It works."

I skipped straight across the room to run my hands along the mantel. "This is amazing, just wonderful." In Manhattan, we have a thing called "apartment porn" that has to do with appreciating an apartment a little too sensuously. I was indulging myself in it. Feeling guilty, I removed my libidinous hands from Mr. Hopkins' mantel.

"It's nice," he said, struggling to look modest. "There's plenty of wall space, and the paintings would look great here. Thing is, in here not many people would view them. Just me."

I understood the slight emphasis on the words "just me." He was telling me that even though he was single, he didn't play around. He wanted me to know that about him. I wanted to deflect without rejecting; was there a delicate way to do that? I smiled and said, in a knowing voice, "Mr. Hopkins, I'm sure anyone you invite here will see them. No one in in their right mind would turn this down."

His eyes flashed as if he enjoyed the parry and, truthfully, it was one of my smoother comebacks. His voice deepened into his chest as he said, "I don't want to invite just anyone. I'm looking for just the right person."

*Aren't we all?*

For a split second my mind brought up the image of Scott Bauer from last week, warm and open after our tumble—but wait, he was Trudi's doctor and Trudi was sick. I mercilessly repressed the image and the information and all of the feelings about Trudi that threatened to erupt.

I was there representing my gallery and installing paintings for a valued client. I wasn't going to muck it up with any awkward and inappropriate sentiment. I turned back to the mantel and placed my hands on my hips as if examining the wall space.

"The paintings would look great here. But since it's not a well-trafficked room, you're right, the dining room is the best option."

He nodded as if expecting to be right, and again his fingers found my elbow.

Downstairs in the dining room, I pointed at the portrait. "Is there room for Nancy in the library?"

"There's a small space on the wall behind the desk. I've had in mind for a while that I'd put her portrait there. Now seems to be the time." He leaned back against the table, crossing his arms over his chest, and stared at the painting.

"How long has it been?"

"Oh, five years and ten months and four days, not that I'm counting." He made a somber, regretful face. "We were together a long time. Forty years. I keep expecting her to walk in the front door, even though she never lived here. It was worse in our old apartment. Somehow, there, I simply could not accept that she was dead even though I watched her die."

"I'm so sorry for your loss," I said softly. I didn't want to inquire further because it seemed painful for him, but I wanted to be receptive if he wanted to talk about it. He was a nice man and I sensed he didn't share his feelings very often.

"Me, too." He looked up, his face losing its habitual guard. "Cancer. Took her so fast. Two months from the time she was diagnosed."

*Cancer.* The word was like a hand clutching my throat. Trudi's face floated in the air before me. Did she only have two months to live? Scott hadn't said much at the initial appointment, just that he was conditionally confirming the diagnosis of pancreatic cancer and that he wanted to run more tests and go over all the results before offering treatment options.

"Sarah, are you all right?" Carl had hustled over to me and taken me by both my shoulders.

I smeared at my eyes with the back of my hand, hoping I was wearing waterproof mascara. "My best friend was recently diagnosed with cancer."

"I'm sorry." The crow's feet beside his blue eyes and the furrows beside his mouth deepened. He looked genuinely distressed. "You know that medicine is constantly making strides forward in cancer treatment. There have been major advances since Nancy got sick. She had a particularly virulent and hard-to-treat form of cancer. Most cancer is much more amenable to treatment these days."

"What did she have?"

"Pancreatic cancer."

I quailed.

"Your friend …?"

I nodded.

His face softened. "Oh, Sarah. Does she have a good doctor? I can make recommendations. I sit on a few boards."

I straightened. Yes, Trudi had a good doctor. Some young wunderkind out of Harvard who had put together a trial and who was creative with plastic baggies. Fold top. I said brightly, "Do you have any tools? Let's get the crates open and install these paintings. They really are gorgeous."

Carl gave me a sympathetic smile. "I can't wait to see the paintings hanging here. But we can get Sergei to do this. Why don't you and I go sit in my den and have a glass of wine? I believe I promised you a nice Bordeaux."

"Mr. Hopkins, I'd be grateful if Sergei could help us, but I wrapped and packed these paintings myself and I'm going to make sure that they're properly unpacked. Then I'm going to stand over Sergei and oversee as he hangs them because nothing is going to happen to them on my watch, not one scratch," I said firmly. "Then, when your beautiful paintings are hanging perfectly I will be happy to accept that glass of wine."

Carl studied my face as if he wanted to argue but was thinking better of it.

"Let me call Sergei."

# CHAPTER SEVEN

I WAS FLOATY AND happy when I got home, floaty from the Chateau Lafleur and nearly deliriously happy to see Clif's river nymphs properly installed in an opulent setting for Carl's benefit. That was one of the great pleasures of owning a gallery: uniting a beautiful work of art with someone who would enjoy it. Knowing that a painting or a sculpture I sold would enhance and uplift, elevate and enrich the space for its new owner. I was truly adding value to another person's life, and I loved the part of my work that matched people with art.

The nymphs looked gorgeous in their new home. The track lighting in Carl's posh dining room showed them off as if specifically placed to do so. My business-self prompted me to ask about photographing the installation for the gallery website; my oenophile-self seconded the plan.

After the installation, Carl and I had, by tacit, mutual consent, sat in the dining room and kept the conversation light over a wine that was a powerful, elegant, overripe, dark-cherry-and-mineral extravagance.

When I was leaving I said, "You know, Carl, now that you're a valued collector of the Paige Realist Gallery, you must come by to browse in a more leisurely way. I have some still lifes with glass bottles and fruit that will rock your world. They'd look amazing in your kitchen."

"Will I get to see dollar signs flashing in your eyes?" he teased.

"Depends on how many you buy," I teased back, opening my arms expansively.

He laughed and kissed my cheek and commanded Sergei to put me in the car that was waiting downstairs. "I hope you don't mind, I asked my driver to take you home," he said in a perfunctory way. I would have told him that it was still early and I could walk across Central Park to the West

Side and enjoyed doing so, but I gave in, because how could anyone mind Carl Hopkins' generosity?

Once home, Groucho greeted me at the door, whining with urgency. It was almost eight-thirty and he was ready for a walk. I slipped off my pumps and slid on a pair of Dansko clogs I keep for that purpose, grabbed his leash, and took him down in the elevator.

Ten minutes later we were back upstairs and he was butting his head against my legs and panting loudly, asking for food. Groucho was a mix of English sheep dog, Labrador retriever, and standard poodle. He weighed about sixty-five pounds and was covered by curly poodle-like hair in a patchwork of colors, including white, apricot, black, and gray. A rescue pup, he had come into our lives some fourteen years earlier when I was still married to George. In fact, I often thought Groucho was the best part of my marriage to George.

I winced.

*Bad Sarah!*

My two daughters with George were way more important than a dog. But Groucho would have none of the toxic programming against me that George dished out, even though Dani lapped it up. Nor was Groucho self-immolating in a heart-shattering and spectacular way, as Alex was.

"I love you more than my own skin," my soul sister Frida Kahlo had said to her husband Diego Rivera, and I thought about that whenever I thought of my love for my daughters. I loved them more than my own skin, but I had to live within my skin, so I couldn't abnegate myself totally for them. Frida hadn't raised children; she couldn't have children after being skewered with a railing in a trolley accident, so she hadn't experienced the heartache I suffered on a daily basis. She'd endured a different kind of pain, and it had imbued her with a human tenderness that was, like her art, a paradigm for us all.

I fed Groucho and promised myself I'd groom him later. Then I realized that feeling floaty was fun but having some food in my belly would be wiser. Hopkins' cheese and crackers were tasty but not filling. He'd started to invite me to stay for dinner but I'd interrupted with a comment about the view from his apartment, and he was canny enough to let the invitation waft away, incomplete.

I hung my coat on the hook beside the door. I called the Thai place and ordered the usual. Then I dialed Alex's number. Sometimes, when it wasn't my week, she'd pick up for me. But not then.

"It's Alex!" her greeting said. "You know what I'm doing. So leave a message and hope I'm not too wasted to get it."

*Lovely*, I thought, but I made my voice sound cheerful.

"Alex, it's Mom. Hope you're OK. Call me later, OK? Tell me how school is. I love you." I hung up and pondered calling Dani to leave a message that I loved her. It was something I considered a dozen times a day.

But Dani wouldn't pick up for me. She never did anymore. My brilliant, talented oldest daughter, the tennis champion, refused to speak to me. A year ago, she had come home at the end of her sophomore year and declared, "Everybody at Princeton has a perfect life, and you're the reason I don't."

"What are you talking about?" I had asked. "No one has a perfect life!"

But Dani had been adamant that I was solely responsible for her life being imperfect, though she didn't explain what she meant. I had struggled to maintain our relationship, but she started coming home from college and staying with her dad without telling me. One of her high school chums or Alex would let it slip.

"Oh, sorry, you didn't know, Dani's in town," Alex would toss off, shrugging as if it didn't matter that my beloved eldest daughter's actions cut me to the core.

I got angry and acted from hurt instead of wisdom. I changed Dani's old AOL password to "Spoiled Brat." I'd told her what I'd done when she finally called me to ask if I knew why her account wasn't working. Things had deteriorated from there. Dani hadn't even acknowledged my birthday in February—not a card, not a note, nothing.

But why was I allowing my thoughts to go down that perilous road? Everyone told me to give Dani some space and she'd come back to me, but I had my doubts. Dani was stubborn beyond the pale, and although her strength served her in competitive sports, I feared that she was immune to other people's pain. Especially mine.

If only I had some wine in the apartment; another glass would go down so easily. I went to the kitchen table and opened my laptop to check for new email. Mostly penis enhancement advertisements.

---

The doorbell buzzed. My food was there. I grabbed my purse and went to the door, threw it open, and laid eyes on Trudi's doctor, Scott Bauer.

"What are you doing here?" I exclaimed.

He held up the delivery bag and patted Groucho, who sniffed him happily. "I brought up your Thai food."

"How did you find me? Trudi?"

"Of course not, I would never involve a patient in my personal life!"

"Don't you dare look offended," I scolded. "If Trudi didn't tell you, then how did you find me?"

"Google and Whois. It wasn't easy. Took me a while to figure out that you have an 'i' in your last name. P-a-i-g-e. I googled you all of last week before I thought to check the sign-in at the Mount Sinai front desk."

"What's 'Whois'?"

"It's a website where you can find out information about the registration of other websites. Your art gallery's website registration shows your home address." He looked past me into my apartment. "Aren't you going to invite me in?"

I felt indignant. "I haven't decided yet."

His eyes focused on mine. He had very appealing dark eyes. They held strength and softness and invitation.

"I bear gifts." He held aloft a box of chocolate like the one I had lost in his elevator.

I reached out to take the box.

He drew it back. "You have to let me in if you want the chocolate."

"How do I know you're not an ax murderer?"

"I'm not an ax murderer, I'm a doctor, which you know because you were in my office," he said. He leaned close to speak confidentially into my ear. "I don't have genital Ebola, either. Apparently, neither do you. I tested myself after our, ah, meeting, and I was still negative for genital Ebola. So we're both in the clear. Phew!"

That struck me as funny and I was still floaty from the Chateau Lafleur, so I giggled.

He took that as a welcome and gently pushed past me to come inside. He walked through my apartment, looking around with interest. "Any chance there's enough food in this bag for both of us?" he called back over his shoulder.

"Pad thai and spring rolls," I said as I followed him. "I'll share if, and only if, you give me the chocolate."

"Deal," he called from the little round table in the kitchen nook where the girls and I ate most meals. Now it was just Alex and me and usually just me. Scott laid the chocolate box next to my laptop and then shrugged off his jacket and hung it over the back of the chair. He unpacked the delivery bag onto the table as if he'd done so a hundred times.

"That's a nice dress," he said as I put a plate down in front of him. "You look great in it." His eyes went to my legs and I could see him noting, with approval, that I wasn't wearing tights. Perhaps he thought my thong would soon be on display for his personal delectation.

Could I be sure it wouldn't be? He was adorable with that chocolate, and I knew how much fun he was in the sack. I asked blithely, "Why are you here?"

"To talk about what happened." He took a spoon from my hand and sat down, then opened the pad thai and scooped it onto his plate.

"Why do we have to talk about it?"

"Because it's important to me."

"What are you, a girl?" I muttered. I sat opposite him and dumped the remaining pad thai onto my plate.

"I never do that kind of thing," he said. "Hooking up. I was with Lisa for a long time."

*I never do that kind of thing either.*

But he was the one who wanted to talk. He'd mentioned his ex-wife, so I could guess the topic he had in mind. I smothered a sigh and asked, "So what's the story with Lisa?"

His face puckered into lines it couldn't yet hold and wouldn't for another twenty years. "We met in college. We've been together ever since. Six months ago, I came home from work one night and she told me that she wanted to be with someone else."

"That sucks," I said softly.

He pushed the spring roll container toward me. "A guy from college. Rowed crew with me. He was in my boat. How do you do something like that to a guy in your own boat? We were closer than brothers."

I shook my head and dipped the spring roll into sauce. I kept my head tilted in listening mode.

"You know what really burns? Salt in the open wound. She hired a great lawyer. I thought we'd do friendly mediation. So I hired an attorney who does that. She hired a guy who litigates. They wrote up this contract, holy crap. You can't believe. She took everything. I'm lucky I still own both my kidneys."

"You got that beautiful Biedermeier table and the birch chairs," I said, remembering. "And your medical license."

He growled, "You sound like her lawyer. Those were my grandmother's. She gave them to me as a gift."

"They're really nice," I offered.

He ran his hand through his short dark hair, combing it straight up—my move when I was distressed. "Can I say that my medical license is still mine when I'll be paying Lisa money for the rest of my life?"

"The rest of your life?" I queried. "Wow, that is a great lawyer. Can you give me his name? I hired a great lawyer and I didn't get money out of my first husband for the rest of his life."

Scott snarled and looked ready to snap at me but then his eyes came sharply into focus. He studied me. "Maybe not for the rest of my life. But I'm paying a hell of a lot of alimony and child support right now on top of my student loans."

"What about the other guy? If she marries him that'll end your alimony obligations."

He shrugged and nodded and ate a spring roll before saying anything else. "They're getting married as soon as our divorce is final. Then they're moving from Boston to New York after that. Janey's starting Kindergarten here in the fall."

"So you came ahead to get things ready?"

"I came first. Then they decided to come. So I contacted all the schools and found a place for Janey in one of the Upper West Side private schools. Everyone says it's a great school. I think she'll be happy." His angular face softened like wax melting into liquid vulnerability, and I knew how important it was to him that his little daughter be happy.

I couldn't help myself; I reached across the table and squeezed his hand. "I'm sure she'll be happy. The schools around here are pretty great, especially at the lower school level."

He looked at my hand on his and then flipped his hand up and clasped mine. "Being with you the other day was the—it was the *liveliest* thing that's happened to me in years."

I was caught off guard.

"It was totally spontaneous, unexpected, exciting! Just when I was lonelier than I've ever been," he rushed on, reaching his other hand over to take mine as well. His hands kneaded mine. "If I'm honest with myself, things with Lisa weren't wonderful for a long time. I mean, we were fine. We were friends. It was all ... cordial. I had my medical practice and research and Lisa had her dissertation and the kids. We were going along, like a ball rolling along in a groove."

Gently I tugged my hand to free it from his grasp. No go. I swayed back in my chair. "Cordial is enough for some people if the relationship includes other things they value, but it's not enough for everyone."

Scott's lips drew together in a straight line. He inhaled and exhaled slowly. His voice was gritty like water over pebbles when he spoke. "Lisa said something like that. The night she—she told me it was over. She said it was boring between us because I put all my real effort into my patients, and she was just a mistress. That she wouldn't settle for boring just because we had two small kids."

"That hurts," I said softly.

"She was right. I didn't know what she meant then. Not until that time with you. It woke me up. I forgot sex could be like that."

I disentangled my hand from his. "Scott, that was a one-time thing. It was exciting and lively because it was what it was. A fling."

"It can be more than that."

"Let's not make it more than that."

"Why not?" he demanded. "We were good together. Is this because I'm a lot younger than you?"

"Yes, and by the way, what do you mean by 'a lot'? How old do you think I am?" I asked, hoping he'd guess at least five years younger than I actually was.

"Late forties," he answered immediately with no hesitation.

I winced.

*Clearly, it was time for more serious cosmetic dermatology than the occasional shot of Botox between my eyebrows.*

"Sarah, don't be upset. You're beautiful," Scott said earnestly. "We're both adults. Age doesn't matter."

I cleared my throat. "You're about thirty-seven or thirty-eight?"

"Thirty-eight in a few months."

I sighed. "Your age is a thing, yes. But there's so much more. I told you, my life is complicated. So is yours. Plus your situation is fresh. I'm in the middle of my second divorce, and when I get involved again, I don't want to be someone's rebound relationship. I already did the whole rebound thing with my second husband. It was a big mistake."

"Your second husband, he's the painter you show in your gallery?"

"Clif is one of the painters, yes," I affirmed. "I show several painters and a few sculptors. All realists doing exceptionally beautiful work. They're not all neoclassicists, even though my gallery's been accused of being a mere 'Neoclassical sanctuary' by critics who lack any sensibility for fine art. Really, they're just lackeys for the toxic art market trade where the ugliest, most meaningless dreck sells for the most money!" I scowled as I remembered the one throwaway line with which the *New York Times* had deigned to acknowledge my gallery.

"You're an art lover, that's for sure," Scott said, his deep voice suddenly amused.

"The point is, I got involved with Clif partly because, well, he was exciting and hot, and partly because things with my first husband were so awful. I was fleeing George and all my bad feelings about how the marriage had failed."

Scott cocked his head. "How did your first marriage fail?"

"I've thought a lot about that. On the surface, it looked like I ran off with an artist. But that was just a symptom of what had been going on throughout the whole marriage, which was that I was a lower-class citizen in my ex's family. His allegiance was always to them, not to me. The whole dysfunctional thing made me angry and hurt and depressed, which gave George fodder to call me crazy and to reject me even more. That hooked me, for some reason I've never figured out, even with a lot of psychotherapy. Except that maybe it had something to do with being exceptionally needy after losing my parents. Needy and alone. I married George hoping to find belonging and acceptance, and I persisted in looking for it long after I should have accepted that I would never find it with those people. I should have either accepted that as the basis of the marriage or moved on."

"But it wasn't over; so you cheated on your first husband with the artist who became your second husband?" Scott clarified.

I nodded. Was he judging me?

"Why didn't you leave your first husband before getting together with Clif?" Scott demanded. "Do you have any idea how much it hurts when your wife does that to you?"

*Yep, he's judging.*

I snorted and rose to put my plate in the sink. "Scott, if I'd had the personal wherewithal to do that, don't you think I would have? Not that we've known each other for more than twelve seconds, but what do you think?"

He seemed to ponder that as I rinsed my plate. He said, "You don't seem like the type to cheat."

I turned and leaned back against the sink, folding my arms over my belly. "Yeah, well, I don't seem like the type to have a fling with a complete stranger whom I met once in a drug store either now, do I?"

That gave him pause.

"Here's a truth I've learned over my forty plus years, and I finally took it in when I realized it applied to me, too: People are not loving and loyal all the time. People we care about get hurt. Even if we're the well-meaning kind of person who goes through life doing our best and trying to be a kind, good, human being, we aren't always. Sometimes we screw up. So my best with George was crappy. I wish I hadn't run off with another man and that I'd made a clean break before I got with anyone. Mostly because I deserve to act like the good person I am. Do you understand?"

One side of his mouth lifted in a wry half-smile. "People are not loving and loyal all the time. Check. I got that one. Got in A+ in that subject, in fact."

"So, yes. I cheated on George. Not one of my finer moments. Not something I'm proud of. But I did it. And you know what? I paid for it. My karmic due came right back at me and bit me on the ass." I was laying all my cards on the table with a man I barely knew, and I wasn't sure why except that he'd shown up at my apartment with a box of chocolate and a need to talk. "Because I married Clif and he's, Jesus Christ, some kind of Peter Pan. A bottomless pit of need and demand, but not a snotty condescending shit who was constantly gaslighting me into believing that I was crazy and worthless, the way George was.

"Oh no, Clif was his own particular brand of hell. A celibate hell, if you must know, which I probably created by becoming his caretaker and his manager—his mommy. So I created it. A celibate hell. As in, NO SEX. Which I never signed up for. Which explains why I asked you to take off your pants and why you, me, and a fold-top plastic baggy ended up in bed together for an electric tumble!"

Scott was shaking his head.

"That's it?" I said, nearly yelling. "You're just going to sit there and shake your head?"

"Lisa isn't the type to cheat either," he said, shrugging. "That's why it hurt so much. I never saw it coming."

"Are you judging me?"

"Maybe I should have seen it coming," Scott went on, oblivious to my internal struggle because he was snared in his own. "Maybe I should have paid more attention to Lisa and not spent all my time working. But I married my work. I left Lisa alone in our marriage. That's a mistake I won't make again." He looked down and mumbled, "I wasn't always loving and loyal, either. I committed the sin of omission. She handled the sin of commission. It took both of us."

"Welcome to the human race," I said, but not unkindly. I was about Scott's age when I'd had the same uncomfortable awakening—that the flaws in any relationship were equally mine as well as my partner's. Not even that realization could save my disastrous first marriage.

His head snapped up and he grinned at me. "It was two plastic baggies. Two, because we did it once and then three minutes later we did it again. That was the word for it, the one you used: *electric*."

I couldn't argue with that.

"Yes, our lives are complicated. But guess what? After the age of thirty, anyone's life is going to be complicated. And life is never going to be perfect, the time is never going to be right. If you wait to meet someone who's your age, he's going to have a life with complications. Because if he doesn't have complications, where's he been? Living in his parents' basement and never venturing forth to live? As soon as you leave home, go out into the world, and make a life you make complications."

"Scott," I murmured. Scott meant well, but he had only a few complications in his life. I was juggling many more and they were all like knives hovering over my head, just a few heartbeats away from raining down on me.

Scott wasn't done. "*Electric*, that's the word for it. For what's between us. *Electric* isn't common. It's rare and magical. It's worth pursuing. That's what I'm saying. That's why I'm here. Let's give it a chance and see what happens."

"I don't know, Scott. You're awfully sweet, but my life is a mess right now."

"So is mine. Welcome to the human race. Let's be humans together." He stood up. "Maybe this isn't the right time to show you this. I didn't just bring chocolate for you tonight." His face wore a sly and triumphant look as he took something out of this pocket. "I brought this!"

It was a box of condoms, and so inappropriate after our soul-baring conversation that I belly-laughed. I couldn't help it, deep chortles churning up from my gut. That's when the front door banged open. I leapt up and Scott swiveled around on his heels as Alex marched in to the kitchen.

Her eyes were barely swollen and her jeans and jacket looked clean and mostly neat. So she was only slightly stoned and she hadn't been screwing some boy in Central or Riverside Park. She looked from me to Scott, back to me and then back to Scott. She sauntered close to Scott and leaned forward. She looked him up and down, appreciatively.

"Way to go, Mom!" Alex sang, as Scott's face reddened. She plucked the box of condoms from his hand, opened it, and took out a few prophylactics. She closed the box and passed it back to Scott, who was doing that frozen-statue thing again.

"Alex," I said.

"I just stopped by for some stuff in my room. I'll be right out of your hair. You two have plans!" She giggled and traipsed toward her room.

Scott opened his mouth, closed his mouth, and shook his head.

I sat down heavily and held my head in my hands, then I jumped up and ran to Alex's room. Her door was closed so I knocked.

"Wait," she called. She came out holding a green Sprite can and her cosmetic bag. "Don't let me interrupt you."

"Alex, it's not like that, it's not what it seems," I said, feeling defensive even though I knew I shouldn't.

She giggled. "Now I know what you do when I'm not around." She blew past me, stopping to wave breezily at Scott from the hallway, then she was out the front door. A second later her head popped back in. "Don't do anything I wouldn't do! Or should I say, don't do anything I *would* do?"

The door slammed and I heard voices in the hall. Alex hadn't come alone; she'd left her friends outside. I ran to the door and threw it open. A wolf pack of teenagers wreathed in clouds of cigarette smoke turned the corner toward the elevator bank. They didn't look back at me. I sniffed and felt relieved to smell regular tobacco smoke. My neighbors didn't like that, either, but it was the lesser of two evils.

I went back inside, closed the door, and leaned backward against it.

Scott came out of the kitchen. He stood in the hallway looking at me. An awkward silence stretched out between us.

"My daughter, Alexandra."

He shook his head.

"Maybe we can talk some other time?"

He nodded. He turned on his heel, disappeared into the kitchen, and re-emerged wearing his jacket. He walked toward the front door.

I was still leaning back into the door.

"Scott, how bad is it with Trudi?"

He looked troubled. "I can't discuss my patients with you."

"Is she getting into your trial?"

"I can't talk about that."

"You think you're going to come into my home and we're not going to talk about my best friend of more than twenty years?" I asked, in a voice that was strangled with humiliation and sorrow and concern.

"Patient confidentiality prevents me from talking about my patients. Privacy is an ethical imperative."

"What about my privacy? Did you think about that when you checked the front desk for my name?"

"You're not my patient." He came close, laid his hand over the side of my face, and kissed me softly on the lips. He lifted his head and said, "Sarah, I'll do my absolute best for her. I do for all my patients. My absolute best."

# CHAPTER EIGHT

A VOICEMAIL AND A fax came in while I was in the shower. I stood with a towel wrapped sari-style around my waist, my hair dripping beads of water onto the floor, and plucked the fax out of the machine while listening to the message.

The fax was the latest love note from George and Katherine. It was a formal letter, cc'd to my attorney and theirs, Dr. Bailey and various other assorted personages throughout Manhattan. I read: "You are a woman who had an affair with a married man so it's unethical and hypocritical of you …"

I figured it was penned by Katherine because it was more lyrically written than George's terse, attorney-esque style. They were referring to Clif, who was married when he and I met, although on the outs with his wife.

At least that's what he'd claimed. I hadn't checked it out because of my desperate need to escape my marriage.

I hesitated.

If I read the letter, it would eventually reveal what they were now demanding, accusing or threatening me with, all because they were the superior people and parents.

*Don't they have anything better to do with their lives than harass me?*

I crumpled the paper into a ball and threw it into a trash can.

Sooner or later their latest hostility would wend its expensive, energy-sucking way to my attorney. George had deep pockets for litigating, and, evidently he got off on it because he constantly took me to court.

In truth, his litigious aggression was just a continuation of the contempt with which he'd treated me during our marriage. I still remembered every single time he stated, "There's only one woman in the world I respect: Rebecca Melnyk." He was referring to one of my roommates from the early days in New York. Becky had a doctorate in mathematics and made millions of dollars on Wall Street. That was the one woman George respected and it wasn't me, his wife.

I wondered if he ever realized how much it hurt me when he said that; when he so baldly let me know that he didn't respect me.

Was it any wonder that our marriage was bad and our sex life worse? At least it taught me to never climb into bed with a man who treated me contemptuously. I might have learned that earlier if I hadn't been so young when I got together with George.

The answering machine had run on while I was engrossed in bitter memories of my unhappy marriage, so I hit the replay button.

"Sarah, it's Carl. My paintings look smashing in the dining room. I really enjoyed our drink last night. Let me take you to dinner. Call me." Carl was issuing an invitation that he expected to be obeyed.

As a general rule, I didn't date clients, even valued ones, and I knew how to let a man down gently. But there was more to it than that.

Carl was more than a client I wanted to cultivate for the gallery. He was urbane and wry and sympathetic, a good listener and an excellent storyteller. Our time over the wine had flashed by—I'd only anticipated staying an hour with him and had ended up staying almost three. I liked Carl.

He served the most beautiful wine and, if I accepted his invitation, he'd take me to an elegant dinner, the kind I hadn't enjoyed in forever because Clif relied on me to pay restaurant checks and I'd invested every dime into the gallery. Going out with Carl meant that I'd be treated royally by a man who appreciated a well-turned-out woman.

It all held a certain allure. It held a lot of allure—as much allure as throwing a leg over Scott and riding him real hard.

That's when I knew I was playing hooky. I dialed Rosa's cell phone.

"Sarah, is everything OK?" Rosa asked.

"Snow day," I said, which was our code word for "I'm taking a desperately needed day off, can you cover?"

She laughed and I enjoyed the rollick of her amusement.

I said, "Gibson from Santa Fe will call to bitch about how low his paintings are being priced and to ask if any have sold since yesterday."

"Oh God," she snorted. "Anything else?"

"The New York Fine Arts Society may call to see if I'll lend them some of Clif's paintings for their realist show, and you can say yes if they'll let him give a talk." Clif loved to talk in front of an adoring audience. He was good at it, too. Whenever he gave a lecture, I made a sale.

"Got it."

"My accountant may call; she emailed last night so probably not." That was it, all the pressing matters for the day.

"Did you finish that article for *American Artist*?"

"Oh crap."

"They wanted it two days ago," Rosa reminded me.

"Tell them tomorrow afternoon, I promise." It was almost done; I just had to tweak a few spots.

"Will do. Sarah, is everything OK?" she asked. "Your voice is funny and you never take days off."

"No worries. It's just been forever since I had some down time."

"I thought you'd be in today writing out checks as fast as your hand could scribble."

I smiled. Rosa knew me. "I'll do it tomorrow morning. I've already paid a few bills online."

"How'd the installation go?"

"You can't believe his apartment, there must be pictures of it online, it's like something out of *Architectural Digest*. The paintings look amazing in his dining room. I'll tell you all about it in detail when I see you."

"And how was *he*?" she pressed. "He's quite the silver fox."

I held the phone to my forehead and squeezed my eyes shut. "He's lovely."

*And that's the problem.*

"Did he ask you out?" she said. "I mean, he was really looking at you when he came into the gallery."

*My business-self really must create better employer-employee boundaries.*

"His dead wife had auburn hair."

"Oh," Rosa said, drawing the word out over seven or twelve syllables.

"Don't 'oh' me, Miss Rosa," I said. "I'm going upstate. I'll bring my cell phone."

"Don't bring your cell phone," she said. "Just trust that everything will be OK for a few hours while you're hiking around the Gunks. But check the forecast in case they expect some wet spring weather. You don't want to get caught without rain gear."

But I brought my cell phone because in a few hours anything could happen, especially where Alex was concerned.

———

I took the subway up to Harlem and got my car out of the cheapish lot where I parked it. I had a navy blue Volvo S70 named Brigit. She wasn't young but her wheels turned just fine. Volvos run forever. Ostensibly the car was a business asset because I used it for deliveries, but I got so much more mileage out of it. I'd driven it to the girls' soccer games, swim meets, and tennis tournaments; to Newport, R.I. on school holidays to drop the girls at their father's family's vacation compound, and to Princeton to visit Dani those first two years when she was still speaking to me.

I made my way up the Palisades Parkway to the Thruway, turned off in New Paltz and drove toward the Shawangunk Ridge. I found a parking spot in the Warwarsing parking lot to the right of the ridge. I walked up toward the Trapps and the carriage trail, wondering if I should have parked where I could hike out to Lost City. The Gunks were well-beloved by rock climbers, so hiking trails and climbing routes were mapped out, but Lost City was to be kept sacred and not to be mapped. The hiking trails were less well known and I'd have more quiet space to myself.

It was peaceful on the carriage trail; the only other hikers were an elderly couple with a golden retriever. They waved as they passed me and the retriever, whose yellow muzzle was shot through with white, wagged his tale. It was the end of April and overcast, with milky gray light filtering in through black-brown tree limbs and riotous splotches of pale green fuzz that would be full-fledged leaves tomorrow or the next day.

It was quiet enough for me to hear myself breathe. Almost despite myself, and marveling at the sensation, I started to relax. The iron bands of tension around my gut and my head softened and loosened. My lungs unfurled like sails filling with wind in an open breeze. My hands unclenched. I hadn't even realized they were curled into fists.

My feet picked their way along paths they knew well. I'd started coming to Mohonk Preserve twenty-six years ago after my parents were killed in a car accident. It wasn't a conscious plan on my part. It was just after I'd graduated from college and I was working at an art gallery and living in Hell's Kitchen with two other women. One roommate's parents had a country home in New Paltz, and I'd fled there after dealing with the funeral and burial. I couldn't look at one more sorrowful face or condolence casserole.

There was something about being out on the trails, walking and walking for hours. I couldn't say it was soothing because that wouldn't be true. I'd come out into the woods day after day to hike and then return to the cabin in the evening, spent and just as inconsolable as when I'd set forth in the morning. Yet I was healing, so there was an undeniable grace afoot.

It was the incontrovertible shock of my life; the ax whose fall severed my life into two distinct pieces one August day when I picked up the phone and heard, "There's been an accident." As an only child, I'd expected my parents would be around until I was good and gray, by which time I'd be choosing their nursing home and lovingly nagging them to take their medications.

Instead, I was twenty-two, shell-shocked with grief, and working with their attorney—one of my dad's legal buddies—to resolve their estate. There hadn't been a lot because my parents were more interested in doing good than in being paid well for it, but there'd been enough for me to realize, around Thanksgiving of that year, that I didn't want to rush into marriage with George. The next compelling step for me was graduate school.

I went to London on an interstice art program. There I met Trudi, whose brother Nick had tangled up his motorcycle with a 'lorry,' and not survived. He was about my age and was riding a Ducati without a helmet. She still remembered hearing the thrum of the Termignoni mufflers as he pulled out of her driveway for the last time.

Our losses bound us as tightly as our shared love of Turner, Vermeer, Raphael, and Fra Angelico. She was ahead of me in the art history program and when she was offered an assistant professorship at Barnard, I knew I was returning to New York with my Master's degree instead of staying on in London to finish my dissertation, as I'd planned.

With no family of my own, Trudi had become integral to my life. While not committing myself to a belief in reincarnation, I felt certain that Trudi had been a fixture in other lives of mine and we'd found each other in this one in the nick of time.

So I came back to New York, which George had wanted anyway. He had a litany of reasons why I should return, the foremost being that he wanted me to do so. Our friends were getting married; it was that time of life. What George wanted had mattered to me back then, more so than ever with my parents gone. His big family seemed to offer the belonging that my orphaned heart craved.

That was before I realized that I could never belong with the Calhouns. There was no place in their purebred, pedigreed tribe for a half-Jewish, half-Baptist mutt with some Cherokee blood thrown into the lineage. When they talked about Jews, they threw sidelong glances over their shoulders at me; when they talked about their upper crust social circle, they angled their bodies toward each other and closed ranks. It was a bulwark that excluded me. I could not figure out what to say or do to walk into their closed circle. The precise cultural mirroring necessary to get them to accept me was beyond my interloper's abilities.

I sighed and found myself scrambling up onto a broad gray quartz and sandstone ledge. I settled under a sycamore tree. How had I got there? My feet had picked out the way without my conscious volition. Even in sturdy hiking shoes I could get up a scramble, an easy climbing route.

I leaned back against the rock, enjoying its grainy rough texture. The spring breeze shuffled my hair across my forehead. I looked up through a crisscrossing network of purple-black tree limbs into a patchwork of sky —gray and white and blue. My body got heavier and more open and sensitive; it, not my mind, sensed the larger invisible suppleness that underlay and supported the visible world, the material world that even with its moments of splendor so often seemed like the lees at the bottom of it all. It was this underlying and ever-expanding elasticity that the great artists communicated in their work along with the glory and the dregs of the manifest world.

Prayers came to my lips, but not the kind that would have appeased my parents. Rather than raising me with no religion, as any sensible parents of differing faiths would have done, my mother and father each sent me to their respective places of worship. I went to Hebrew school and Sunday school, church and temple, vacation bible school and United Synagogue youth camp. I was inundated with traditions and felt awkward in both and so, naturally, I rejected everything. But I couldn't deny the spirit that informed everything, not when I could feel it so palpably. So when I was 16 years old, I embarked on a genteel pantheism and quit attending services altogether.

When I was 17, my parents, with great solemnity, sat me down and asked if I would consider studying Buddhism. They had a friend who knew a Rinpoche. I laughed in their faces, not kindly. What were they thinking, force-feeding me all that doctrinal nonsense? What was I thinking, sneering at them like the teenager I was? Would I have behaved more lovingly if I'd known they'd be gone only five years later?

Some regrets are never resolved. I wondered if that would be the case with my daughters. The prayer that emerged, whispered into the thick Shawangunk air, was a blessing for them.

A black snake swirled itself up onto the rock and stretched out to absorb the wan sun. Its eyes stared unblinkingly but it didn't aggress toward me, and I figured we could co-exist on those terms.

I asked myself how much I was to blame and what I could do to fix things. Trudi stoutly maintained I was a good mother and that George was vindictive because I had left him, and because George was rich, the girls sided with him. George paid their tuition bills and brought them along on luxurious vacations with his parents and brothers. He encouraged them to bring their friends to the posh Calhoun compound on the beach in Newport. He had all the goodies. I had only love, and George declared my love to be false and wrong because I refused to see the girls as perfect. I persisted in correcting my daughters when they behaved in ways that were unkind or dishonorable. No Calhoun could abide any kind of criticism, no matter how lovingly tendered or how well deserved; it might dent their shiny chrome image of themselves as the perfect American family.

Time spooled away from me, the afternoon shadows lengthened and the snake, rather than creeping away, simply dissolved in an errant beam of sunlight, its white chin and yellow underside rolling out like scattered dust. I hadn't eaten lunch and my stomach grumbled. I rose and stretched and decided to return to the car and drive to the deli at the foot of the mountain.

---

I hiked quickly back to the parking lot and found Brigit waiting patiently. Volvos were like that. Inside I rummaged through my handbag for my cell phone. Twelve missed calls. The first one told the story, the rest were elaborations on the details. It was the principal of Alex's school asking me to come immediately to pick her up. She was being expelled. She had brought synthetic pot with her into class.

*She went to class? That's progress.*

But the principal didn't think so, and neither did George, who left some typically disgruntled and accusatory messages. How could I be so thoughtless as to be unavailable for my daughter?

I called Alex.

"Mom! Where are you? We couldn't reach you! Why didn't you pick up?" Her voice sounded as petulant as always; as if getting expelled from school was an ordinary occurrence. For her, it was becoming that.

"I had something to do," I answered.

"What?" she demanded.

"You've been expelled, Alexandra? Where are you? Are you still at school?"

"I'm in dad's lobby. He had to go back to work, and he and Katherine don't want me in their apartment by myself."

*That's because you steal things to sell for drugs.*

Twenty-dollar bills went missing from my purse all the time, as if they evaporated into thin air. "Sit tight. I'll be there in an hour."

I phoned the principal as I drove past the deli. "Hi, Mr. Villanova? This is Sarah Paige, Alex Calhoun's mother ..."

He launched into a rant. "I knew I was taking a chance when I accepted Alex to Devon Town School," he began.

I let him run on for a while.

After five or six minutes, he took a breath for air.

"Can she come back?" I asked, gently. "Is there any possibility that she could redeem herself? Redemption is, you know, everything."

"Some parents take their children to their pediatrician to get a blood test to determine just how much THC is in their system. Anyone who thinks that pot isn't a gateway drug hasn't worked in a high school," he grumbled, evidently referring to an ongoing argument.

"I'd like for Alex to have a chance to graduate high school with her peers," I said. "I know you've gone out of your way to help her, Mr. Villanova. I appreciate it, I really do. More than I can say. You've been amazing. Can't you just give her one more chance?"

"Alex needs stability, structure, strict boundaries, consistency, and parameters."

"I totally agree, Mr. Villanova. You are right in everything you say. But there's a difficult situation with her father and me. I can't correct it."

"Get her out of the city, then. Put her in a boarding school."

"I am willing to explore that for her."

"You know we have repeatedly talked to her about her behavior with boys," he said, apropos nothing. "She behaves in a highly inappropriate fashion. The other day she stuck her hand down a boy's pants."

"I didn't know she was behaving so outrageously in class. You're right, that's not acceptable. I will make sure that is addressed."

"That boy's parents could sue the school for sexual harassment."

"I will be clear with Alexandra that inappropriate behavior must stop."

"If she goes to therapeutic school and completes a program about substance abuse, we'll give her a second chance," he said finally, at a growl.

"Is there one you recommend?"

He gave me three names and hung up on me while he was still complaining about Alex.

I didn't blame him. I felt like calling Trudi but I didn't want to bother her when she was so ill. Before I quite knew what I was doing, my fingers were calling Dani.

"Mom, what," she answered, in a chilly tone.

*Dani picked up!* I thought, rushing and breathless, shocked and hopeful for even the meagerest connection. "I suppose you heard that your sister has been expelled again. Her principal is recommending a therapeutic school."

"Um, I don't have to get involved in your toxic drama," she said. She hung up.

I knew I was going to need support to deal with Alex's expulsion, so I phoned my shrink Dr. Maitra. Everyone in Manhattan had a shrink and he was mine. I didn't see Dr. Maitra weekly anymore and hadn't in years, but I called him sporadically, when I felt the need to talk—like now. His secretary gave me an appointment right away.

The only person left to call was Dr. Bailey. I just hoped that after he was done blaming me for Alex's choices, he would have an equally lucid evaluation of the three schools Principal Villanova had recommended.

# CHAPTER NINE

EVERYTHING WENT ON HOLD while I dealt with Alex's latest crisis. It was always that way: Alex engineered a catastrophe; King George perched up on his high horse, blaming me and issuing orders for how to deal with it; I scrambled to take care of matters while my gallery—my livelihood—was put on the back burner.

On the day of both my appointment with Dr. Maitra and Trudi's next doctor's appointment, I brought Alex into the gallery with me. Rosa had agreed to babysit my sixteen-year-old daughter.

Rosa greeted us at the door. "Mamacita, Alex." She smiled but her gaze was troubled.

Alex marched past her.

"You look like hell," Rosa said, in a low voice.

"It's been hell." I closed my eyes for a moment and promised my eternal self that I would be a celibate nun in my next life: no men, no children.

"Let me guess, George has sent you about a hundred scorching emails?"

"Faxes and texts. I haven't given him my new email address," I said blithely, coming in and closing the door. "How was it here yesterday?"

"Quiet."

I frowned. That was all too common with the art market teetering on the brink of oblivion. "No foot traffic?"

Rosa shook her head. "Gibson called. Daniele called from Italy, there's some young painter he loves, he wants you to show the kid here in the US after the Art Miami New York Fair."

"I'll look at the images." I scanned the back for Alex.

"She's probably in the office talking to Geoff," Rosa offered. Geoff was Rosa's boyfriend and my tech guru.

That was good news. "Geoff has time to tweak the website? Yay!"

"Finally," Rosa said smiling, but I had the distinct impression that Rosa brought him along for moral support. Alex could be a tough customer.

"Rosa, thank you!" I squeezed her arm gratefully.

"No, no, Sarah, thank you for all the times you let me go to auditions," she replied, as I was trotting purposefully toward the back.

Alex came out of my office. She avoided my gaze and seated herself on a wooden stool in a corner between two landscape paintings. She dug through her backpack and got out a dog-eared copy of Steinbeck's "Of Mice and Men." The joke on all of us, most of all Alex, was that she had a quick and penetrating intellect and could easily have aced any of the high schools she'd attended to date.

"Call me if you need something, I'll be in the office," I said. "You're welcome to sit with us in there."

"I need my phone. Give it back to me," she snarled.

"Alexandra, you're sitting in my gallery within a few yards of me, you don't need a cell phone," I said. "And we discussed consequences. If you're going to get yourself expelled—"

"Dad doesn't talk about consequences, Mom," she sneered. "Dad tells me to do whatever I'm going to do. Why can't you be like him?"

*Because I actually care about you, and life brings consequences, so I want you to understand that. And since I care about you, I also care about your character, and I don't want you to turn into an entitled, spoiled brat.*

But I didn't say that aloud.

"No school, no cell phone."

"You're such a bitch. I bet dad will get me a cell phone." She opened her book with exasperation and stuck her nose in it.

I looked at her for another moment. She sat bowed over with her long fair hair hanging over her fully made-up face that was thrust close to the novel in her hands. Her fingernails bore fading crescents of sparkly teal nail polish. She was wearing a midriff-baring shirt under a denim jacket, low-riding blue-jeans that we'd bought at Bloomingdale's especially for the astronomical expense of chic worn patches, and Converse sneakers on which she'd drawn red hearts and green marijuana leaves in ink. If she took off her jacket, the entire expanse of her tummy from just below her breasts to just above the rise of her pubis would be revealed, as well as the pink-magic-marker peace sign with which she'd embellished her hip bone.

Alex studiously ignored my gaze.

I turned and went to my office.

Geoff sat at the big iMac in the office. He waved without looking up. He was a square-jawed, all-American looking kid in his late twenties. He freelanced doing tech stuff and had built the gallery website and maintained it for a low price, basically a few free meals, thanks to Rosa. "Hey, Sarah. I'm loading that last batch of pictures onto the site, the ones from the opening in February."

"Great. Oh, and a few questions. One, can you show me what a 'Whois' is? Can I get my name and personal address taken off it?"

He looked up, crinkling his forehead. "I should have thought of that." His fingers flickered over the keyboard and then he pointed at a web page. "It's a registry page for your domain. It's easy to put ID protect on it and it's not that expensive."

"Great, let's do it," I said. "Can't have strangers finding out where I live that easily, right?"

*Not even hot strangers with chocolate and condoms.*

"What's the other question?"

"StatCounter," I said, referring to the free web tracker that he'd installed on the gallery site. It monitored activity on the website, tracking IP addresses in real time, which was useful for all sorts of business purposes.

His fingers flew again, little hummingbirds zipping along, wreaking magic. The StatCounter page for the website opened up. "Whoa! Someone's on your blog page all the time!"

Rosa poked her head in. "You two are good?"

"Rosa, did you know about this?" Geoff gawked at the listing of IP addresses. "This is a form of internet stalking."

Rosa came all the way in and leaned over Geoff's shoulder. "Ah, yes. That would be Sarah's ex-husband George."

"Could be his wife," I murmured.

"Look at this, he accesses the gallery home page and then goes to the blog site. Like, every day." Geoff pointed to the repetitive IPs. "It's creepy."

"I think that IP is his home computer here in Manhattan," I said. "See this one, in Newport, Rhode Island? That's probably his family compound

—it only turns up on weekends."

Geoff shook his head and stabbed at some keys. "This one, Verizon wireless, it counts up visits and then resets back to zero, that must be his cell phone."

"Can you do anything about it?" I asked. "I don't have to let him stalk my blog just because he pays me child support."

"Yes, you do, Sarah," Rosa straightened and crossed her arms over her chest. "George owns you, don't you know that by now? You're a thing for his personal use and abuse." Her voice dripped with sarcasm. She had laid eyes on some of George's contemptuous missives to me, had heard some of his scornful voicemails, and formed an opinion of the man—an opinion with which I couldn't argue.

Ok, so I'd cultivated her opinion. And not just with her but with other friends like Trudi and Marcia. I wasn't a model of discretion about my children's father. I should've been, I knew. But one of my meaner selves felt vindicated when my friends understood what I was going through and, anyway, I never said I was a perfect, faultless human being. I had my shadow and sometimes it went walking around without me.

"Ha ha," I said. "What do you think, Geoff? Can we keep him off my site? It *is* kind of creepy. I don't understand why he does this. There's nothing all that exciting on the blog page. It's promotional, mostly, along with some of my rants about the corrupt art market. It's not like I write about sharing hazelnut praline chocolate with a hot stranger in a candy store, and then shagging him senseless in a nearby apartment."

Rosa and Geoff exchanged a glance. Geoff's eyebrows rose up to his hairline as he returned to the computer screen.

Rosa cleared her throat. "Maybe he's looking for stuff he can use against you in court next time he sues you."

"I can block the static IPs, like this one and the Newport one," Geoff said, pointing. "But I can't block his cell phone because that IP changes all the time. If he wants to see your blog, he'll be able to see it on his cell."

"You ought to write a blog post that says, 'George, quit reading this, you pathetic excuse for a human being,'" Rosa said, giggling.

I giggled, too. "My lawyer says not to give it away that I know he's obsessed."

"How is good ole Marty O'Shea?" Rosa asked.

I sighed. "I have to call him and let him know the latest news about

Alex. Speaking of, Rosa, do you mind?" I gave her a hopeful look.

Rosa swiveled on her heels and went out to check on Alex.

I took my cell phone and walked out into the street to call Marty. He thought I was calling about Clif and assured me that everything was moving ahead correctly and it wouldn't be long before that marriage was legally over.

I explained the situation with Alex.

"Never a dull moment," he said, and I could hear him shaking his head. "Conduct all your communications with George regarding Alexandra's school situation via email. Politely."

"Don't worry, I can't bear talking on the phone with him, he's so patronizing and awful."

"He's patronizing in his court briefs, too," Marty observed. "That's the dynamic. He hooks you in with his aggression. You fight back and he's got you. You don't hafta take the bait just cause he's dangling it."

"What are you, Marty, my shrink?"

"1-800-Marty-knows-best," he answered, pointedly. "Do not send any nasty emails, Sarah. Just resolve the situation for Alexandra's best interest. Make sure her psychologist is on board with the course of action you and George decide on."

"I will. And I've been good. No emails to George. None at all—he doesn't even have my new email address."

Marty grunted. "Do I?"

"I'll send it to you. Alex was using my old address to forge absence notes to her school."

"She's so creative," Marty observed. "If she ever harnesses that brain power for good, she'll be a dynamo." Before hanging up, he told me an off-color, wickedly funny joke that left me chortling, thinking how lucky I was to have hired him five years ago when I left George. Marty was stalwart. He was of small stature and large personality, with the thick jet hair, green eyes, and the crisp wit of the black Irish. He looked good in a suit and he didn't believe in fanning the flames of bitterness in a divorce even though he enjoyed being in court in front of a judge. I suspected he was a brawler at heart. He was the attorney other attorneys hired for their divorces, and he'd stood staunchly at my side during all of George's legal shenanigans.

I went back in and Alex was still reading. Rosa was dusting the frame of one of Clif's paintings—a standing male nude, *Mars with Olive*

*Branch*, which always reminded me of Guido Reni's Saint Sebastian but without the homoerotic overtones.

Geoff was waving to me from the office. It was only an hour until the first of my appointments—long enough to send an email to George about the three schools. A polite email.

———————

I walked into Dr. Maitra's office and he rose from his chair to greet me. Dr. Maitra was tiny, brown-skinned, contained, thoughtful, and brilliant. In my eyes, he was altogether perfect. I had taken enough psych courses at Princeton to know that such an opinion was my transference. No one was perfect. But I couldn't help feeling that way because he had helped me so much and he had often been so eerily accurate about my life and feelings.

He'd helped me through a few years of struggle in my thirties when I realized how angry I was with my parents for dying—it was the ultimate abandonment. I was left entirely, shockingly alone; the last of my grandparents had died when I was a child, and the strained situation between the two families because of their religious differences meant that I wasn't close to any of my cousins. Nor was I given the time to confront my parents on what I perceived to be the flaws in their parenting, like their inability to accept that I didn't want to be either Jewish or Christian. It felt like a lack of acceptance of me. There would never be a resolution for that, but Dr. Maitra helped me put it into a working perspective.

He also helped me through my despair at the end of my marriage with George and he helped me when I'd realized that I could not stay married to Clif and be a happy, fulfilled human being. In fact, Dr. Maitra helped me craft the strategy by which I'd arranged for Clif to think that splitting up was his idea.

When I first started my sessions with Dr. Maitra, about fifteen years ago, his hair was thick and black. Now it was salted through with white and receding on his forehead.

*Time is passing and maybe he'll die*, I caught myself thinking.

But he still wore the same wire-framed glasses that he'd always worn, no matter the style in eyewear, which seemed reassuring. He gave me his crooked grin and I beamed back at him. Years ago, I had asked him where he was from, meaning his family's ethnic origins; he had replied, "New York," which was a sublime answer.

"Hello, Sarah."

"Dr. Maitra, how are you?" I took a deep breath. "You're not going anywhere soon, are you? Not retiring or moving?"

"I have no plans to retire or move," he said in his quiet way. "I'll give you ample notice when I decide to do so."

"But 'when' doesn't mean you're actively considering it, does it?" I quizzed him. "You didn't say 'if,' you said 'when.'"

He smiled and shook his head. "I'm not considering moving or retiring or anything."

With my abandonment fears addressed, as per our ritual, I threw myself on the couch across from him.

He sat back down in his chair and pulled a notepad into his lap. "Sarah, I spoke with Dr. Bailey. You've got a problem."

I stared up at the white ceiling of Dr. Maitra's office. "It's like watching a freight train collide with a car in slow motion. I know what's going to happen and I can't stop it."

He nodded. "Dr. Bailey doesn't like you. Of course, I made nice with him so he'd open up to me. He finds you intrusive and controlling."

"I knew that," I said wearily. "He's made that clear. He tells me that regularly."

"He's too grandiose in his psychotherapy," Dr. Maitra continued, in his placid but direct way. "Long after he rides into the sunset, you'll be left holding the bag with Alex. He's hoodwinked himself. He works for you, he has no right to say these things to you."

"He doesn't get it about mothers. And I think he over-identifies with Alex. He's constantly scolding me and putting me down."

"His role is not to tell you how to raise her, but to help you get her to where you want to get her, in terms of her character. Where is Alex's character?"

"Nowhere good," I muttered.

"Sit down and make a wish list for Alex, for what you want for her character. From what I can tell from talking with you over the years, when she feels lonely or rejected, she goes out and does drugs and has sex. When she feels lonely or rejected, she should reach out and have the courage to say, 'Can we talk? Have I offended you?' She needs effective coping strategies in order to be successful in life. She doesn't have them." Dr. Maitra gave me one of his piercing looks. "You need to be Alex's teacher."

"I'm going to be her teacher when all she does is mock me?"

Dr. Maitra tilted his head, the way he did when he was reflecting on something I'd said. Maybe he was just reading my mind, which I could swear he did, transference be damned. Then his black eyes focused on me. "Yes. She's watching you, even if she doesn't seem to be. With Dr. Bailey, you can say, 'Look, I think we've got to get something straight. What I'm concerned about is that Alex's coping strategies are completely ineffective. I want her to learn good coping strategies and to develop an interest in something that sustains her.'"

"He's being paid by George. And George's agenda is about hurting me."

"That's not your agenda," Dr. Maitra pointed out. "Your agenda is Alex's character development. You want her to have effective, thoughtful coping strategies. You want her to relate to people respectfully. You want her to show discernment with her peers and to keep her pants on with boys. You want her to develop an interest in something that sustains her, something she commits to. You want her to work on problem-solving. You want her to understand that nothing in this world is free or entitled. Most especially, you want her to take ownership of, and responsibility for, her wrong-doing, so that she can reclaim her self-respect after messing up."

I was frustrated and my hands clenched and unclenched of their own accord.

"George and Bailey have done everything possible to prevent her from taking ownership and responsibility. They actively encourage her entitlement. Bailey acts as if I have no moral authority with my daughter, exactly like George does. And both of them distort my every action to make me look like a bad mother."

"Bailey's trying to turn you into a perfect person in order to be a good enough person. That's a clear sign of a problem. I'm not sure what his counter-transference is, or what the hook is with Alex. I've printed out an article by Phyllis Greenacre for you to read." He reached for a stack of clipped together papers on the stand beside his chair and held them out.

I got up and took the sheaf of papers. "'Problems of Overidealization of the Analyst and of Analysis,'" I read, as I returned to the couch.

"There can be a projection of omnipotence onto therapists. It's the therapist's responsibility to clarify to the family that he's not a magician. He shouldn't buy into the projection of grandiosity and helpfulness, which is called splitting. He does so to meet his own unconscious needs."

"I'm sure this is a wonderful article," I said. "But is it really going to help me wrestle Bailey into an appropriate relationship with Alex and me?

Will it help me get George on board to help Alex?"

"Getting George to encourage the formation of positive character traits in Alex is another thing," Dr. Maitra admitted.

---

I tried to put Dr. Maitra's words and Alex out of my mind when I met Trudi and Robert at a Starbucks near Mount Sinai. None of us felt like ordering anything so we walked slowly to the hospital. I chatted about the sale to Carl Hopkins and how it meant the gallery was afloat again.

"You fancy him," Trudi said, smiling. She was tall with blonde hair cut into a pageboy and she wore black horned rim, cat eye glasses. She had an ironic British affect that belied her native good humor and kindness.

"I'm certainly grateful to him, he bailed out the gallery."

"There's more to it than that, you fancy him," Trudi insisted.

I flushed a little. "He is rather a silver fox."

"I always saw you with someone older, someone polished, a man with some refinement," she said. "So when do we get to meet Hopkins?"

"Sheesh, Trudi, slow down," I said. "I don't even know if I'll see him again."

"I wager he's already asked you out."

I gave Trudi a sidelong look. Did I mention that she's so astute that she's practically psychic? Her students at Barnard loved that about her, that they could go to her office hours and she'd take one look at them and know what their problems were and how to solve them. "Trudi, stop that. Please."

"If I didn't have cancer you'd be yelling right now," she said with an innocent tone but a definite smirk. "So he *has* asked you out."

"I'm swearing off men. At least for now. And when I do get with someone, he'll have 'I am not a narcissist' written on his chest."

"Hopkins doesn't sound like a narcissist. He sounds bloody lovely."

"Oh," I exclaimed, changing the subject, "Clif is giving a talk next week at the New York Fine Arts Society, they're by Grand Central. Why don't you guys come and we'll go out for dinner afterward? If you feel like it, Trudi."

Trudi's face changed slightly as she turned inward. No one except me, Robert, and their son Peter would notice it. She said quietly, "If I'm well enough, we'll be there."

"I will give you all of my strength so you'll be well enough," Robert said. He threw his arm around her shoulders and squeezed her and kissed her cheek.

———⁓———

We saw Bauer's research assistant first. She was a young Pakistani woman who asked Trudi a battery of questions. She left and sent in a nurse who took Trudi's blood pressure and a few vials of blood. She gave Trudi a cup and asked her to provide a urine specimen. She and Trudi went out together so she could show Trudi to the lavatory.

Robert and I stood in the little exam room, shoulder to shoulder, leaning against the wall.

"Robert, don't let her come to the talk next week if she's not feeling well. You know she'll want to support me, but I don't want her to do it at her own expense."

He nodded.

"I guess she'll be on meds by then. Chemo or whatever. I hope. I guess Dr. Bauer will tell us," I continued.

Robert took a deep inhale.

Trudi came back grinning. "I left them a generous sample that should fulfill their needs."

Nurse practitioner Janet Finley came in, throwing her arms loosely around Trudi in a half-embrace. "Mrs. Waterston! Right this way; come with me. Dr. Bauer can see you now."

She kept her arm lightly draped around Trudi as she marched her toward Bauer's office.

Scott stood near the door and shook Trudi's hand as she walked in. "Mrs. Waterston, how are you feeling?"

"I have some back pain," she said. Her neutral tone of voice told me how much it hurt. Trudi never complained about anything.

Bauer frowned and touched her arm. "Come in and sit down and we'll talk." He shook Robert's hand and then turned to me, visibly brightening.

*He should never play poker*, I thought. But I just shook his hand politely. He held on a split second longer than was necessary.

Three chairs were arranged in front of Bauer's desk. Trudi sat in the middle and Robert and I flanked her.

"We're still in the midst of the work-up for you that I require," Scott said. He looked Trudi full in the eyes. "There are more tests to run."

"I understand," Trudi said.

"But I can now confirm your internist's diagnosis. You have stage three pancreatic cancer with locally advanced exocrine tumors," Scott continued. "These tumors are a type of adenocarcinoma. They are unresectable."

"That's what makes it stage three," Trudi observed.

Scott made a small head gesture of acknowledgement. "That's right, you're a professor at Barnard. You're good at research."

"My real skill is reading stockbooks from Parisian art dealers in the nineteenth century," Trudi joked. "But in a pinch, I can find my way around WebMD."

"Be careful what websites you search, some contain inaccurate or even misleading information," Bauer cautioned.

Trudi raised her sandy eyebrows at him. "Dr. Bauer, that is exactly what I say to my freshmen."

He smiled back frankly, meeting her eyes with fierce intelligence. "I don't mean to be patronizing, Mrs. Waterston. I just want you to have the absolute best facts as you battle this cancer. You have my cell phone number and email address from our first appointment. I encourage you to contact me whenever you have questions. If I don't pick up for you, it means I'm with a patient. I'll call you back ASAP. You can also text me. I will respond."

"That's service with a smile," Trudi noted.

"This is a battle and you and I are down in the trenches fighting it together."

"You know, Dr. Bauer, I *am* an expert at research. By the time I see you next, I'll know almost as much about stage three pancreatic cancer as you do," she said. "My research will be a great aide in our battle."

"I welcome the support." He continued to meet her gaze without blinking. "I'm concerned about one of your lymph nodes. So we know exactly what we're up against, I'd like to get an updated CT scan."

Trudi's hand touched her breastbone, just above her great grandmother's cameo pendant. "What about treatment?"

"There are standards of care for treatment. That is, a combination of low dose chemotherapy given simultaneously with radiation to the pancreas and surrounding tissues. Radiation therapy can destroy cancer cells. Chemotherapy can prevent pancreatic tumors from growing and sometimes it can shrink them. I recommend an aggressive approach."

"What about your clinical trial?" Trudi asked quietly.

"You'll have to sign an informed consent form first before we proceed to anything research related. I will go over that with you in detail. In terms of my trial, I am using a vaccine therapy in combination with three chemotherapy drugs. The vaccine is made from gene-modified tumor cells. Two of the chemotherapy drugs have been approved for the treatment of pancreatic cancer while the third has not. If you qualify for the study, you will receive the drugs and vaccine therapy on a three-week schedule that repeats for up to six courses."

"I hear your trial has been getting good results," Trudi said.

Scott took a breath and tilted his head. "It's a trial. Some of the initial results are promising. I won't make you any promises. Also, there are strict requirements for the trial. I'm not yet certain you're a candidate for it. We need to run a few more tests."

"I spoke to someone from your trial who said that after six treatments, her tumor growth had been halted, and her carbohydrate antigen marker had fallen by 80%," Trudi said. "She said she's coming in for six more treatments. So your six-course protocol gets extended if it's working."

Scott's eyes gleamed behind his glasses. "You are exceptionally good at research, Professor Waterston. If you don't mind telling me, whom did you speak to?"

"Patricia Wexworth, a friend of mine at Boston College."

Scott smiled, the small, tight smile of an athlete who knows he's winning a contest. "A remarkable and courageous woman."

"You should read her book on J. W. Waterhouse, you'll never look at *The Lady of Shalott* the same way," Trudi said.

Scott blinked at her for a moment. His deep, smooth voice grew even more melodious. "Suddenly I'm hearing a lot about art. I'll have to brush up on art history so I have something intelligent to say about it."

His comment was meant for me and I felt a wisp of his energy extend toward me, like a private, invisible caress, but I didn't respond.

"You're welcome to sit in on my lectures," Trudi offered. "I'm teaching a survey course during the summer session. European art from The Black Plague to the Reformation."

Scott shook his head. "Don't plan on teaching this summer. If you qualify for the trial, you're going to feel lousy. Treatments are infusions that take eight to nine hours to complete. If you don't qualify, it's almost as bad. You'll have anti-nausea and anti-fatigue medication but still, you'll lose your hair and feel extreme fatigue. Some women and men too, experience depression and embarrassment about their hair loss. That's on top of depression about the cancer. If you don't have a psychotherapist, I can refer you to one."

"I'm British, I have hats. Almost as many as Her Majesty. I'll perch one at a jaunty angle atop my shiny bald head," Trudi said, gesturing with her hands to demonstrate. "Don't worry about me, Dr. Bauer. I'll carry on."

"Oh, I'll worry about you, you're my patient now," he said, gazing at her solemnly.

She took a deep breath and visibly steeled herself. "What's my prognosis?"

"The median survival for untreated advanced pancreatic cancer is three and a half months. But we're going to treat it, and we will do so aggressively. We'll employ systemic therapy that targets the micro-metastases, too."

"I do hope I qualify for your trial," she answered.

Robert and I sat there like two proverbial bumps on a log.

---

Back at the gallery, all was as I'd left it. Alex sat with her nose stuck in her book. Rosa stood at the door to the office, looking anxiously at Alex.

"Any foot traffic?" I asked.

Rosa shook her head. "How's Trudi?"

It was my turn to shake my head.

Rosa squeezed my arm. "I'm sorry, Sarah." Her eyes searched my face for a moment and then they sparkled at me. She crooked her finger and led me into the office.

Geoff was gone, which I hoped meant that the gallery website was updated. Rosa reached into her purse and tucked something into my hand. She closed my fingers around it. "I keep some in my purse, I want you to have these."

I opened my fingers: two condoms. "Uh—"

"No judgments," Rosa whispered. "Just, be safe, OK?"

Steps thumped behind me as Alex stomped toward the office.

I stuck the condoms in my jacket pocket.

Alex asked, in her usual pissed-off voice, "What's wrong with Aunt Trudi?"

"She has cancer," I said. I had my back to her so she couldn't see my face twist with sadness and worry.

Alex was silent for a moment. "Bummer." She stomped back to her seat.

*Bummer?* After all the times her godmother had been in our home, having dinner and celebrating holidays, presenting Alex with birthday gifts and Christmas money? *Bummer?*

What have I done wrong as a mother and a person to have created such a cold and insensitive child?

Rosa put her arms around me and hugged me.

If there'd been any fat at all in the gallery budget, I'd have doubled her salary.

# CHAPTER TEN

THE FOLLOWING MONDAY, MY bi-coastal friend Marcia Mensdorff was in town staying at the Four Seasons. She kept texting to invite me out: lunch at the Carlyle restaurant, dinner at the Landmarc at the Time Warner Center, drinks at the new hot bar in Chelsea, a cocktail party in Tribeca. I texted back that I had a catastrophe with Alex and was glued to my daughter's side for the time being. I hoped to see Marcia before she returned to Los Angeles.

Bailey got on the phone with me numerous times. As I said, he cared about Alex. I was going to have to take Dr. Maitra's advice and meet privately with Bailey, but first I had to get Bailey's opinion on what to do next with Alex. After his usual snarky lecture that suggested that I was too controlling and intrusive, he approved of therapeutic school and suggested one in upstate New York. I followed up with an email to him asking for clarification. When he emailed back a summation indicating his preferences, I composed a brief email to George, relaying what Villanova and Bailey had said.

George emailed back commanding me to apply to the school. He kept his email brief and didn't add any of his usual putdowns of me. I was surprised at how relieved I felt. I couldn't help but wonder how much worse my resistance to George's hostility made the whole situation.

I phoned the Brookton Academy, which billed itself as a "coeducational therapeutic boarding school for bright but underachieving kids" and talked honestly with their admissions person. She was warm and kind and went over all the school's offerings and protocols. She described their college preparatory program, which included a summer semester so Alex could finish her sophomore year. That was an important consideration since it was already May and the end of the school year.

The admissions lady also went over their support program, which included a substance abuse component and therapeutic interventions such as wilderness camp. She told me that Alex's story wasn't unusual. "Especially in cases of high conflict divorce, teens can struggle with a range of behavioral problems, including drugs and delinquency," she added.

I winced, though the way she said it wasn't judgmental. I wished for the millionth time that George and I had been able to come to some sort of courteous peace. Other divorced parents did it all the time.

It was true that my resistance to—yes, my loathing of—George exacted its own toll. He wasn't solely responsible for the mess. There was a need here for me to tiptoe on eggshells all the time, and I was no ballerina. I was more like a rhinoceros wearing combat boots. In the roulette wheel of my soul, sometimes the ball landed in a red pocket marked "Reactionary self" or a black one marked "Vengeful self" rather than in the green pocket marked "Better self."

I sat at the kitchen table amidst the ruins of our Mexican delivery food, typing in the application on my laptop. Alex was in her room with her door shut. Periodically I rose and knocked on her door and peeked in to ask her a question: "How about some tea?" or "Walk Groucho with me? It's a beautiful night."

Alex was mesmerized by Netflix on her laptop and just grunted.

I hoped she wasn't getting too depressed, although a little depression wouldn't hurt her. I wanted her to feel upset about the hell she was wreaking.

I finished the application and emailed it to George. An incoming email chimed; it was from the editor at *American Artist* magazine. I groaned and smacked my head with both hands because I had, of course, forgotten to finalize the article and send it to him. The furor around Alex's expulsion drove most other thoughts out of my mind.

The email was suitably nasty. "Sarah, our magazine relies on contributors to meet our deadlines so we can produce our print magazine on time," it began. It devolved from there, and the editor closed by suggesting that I not submit articles to them in the future.

I couldn't let that stand because my articles generated traffic to the gallery website, speaking engagements for me, and ultimately interest in my artists. With the art market changing because of recession and the internet, I had to be creative about marketing and promotion. It was all about drumming up business. I sent an apologetic letter back, humbly begging forgiveness and explaining that a family crisis had arisen.

I phoned Rosa without realizing how late it was until I heard her groggy voice. I apologized and thanked her for her good work promoting Clif's talk, then warned her that I might be absent to take Alex to the therapeutic school.

She muttered the appropriate words of reassurance and hung up.

I sat for a moment wondering, have I become *that* boss?

———

In the morning, George sent back a short response to the application: "Submit it."

So I did. Then I got Alex up and dressed. She was spending the day with her father and I was going to the gallery to put out the fires that had started while I was attending to her. I was pleased that Alex only cursed at me for five minutes instead of her usual twenty.

I walked a morose Alex the few blocks over to her dad's apartment. He lived on Central Park West across from the Museum of Natural History, a location suitably upscale for a Calhoun, though it was a radical enterprise for a Calhoun to reside on the West Side. Calhouns in the city had hitherto resided on the East Side, in an enclave with other people with similar last names, like 'Dewey' and 'Ferguson' and 'Taft.' George's abode on the left side of Central Park was a sign of a brave new inclusive world. We stopped under the awning and I kissed her cheek despite the forearm she stuck in my chest to prevent it.

"Have a good day, Alex. See you later."

"At least I'll get some real dinner tonight," she snarled as she trudged past the doorman.

I walked out a few meters and found myself stopping to look around and breathe. I paused to take in my surroundings and appreciate them. It was May, perhaps New York's most beautiful month; the rains cleared up and the sun showed itself bright and strong but not yet scorching, the way it was in August. A fresh breeze fluttered the green leaves on the trees and people's steps quickened with new life. George's apartment was directly across from the Natural History Museum, and I looked over the trees in front of the planetarium, up into the infinite, brilliant sky that arched above us all.

Something about the specific cadence of the steps approaching me snagged my attention. It was Katherine, George's wife. She was a tall skinny blonde, the type who proliferate on the Upper East Side and who make the Calhouns feel that all is right and good with the world. She was some kind of fancy caterer or blue-ribbon baker, I'd never figured out which. She speared me with eyes widened with feeling. High color slashed across her cheeks, her patrician nostrils quivered, and her face contorted like a broken theatrical mask. She actually shook as she marched past me.

It took me a moment. Then I realized that she was shaking with rage. At me.

There was no love lost between us. I had dissed her zipless, Pollyanna-ish philosophy of life on more than one occasion, which George and Alex had reported to her.

Katherine looked back over her shoulder, throwing me a glance of furious contempt. She was turning up the volume on her thoughts so that I would be sure to hear them. She despised me and she wanted me to know that; she wanted me to feel bad because of it.

She hissed, "Alex is always starving. Why don't you ever feed her?"

I just stood perusing her quizzically.

I usually wasn't good at detaching, but today, for some reason, perhaps because Dr. Maitra had told me to be a leader and demonstrate character for my daughter, Katherine's scorn didn't hook me.

I looked at her, a slave to her anger and loathing, consumed by her own bitterness and thought: *So that's why all the great spiritual leaders tell people to forgive.*

I shrugged, turned my back to her, and walked away.

Another day in other circumstances, I might have spit in her face. In my mind I had every reason to do so. From what I could tell, Katherine's viciousness toward me had wrought terrible damage to my relationships with my daughters and thus to them. Even if they didn't know it, my children needed me for their own psychological wholeness. It was hard for them to understand that when they'd been breathing the poison of Katherine's and their father's enmity toward me. She contradicted anything I said and went to lengths to invalidate me. She led them to believe they didn't have to respect me. She encouraged Dani to cut me out of her life. She did it all with a self-righteousness bordering on self-canonization.

George went along with it because of his own malice. He would never forgive me for humiliating him by leaving him for another man. Seeing the bonds of my relationships with my daughters erode must truly have delighted him.

It was a powerful burden of pain for me to live with. But today, the whiplash of negative feelings I had about Katherine didn't happen. I felt bad, but not because she wanted me to feel bad about myself. I felt bad for *her*.

It was a strange, unsettling realization to carry with me to the gallery. I wasn't enlightened enough for it.

———

I texted Marcia from my office and asked to meet her for a late lunch. I finished editing my belated article and emailed it, with another apology, to *American Artist*. I opened Rosa's notes on her email correspondence with our collectors regarding Clif's talk.

My cell phone rang. It was that lovely admissions lady from the Brookton Academy. "She's in," the lady said. "Bring her up as soon as possible. Let's get her enrolled and get her started on healing."

I exclaimed with hope, the first hope I'd felt in a while for Alex. I emailed George right away, telling him the good news and suggesting that I drive her to Brookton the next morning. Then I emailed the same to Bailey and Marty. The latter two responded quickly and positively.

Just as I was leaving to meet Marcia for lunch, George got back to me. It was a typically shitty George email. "I won't pay for it. Find her a public school in Manhattan. She can live with you and go to summer school. She'll be at your place after dinner."

I texted, emailed, and phoned Bailey, Dr. Maitra, and Marty. I texted Marcia and canceled, telling her that I loved her and another crisis had arisen around Alex. Marcia phoned back immediately but I couldn't talk, I was heading out the door to collar Bailey at his office for a quick word.

What was I supposed to do with Alex? She needed help. It would be disastrous to stick her haphazardly in yet another school in Manhattan. The city was a moveable feast of vice and indulgence for wayward teenagers, and Alex knew the menu better than she knew her own name. Her regular therapy wasn't helping her, even Bailey acknowledged that.

If I took her to Brookton despite George's capricious commandment, how was I going to pay the tuition? George was the one with the rich family who catered to his every whim and the endless deep pockets for everything from litigating to buying Dani a car. I was the one with all her worldly assets sunk into a gallery for beautiful art. I was the one who was teetering on the precipice of financial ruin.

———————

Bailey was at his office on Central Park West and Seventy-Eighth, seeing a client. I paced around his waiting room. A dodgy-looking young guy came in and seated himself, ostensibly Bailey's next client. I glared at the guy so he'd know that I was going in before him.

He huddled down into the chair and played a game on his iPhone.

Bailey's door opened and a woman wearing tall platform shoes hurried out. Bailey peeked around the corner. He spied me and frowned. "I have someone waiting."

"Five minutes," I said, throwing my weight against the door to get him to let me through.

Bailey was a pudgy, medium-sized guy with a round face, thick glasses, and thinning scraggles of gray hair on his pink pate. He scowled but let me through and closed the door behind me. He said, a bit testily, "I thought you were taking Alex to Brookton?"

"So did I. But a few minutes ago George emailed that he won't pay. He wants me to send her to public school here in the city. Ordered me to."

Bailey grimaced. He stroked his chin and shuffled his feet and didn't say anything.

"What am I going to do?" I wailed. "She's out of control! I never know if or when she's coming home or what she's up to. When she does come home, she's stoned or drunk or both. She's been stealing money from my purse. Other parents call because she's vomited in their homes. She won't go to class except when she's terribly stoned. Now she's brought a banned substance to class."

"I know," he said. "Alex is spinning out of control."

"So what do I do? I'm so afraid she's going to do terrible damage to herself!"

"So am I," he muttered. He pulled at the collar of his polo shirt. "Do you have the right to make the decision to take her to Brookton?"

I took a moment to wonder how I was going to pay Brookton's tuition. I had the right to take Alex to Brookton; I knew that. But Bailey was the kind who'd have to hear it for himself. I took out my phone and got Marty on the line.

Marty said, "According to the settlement agreement, you have final decision-making authority regarding schools."

I put him on speakerphone. "Marty, would you repeat that for Dr. Bailey and me?"

Marty repeated himself.

Bailey said, "Take her to Brookton."

# CHAPTER ELEVEN

ALEX STARED STRAIGHT AHEAD through the front window. Her eyes were glassy and reddened; she'd been crying.

My eyes were glassy and reddened, also. I'd been crying, too. For Alex mostly, but truthfully also for myself. It hurt to have come to this eventuality—I loved Alex and wanted the best for her. I wasn't going to be able to teach her, as Dr. Maitra had counseled, with her living at therapeutic school, but I felt it gave her the best chance to get clean and get herself together in a wholesome way. I was also scared about the expense of Brookton.

Alex's duffel bag sat in the back seat, the giant one she used for summer camp. I made a mental note to call her summer camp and ask for a refund. Alex wouldn't be going to Maine to play soccer, paint ceramics, and swim in a lake with the younger kids she was supposed to be overseeing. She was enrolled in a junior counselor program that would have led to a paying job next year, but that didn't matter now. As with so many plans involving Alex, it was simply shattered like a porcelain vase.

"I think this school will help you, Alex, I really do," I said. "It's a good program. Dr. Bailey recommends it."

"You're taking me to loser school," she said, her voice thick with anger.

"No, it's for kids like you who are smart but troubled."

"It's jail." She sobbed and chartreuse snot trickled down from her nostril.

After a while, she stopped crying. She fiddled with the brand new iPhone her dad bought her when I'd confiscated her old one and plugged it into Brigit's dashboard. She turned on a streaming music service.

She saw me glance at the iPhone. "You should cancel my old number. Dad put me on his account. I've got a new number."

*To go with your fancy new phone, a reward for getting yourself kicked out of another school. It's great the way George supports my parenting decisions.*

"They won't let you keep the iPhone, Alex. The school has a no electronics policy."

"You're such a bitch," she shrieked.

Meredith Brooks' song *Bitch* came on. Once upon a time, not so long ago, we had declared that our song. We used to sing it together at the top of our lungs, it was our thing, and then we'd collapse in laughter together, feeling our silliness and our adventurousness and our shared femininity and above all else, our closeness to each other: "I'm a bitch, I'm a lover, I'm a child, I'm a mother, I'm a sinner, I'm a saint, I do not feel ashamed."

After about five hours of driving we arrived at Brookton Academy. We were met in the front lobby by Jody, the admissions lady, and Ted, the director of the school. They were serious but welcoming, looking Alex in the eye and explaining what was expected of her as well as what would be offered to her. There were forms to fill out and the school's physician's assistant to speak with regarding Alex's medications. The staff psychologist who would be supervising Alex's recovery met with us, as did the academic director, who plotted out Alex's courses.

We toured the grounds that were unexpectedly verdant and filled with tall old trees. The land was good, which comforted me. The dormitories were strictly separated by gender, which was also comforting, though I knew that wily Alex would find her way around any barrier to get to a boy she wanted. But I supposed that Brookton had plenty of experience dealing with rebellious kids and their agendas.

I met with the registrar and put the summer session on my credit card. I'd only once ever made a five-figure purchase—when I'd been in a gallery on the Isle of Capri and spotted a painting I knew I could flip for double its price. That had worked out—this might not.

I felt numb and exhausted. It was not what I ever expected when I was raising my beloved children, trying to give them everything—especially what I didn't have. Trying to be there for them always. Who would expect that my child, who was wonderful in a million ways, would go completely off the rails? That I'd be putting her into a school that was one step up from boot camp?

I grabbed her and hugged her for two whole minutes before saying goodbye.

Alex didn't say anything, but neither did she swear at me or push me away.

---

I got back to the city well after dark. I hadn't eaten dinner and I'd lost all sense of time.

I parked Brigit and found the Manhattan air cool and indigo, so I shrugged on my jacket. I placed my keys in my pocket and found the condoms from Rosa.

I took the subway to my neighborhood on the Upper West Side and walked a few blocks south to the Chirping Chicken Ristorante for a meal. I sat at a banquette, swallowing big mouthfuls of steaming, succulent white meat and washing it down with icy cold water in a paper cup. It was delicious and put me back inside my body.

Checking Alex into Brookton had been surreal, disembodying, almost an experience of astral projection. After the meal, I started to feel like myself again.

I sat back in the vinyl banquette and thought about calling Dani to let her know her sister was safely ensconced in a school where she would be well looked after. Maybe she would even start to heal and grow. But calling Dani would be an exercise in futility. Dani didn't want to hear about Alex's travails; she would only hang up on me again. In other times, I would have instantly called Trudi, who would have spent an hour on the phone with me scolding me into feeling better. But not now; I wasn't going to bother her now.

I was lucky to have people like Trudi who did care about me. Trudi and Scott, her doctor.

My feet started moving before my brain quite picked up on what was happening. I dumped the sparse remains of my bird into the trash and bussed my tray. I was out the door and nearly skipping the next few blocks to the candy boutique.

Had I realized before how close Chirping Chicken was to the candy boutique?

But it wasn't chocolate I was interested in, and a polite older man emerging from Scott's building held open the front door for me. Was it the sixth floor or the fifth floor where Scott lived? My hand hovered over the panel, considering. I closed my eyes and thought back to the moment he'd pressed the button, and then again when we stumbled out of the elevator, entwined. I caught it out of the corner of my mind's eye, the plaque saying "5."

I got out at the fifth floor and walked toward Scott's door. I knocked softly.

He opened the door and his face lit up. He was a little scruffy with beard stubble and he wore grungy sweatpants and an even grungier tee shirt, but I was so happy to see him.

I leaned up on my tiptoes and kissed him and his mouth responded and he dragged me inside. Our tongues were busy inside each other's mouths while he locked the door behind me. I pressed myself against his long, lean form and enjoyed the warmth and tautness of him. He was rank but in a good way, as if he'd worked out and hadn't showered yet, so he was plastered over with testosterone and sweat.

"What are you ..." he started.

I plucked the condoms from my jacket pocket and held them up.

"I have a few boxes, too!" he said jubilantly.

"But only if you don't talk," I said firmly.

He tilted his head, and this was the phenomenal thing about Scott: I could actually see him thinking. His dark eyes percolated and his face underwent a series of narrative expressions. He said, as if I hadn't told him not to talk, "This isn't the way I'd have arranged it, but I'm not going to turn down some company. Will you take off your skirt this time?"

"Hell no, and don't say another word."

He kissed me again and dragged me to his bedroom. He swept a stack of charts and an iPad off his bed before lowering me onto it.

I kept my skirt on.

Afterward, I was soft and unhinged with release. I figured it was better to leave before I started crying.

"Don't go," he said. "Come on, Sarah. Can't we talk now?" He lay on his side next to me. He was naked except for the appendix scar on his side. His long thigh was curled over mine, just below where my skirt was bunched up.

"You talk too much."

I touched the scar with my index finger and marveled at his smooth, perfect olive skin. His chest and belly were lightly furred with dark hair, his nipples were dark peachy-pink, and his shoulders curved and rolled with delectable muscles in all the right places, like a Jacques-Louis David painting.

"You don't talk enough."

I gave him a wry look.

"Can't we just enjoy this without making something out of it?"

"What's wrong with making something out of it?"

"I don't want to."

"I do."

I uttered a sort of sigh with an exclamation point attached. I ran my hand again over his appendix scar. How old was he when he had the operation? Six? Ten? I could imagine a young, serious, all-too-talkative Scott. He probably already had glasses and spoke like a computer.

"Why did you come here today?"

He was watching me. His face was relaxed and his voice lazy but direct.

"Long day."

"I feel so used," he muttered.

"I thought you were glad to get company?"

"Yes, glad, and used," he said. But my hand was stroking his abdomen, and he was getting an erection.

"Care to be used again?" I asked.

"Take your skirt off?"

I shook my head and stroked along the inside of his thigh.

He pulled the other condom off his nightstand and sheathed himself more adroitly than the first time around. Then he rolled over on top of me. He was getting the hang of not talking.

---

I made it to The Mark for lunch with Marcia the next day. I wore a prim, lightweight gray wool dress and jacket suit—my librarian outfit. As I approached the table, Marcia looked up from texting on her iPhone and sang, in her lyrical contralto voice, "You've been a naughty girl, and had a good time at it!"

*How could she tell?*

I tried not to blush furiously. I failed.

"Tell me everything," she said, rising to kiss the air next to my cheek.

"How are you, Marcia? Wonderful to see you," I murmured, air-smooching back and then seating myself next to her. I looked her over and my heart lifted. Marcia was blonde, curvaceous, and gorgeous, and always the most glamorous woman in any room. But more than that, she was a good friend. There wasn't a bitchy bone in her six-foot-tall body and she was unfailingly supportive.

I said, "You look gorgeous!"

"I was just thinking exactly that about you. Obviously shagging agrees with you," she said, eying me just as closely. "New lipstick color? I like it. It's brighter than what you usually wear."

"The suit is so demure that I felt I needed a jazzier lip color."

She giggled. "That color's not about your suit, darling. It's about the lucky man who's receiving your attentions. I hope he's properly appreciative."

I shook my head a little. "Marcia, I have to ask, what is it you do that keeps your skin so beautiful? You have the best complexion—you look twenty-five years old. Share your secret."

Marcia grinned widely. "Oh, I see. A *younger* man, then. Good for you. I prefer them, they have such life force energy."

I blushed again.

Fortunately, a waiter appeared and bowed several times, something Marcia frequently elicited. Perhaps it had to do with the Hungarian nobility in her lineage or perhaps it had to do with her striking and graceful presence.

I said, "I really am happy to see you."

"I want to hear all about what's going on with your daughter. I suppose your ex is being completely vile. Ex number one. But first, tell me about the new man?"

I said with a sigh, "If I'm going to talk about all this, I need wine."

"I've already ordered us a bottle of Barolo," Marcia said merrily.

Two bottles of Barolo later we were giggling, and the lunch crowd was sliding into an afternoon tea and cocktails clientele. Make that late afternoon cocktails. OK, early evening, four hours later. I should have gone back to the gallery but Rosa was minding it and that was one of the great perquisites of being my own boss, I could give myself some afternoons off.

Marcia and I sat near the bar, observing the parade of chicly dressed people of all ages. She filled me in on her latest beaux, her mother, her nieces, her brother in Paris, her sister in Vancouver, and her work as a producer of commercials and music videos.

I related my recent events: Alex, Trudi, Scott, the gallery narrowly escaping its demise. I didn't say much about Carl because there wasn't much to say.

"Now that you're sampling younger men, Sarah, I'll make some introductions," Marcia said. She was scrolling through her contacts list on her phone, deciding who was good enough for me or perhaps simply tumble-able enough.

"I don't know, Marcia, my life is pretty complicated."

"Darling, that's precisely why you must enjoy yourself!" she admonished. "You've been married far too long. It's about time you let yourself play."

"I think I've got all I can manage right now. I don't want any more commitments."

Marcia looked up and wrinkled her nose. She had a finely modeled face, as feminine as any Botticelli goddess but in more of the Bouguereau style of strong yet delicate features.

"Who said anything about commitment? Play around for a while. Date a few men. You've got to stop marrying everyone you sleep with, Sarah. It will save you a fortune in legal fees for divorce."

"And will dating younger men save me a fortune in suing my ex-husband when he tells me to send our daughter to a therapeutic school and then, after I've submitted the application he approved—"

"Here. Enrique Rivera," Marcia interrupted. "Hottest young telenovela star in Central and South America. There are a gazillion pictures of him online and you can check out everything, I mean everything, before you go out with him. Isn't he altogether yummy?"

She handed over her phone for me to see an image of the aforementioned actor in his altogether. "Doesn't that make you forget about this dreadful business with your ex?"

"Yes. You're a terrible influence," I said giggling and perusing the image—I couldn't help myself. It was a still from a film, perhaps a naughty one. I mean, it wasn't certain the film was NC17. But what was the point of a plot when the star was so delicious? Enrique Rivera was a spectacular dish. I'd have to be dead not to see that. And I knew I wasn't dead because everything hurt so much.

"Influencing you terribly is what I'm here for," she returned. "I'll call Enrique and set up a meeting."

"A blind date?" I shrieked. "God no!"

"It's not blind at all. You've seen him. He's seen you, too. I sent him your photo ages ago, from that character ball last Halloween."

"Oh, no, fishnets," I said, remembering my costume. "He'll get the wrong impression of me."

"You mean he'll get the right impression," she said, giggling.

"What is he, like, thirty? What if he doesn't like older women?"

"Enrique likes women and he'll adore you. Wear that black bustier dress when you meet him. No stockings and your highest stilettos."

Then I laughed out loud. "Those make me fall over!"

Marcia tilted her head with a whiff of exasperation. "Your second highest stilettos. Practice walking in them before you go out."

# CHAPTER TWELVE

I'D DRUNK ENOUGH WATER to float an aircraft carrier, taken a couple of multi-vitamins, and swallowed a fistful of analgesics. The hangover from being out with Marcia until the wee hours was greatly diminished. I'd put on a navy blue lace cocktail dress that showed some cleavage—which was enhanced by a brassiere made in Italy for the explicit purpose of elevating a woman of a certain age—and I'd donned some dangly pearl and turquoise earrings made by a jeweler in Santa Fe. I was dressed like a successful, confident art gallery proprietor. I was ready for Clif's talk.

I arrived at the New York Fine Arts Society's showroom early and greeted Jenna Shaw, Leah Goldberg, and John Whitford who ran the organization. I spread out some flyers for my gallery on the designated table and then found myself with little to do. I stood near the entrance and texted Marcia, who let me know from her plane that she'd slept so late after our evening out that she'd almost missed her breakfast meeting.

"I laughed 2 hard," she texted. "my cheeks hurt!"

"Me 2," I replied. It was always fun to go out with Marcia. My inner-goofball seldom got let out to play; I had responsibilities and obligations and duties, children and a gallery and an employee. George and Clif both looked askance when my innate silliness erupted.

But Marcia, ah, Marcia understood that part of me. When my goofball self emerged, she greeted her with "Oh, goody!"

It was redemptive to remember my friends when all Hades was cluster-fucking my life.

"Sarah," said a voice. It was Clif, standing near me—my soon-to-be former husband. "You look good."

He gave me a smoldering look, the kind that had weakened my knees into overcooked egg noodles when we'd first met and even during the early years we were together after he'd stopped sleeping with me. I had a weakness for good-looking men and Clif hit my Achilles' heel like an arrow dipped in poison. He had his Italian father's dark hair and brawn, and his Philadelphia high society mother's classic movie-star features and brilliant blue eyes. He had a deeply-ingrained sense of his own physical person and carried himself with superb posture. He walked into a room and was instantly 'on,' like a motion-sensor light bulb, radiating charisma. The amazing thing about Clif was that his talent backed up his attitude. He could paint a figure like no one since Caravaggio. He was an expert at the anatomy that gave architectural structure to the body, the spiraling organic forms of muscles on bones, and the palette of colors that depicted flesh. He truly was the cream of his generation of artists, even if the art world hadn't yet embraced him. I thought he was one for the history books. So did he, of course.

He said softly, with a wistful edge to his voice, "You look beautiful, Sarah."

"Oh, I have something for you," I said. I went to get a check out of my handbag, which was secreted away in Jenna's office. It was Clif's cut of the sale to Carl. It was his full cut. I didn't play fast and loose with my artists' monies, the way many gallerists did. It always surprised me how many seemingly reputable gallery owners dummied up false invoices for their artists or simply verbally relayed a lower price than the piece actually sold for, in order to take a bigger chunk of the sale than they were entitled to. People might be shocked if they knew how often that happened and which important, famous galleries were defrauding their artists. The artist always got screwed.

But, in all truth, it was partly the artist's fault. Like Clif, most of them were allergic to business in all its forms and preferred to let Big Daddy Gallery hand them their allowance. There was something in the zeitgeist that encouraged, in an artist, the complete abdication of a mature person's financial wherewithal. Historically, it wasn't always that way. Michelangelo, the best of all artists, was as shrewd and cutthroat a businessman as any Medici. Canova ran a thriving enterprise. But currently, few artists exerted themselves in that arena. I couldn't change that, but I could be meticulous with my artists. And I kept my mouth shut about the shady goings-on in other establishments.

I trotted back out of the office to find Clif coming toward me, and laid the check in Clif's hand.

His eyes dimmed and he stared at me as if commanding me to pet him. "It was so much better when you'd deposit it for me and tell me it was there for me to buy paints with."

*Better for you.*

I fought the urge to tell him to buy his paints with cash or else to use debit—it was not my problem anymore. Clif liked to run up his credit cards into the five figures and then make minimum payments. Much as I had tried, I'd never been able to make him understand the concept of compounding interest.

"What are you working on these days?" I asked, changing the subject.

He gazed soulfully into my eyes. "A multi-figure composition based on the Trojan War. Aphrodite, Hera, Helen, and Paris. I call it *Fury and Lust*. It's my best piece yet and it's large. I'll be done in a few days."

"I'll show it right away."

"You're so good at promoting my art," he said. He snaked his arm around me so that his hand rested on my sacrum. "It's because you understand my process."

"Isn't that your new lady friend, Clif?" I asked, shrugging off his hand. I nodded toward an elegantly dressed woman of about fifty who stood in the entryway, perusing the room.

She was petite and blonde, very well coiffed and dressed in Chanel from toe to widow's peak. She wore several strands of creamy white pearls whose thick, lustrous nacre proclaimed them the real thing. She bustled over and stood close to Clif, laid a proprietary hand on his shoulder, and gave him a look indicating that he should introduce us.

"Sarah, this is Nicole; Nicole, Sarah."

"Hello," I said cheerfully, wondering where I had met her before. She was probably an art groupie and I'd seen her at events around the city. I couldn't keep track of all the sexually desperate forty and fifty-year-old women in Clif's entourage.

"Hello," she said sourly, not meeting my eyes.

I felt for her. It wasn't easy being with Clif.

"Nicole, you probably want to help Clif get ready for his talk. I won't keep you." I looked across the room and waved as if spying someone I knew. I smiled vaguely at Clif and Nicole and then hurried off toward the small knot of people gathering by the door.

In truth, two of my better clients had arrived or rather, two pairs of clients. One was a gay couple: a surgeon and an interior designer. The designer was a stay-at-home dad for their two children. At the risk of sounding cliché, they had fabulous taste. I never sold them a painting without wishing I could keep it for myself.

The other clients were a youngish couple who lived well on the lavish bonuses from his job on Wall Street. The model-thin, pleasantly harebrained wife had taken a liking to me after I'd invited her to lunch and plied her with kiwi-and-passion fruit margaritas; I think that was the most calories she ever consumed in a single day. The husband, her age and a hundred IQ points her better, was going to buy whatever his wife wanted to keep her happy. It was an arrangement that worked splendidly for me because she regularly wanted beautiful art for their apartment on the Upper East Side or their house in East Hampton.

I greeted all four of them happily and made introductions all around. It seemed the skinny wife and the designer husband attended the same spin class. I suggested we all get together for a private viewing in the gallery, complete with champagne and hors d'oeuvres; I could arrange for them to see works that hadn't yet been shown to the public. The designer and the skinny wife lit up and the two husbands grimaced respectfully: they'd be spending money at my gallery.

"Well played," whispered Donald, the surgeon.

I was going to whisper something cheeky back but someone touched my arm from behind. I turned and exclaimed, "Oh, Carl!"

"Sarah, I thought I'd see you here." He squeezed my upper arm and kissed my cheek affectionately.

"Everyone, this is Carl Hopkins." I relayed their names to Carl.

"I've heard of you and your funds, of course, Mr. Hopkins," said Eric, the Wall Street guy, with awe in his voice.

Carl's posture straightened a bit and his gravelly voice dropped deeper into his chest. "Where are you, Eric?"

Eric mentioned an investment bank and Carl responded with a few names that must have belonged to important personages, since Eric's eyes got as impossibly large and round as UFOs flying overhead.

I glanced across the room to see the editor from *American Artist* magazine and I excused myself. I stepped away with every intention of groveling abjectly at the editor's feet in apology for the late article. I already had in mind a few juicy slices of humble pie to eat in front of him. Anything to keep my business afloat. But Carl caught up with me.

"I know this is a business event for you and you have people to talk to," Carl said in a low voice. "I was wondering if I could take you to dinner afterward?" His blue eyes sparkled.

I was surprised by how pleased I was with his invitation. I found myself sparkling back at him. Before I could respond, however, another voice sounded from behind him.

"Sarah," called Trudi. She had a wicked gleam in her eyes. On one hand, I was happy to see her looking so chipper and, on the other hand, I knew exactly what she was thinking: she was about to meddle in my life.

"Why, hello there. I'm Trudi Waterston and this is my husband Robert. Are you a friend of Sarah's?"

"Indeed, I mean to be one. Carl Hopkins," he responded warmly, shaking her hand and then Robert's.

"Sarah, we'd like to have dinner with you after the talk," Trudi said, her British crispness accentuating itself as it always did when she was revved up about something. She arched one eyebrow at me in her best inquisitive professor mien.

"Oh, it's going to be a late evening," I murmured.

"Actually, I just invited Sarah for dinner tonight, why don't we all go out together?" Carl suggested. "I know just the place for a late dinner. I'll call for reservations." He pulled out his cell phone and stepped back to make the call.

"Damn it, Trudi," I whispered in admonishment, before bussing Robert's cheek.

She grinned widely and looked around. "This is a wonderful turnout."

"Are you feeling OK?" I asked, squeezing her in a quick, fierce hug.

She patted my arm gently. "If I wasn't, I wouldn't be here."

Carl returned to our circle. "Good news, the maitre d' at the bistro will hold our table as long as we need."

"I do enjoy good bistro fare, it's increasingly hard to find," Trudi remarked.

"Then you'll love this place, the food is wonderful," Carl assured her.

"I'd love to chat but there's someone I have to speak with," I said.

"No worries, we'll be waiting," Trudi said with a smug smile. "Carl, why don't you sit with Robert and me?"

I thought about kicking her—not a giant donkey kick, but a small, discrete tap on the ankle—but then I wondered: is it acceptable to kick someone with stage three pancreatic cancer?

Clif talked about modern classicism in a way that made everyone in the audience feel as if they expertly understood it and therefore naturally loved it. He spoke of the New York Fine Arts Society as if they were the Don Quixotes of the art world, visionaries who were nobly bearing the sacred torch of art at its most beautiful. By the time he finished, all the women in the audience wanted to shtup him and all the men wanted to be him. If only they knew what I knew, that Clif's sexual magnetism was a clever mask for his bottomless desire to be taken care of as if he were an infant. But that unacknowledged longing didn't crack the veneer of Clif's social persona which was, in its way, as artful as his paintings. Regardless, his talk was a wonderful introduction to the realist show and it teed me up perfectly to pass out my business cards and invite folks to my gallery—I was Clif's sole gallerist in New York and the divorce agreement Marty had proposed maintained that arrangement.

Following the talk, I did the requisite mingling and we were out of there by nine-thirty. Our table was waiting at the bistro, which was in the eighties off of Madison. The maitre d' ushered us in, and Carl ordered a beautiful cabernet before we were even seated.

I beamed at him.

Once we were seated with menus, Carl said, "The mussels are terrific and they do a first rate steak frites."

"Steak frites sounds perfect to me," I said happily. I laid down my menu and excused myself to go to the ladies room.

When I returned, Trudi and Carl were clasping hands across the table and Robert had his arm around Trudi's shoulder. There was an air of revelation and heightened emotion, like the hush after a powerful symphony ends. I had missed something important.

Trudi looked up with an apologetic wag of her head.

"I declined a wine glass. I'll be starting chemo soon, I think. I hope. Still not sure if I made it into Dr. Bauer's trial but the tests are almost done. I went for the last MRI this morning."

Carl was looking at her with warm compassion written all over his craggy, lined face. I could see him willing her to be strong, to fight well, and to survive. She was taking it in too, which was rare for Trudi, whose professorial facade of good-humored self-reliance kept people at bay.

He said softly, "I'll ask around about this Bauer, see what I can find out about him and his clinical trial. We'll make sure you have the top doctor and the very best treatment."

Robert blinked a few times, his eyes filling with tears.

My eyes filled, too. I turned around and walked back to the bathroom so that Trudi wouldn't have to see me cry. I had never appreciated a man as much as I appreciated Carl at that moment.

# CHAPTER THIRTEEN

ON SATURDAY, I SWEATED through a long, hard yoga class early in the morning. I went to the gallery and answered emails, sent inquiries to Brookton about Alex, and followed up with potential customers I'd greeted at the New York Fine Arts Society's event. A nice, well-dressed, middle-aged couple from Poughkeepsie wandered in and I chatted with them. They weren't buyers, not yet, but they had some means and I could maybe cultivate them. I made a list of errands and tasks for home that included doing the laundry, grocery shopping, and ordering dog food for Groucho.

Rosa came in to do the four-to-seven shift and given how few walk-ins there were, I went home. I stopped in the mailroom to get the mail and my cell phone bill was there, which reminded me to take Alex off of my account. I stepped into the elevator and so did Jack, a young man who'd grown up in the building and used to babysit for me. He and I formed a friendship over the years and I was delighted to see him. I squealed and hugged him.

"Sarah, how are you?" he asked.

"I never see you now that you live in Chicago. How's it going? You're doing management consulting, right?"

"Yep. I'm home for two days visiting my parents," he said. "How are Dani and Alex?"

"Alex is in therapeutic boarding school. Dani doesn't talk to me."

"That sucks," he said. "I try to talk to Dani sometimes but she's an angry young woman. What can you do?" He scanned my face intently and chewed his lip. Then he said, "I never told you this, Sarah, but there's this thing that happened that I always felt uncomfortable about. After you and

George split up, George and Katherine invited me and my girlfriend out for dinner. I just thought it was so weird. I went but I always felt guilty about it."

"Don't feel guilty about a free meal, Jack."

"It was just so weird because I'm friends with you, you know. It was like they wanted me to like them more than you. Like George wanted to show me that Katherine was better than you."

I just shook my head and shrugged and the elevator doors opened for my floor. "Come up and visit before you go back to Chicago, OK?" I said.

I got into my apartment, dumped everything on the kitchen table, opened the cell phone bill, and glanced through it casually. My eyes fell on the summary of Dani's usage and it made me wonder. I logged in to my wireless account on my laptop. Dani's usage details scrolled up, and there was my number as an incoming call. That call was one minute long. It was sandwiched between twenty-minute calls to her father and her stepmother. She had originated many calls to both of them throughout the cycle of the bill. I was sure she did not speak to them with the contemptuous disregard for their feelings with which she treated me. They were her intimates, not me. She had established that.

The sting was immediate and sharp, a scorpion's lash across my heart. My beloved oldest daughter was rejecting me. That was not news. I had known that for a while. Each new proof of it brought a fresh round of pain.

What happened to the twenty years I had been there for her, taking care of her, raising her and sacrificing for her and giving her the best of everything I could? Why didn't that matter to her?

I closed the laptop and walked around my apartment with my arms crossed over my chest. I went into Dani's old bedroom, which still had some of her belongings. It was now a storage room with paintings that should be taken to the gallery and boxes of old client files. The apartment, which George and I had moved into when we first got married, was a classic six. It had two full bedrooms and a small maid's room that was a third bedroom. Alex had slept in the small bedroom until Dani went to college, then Alex got the big bedroom.

I picked up one of Dani's old tennis trophies, a simple engraved cup, and remembered Dani as a six-year-old, holding her tennis racket and wearing a white dress with her long fair hair in a ponytail. I'd enrolled her in an after-school tennis program as a lark because a friend of the

Calhoun's owned the program. George and I were so happy when Dani turned out to possess a full measure of the famed Calhoun athleticism— she was slim, powerful, and fast, a natural tennis player.

I enjoyed bringing her to matches, even though I didn't play myself. Swinging a racket wasn't my gift. But I enjoyed the time together as we took the subway or a bus or drove out to Long Island or New Jersey in George's car. In the in-between time and space of transit, we would talk and talk and talk. Dani had a thoughtful curiosity about the world that enchanted me. I loved watching her play tennis with growing skill and self-confidence, and I shared her joy when she won and her determination to prevail in the next match when she didn't. She was a marvelous person, this oldest daughter of mine.

For a few minutes, I could barely breathe. Then my yoga training kicked in. I forced myself to inhale slowly then exhale at the same measured pace. At first it made my heart ache keenly. Then the ache softened into something more manageable.

On other days, I would have called Trudi. But now she needed to marshal her forces for her own battle. I needed to support her with my forces, in fact. I could text Marcia and drum up a phone conversation with her, but Marcia was more accessible in person than on the phone and anyway, she would just tell me to get laid.

Which was not bad advice. Not that sex was the answer to anything, but the point was I had to keep living as fully as possible.

It was too late in the day to drive the seventy-five miles up the New York Thruway to the Gunks but there were precious, carefully curated patches of nature to be found in Manhattan. I found my sneakers and took Groucho on a walk up Riverside Park. It was another sunlit May day, with pink and orange tulips blossoming in the block-long community garden at 91st Street, bicyclists whizzing past, children scootering and running in zigzag patterns, and boys playing catch on the lawn. Red-breasted robins hopped on the ground, gray squirrels ran up and down tree trunks and pigeons pecked the earth around the benches, hoping for food droppings. Other dog walkers let their dogs sniff Groucho's butt. After years of taking Groucho to the park, some were acquaintances of a sort and we exchanged pleasantries and congratulated each other on the fine weather. Wasn't it a cold winter and weren't we all ready for summer?

Groucho and I returned home and he flopped down on the living room sofa for a snooze. I rolled out my yoga mat and streamed a short online class, twenty minutes of sun salutations. The plan was to get me out of my pain body and into the present moment.

Somewhere between trikonasana and virabhadrasana, I had the wisp of the thought that maintaining my own courage and happiness was the most loving and beneficial thing I could do for my daughters. Someday, each in her own way, they would face a reckoning. Someday they'd have to look within themselves and face the internalized pieces of me, the bad mommy, the mommy their father and stepmother had dehumanized and demonized so relentlessly. When that day came, if I was still me, still filled with the wonder and exuberance of life, Dani and Alex would learn something and grow.

After yoga, I took a shower and shaved my legs and thought about Carl. He looked like he'd know exactly what to do in the sack. He had that confident way about him, that aura of power and accomplishment that made a man luscious, like a perfectly cooked prime rib. Alas, he was a proper sort. He'd want to wine and dine me before letting me have my way with him. He just wasn't going to appreciate my randy and ready, non-communicative style of discourse.

Scott's long, lean body came to mind in a visceral way. My lady parts filled with warmth. In fact, my thighs had an appetite of their own to wrap themselves around him.

I got out of the shower and slid into leggings and a slouchy cotton top and peered into my closet. I went to the section of my closet where I'd hung several items of lingerie purchased during the year Clif had stopped sleeping with me.

When Clif had first taken to rolling away from me at night instead of toward me, I did what women do when their husbands stop wanting them: I tried to make myself more desirable. I exercised more and I dieted. I bought matching lace bra and garter sets, sheer negligees, boned corsets that drew my curves into an hourglass, a zip-front leather teddy, and even a few costumes. I was willing to do what it took to turn on my husband.

It was all for naught. Nothing worked with Clif. But I'd made the effort and so I had a wardrobe of lascivious garments, one of which would surely please Scott. Not that we needed slinky underthings at that point when it was all so new and hot; but he'd surely appreciate the look and I'd enjoy his pleasure. Maybe I'd even perform some sorely needed hygiene of the lady parts. Marcia had informed me that all the young women kept themselves neat and trimmed. Maybe Scott expected that? He was of that generation.

Then I winced because I was *not* of that generation. And part of my reason for an erotic fashion statement was to distract Scott from the puckered white line that ran across my pelvis just above my pubic bone.

Later, after modeling several outfits in front of the mirror, I called the cell phone number he'd left on my answering machine.

"Bauer," he said, briskly.

"Paige," I answered.

He smiled. I could hear it or feel it through the ethers. "You realize that the telephone is a device for talking?"

"What are you doing tonight?" I walked over to the window and looked out into the leafy treetops of Riverside park.

"The usual. I was going to go for a run and finish some charts. Skype with my kids. Bake salmon for dinner and read through some recent medical journals I haven't had a chance to look at. Why?"

*You need to get out more.*

"Care for some chocolate?"

He was smiling and thinking. It was a few beats before he answered. "This is a booty call."

"I believe that's what it's called."

"I'm not available for booty calls."

"Yes, you are."

A few more beats. "Yes, I am. Beats the hell out of another night alone." Another pause. "Will you take your skirt off this time?"

"I have a peignoir set I thought I'd model for you. It's a red silk charmeuse, babydoll chemise and thong with a matching robe." I swear I felt him get an erection through the phone lines. It was so flattering that I giggled.

*Marcia's right about younger men.*

I added, "But you have to promise you won't stare at my c-section scar."

"What time? Your place or mine?"

"Mine, no kids to interrupt us," I said. "When's good for you?"

"I'll go for my run now, and then shower and head over. Give me an hour, make that an hour and fifteen."

"I'll be ready."

"I'll bring the salmon. There's enough for both of us for dinner."

"I thought this was about chocolate," I objected. "That's dessert. Now you're talking cooking and fish. That's a lot of effort for a booty call."

That got his attention. "We can start with dessert. And salmon's a good source of protein. A man's got to keep his strength up."

"You don't," I said.

"I don't," he agreed.

"An hour and fifteen then?"

"Precisely," he promised.

But an hour and a half later, Scot still hadn't arrived, and I was worried. Scott was the type to be punctual. Even his office appointments started on time, which was a Biblical miracle for a doctor.

It occurred to me to check the answering machine. He must have called when I was in the bathroom because he left a message: "Sarah, I'm going to be late. And I've got a surprise. Two, actually."

Two surprises? Chocolate and whipped cream?

A few minutes later, the bell rang for him to be buzzed in. Somewhat tremulously, I went to stand by the door. I was about to expose my flaws more fully to Scott and I felt nervous. I was, as promised, clad only in the silky red chemise and matching thong. I lightly wrapped the diaphanous robe around me and what was concealed was all the more alluring for it. The overall effect, despite the mostly hidden scar and my slightly drooping boobs—I had nursed two babies—was good. Not perfect like Rosa in her dancing twenties, or perfect like thirty-eight-year-old Scott. But good enough. Suddenly I was grateful for all the yoga classes I'd toiled through and all the wine and chocolate I'd foregone. I could tolerate the glaring infelicities of middle age.

He knocked lightly and my heart leapt. I threw open the door.

There stood Scott with two children. A little boy, maybe all of two and a half years old, was curled up on his chest, asleep. A serious-faced girl of five or six stood by his side, holding his hand with one hand. In her other hand she held a plastic purse covered with pictures of Barbie doll heads. The two children were lightly mocha-skinned and extremely beautiful, the product of two exceptionally good-looking people—one of whom I'd expected to tear the lingerie off my all-too-willing person.

"Surprise," Scott said.

"Uh uh," I stammered.

Scott's eyes were taking in the silk babydoll set. In a quiet voice that I couldn't read, he asked, "Would you please put on a robe?"

I turned and raced back to my bedroom for my longest, woolliest robe, which I threw on over everything. I raced back out. Scott had taken the kids to my living room sofa. The little boy was curled up in a ball, still asleep. The little girl sat with her back straight and her slim brown hands folded over her purse in her lap.

"Sarah, these are Janey and Max, my children," Scott said proudly. "Janey, this is Sarah."

"Hello," Janey said. She looked at me wide-eyed out of a triangular, high-cheekboned face. Her shiny black hair fell in thick waves to her shoulders, and matching pink bows on barrettes held back the right and left wings of her hair from her exquisite little face.

"Hello," I managed.

"I can explain," Scott said. He grasped me by the upper arm and dragged me back to the foyer.

"Um. Uh?"

"Right after I talked to you, Lisa called to say they were in town. She hadn't told me they were coming in; it was going to be a surprise. At the last moment they got theater tickets and she asked if I could babysit. But you know," Scott shrugged, "it's not babysitting when I'm with them. It's parenting. Of course I said yes, I'd be glad to be with them."

"Why didn't you just tell me your kids showed up? We could have rescheduled."

"I was going to and then I got another call. Sarah, I need you to babysit."

"What?" I shrieked.

"Please, Sarah. I wouldn't ask but it's an emergency and my secretary is sick, my assistant is out of town, and my nurse is moonlighting for a private patient. There's no one else for me to ask."

"Take them to the hospital with you."

"Lisa will kill me," he said, with an expression of naked fear.

*If you're still that afraid of her, you're still married to her in some way.*

"Call a nanny service, there are plenty of reputable services in New York."

"I would and I will next time but I haven't vetted any of them yet, and anyway, I don't have time. It's a patient. She's dying. I have to be there."

"That is not my problem. You take your kids back to your place and look on the internet for a service!" I drew the soft lapels of my plush robe closer around my body. I was just furious.

"What if it was Trudi?" he asked, putting his hands on my shoulders and slipping his fingers under the collar of the robe to stroke me gently around my neck on my cervical vertebrae. "What if I was with my kids and I got the call that it was Trudi who was dying, wouldn't you want me to be there for her? Wouldn't you want someone to take them so I could be?"

I shook off his hands and marched a few steps away.

*What if it was Trudi?*

My heart constricted with fear.

*What if it is Trudi a year from now?*

"That's dirty pool."

"Please take them. It won't be long. Lisa will be back in a few hours, as soon as the show ends, probably before me. I texted her your address."

"OK, OK, Scott. I'll do it. But we're going to make a bargain."

"Anything you want, anything," he swore. "As much chocolate as you want! I'll owe you big time for this!"

I gave him a scathing look. "Don't even mention chocolate to me. You'll probably never get chocolate again."

A chagrined expression came over his face and he started to talk but I held up my hand.

"I'll take care of your kids so you can go be with your patient. On one condition. You have to let Trudi into your trial."

Scott recoiled. "I can't do that! I'm not sure she fits all the criteria! I haven't finished my workup!"

"I don't give a rat's ass if she fits the criteria," I snapped. "If you want me to babysit your children right here and right now instead of getting laid like I thought was going to happen, then you will promise me that Trudi's in your trial. Because that's her best chance at surviving, isn't it?"

He nodded slightly, once, and stared off into the distance, his eyes narrowing.

"So this is my nonnegotiable condition. Yes or no. Take it or leave it," I said, folding my arms over my chest in a defiant posture.

He didn't say anything but he didn't need to; his ruminations were writ all over his face like neon letters advertising a seedy shop. He was conflicted. His integrity was at stake. Being there for a patient meant everything to him. What was he going to do with his children if he didn't concede?

It was the most articulate nonverbal conversation in which I ever participated.

I was pretty sure it was his fear of his wife that carried the day. Ex-wife.

He swiveled on his heel and strode swiftly back to the living room. I followed. He squatted down next to Janey. "Sweetie, Sarah's going to watch you for a few hours. Daddy has to go to work."

Janey nodded solemnly.

"You'll be good for her, won't you?" he asked, anxiously.

She nodded again.

"Mommy will come get you." He kissed her cheek. "See you tomorrow. We'll have waffles at the hotel restaurant. Then I'll take you to FAO Schwartz." He passed his hand over Max's head without waking the boy and then marched out.

I followed him.

"She probably qualifies anyway, I'm almost certain," he muttered. He opened the door and paused. "They haven't really eaten, it all came about so quickly. Would you please give them something healthy to eat? If you're going to order in, there's a Chinese place on 72nd that doesn't use MSG and offers gluten-free alternatives. Be sure to include vegetables." He went out and closed the door.

I stood there looking at the door and shaking my head in equal parts disbelief and indignation. I took some deep breaths to calm myself so I'd be pleasant for Scott's kids—none of it was their fault. I wasn't going to visit my feelings on them. I was just about to go to the living room when the door opened again.

Scott stepped back in and put his arms around me, loosely but firmly. He kissed me softly in the center of my forehead. He lifted his head and murmured, "You don't have to wake Max to feed him. But if he does wake up, he'll be hungry. Feed him quick." He let go and went to the door. He turned and gave me an unquashed and raffish look. "That red outfit, wow! I am so getting chocolate again."

"No, you're not," I replied, automatically.

"Yes, I am," he said.

# CHAPTER FOURTEEN

I WENT BACK INTO the living room and looked at Janey.

Janey looked back at me.

Neither of us knew what to say. We were being awkwardly quizzical with each other.

"This is weird," I finally said.

"Yes," she agreed.

"Do you mind if I take a minute to put on some comfy pajamas?" I asked. "I think I have some of my daughters' old books for you to look at."

Janey brightened. "I love to read!"

I trotted over to the bookcase by the television and pulled out *Madeline and the Bad Hat*. "It might be too advanced for you," I said, showing her the book.

Her face fell.

"You don't like Madeline? Maybe I have *Goodnight Moon* in here."

"I like *Harry Potter*," she said. "Do you have any of those books?"

I did a double-take. "How old are you? Five?"

"I'll be six in three weeks," she smiled.

"Are you having a birthday party?" I never yet met a kid who didn't like to talk about their birthday party, though some of them had strong negative opinions about cake. And clowns.

She nodded and lit up with a serene inner radiance. "We're having an animal lady bring a bunch of animals to our house. There'll be a rabbit, and a chicken, and a snake, and a baby goat. And a lynx. I'm going to be a zoologist when I grow up. My friends from school are coming and Daddy's going to come and Mommy's getting a cake in the shape of a monkey. It's a vanilla cake inside but it has chocolate frosting for the monkey fur and it has licorice drops for its eyes."

"That's pretty exciting." I asked, hesitantly, "Your parents really let you read *Harry Potter?*"

She nodded. "I'm on the third one, *Harry Potter and the Prisoner of Azkaban.*" Her young voice lisped deliciously over 'Azkaban.'

I smiled. Alex the great reader had adored Harry Potter. She probably still possessed some of the books. I said, "I think there are some Harry Potter books in my daughter's room. I can't say which ones. I'll go look."

I went into Alex's room, which she kept locked when she was home. But she was at therapeutic boarding school and I had unlocked her door so I could clean the room. I'd opened the windows to air it out but hadn't yet gotten around to the thorough cleaning it needed, there was just too much else on my plate.

Alex's room was an epic mess. The bed was disheveled and heaps of clothes lay everywhere. Belts and shoes and jewelry and cosmetic items and plastic bags were scattered in and around and atop everything. It was disgusting.

I looked in the bookcase for a Harry Potter volume and noticed a can of Sprite on the shelf. Didn't I always see Alex with that can?

I picked it up and it had some weight but no liquid sloshed within it. Curious. I turned the can in my hand and, I don't know why, but I thought to twist the top. The aluminum exterior came loose and the bottom of the can slid out, revealing a secret compartment. Inside the compartment was a slimy brown ball of vegetal matter. I was no expert in the field of drugs, never having been drawn to them, but I knew it was probably some form of pot. Or maybe it was another illicit substance.

So Alex hid her stash in there under my very nose.

I swiped at my eyes and gulped some giant breathfuls of air like a drowning person. Janey couldn't see me this way. I put down the can, knowing I'd have to face Alex's room and thoroughly search it for paraphernalia and substances. But not this moment.

This moment, I had to find a book for Scott's preternaturally gifted child. I remembered something Frida Kahlo said, a quote that was often printed on refrigerator magnets and coffee cups: "At the end of the day, we can endure much more than we think we can." That would have to be true for me.

I went back out with the first book of the series in my hand. I said apologetically, "This is the only one I could find."

Janey smiled shyly. "I like that one. Thank you, Sarah."

*Oh my god, and she's polite too.*

"Are you hungry, Janey?"

She nodded while opening the book.

"What do you like to eat? I don't know what I have because I haven't been to the grocery store in a while, but maybe I can figure something out."

"I like a lot of stuff," she said. "But I don't eat anything red."

I put my hands on my hips. Kids have food rules; it's a thing. Dani used to arrange her food in patterns and she refused to eat "squishy food." Alex once ate ravioli for fifty-two days straight. "So, no tomatoes or tomato sauce?"

Janey crinkled her nose, frowned and shook her head.

"Got it," I said. "But first I'm going to change."

She nodded and her fingers ruffled through the pages of the book.

I peeked at Max and he was still sleeping soundly, drooling on the sofa. I went to my bedroom to change into something a little more demure and a little less, "Hey, I'm going to shag your dad!"

I pulled soft yoga pants and a drapey white tank top out of my drawer, and then slipped on an oversized cashmere wrap cardigan. I tied it around my waist and wiped my eyes again because somehow, being out of Janey's view, they'd leaked again. I went into my bathroom and splashed water on my face, wiping off some of the makeup I'd put on in anticipation of Scott's arrival.

I stood and looked in the mirror and told myself it would all be OK and wondered what it would be like if my parents were still alive and I could turn to them for advice and support.

But that ship with its black sails had slipped away twenty-six years ago, and there was a hungry kid in my living room.

A box of Annie's Mac n' cheese was in the pantry, and there was a carton of eggs. There was even a not-too-old cucumber in the crisper drawer of the refrigerator. I assembled all the items on the kitchen counter. A starch, a protein, and a vegetable. That should satisfy Scott's nutritional rules.

*God, I hate to cook.*

I'd raised my girls on rotisserie chickens and other hot food deli take-out from the grocery stores on the Upper West Side. When they got older,

I encouraged them to learn to cook. I had long ago decided that the apple-pie cultural fantasy of mom in a white apron didn't suit me and didn't define good mothering. I had something else to give my daughters, along with the mixed Cherokee, Baptist, and Jewish blood: an adventurous spirit and a willingness to learn.

Janey came in with her book and stood at my elbow.

"Do you like Annie's? It's not red. Not even the package. The package is blue and yellow."

That made her giggle. "It doesn't matter what color the package is, the package can be red. Does it have MSG?"

"No, no, I don't think so, and no high fructose corn syrup either," I murmured, scanning the ingredients. "It's even organic."

She nodded.

I held up the cucumber.

She nodded again.

Last of all, I held up the carton of eggs.

She said, "Scrambled, but no ketchup."

"Fair enough. Why don't you sit at the little table over there and read your book while I cook?" I suggested. "I'll give you a glass of water to drink. Unfortunately, I don't have apple juice."

*Or grape juice, the fermented kind, which I could really use right now.*

She nodded and hopped up into the chair. She spread her book out on the table in front of her and looked at me. "Are you daddy's girlfriend?"

*Oh sheesh, another talkative Bauer.*

"Not exactly."

"My mommy gets a magazine in the mail and the ladies dress in pajamas like the red ones you had on when you opened the door. But they're skinnier."

"They're a lot younger than me."

*And have perkier boobs and don't have caesarean scars.*

She nodded. "Victoria's Secret magazine. I get *Highlights* Magazine and *National Geographic*. I like magazines. I could read them on the iPad but mommy and daddy don't believe in screens for me so I get them printed on paper. But it's fun to get the mail, anyway. Are you going to be daddy's girlfriend?"

*No way, José.*

"I think that's between me and your daddy, don't you?"

That gave her pause.

I cracked the entire dozen eggs into a big bowl for scrambling because I was hungry and Max might wake up. Also, because the expiration date was tomorrow.

As if she were reading my mind, Janey said, "Max won't eat anything brown. Mommy gets really upset about that when she burns the toast. He won't have a piece of my birthday cake."

"Thanks for the warning."

I made a small plate for Max and put a lid over it to keep it warm. I divvied the remainder between Janey and me, although I gave her all the cucumber because, despite Scott's beliefs on the subject, I really felt my nutritional health wouldn't suffer if I failed to have a vegetable at that particular meal.

She read while eating, so I leafed through a Sotheby's auction catalog of items from an Italian sale. I couldn't believe the prices they were asking for a little known, and frankly not very good, futurist painter. He wanted to be Severini, whose work actually was rather fascinating, but instead he looked like a slavish emulator to me—and one who hadn't properly steeped himself in Marinetti's manifesto.

Marinetti had written that "Art … can be nothing but violence, cruelty, and injustice," and he celebrated speed and war, youth and danger. The unknown artist gave a Futurist-like wash over subjects that would have made Marinetti flush the artist's head in a bidet. It was a travesty of Futurism and not one of wit but of ignorance. I felt that artists should know their tradition intimately. Many current artists were too lazy. With the prestige of the Sotheby's tag, this totally undeserving artist had a new validation. That kind of branding always pissed me off a little. It was solely mercenary, without regard for the field of art, the people who made art, and the people who bought art.

"Are you a doctor?" Janey asked when most of her food was gone.

"No."

"Do you have a PhD?"

"Almost. I'm an art lady."

Janey looked skeptical. "What's that?"

"Someone who loves art. I own a gallery and I sell beautiful art to people."

"Why do you do that?"

"Because I love art and I know a lot about it, so I can help other people choose art that they love."

"If you had a PhD, you'd know a lot about art; that's what a PhD shows, that you know a lot about something," Janey observed. "My mommy is getting a PhD in culture anthropology. She's going to defend herself in a few months."

"I did everything but finish my dissertation," I said defensively.

"Mommy says a PhD is really important. I'm going to get a PhD in zoology. I'm going to Harvard like my mommy and daddy."

I put my fork down and looked at her. "Do you know what zoology is?"

She nodded vigorously. "It's the scientific study of animals and their behavior. I like animals. We have a Bernese mountain dog named Toto, like the dog in the *Wizard of Oz*. But it's funny because Toto was small in the movie and our Toto is big. He needs a lot of exercise. Mommy runs with him."

"My dog is named Groucho. He's a mutt. He doesn't run anymore."

"Groucho is sleeping on the couch with Max."

"Who's drooling more?" I wondered aloud.

Janey giggled and her big, melting brown eyes sparkled. She had that quality that Scott did of showing her thoughts on her face without any mediation whatsoever, as if the thought was her being and the flesh was just a convenient side effect. "Max drools a lot, but he's too little to tell him that. Do you think my new daddy will run with Toto? He says he's my new daddy. But I don't want to call him 'daddy.'"

*This could be a tricky conversation.*

"Your daddy will always be your daddy, but your mum's new husband will be like a bonus dad who's a friend. Maybe he'll let you call him by his first name. Or something like 'pop' or 'poppy.' Sometimes kids do that."

"He used to be Uncle Rick, before." Janey's small face was suddenly bereft. "I liked it better when he was Uncle Rick and daddy was at home with us. I liked it when daddy lived with us in Boston."

I couldn't help it; I reached across the table and squeezed her hand. "Sometimes grownups do things that kids don't understand. But I know your parents love you and want the best for you."

Janey didn't say anything. She looked at my hand mournfully and squeezed back.

After dinner, she needed to use the bathroom. She also asked for soap to wash her hands. I unwrapped some cedar and lemon Antica Farmacista soap that she spent time sniffing before she washed her hands.

We sojourned to the living room to keep Max and Groucho company. I sat at the end of the couch with a stack of auction catalogs and Janey sat beside me. Occasionally she hopped up to use the bathroom. I wasn't sure if she was really peeing or just washing her hands with the fancy soap because she came back from her trips wreathed in a big cloud of scent. After a while, she huddled into me and fell asleep. I must have dozed off too because suddenly someone was knocking at the door and I was startled awake.

I extricated myself from what was then a puppy huddle of Janey, Max, and Groucho. I went to the door, yawning and stretching and trying to focus. "Yes?"

"It's Lisa Bauer," a quiet voice said.

I opened the door and beheld an uncommonly beautiful woman and a tall, good-looking blond man. The woman almost literally took my breath away. She was tall, long-limbed, willowy, and mahogany-skinned, with almond-shaped dark eyes that were thickly fringed with minky dark lashes. She had the same triangular face and high cheekbones as Janey, and her graceful head was framed by a halo of black ringlets. I knew a dozen artists who would give their left testicle to paint her.

"You're watching my children?" she prompted, probably because I hadn't spoken.

I shook myself. "Of course, yes, sorry. I must have fallen asleep on the sofa. I'm Sarah Paige." I extended my hand and shook hers.

"Lisa Bauer and this is Richard Mitchell." She peeked past me into the foyer.

I stepped aside and ushered them into the living room.

"That's a sweet picture," Lisa said with a small smile. "I hope they weren't any trouble. I wouldn't have gone to the theater if I'd known Scott was going to be called in to work."

"They were wonderful," I assured her. "Max slept the entire time. Janey ate dinner and then read Harry Potter. Pretty amazing reading for a kid her age."

"She's been reading since she was two," Lisa told me. "Scott and I were both early readers. I guess it was in her genes." She was eying me, scanning my face as if watching for a reaction or looking for a clue.

I nodded.

She asked, curiously, "You're a friend of Scott's? Since he moved to New York?"

"Yes, uh uh," I answered. What else was I going to say?

"Do you work with him?"

"No, I own an art gallery in Chelsea."

She nodded and studied me for another few seconds, clearly trying to parse the nature of my relationship with Scott. My age meant that she didn't immediately conclude that we were lovers. Then Janey stirred on the couch and Richard scooped up Max into his arms and gave Lisa a pointed look. She went over and gently touched her daughter's cheek. "Janey, wake up, mommy's here."

There ensued a few minutes of groggy children murmuring greetings, and of Lisa and Richard thanking me for taking care of the kids. I made all the polite, appropriate responses.

They left my apartment and I stood at my door waving goodbye as they walked down the hall toward the elevator bank. I was just going to close the door when I heard Janey say, "Mommy, Sarah wears red pajamas like the ladies in your Victoria's Secret magazine."

Lisa spun around and looked sharply at me.

I closed the door.

It was none of her business.

# CHAPTER FIFTEEN

SCOTT CALLED THE NEXT day and left a few messages, but I didn't pick up for him nor get back to him.

After a late brunch with Trudi and Robert at their place in the West Village, I drove to New Paltz and hiked around Lost City. Lost City enjoyed a reputation as being a secret, local's only rock climbing preserve, but it was really just an exquisite and undocumented corner of the Gunks. The routes were steep and challenging and mostly only diehard climbers ventured there. I seldom encountered any casual newbie types throwing themselves at the walls for the thrill of the moment. Of course, I wasn't climbing; I was hiking.

I spent a few hours staring at the high stone monoliths of Wishbone roof and the famed Lost City crack. I was surrounded by hemlock, spruce, sugar maple, oaks, tupelo trees, and old pitch pines clinging to cliff tops. I scrambled over a scree field and avoided the poison ivy. The quiet exertion of hiking very nearly screwed my head back on correctly. Falcons, red-tailed hawks, and turkey vultures wheeled above the sheer escarpments, and coyotes yapped before falling suddenly quiet. Scattered deer ambled through the paths; I hoped they weren't carrying ticks that would bite me into lingering illness. Talus caves and dens harboring various sorts of creatures studded the cliffs. They were hidden and indiscernible but I knew they were there, replete, used continuously by their manifold, speechless inhabitants for vast swathes of time.

In the sunny peacefulness I was able to find my way back into my own being. It was like a homecoming and I was grateful for it. I felt pretty burnt out lately by Alex's troubles and Dani's coldness; by George's hostility and the gallery's demands and yes, as much as I loved her, by

Trudi's cancer, which tore up my heart.

I was angry that I'd babysat for Scott, and that he'd brought his kids over and I'd submitted to the exigency of the moment. Yes, I'd negotiated something in return, something precious, Trudi's inclusion in his trial. But still. How could Scott put me in that position?

I liked his kids. Well, I liked scary precocious Janey; sleepy Max with his drool seemed sweet but I hadn't interacted with him.

It was just that I'd already paid my dues with little kids. I'd done all the sleepless, colicky nights and pediatrician visits, tooth fairy gifts, piano and ballet recitals, travel soccer junkets and swim meets, class plays, parent-teacher conferences, class parent bake sales, Halloween costumes and Trick or Treat parties, children's vitamin administration, lice infestations and strep throat plagues and sleepover birthday parties. I had done them with love and with joy and with a strong sense of duty because I wanted to do them well. I had moved on to paying the pound of flesh and liter of blood that was the toll for raising a teenager and a young adult well and truly alienated from me by their spiteful father.

Not that George would admit to his spite. In his mind he was perfect, and I was the problem. I remembered our last argument on the day before I told him that I was in love with another man. It didn't matter what we were arguing about; by then we fought more or less continuously. He stood in our bedroom shaking his head at me.

"You're full of rage," he spat. "You're crazy!"

"Fuck you!" I shouted—my screaming proving him right. "Don't think I won't leave you!"

He sneered. "No one but me will ever want you. You couldn't function without me."

I vividly remembered staring at him when he said that. The boil inside me subsided, and I knew in that moment that it was only a matter of time before I left George for Clif, as Clif was pressuring me to do.

George added, "You're crazy, Sarah, everyone thinks so. Everyone you ever met would say you were crazy."

That's when I knew it was only a matter of days.

Truthfully, I was angry when I was married to George. The third class citizenship that I was accorded, and for which I was expected to be grateful, had continually pissed me off like a low-grade fever that never quite resolved.

I thought of Frida Kahlo, as I did in quiet moments. I wrote a paper about her in college and was impressed by the life of that passionate, creative, damaged woman. I thought of how much she had endured, physically and emotionally. I thought of her heartfelt *"The Two Fridas."* It was a double self-portrait, with two versions of the artist sitting together. She was completing the painting as her divorce from muralist Diego Rivera was finalized. One Frida was the woman Diego had loved; the other Frida he scorned. Both Fridas literally wore their hearts on their chests. The painter had communicated with exquisite poignancy the pain that divided two of her selves.

Frida transmuted her suffering into art. In the process, she came to accept herself as she was. "I used to think I was the strangest person in the world but then I thought there are so many people in the world, there must be someone just like me who feels bizarre and flawed in the same ways I do. I would imagine her, and imagine that she must be out there thinking of me, too. Well, I hope that if you are out there and read this and know that yes, it's true I'm here, and I'm just as strange as you," Frida wrote.

Her words, along with the time I spent with Marcia and her unconventional Los Angeles crowd, as well as the time I spent with Clif and other artists, serious collectors, and gallerists in the complex, protean, imperfect but mesmerizing world of art, helped me to understand that I fit into a different mold than any Calhoun, for sure. But it didn't make me crazy, as crazy-making as it was to hear myself disparaged that way.

The sun set, and I drove back to the city. I took the subway down to the gallery to catch up on paperwork. Sunday evening was transcendentally quiet and therefore perfect for getting work done.

The gallery phone rang and I picked it up by rote.

"Sarah Paige."

"Sarah, it's Carl," said a familiar gravelly voice that suddenly struck me as throaty and sexy.

"Carl! How come you called me here?"

"Calculated bet," he answered. "You weren't at home and I don't have your cell phone number. I asked myself, where would I be on Sunday night if I were a dedicated gallery owner who cared passionately about her business? *Laboro, ergo sum.*"

I laughed. "You caught me."

He chuckled warmly. "I used to do that, too. No one's around on Sunday night, you can get a lot accomplished that's not possible with the phones ringing and people wandering in to ask you questions."

"Exactly."

"I really enjoyed dinner the other night. So how about I come downtown and take you out for a drink near your gallery? There are some great bars in Chelsea and you have to live a little. Take it from me, you don't want to invest your whole life into work."

I leaned back in my chair, smiling. What a lovely invitation.

"I'd love to, Carl, but I spent the day outside and I'm in ratty hiking clothes without a lick of makeup. I'd hate for you to see me like this. My hair's not even combed."

"Nonsense," he expostulated. "You should see me when I come home from a fishing trip. My own mother would pretend she didn't know me."

I giggled. "I can't imagine you being anything but elegant, Carl. Even in hip waders, you'd look like something out of *GQ*."

"I'd better be wearing hip waders if you're going to flatter me like that," he returned. We both laughed. He said, "Come on. You can't work all night. I'll dress casually if it'll make you feel better."

I sighed and remembered the secret cache of makeup, toothbrush, and hairbrush in my desk drawer. There was even a clean white silk shirt, a black blazer, and a pair of pumps in the closet to dress up my jeans.

"Plate of French fries to go with my wine?"

"You got it," he promised and we were on.

———

Carl and I took stools at a bar on 23$^{rd}$ Street. We were seated beside each other but he swiveled around and gave me the once over.

"This is your idea of ratty hiking clothes? You look pretty good to me."

"I had some stuff in the gallery," I said, blushing a little. Carl looked pretty good to me, too, in a distressed leather jacket over a classic long-sleeved, navy blue button down shirt and graphite-colored denim pants, very John Varvatos, a good look on him and one he carried off very well, indeed.

He nodded. "I still keep spare shirts and shoes in my office, even though I don't work a hundred hours a week anymore."

"I wouldn't say I work a hundred hours a week," I murmured. "I mean, it's my own business, so I don't count the hours. I just do what needs to be done. Something *always* needs to be done."

"I felt that way, too," he remarked. "But the gallery is a more recent venture for you, yes? You've been raising children?"

"Two daughters. They're both out of the house."

He caught the bartender's eye and asked what I wanted.

"Red wine, always!"

He ordered a soft, fleshy merlot for me and a scotch for himself. How did he know? The merlot was just what I felt like drinking.

He said, "I gather from Trudi that there are some issues with your children. She's worried about you."

"You were awfully nice to Trudi, I really appreciate it," I said earnestly.

The bartender was back with our drinks.

"A plate of French fries for the lady," Carl told him. He turned to me and held up his glass. "To being at the office on Sunday night."

"Hear, hear," I said and clinked my glass against his.

"Your younger daughter just went to a therapeutic school?"

I grimaced. "Trudi was feeling loquacious. Did she tell you my shoe size and blood type, too?"

He tilted his head. "We don't have to talk about it, if it makes you feel uncomfortable."

But of course, I was all too ready to disgorge everything. Much of the story about Alex poured forth in a torrent of words.

Carl sat shaking his head. "We had some trouble with my son. We were lucky with my daughter and yes, good luck had a lot to do with it. She had good friends who didn't lead her astray, she received a lot of validation from playing the flute and riding her horse, and she was a good student. My wife kept her busy. I think that when teens have an activity they're passionate about it helps keep them out of trouble. It focuses them away from sex and drugs where their hormones and their lack of a frontal lobe lead them.

"But my son was an entirely different beast. He just couldn't find his place. He had a chip on his shoulder about our station in life and yet he felt entitled to the privileges and benefits of it. He was troubled and often a troublemaker. We had a lot of meetings with his headmaster."

"How'd he come out of it?" I asked, swirling the red wine around the glass to watch the skirt.

Carl shrugged. "I can't say there was one specific moment when it resolved for him. Alan did better than we expected on the standardized tests. He was interested in computers and taught himself how to program. He wrote a game that the gaming community embraced—that was early in the online gaming industry, so he was able to break into it without formal training. He just grew out of his inner chaos. It wasn't because of anything my wife or I did, though my wife certainly tried everything to help him. She spent a fortune taking him to various specialists, and she spent precious time she didn't have worrying about him and crying over him. Now he's got his own telecommunications business in Boston. We go fishing. He actually paid to take me to Iceland last year!" Carl laughed softly, shaking his head at the very notion of someone else paying for him.

"It's good of you to let him," I murmured.

"Ah, the old king must die," Carl said, in his growliest voice. He tilted his glass and looked into the amber surface of his scotch. "Kids. I'll tell you what I've learned. Teenagers are beasts. They're just hormonal and nuts. Then in their twenties, they know everything. You can't tell them anything because they have all the answers. Why even bother? But they get to their thirties and life catches up with them. Things become a little more nuanced. Maybe they didn't end up in the career of their dreams or they didn't get a job they wanted. Maybe a major relationship failed. Maybe someone close to them died." Carl nodded. "In their thirties, they come back to you."

"My oldest daughter barely speaks to me," I confessed with the pang of longing, shame, and sadness I always felt when I acknowledged Dani's alienation. "She's twenty-one. She's in San Francisco with her boyfriend for the summer and the only reason I know that is because a friend of mine told me. She came home from college a year ago and told me that everyone at Princeton had a perfect life and I was the reason she didn't. We used to be so close. We used to laugh together. We used to talk. We went to Paris together. Now she barely picks up for me and worse, she goes around saying terrible things about me, things that aren't true and that are just distortions taken from some alternate reality where she's justified in demonizing and dehumanizing me. Am I supposed to wait until she's thirty to be close to her again?"

"You are if that's how long it takes her," Carl said sympathetically, looking at me quite directly, the way Scott had looked at Trudi while confirming her stage three pancreatic cancer.

I wondered if Trudi wasn't the lucky one, after all. An alienated child was a scourge in a way even cancer wasn't.

"Sarah, give her some space and pray for her," Carl said sympathetically. "Daughters are hard on their mothers. Even Jennifer, who was a great girl, was tough on Nancy. But there's some of you in your daughter and you're terrific. Give her some time and she'll circle back around to that eventually. You'll see."

But I wasn't sure. Whatever natural impulses for rectification arose in Dani had to withstand her father's steadfast malice toward me.

"Maybe your younger daughter will be like Alan and, in her own time, she'll find her way out of the wilds of the labyrinth."

"I hope so," I murmured.

"In the meantime," he said, his blue eyes twinkling as he gently touched my chin with his thumb, tilting my head up slightly, "I'll come around and take you out for wine and fries. And dinner. Whenever you let me."

I couldn't restrain a smile.

I was relaxed and tired in a good way when Carl's driver dropped me at my apartment. I was thinking that I'd have the silk shirt dry cleaned so I could replace it in the gallery closet, and that Carl was excellent company. I wondered if I could invite him over and order in pad thai and see if I could loosen him up into dispensing with his John Varvatos togs. I had a hunch that he had it going on under them.

Propped up against my door was a large box of chocolate. A note was tucked into the ribbon.

"I waited, no sign of you. Thanks again for last night. Til soon? Call me, S."

# CHAPTER SIXTEEN

I CAME DOWN IN the elevator, tottering on the stilettos despite the hour I'd spent practicing walking in them. The elevator doors opened, I took a deep breath and launched myself precariously into drinks and dinner with Marcia's friend.

It was a glorious, balmy May evening. People were returning to the Upper West Side from work, and parents and nannies schlepped kids to and from after-school activities. Neighbors walking dogs waved to me. The sidewalks bustled with people, yellow taxis careened around corners and it was warm enough that I draped the black silk shawl around my arm instead of my bare shoulders.

I used the distance to West End Avenue, where I could catch a cab, to practice striding in my stilettos. I was trying to keep my neck atop my spine while my hips sashayed. I was so fiercely focused on not falling over that I strolled right past a tall, familiar shape who had stopped to ogle my progress. I turned to see who it was.

"Scott!"

"That's some dress," he said, eying the black satin bustier. His eyes weren't as far above mine as usual, now that I had added five inches to my height, so the downward angle of his glance was more obvious.

"My face is up here," I said, pointing.

"If you don't want me looking, why are you wearing that dress?" His eyes swiveled back upwards. "I left twenty messages. Were you ever going to call me back?"

I turned and resumed my way toward West End. "Eventually."

Scott walked beside me. He wore a pinstriped blue suit and a purple paisley tie and he was carrying a beat-up leather briefcase as if he'd come directly from work. He probably hoped to waylay me in my apartment. He frowned.

"I said I was sorry. I want to make it up to you. We should have talked."

"OK." I didn't want to get into it, not when I was on my way to meet Marcia's friend, the hottest young telenovela star in South and Central America.

"I have a gift for you, to thank you for babysitting for me."

"I can't take it right now, Scott," I said, with a gesture toward my dress. "I'm on my way out."

"You're going on a date. Who's the lucky guy?"

"No one you know," I felt safe saying.

He took hold of my upper arm and swung me around to face him.

"Sarah, you're meeting some guy in a dress that begs for a good time. Why him? Why don't you let me take you out? I'd like to. You'd enjoy yourself."

"No, I wouldn't. I'd have to listen to you talk," I said. It was mean-spirited and I regretted it the instant I delivered it. He recoiled, his cheeks flushing and his mouth narrowing into a hard, straight line. I grabbed his arm.

"Scott, I'm sorry. That was nasty. I didn't mean it. I'm sorry. Sometimes my worse self takes control of my mouth."

"You've been perfectly clear that you're just looking for some quick fucks."

"Not necessarily quick but definitely uncomplicated. That was what I was hoping for when I called you the other day," I admitted. "I went to some trouble to prepare for it. But what I got instead was your freaky genius daughter and your sleeping son, and then an encounter with your ex-wife who happens to be the most beautiful woman I've ever met in real life. Why didn't you tell me she was insanely gorgeous?"

"Janey's not a freak, she's a precocious reader," he answered sharply.

"Janey's great. Don't get me wrong, she's adorable. I really liked her; she was fun to talk to," I said. "I've met twenty-year-olds who were less articulate."

"Lisa and I were early readers."

"So I've heard. From Lisa. Couldn't you have warned me about her so I didn't have to feel like Granny in her rags when she came to the door?"

"Are you angry with me because you babysat for me or because of the way my former wife looks?"

"No! I don't know. I'm not jealous."

"Yes, you are."

"No, I'm not. The thing is, Scott, I'm not at the stage of life where I want to babysit little kids. Been there, done that, got the tee-shirt and wrote my name in the wet concrete." I could feel myself gathering a full head of steam, which I didn't want to do en route to the hot date Marcia set up for me, but I couldn't seem to prevent it. "I'm not jealous, but how do you think I'm supposed to compete with an ex-wife like that? I'm about a million years older than her. And you."

"It's not a competition," he said in a growly voice that reminded me of Carl.

We reached West End Avenue and I paused at the street corner. I looked into Scott's angular face and noted that, behind his glasses, dark circles ringed his eyes.

"How's your patient?"

"Dead." His face sagged inward and he scrubbed his free hand straight up through his hair, wrecking the neat combing job he must have done before coming to my street.

"I'm sorry," I said softly. "I know you did everything humanly possible to help her." I stepped into the street and waved for a cab.

"I can't save everyone. But there is good news. Mrs. Waterston got some good news."

I gave him a level, sardonic look. "Good to hear."

He muttered, "I called and told her. She said she was going to tell you right away, so I'm not breaking her confidentiality."

"She probably called but I haven't picked up my voicemail for the last hour," I murmured, hoping that the practice walking in stilettos would save me from falling on my ass.

"She qualified for the trial on her own merit. This isn't about you babysitting."

I gave him a look and my lip curled a little.

"So when are you going to call me?" he challenged. "Let me take you out."

"Maybe," I said. A free taxi spied me and veered over to where I stood.

"I won't talk. We can sit there at a restaurant in total silence from the appetizer until I pay the bill."

I had to grin. "That sounds like a lot of fun, Scott, thanks, I'll give it some thought."

"Chocolate for dessert," he offered under his breath.

I compressed my lips and reached for the handle of the cab but Scott stepped around me and opened the door.

"Janey told Lisa you were the nicest, prettiest art lady she'd ever met, and Lisa had some unnecessarily snippy things to say about our children seeing you in red Victoria's Secret pajamas. So I'd say that female jealousy thing cuts both ways." He sounded a little mad and a little disgusted as he put his hand under my elbow to steer me into my seat in the taxi. "In that dress and those shoes, you don't have to worry about your age, Sarah."

———~———

The date was ruined by my encounter with Scott. I just couldn't put my heart into smiling at some hot young thing who was gorgeous but only interested in himself and certainly not in Renaissance art. Back home, I changed into soft comfy things and wrapped myself up tightly in my cashmere robe as if swaddling myself. I turned on my laptop and went through my emails.

Brookton: Alex was settling in. When might I drive up for a counseling session with Alex?

*That requires some mulling.*

A client out in Scarsdale had chipped a frame and asked me to recommend a restorer. I sent back an email offering to repair it myself. I was pretty competent that way. Also, if I saw the house I might be able to suggest something for her. Her husband was a real estate lawyer and they could afford more art.

Clif wanted to talk. I didn't respond.

Daniele, who owned art galleries in Rome, Positano, and Venice, sent jpg's of paintings by a young artist he discovered. I liked Daniele, who was tall with a mop of black and gray hair and limpid dark eyes that took women in all too admiringly. He was suave and intellectual, charming and operatically seductive in the way only an educated Italian could be. He had a way of clasping your hand and saying, "Magari ..." that made you want to lift your skirt. He was successful, which was a neat trick in Italy where the government was sticky-fingered and incompetent, whether it was leftist or conservative.

I clicked open the first image and my breath caught in my throat. It was a reclining nude woman, a dark-haired coquette with a furry golden boa draped over her shoulder. She was seen from behind, twisting her head to look back at the viewer, and the golden-brown fur picked up the gold in her eyes and hair and flesh. A blue, blue sky held her the way a sumptuous gold ground embraced a Cimabue Madonna. It was good. Really good.

What was the painter's name? Alessio Abbate.

I let my eyes travel over the image. Did I lose interest or lose track of what I was supposed to be taking in? No, Abbate knew precisely what he was doing. His painting kept a grip on my eye. The surface was skillful and mostly finished, nearly photo-realistic like Bouguereau in the highlighted parts but with a bit of unevenness in other places; John Singer Sargent painted that way, finishing some bits of his paintings more than others, where the impasto was thick and the brushwork was flashy. I liked the artist's creative way with the technique.

One after another, I opened the six images. They were all nudes, three women, one man, and two multi-figure compositions. I experienced that thrill of delight and discovery that was one of the reasons I had gone into the gallery business.

The images inspired me to consider how I could present Abbate's work in Manhattan, how I could show him best while also educating the public about the value of his paintings. That's what a good gallery did: cultivated clients, educated the public, encouraged artists, explained the importance of an artist to a press jaded by balloon animal sculptures, gay Christ figures, and urine exhibitions. Owning a gallery never was supposed to be solely about making money. Making art never was supposed to be solely about shock value. I wasn't naive enough to believe that we could return to the glory days of Paris between the wars, when artists were innovating for real and galleries were at the center of a lively, engaged community. But surely art galleries could do more than swindle both customers and artists.

Just as bad as the swindling was the branding. Branding was an exploitative byproduct of the incestuous relationship between a few top galleries and the majority of the world's art museums. About a half-dozen "blue chip" galleries accounted for a great proportion of solo shows in museums. More specifically, museums weren't curating anymore; they were simply showing the artists whom the most profitable galleries told them to show. The galleries would then underwrite the expense of the show.

It was an insidious, thoroughly corrupt, good old boy network that grew up over the last few decades and it resulted in the same fifty artists being shown around the world. At least forty of the anointed ones produced nothing but crap; the general public was too intimidated to say that the emperor had no clothes, and those lousy branded artists were nasty to artists with real talent. I saw it all the time with Clif, who had serious chops as a draughtsman and painter. He had mad skills but because there was no separation between the market and the museum, he couldn't get a solo show.

Yet. I was working on it and I was the tenacious sort. I'd get him a solo museum show if it was the last thing I did.

I'd have to bring that tenacity to bear with regard to Abbate's paintings. He deserved some acclaim. I decided to let my unconscious mull over the problem of how to engineer that for him, and that led me to the idea to hold a series of lectures at my gallery. I could get Trudi to give one—if she felt well enough. She was a compelling speaker and she was on the same page as me when it came to loving representational art. Clif could give a talk. I wondered if that snotty editor from *American Artist* would do one lecture; the public exposure might soften some of the pissed-off-at-Sarah right out of him. I could practice being unctuous.

As I was contemplating how unctuous I could be, an email came in. It was another shitty email from George. He was still refusing to pay for Brookton and complaining because he had to drive upstate to have a counseling session with Alex.

I had enough. Before slowing down to think or to remember my attorney Marty O'Shea's excellent advice, I abdicated my discretion. My angry, sarcastic self took the reins. My fingers flew over the keyboard in response. I wrote, "You're an asshole, you've always been an asshole, and you'll always be an asshole." It devolved from there. I threw in some ethnic slurs about Yankees and Episcopalians. I made snide comments about people married to their families. It was not my finest hour; it was downright ugly, and it would reflect poorly on me if it ever made it into court, which it probably would.

But I didn't care.

I was sick and tired of trying to demonstrate more virtue than what was required of Caesar's wife. I was fed up with George Calhoun. I wished he would go die in a hole, a sentiment that also managed to make it into the email, but even more strongly worded, and with language that wasn't standard English.

I hit send.

I couldn't claim to be drunk because the buzz from the wine with dinner had long since worn off. Part of me felt light-headed with relief at expressing myself. Another part, the Princeton-educated self, wished I had carefully crafted the email. I mean, if I was going to fire off an email telling George to go fornicate himself while servicing a male donkey, I could have done it with style. I could have written, "Dear George Calhoun, Mongoloid Esquire," with a nod to Ignatius J. Reilly, the patron saint of indignant correspondence to the idiots of the world. I was sure, as Ignatius was, that Fortuna, that temperamental slut, would spin me down on her wheel.

And then I was giggling and rising and stretching.

*Sometimes I enjoy my lower self.*

Negative pleasure, to be sure, but I wasn't above it. I went to find my dog-eared copy of *Confederacy of Dunces*. I curled up in bed with it. I reached the part where Ignatius was having some fun with an oven mitt and that reminded me that I was due for some fun myself. I mean, oven mitts and wacky New Orleans characters do not ring my bell. It reminded me that I had been keyed up and frisky for most of the day and now I could do something about it. Something about swaying on those heels lit a fire in the sweet spot beneath my navel.

I opened the drawer in the nightstand by my bed and pulled out my vibrator. It was a relatively new device, tastefully colored pink and white, and shaped to fit easily into one hand. I'd thrown out my old one the day Clif moved out. I'd had enough of the humiliation of pleasuring myself after being rejected by my husband. But I soon realized that 4000 rpm's was faster and more efficient than my right hand. Despite my sacred vows that I'd find an equally libidinous man so I'd never again have to masturbate with a machine, I placed an order online.

But, you know. There was a frisky guy orbiting my sphere these days. I didn't necessarily have to get myself off with a machine.

I put away the vibrator and picked up my cell phone and dialed Scott's number.

"Sarah!" he said in a glad tone.

"I'm still mad at you."

"So your date didn't go well." His deep, smooth voice sounded pleased.

"Don't gloat."

A few beats. "What are you wearing?"

I stretched out on my bed and wiggled my toes. "Flannel pajamas over a flannel turtleneck. Under a flannel robe."

"Sexy," he said. "See you in fifteen minutes?"

"Bring condoms. And that present you got for me."

# CHAPTER SEVENTEEN

"I COULD STAY THE night, leave at five thirty and that would give me enough time to get home and go for a run before work," Scott offered. He lay on his side and crooked one eyebrow at me. His dark hair was rumpled and his angular face was soft, unguarded, and stubbly, with red indentations on the bridge of his nose where his glasses usually sat. It was about one in the morning.

"No, thank you," I said, withdrawing my hand from his belly and pulling the sheets up around myself. We were a little sweaty and a little stinky, all those good musky, sticky smells that people make in bed together when they're getting theirs and making sure the other guy gets his, too.

Turns out my c-section scar wasn't such a big deal. At least, it hadn't affected Scott's enthusiasm. I hadn't even noticed him looking at it. If he'd peeked out of the corner of his eyes he'd hidden it well enough that I couldn't tell. Of course, half the time my eyes had been closed in bliss, anyway. He could have gotten an eyeful of whatever he wanted and all I could notice was the rising tide of pleasure.

"Why can't I sleep over?"

"We're not at that stage," I said.

"What stage are we at?"

"The booty call stage."

Scott was reaching toward the nightstand for his glasses and he turned half way and gave me a skeptical look over his shoulder. It reminded me of the way Janey looked at me when I told her I was an art lady.

"Your daughter makes the same expression." I smiled.

"Janey has precocious common sense in addition to being an early reader," he commented. He related an anecdote about Janey's superwonderfulness.

I listened with half an ear while shrugging into my robe. "Thank you for coming over," I said, at a pause in his story. "I'm grateful."

He was pulling up his pants and he froze and glared. "Did you hear a word of what I just said?"

"Ah, yes, Janey."

"Liar. You tuned me out."

"Not totally."

"Yes, you did."

"Yes, I did," I sighed. I went over to him and put my arms around him. His flesh was warm and taut and full of a faint thrum like something vibrating deep in the core of the Earth. "That was amazing. You're amazing. Thank you."

"When can we do it again? And how about dinner?"

"What is it with you and dinner? You're always talking about cooking dinner and eating dinner out. It's like a thing with you."

"Can't we do more than have sex?"

"Why? This is awesome. Let's do this a lot!"

He started to grin and then shook his head. "You're not buying me off that easily. So? Dinner Friday?"

"If we go to Gray's Papaya, we can eat quick and then get to the bedroom for dessert. They make a great Recession Special: two hot dogs and a papaya drink for a few dollars. I really like their onion sauce. Just so you know, the onions are a both-of-us or neither-of-us kind of thing and I'll definitely order them. Don't say I didn't warn you."

Scott put his hands on my shoulders. "Sarah, I like you."

"I alleviate your loneliness," I said. "You were married a long time and you're still not used to being on your own."

"There's more to it than that. I enjoy you. I would like a proper date with you. And don't tell me the improper ones are more fun," he said, as I started to say just that. He leaned down and kissed my forehead. "Are you going to tell Mrs. Waterston that we're seeing each other?"

"We're not seeing each other. We're booty calling each other."

"Dinner Friday," Scott said firmly. "Play hard to get. Make me work for it. You don't have to jump me."

"I like jumping you." I kissed him and walked him to the front door.

He stopped en route and a brooding, almost melancholy, mood swept over him. "I like that you want me. When Lisa first told me that she was leaving me all I could think about was when she stopped reaching for me. When she stopped wanting me. If I had paid attention then, maybe things would have turned out differently for us. Maybe I'd still be living in Boston with my kids. Even if they live two blocks away from me here in Manhattan, it's not the same. I don't get to see them every single day and every single night. I'm going to miss out on parts of their lives. It's inevitable."

Part of me wanted to respond with a joke; I already had so much turmoil in my life that I didn't feel I could take on one more person's pain. But my silly soft heart opened to him because this was the crux of it for him: could he have or should he have done something to save his marriage and his family?

I met his eyes straight on. "Scott, there's no going back to do it over. You did your best at the time. Maybe your best sucked. That happens to all of us."

"My best is an A, and I get A's at everything," he said, his mouth pulling down. "I got an A in organic chemistry. I aced the MCATs. I went to Harvard Medical School right out of Harvard. I'm looking for an effective treatment for pancreatic cancer. I'll find one sometime in the next decade, you'll see."

"No one gets A's at everything in life. Sooner or later, life catches up to you. We all graduate from life with a few F's."

He didn't like that one bit. He stood at the door and kissed me with his hands cupping my bottom. "If we're going to do this regularly I need to bring over a toothbrush."

"Let's take it one booty call at a time."

"Friday at seven?"

I nodded and kissed him one last time and pushed him out the door.

———

Fortuna, that vicious slut, had indeed spun her wheel downward on me. I wasn't referring to the passage of Mother's Day without a card or any other form of acknowledgment from either Dani or Alex. Alex was angry about being taken to therapeutic school and, anyway, she didn't have access to electronics. Maybe a handwritten letter would come next week, but I couldn't count on it when her father was telling her that I was wrong to enroll her at Brookton instead of a Manhattan public school where she'd be free to indulge herself. And Dani hadn't sent a birthday card to me in February so I couldn't expect any remembrance on Mother's Day.

My daughters' thoughtlessness toward me was, sadly, par for the course. Fortuna's displeasure took another form: a giant tax bill from New York State. It shocked me how greedy the state had become, thanks largely to the benighted health care reform act that had targeted resource-stretched states instead of the fat cat health insurance companies. So small businesses like mine were squeezed more and more in an already tough market.

I was politically agnostic, but I didn't know how small businesses would survive with the current socialist climate screwing us to the wall. Not that the Right would do more for small businesses, the Right was too busy toadying to big multinational corporations to care about the mom-and-pops like me. When it came to small businesses, it seemed as if both the Democrats and the Republicans were conspiring to create a world with only two classes. One class was the lower middle class, who worked either for the government or for the government's senior partner, the big corporations. The other class was the fabulously wealthy upper class comprised of executives at banks, stock market firms, tech companies, and giant corporations that functioned as sovereign nation-states without accountability or oversight.

"Oh my god, where am I going to get the money to pay this?" I asked myself. I stared blankly at the computer screen and my accountant's semi-apologetic letter. Maybe if I had known the bill was coming, I wouldn't have paid all those other bills with the proceeds from the sale to Carl.

I walked around the gallery and stared at the various paintings, wondering which ones I could sell quickly. Then I remembered suggesting an evening at the gallery to the banker's skinny wife and the gay interior designer. I could make that happen. I couldn't be sure to sell something but I'd pull out all the stops and see what happened. It was also time to set up those gallery talks for introducing Abbate's work. The process of drumming up interest in the lectures would attract attention to the gallery and that attention might bring some sales.

———

Alex and I sat next to each other on a small beige sofa in her therapist's office. I had risen at four in the morning on the Friday before Memorial Day and got Brigit rolling before dawn had even cracked the horizon. I arrived in time to hug Alex ferociously, grab a cup of coffee, and head over to a second-floor room with her.

Lindsay, the therapist, said that Alex was getting used to the routine at Brookton.

*What a curiously plain statement.*

It wasn't positive—it wasn't a statement like "Alex is doing well here." I wondered if it concealed wrongdoings by Alex. Probably.

Lindsay reported that the nurse practitioner that handled the kids' meds had tweaked Alex's prescription. A few covert looks I couldn't read passed between Lindsay and Alex.

Lindsay asked Alex to talk about her feelings. It was nothing more and nothing less than an invitation for Alex to rant about the unfairness of it all, and Alex ran with it.

"Why can't you treat me like dad does? He doesn't try to control me! Dad and Katherine say I shouldn't be here, that I should be in New York going to public school," she declared, accusingly. Steam rose off the top of her head. She kept going with her usual defiant litany of excuses, justifications, and demands.

"I found what was in your Sprite can," I said when she finally paused to take a breath.

That set her off again. It was another round of how could I be such a bitch? Dani and Katherine agreed that I was awful. So why didn't I just leave her alone, and why couldn't she just do what she wanted without my interference?

"Because I'm your mother and I do care, and I'm always going to," I said.

Another tirade about the injustice of it all.

In no way did Alex ever acknowledge her own behaviors: truancy, marijuana abuse, refusal to do homework, inappropriate behavior with boys in class, screaming curses at her mother, missing curfew, stealing money out of my purse, or bringing a banned substance to class.

I tried to interject a few thoughts about personal responsibility but Alex attacked me with a torrent of vicious words when I did.

Lindsay sat there with a carefully blank expression on her face.

I could feel myself starting to boil. It was always that way with Alex; she didn't care about the consequences either to herself or to the people closest to her or to her community. She was blind to how her own behaviors resulted in serial humiliations at school. Statements rose to my lips but I didn't want to speak them because they wouldn't be "therapeutically approved." That is, they would direct Alex to hold herself accountable for the constant trouble and protracted failures she had created through her own choices, an accountability that child and adolescent therapy seemed designed to prevent.

Alex didn't notice my silence and anger because she did not comprehend my anxiety and grief over her. She continued to declaim in a loud voice about how aggrieved and put upon she was.

Why couldn't she run her own life?

Why did she have to be under my thumb?

Her father and stepmother said she should do whatever she wanted because that's the only way she'd find herself. It was the same nonsense I'd heard for the last two years.

I rose and walked out of the therapist's office.

I walked out across the rolling green land and was glad I had left before saying something awful. It was a brilliantly sunny day and tall treetops swayed in the breeze. The air smelled like the Adirondacks, like Balsam fir and lakes and mountains and cold air from the North. I realized that therapeutic school would fail Alex. It would fail because it was failing to address the root of her problem: her entitlement, her surety that only her feelings mattered, her lack of empathy, her lack of a moral compass. She would continue to believe what she was taught in the bosom of the Calhoun tribe: that she was the grandiose center of everything and everyone around her was at best a pale reflection of her superiority.

In the artificial laboratory of therapy where so much was supposed to be played out, examined, and rectified, Alex would not meet her authentic self, because a therapy that condoned everything except uncomfortable feelings would not provide her with the necessary realness to heal.

As Dr. Maitra pointed out, I had been dealing with this with Bailey: the systematic undermining of a moral center that would have led Alex to think carefully and to feel deeply, to squirm with regret and shame, to quiver with sadness and loneliness, to understand the necessity of wise guidance, and to wrest her true self from the pain despite the barrage of stimuli and the festival of vices in the city. When I had wanted Alex to become competent, self-disciplined, responsible, motivated, empathic, and well-behaved, I had been slapped down as over-bearing and intrusive. Of course, that was George's shtick, and he paid Bailey's bills.

I had hoped that up there in this green and forested land, unplugged from her drug dealers and her text messages and social media, Netflix and other entitled teenagers—especially the unending parade of horny boys—

Alex would be able to let down into something more soulful. I had hoped that she would start to understand the importance of deferred gratification and self-discipline for safety and growth. I had hoped that she would start to mature.

I had gone out on a limb, financially and personally, to put Alex into that school. The tuition cost a fortune. The first payment sat on my credit card like a gaping chasm. George, with his pathological need to hurt me, would not forego the opportunity to use the system of American jurisprudence as a forum for proving, yet again, how I was a terrible, crazy person.

Nor would any of these therapists, not Bailey and not Lindsay, ever admit that George's unrestrained aggression toward me was a primary cause of Alex's problems.

I sat on the ground and leaned back against the bole of a giant, ancient white pine. It was massive and straight as an arrow, branchless for at least sixty feet. It didn't have much to say, but it let me lean and pause and empty myself into the moment, into my sadness and disappointment over Alex and this latest school that would not be the panacea I hoped for. It was probably my own fault for wanting a panacea.

It's just that I loved Alex.

I loved her with all my heart. Loving her, I wanted so much better for her than sneaky misbehavior, risk-taking, substance abuse, constant floundering, lack of cooperation, defiance toward adults, rampant promiscuity, and functional failure.

But I was being pessimistic. Not enough time had passed for Alex to begin to be educated at Brookton. Maybe with a few more months here she'd show a dawning consideration of other people. Maybe she'd stop throwing tantrums and begin to lay out goals for herself. Maybe she'd begin to see the difference between honorable and contemptible—and why that difference mattered.

I should have stayed for the counseling session. Certainly, I should have. Dr. Maitra had advised me to be a leader and walking out of the session did not show leadership. It's just that I was human. I had feelings. I was tired of being Alex's punching bag. And George's. And Dani's. I was sick of hearing how my hopes and dreams for my daughter were bad and wrong. It often felt as if the only way to have a relationship with Alex or Dani was to abnegate myself totally, and I just didn't want to do that. I couldn't.

I went back in to the school and found Alex waiting in the lobby. Her pretty face was puckered with its usual petulance but she didn't talk about the therapy session—not one word about me walking out. We walked shoulder-to-shoulder to the cafeteria and stood in line for lunch. We filled our trays with what looked to be healthy fare, roast veggies and hamburgers and potato chips, and took seats at a long white melamine table. Some of her teachers stopped by and shook my hand in greeting. I wondered if any of them would model a higher consciousness for Alex so she would get some of what I'd hoped for from this place.

# CHAPTER EIGHTEEN

JUNE 1: THE FIRST day of Trudi's treatment.

Robert and I stood beside Trudi at the door to the chemotherapy suite. It was a long rectangular bay jammed with recliners. Curtain dividers hung between some recliners, others stood shoulder to shoulder, separated only by small end tables with lamps.

Surprisingly, it was a cheerful room with yellow walls, oversized landscapes on the wall, and gentle, diffused lighting. There appeared to be some private cubicles off to one side.

It was eight a.m. and some of the chairs were already occupied with people connected to their IV drips. They were looking at their tablets or smart phones, reading books or newspapers or magazines, or chatting with a visitor who sat on a stool or in a wooden chair beside them.

"I've done the research so I know my hair won't fall out instantly today," Trudi murmured. "Still, somehow I look at this room and I imagine it will fall out today. I feel as if I should have brought a hat."

"We'll go shopping and I'll buy you a bunch of new hats," I promised, knowing my voice sounded hoarse.

"To go with the hundred I already own?" she asked, in her tart Trudi way. Her hands clasped and unclasped in front of her solar plexus. She wore a fresh coat of crimson polish on her fingernails. "This is the room where I will face the foe."

"This is the room where you'll win," I said. It was the prayer in my heart.

"I will certainly give it my all," Trudi said, almost defiantly.

A nurse bustled over, beaming at us. She held an iPad and swiped her finger over Trudi's name. She said, "This is your first treatment, Mrs.

Waterston, so we'll allow both of your visitors although we usually allow one visitor per patient."

"It'll just be my husband today," Trudi told her. She turned and patted my cheek. "Sarah, you can bring me next week. But don't plan on staying for the whole treatment. It takes several hours."

"Will do," I said, blithely, even though I didn't feel that way. Sappy sentiment would only piss Trudi off.

Trudi nodded briskly and trotted off behind the nurse. Robert followed them.

———

I went back to the gallery and locked the door behind me. Technically, the gallery didn't open until eleven; it was only nine so I had some time to catch up on administrative stuff. The wine delivery guy rapped on the door, so I waved and ran back to unlock the door and usher him in. Tonight was champagne and hors d'oeuvres for two of my best and favorite clients. I took the case of Moët & Chandon and loaded several bottles into the small fridge in the office. I liked the fruity brightness of that bubbly and I intended to pour it plentifully enough to lubricate some sales.

Around noon, Clif sent a courier over with his new painting *Fury and Lust*, finished just a few days ago. It was larger than most of his works, seventy-two inches by eighty-four inches. I pulled off the bubble wrap and found a playful seascape with three female figures and a male: Aphrodite, Hera, Helen, and Paris. On the right side of the canvas the beach curved off toward a gate. If you looked at the gate you realized it was burning.

But it was the figures that commanded attention. They were masterfully done. Aphrodite was an ethereal goddess with flaxen hair. She smiled at the golden apple she held in one exquisite hand, the luminous and delicate hand of a Bellini Madonna. Her other arm was wrapped around Helen's waist. Helen was also blonde, but taller, earthier, full breasted, round-limbed, and milk-maidish—a kind of Vermeer voluptuary. She exchanged a salacious glance with black-haired Paris, who knelt in front of her on one knee, and who bore a striking resemblance to the artist himself. Auburn-haired Hera stood aloof to the left of the triangular central grouping of her cohorts. She was slightly recessed and her head was tilted because she was looking at the burning gate. One soft white arm was raised, a finger pointing to the heavens, a curiously St. John the Baptist gesture.

I could not miss the resemblance between Hera and me.

I propped the painting against my desk and knelt to examine it in detail. It was a treat for the eye to behold. Clif's paintings never failed to elicit wonder and admiration. However I felt about the man, and however happy I was to be starting a new life apart from him, I could not deny his prodigious talent. His genius was not just in the perfection of his forms, but also in the resonance they had with the causal deep. In a Perini painting, the apparitions of time—human bodies—were portals for transiting the worlds. The viewer was drawn in by the figures—drawn in and in and in—into the mystery of transcendence and immanence, two worlds in one. Aphrodite wasn't just a bosomy blonde, she was a mandala for Beauty itself, for the Way of Beauty that leads into Truth and Oneness. Helen was all that was seductive and pleasurable about the human condition. Paris was the hero and the supplicant, lured into adventure.

"Knock, knock," said a gravelly voice at my office door.

I rose. "Carl! Good to see you. What brings you here?"

"I haven't heard from you for a while, so I thought I'd lay eyes on you," he said. He was wearing a well-tailored British suit and he smiled and kissed me warmly full on the lips.

*Are we kissing for real now? Oh, goody.*

But on the heels of that little burst of pleasure followed another, less enthusiastic thought: *Now I can't sell him anything.*

I just wasn't going to mix business with my intimate life. There's a word for women who do that, and it's not a nice one. Even to save my gallery, I wouldn't go there. Sometimes it really sucked to have values.

"Wow, that's some painting!" Carl exclaimed when he stepped back from me.

"I know; it's amazing, right? Gotta hand it to Clif. He can really paint."

Carl bent over to peruse the piece. "The Trojan War. The burning gate and the golden apple."

"You're the classics major," I acknowledged.

"Is that you?"

"That would be Hera."

Carl straightened and his blue eyes glimmered. "Sure."

I shrugged. "I've been around artists enough so I know not to take it personally."

He turned back to the painting. "Interesting, the way he's positioned the golden apple in the very center of the canvas. I might have expected one of the goddesses. Hera's state of dishabille does make one wonder how close the resemblance is to you, Sarah. Hera is just gorgeous."

I meant to tell him that Clif had taken artistic license and although I wanted to encourage Carl's thoughts in the general direction of dishabille, I didn't want him to be disappointed when I didn't turn out to have a heavenly body. But then Clif poked his head in behind Carl.

"You got it? What do you think?" he asked eagerly, like a kid seeking his mom's approval for a kindergarten art project.

"Clif, you know it's amazing," I said simply. "Carl, this is Clif Perini, the artist; Clif, Carl Hopkins, who bought your river nymphs a few months ago."

"Your work is extraordinary," Carl said, shaking Clif's hand. "It's a pleasure to meet you."

"Thank you, that's always good to hear," Clif said. "How do the nymphs look in your home?"

"Absolutely gorgeous," Carl said. "Sarah did the installation."

"She's good with my work," Clif said.

"Yes, she chose the perfect place for them. They are magnificent pieces and they show superbly." Carl nodded a few times.

"I'd love to get some photographs," Clif ventured.

"We'll do better than that, we'll invite you over to see for yourself," Carl returned, in a sprightly voice. "In fact, I have an idea. Sarah, why don't we make a cocktail party in honor of Clif and the paintings? I have a number of friends who should see Clif's work in person. They'd really enjoy the river nymphs."

Clif glowed. He enjoyed nothing more than attention and adulation, which would be pathetic in a man who didn't deserve it so much, and was slightly pathetic even though he totally deserved the acclaim.

He said, "That sounds great! I'd appreciate that, Carl."

"Sarah will be in touch to arrange a day that works for you," Carl said. He shook Clif's hand again, which was clearly the signal for Clif to leave.

Clif was not one to miss a public cue. He took gracious leave of me and departed the gallery.

I stared at Carl with true, if sardonic, appreciation.

"What?" he asked, with a small smile.

"That was impressive," I said, raising my eyebrows and doffing an imaginary hat. "I've never seen anyone finessed quite so adroitly. That was quite the display of virtuosity."

Carl stroked the top of my wrist with one finger. "Don't be mad. I've had this idea about a cocktail party for a while. I've been meaning to ask you about it. I haven't hosted my friends in forever, and they'll love the paintings. Won't it be good for your gallery?"

"That's not the point. You do realize that I didn't say a single word during that entire interaction?"

Carl's flush deepened. "I get carried away trying to help. It's a flaw of mine, I know. My kids tell me all the time. Don't be mad at me, Sarah."

"It's hard to stay mad at you when you're so nice about it," I grumbled.

The juicy light of victory flooded his countenance. "Let me take you to lunch to make up for it."

"I can't leave the gallery until two o'clock when Rosa comes in," I said. "I was going to order in. You're welcome to join me. How do you feel about pad thai?"

"I like it," he said. "Happy to stay, as long as it's my treat." He pulled off his jacket and hung it over the back of one of the rolling chairs in the office. Then he loosened his tie. "What are you doing with this painting? Should I buy it?"

"No, Carl, you may not buy it," I said, not entirely able to smother a sigh.

*Wouldn't it solve my tax bill problem if you did?*

I imagined a giant, fat check for what Clif's exquisite, museum-quality painting was worth. My tax bill would be paid and there'd be plenty leftover. "I'm showing it to some special guests tonight."

"They'll love it," he assured me. He seated himself in the chair and stretched out his legs, wagging his feet back and forth. He was completely at ease in my office, as if he sat there every day.

"Shouldn't you be at work?"

"I'm the boss. I'm eating lunch out. At an art gallery." He looked around my small office crammed with art catalogs, books, brown-paper-wrapped canvases, and files of client information. He smiled to himself. Then he focused his eyes and directed a blue-laser gaze at me. "I hear that Trudi started chemo today. How are you doing with that?"

"Oh, so, now it comes out: the real reason you're here!" I said, in a laughing and scolding tone. Gently I kicked the sole of his hand-made

Italian shoe. "I thought you stopped in to lay eyes on me, but you have ulterior motives."

"I always have ulterior motives," he admitted. "Dr. Bauer has a good reputation. He's young but he's made a reputation for himself in the field of pancreatic cancer. His trial has shown mixed results, but the good results are very, very good." He breathed heavily and his vision turned within, and I knew he was thinking about his wife. She had been with a different doctor, certainly the best he could find at the time, and her results were not good.

"That's what I hear, too," I murmured. I seated myself at my desk and pulled open the top drawer. I fished around for the Thai restaurant menu. "The food here is fresh and tasty. What do you like? And Carl, I'll be meeting your friends at the cocktail party, won't I?"

He nodded and kept his eyes on the menu as if he really needed to study it, which he didn't. "Is that OK?"

"Would it matter if it wasn't?" There was an edge to my voice. "I mean, isn't that the plan, for me to meet your friends?"

"I don't want you to feel uncomfortable, Sarah." He gave me a guileless look. Then his smile broadened. "Why don't you come out to Sag Harbor this weekend? I've got a house there. Plenty of room. A stretch of private beach. It's supposed to be beautiful this weekend."

"Come to Sag Harbor to discuss a cocktail party we're making together?"

He nodded.

I got the feeling he was holding his breath. I had to think about his invitation. "Let me see what I've got planned for this weekend. Also, I have a dog."

"Bring your dog. You can ride out with me or I can have my driver bring you."

"I can leave my dog with my neighbor. And I can take the jitney." I furrowed my brow at him. "If I don't have something else going on."

He said, "Pad thai and lemongrass soup. Ask them to make it extra spicy."

———◦———

The evening at the gallery did not go as I hoped. It was great fun and we all had a blast, but no sales ensued, and a blast wasn't going to pay the tax bill. Skinny Mrs. Banker had gone and gotten herself knocked up, and they were now putting their money into making a nursery in each of their two homes. She was radiant and sat drinking water with a stupidly happy expression on her face. I couldn't help but feel happy for her and hoped that she didn't have the same troubles with her progeny that I had with mine.

The surgeon and the designer were facing two private school tuition bills as their youngest was just accepted to Ethical. They didn't feel they could splurge on art at this juncture. I let them out the door after we had all swilled copious amounts of champagne. Donald leaned in and whispered, "Sorry."

I licked my fingertip and drew a line in the air. "One for you."

He giggled once and shrugged, then he and Todd smiled and waved goodbye.

I tidied up the gallery and then shut down the music, a blues channel on internet radio. I was tempted to sit at my desk and brood, but I knew that wouldn't truly do any good. It was ersatz work, designed to make me feel like I was succoring my business even though I wasn't accomplishing a damn thing. I shrugged on my blazer and my cell phone vibrated.

"Sarah," said Scott.

"Scott!" I was happy to hear his deep voice.

"I'm calling to say I can't make it tomorrow. Something's come up at work."

I wondered if another one of his patients was dying and I thought warily of Trudi. "Another time."

"You could sound disappointed."

"Do you want me to be disappointed, Scott?"

He hesitated for a fraction of a second.

"Yes. I want you to be disappointed because I'm disappointed. This is the second time I've had to reschedule. Friday or Saturday won't work, either. Lisa is bringing the kids in, and they'll be with me while she goes apartment hunting. Unless you want to join me and the kids for dinner?"

"Another time, Scott. I understand about kids."

"I suppose you do. How's your daughter? She hasn't been around much lately?"

I flipped off all the lights in the gallery, both in the office and the showroom. I walked across the darkened front room with its long glass windows looking onto Eighth Avenue. Street lamps sparkled above the street, glinting through the windows and bathing the gallery in a fluid, milky radiance. Some of my paintings looked even more beautiful in the exotic half-light, some disappeared totally. Light was everything in art.

"I have two daughters, Scott. My older daughter will be a senior at Princeton next year. This summer she's in San Francisco, interning at a law firm. The daughter you met is now in therapeutic school upstate."

"I didn't know," he said simply.

I stepped outside and held the cell phone between my ear and shoulder while locking the front door. "There's no reason you would."

"That's why we need a real date. To get to know each other better."

I stuck the keys in my purse and laughed softly. "My life is way too full of realness. I like what we're doing. The booty calls. The fantasy. It works for me. It's real enough that you're my best friend's oncologist."

He didn't say anything for a few beats.

I walked toward the subway but I didn't hang up on him.

Finally he said, "I'm more than that. I think you should acknowledge that."

"I have a really complicated life," I said. "A lot of things suck for me right now, Scott. I'm enjoying you. Your life is complicated too, with Lisa and Janey and Max and Uncle Ricky and starting over in New York."

"Rick," he snarled. "We can get to know each other better and that doesn't make it heavy. It'll make things even better in bed."

I stopped at the street corner to wait for the light to change on Seventh Avenue. "I can't imagine it getting better, it's pretty damn good!"

He was smiling again; I could just feel it. He said, "I'm inviting you over."

*Now there's a thought.*

I couldn't stop myself from smiling almost as stupidly as skinny Mrs. Banker.

"I've been drinking champagne with clients. My defenses are down. If I come over, it'll be way too easy for you to take advantage of me."

He laughed outright. When he stopped, he asked, "How long?"

"Depends on the number one train. I'm at 23rd Street."

"You're at 23rd Street? Twenty minutes," he calculated.

# CHAPTER NINETEEN

I DROVE OUT TO my client's house in Scarsdale and repaired her frame. I failed to sell her another painting because she and her husband just bought a condo in Palm Beach. If I didn't have bad luck, I'd have no luck at all, I concluded. Fortuna was having her way with me.

The following day, Trudi met me at a diner a few blocks from the chemo suite. She arrived first and early and was seated in a banquette. I slid in across from her and checked my cell phone. It was seven-fifteen a.m.; I was exactly on time.

"Your omelet is on its way," she said before sipping her tea. Her face was gaunt, her eyes were hollowed, and was I imagining things, or was there a yellowish cast to her complexion?

"Onion and peppers?" I asked hopefully, and not because I cared about the flavor of my breakfast but because I cared about her. Trudi disliked displays of messy emotion. She considered them an American invention and called them "pure rubbish," according them almost as much sarcasm as the inveterate American habit of wishing people a nice day. I eyed her and my heart constricted. She had lost more weight. She did not look well.

"No cheese."

She nodded and then wiped her lips, leaving some of her coral lipstick on the paper napkin. "Here's how it will go: you'll get me settled and we'll chat for a while. Then you'll be off on your day. I will text you about an hour prior to the end of treatment. You may retrieve me at that time."

I smiled beatifically and held up my canvas tote bag. "I'm staying. I brought a day's worth of things to do. Herrera's bio of Frida Kahlo. My iPad, so I can answer emails."

"You're not sitting around the chemo lounge with me all day."

The waitress set a plate in front of me. The omelet was steaming hot and I could see the translucent onions peeking through the soft yellow skin.

"Yes, I am. You won't be able to make me leave because you'll be plugged into an IV. Also, last time we arm wrestled, I won." I took up my fork. "This looks delicious! I love diner food."

"I don't have it in me to argue with you, Sarah," Trudi murmured. "I don't have the energy. But what about your gallery? Shouldn't you be there minding the store?"

"Rosa's there all day."

"You'll get depressed sitting in the chemo lounge. The colors are cheerful but, ultimately, it doesn't distract you from what is really happening: dying people are grasping at straws, trying to stay alive." Her voice was draggy.

I gave her a sharp look. "Many of those people will succeed."

Trudi sipped some tea. "Did you have to bring suit against George for payment of therapeutic school? What's the latest word?"

"I did, and Marty called last night to say they finally managed to serve George."

"Finally?" Trudi asked. "Didn't they serve him right away?"

"He had directed his attorney not to accept service, and then he was running away from the process server. That's what Marty said. He didn't tell me about it earlier because he didn't want to drag me into it."

Trudi nodded brusquely. "George is at it again with his usual gamesmanship."

"Marty said he's only trying to get me hooked into that dynamic." I felt the simmer of frustration that George's antics always provoked.

*God, I dodged a bullet when I left him.*

"I told Marty not to protect me but to tell me next time if that happens again."

"Maybe this will be the end of it, and there won't be a next time," Trudi said. She didn't sound convinced.

"You know George. He's richer than sin, his family is richer than that and they cater to his every whim. This is how he gets his jollies. There'll be a next time."

Trudi scowled. "How are the girls?"

"Same. Dani doesn't want to have anything to do with me. Alex is still in therapeutic school."

"Is it helping her?"

I shook my head.

"Why not?"

I shook my head again.

"You must have some idea, Sarah," she prodded. "You always do."

I sighed explosively. "It's not Brookton's fault. It's a problem with contemporary psychotherapy."

Trudi smiled for the first time. "Are the hoofbeats thundering in the distance? Do I hear a diatribe coming on? You're taking on the field of psychology instead of the art world this time?"

"You asked," I pointed out, before plunging in. "So there's this trend in contemporary psychotherapy that anything you want to do is fine as long you don't feel guilty or bad about it. Shrinks write a million scrips to make sure that peoples' feelings stay within a narrow range: not too bad and not too good. But whatever those hopped-up-on-psychopharmaceuticals people do is fine!"

"Whatever they do?"

"Yes!" I slapped the table, making the fork clatter on my plate. "People can be unconscionably selfish and cruel to other human beings because it isn't their actions that matter, it's their self-esteem. It goes like this: 'So, you lure people deep into the woods, murder them with an ax, and chop them into tiny little pieces. How do you feel about that? Not so good? Let's give you an anti-depressant, you poor thing.' That's how it works. That's why I don't know if therapeutic school will help my daughter. I don't think it will address the problem of her behavior in the world. It's not going to teach her that accepting her responsibilities with dignity, finding her work in the world, and treating other people with kindness and respect and consideration, is what will fulfill her. Ultimately that, not the fake high of a drug, will bring her real happiness."

"Alexandra hasn't been at the school very long," Trudi pointed out.

But I wasn't done. "You know what else sucks? These stupid therapists can see George being crazy aggressive toward me. They must know that has an impact on Alex, but none of them ever call him on it because they're too busy trying to maintain 'therapeutic neutrality.'" I made quotation signs in the air with my fingers. "But you know, Trudi, there's no such thing as neutrality. If you live in a body, you're not neutral.

I believe that everyone should have figured out after World War II that neutrality is an excuse to give free rein to a bully!"

"World War II no less? This doesn't go all the way back to Marcel Duchamp foisting a urinal on a gullible public, the way bad art does?" Trudi teased. She was smiling for real now. Trudi always got a kick out of my rants.

"Give me a few minutes, I'm sure I can pin the failure of contemporary psychotherapy on Duchamp somehow," I grumbled.

Trudi laughed shortly. "You're correct in all you say, Sarah. You make good points. And you know the English do not necessarily accord psychotherapy the reverence that Americans do. But the question is, what else is there?"

My eyes snapped to her face.

Trudi shrugged. "It's what we have. An imperfect solution in an imperfect world. That's why you put your daughter in therapeutic school. Because it's the best option available to help her. In the end, you go with the best option even if it's not perfect."

I nodded but didn't say anything. She was right and she knew it, and she wasn't just talking about therapeutic school.

After a while, she asked, "How's Carl?"

I gave her a cynical half-smile.

"Carl, Carl … the control freak who manipulated me into hosting a cocktail party with him and invited me to his place in the Hamptons? That Carl?"

"A jolly good bloke. I like him," Trudi answered, her voice livelier. "We're coming to the cocktail party. I think you should go to Sag Harbor. It sounds lovely. He has a stretch of private beach."

I gave her a dirty look that made her grin gleefully. I was glad to see it.

"You and Carl are now BFF's?"

"He phoned to see how I was doing. He sent over some imported tea. He's very thoughtful. Perhaps later in the summer, depending on how I'm doing, Robert and I could join you out in Sag Harbor."

"I didn't say I was going to Sag Harbor."

"If you agree to go I'll let you stay for the whole day."

"No deal, lady. I'm staying all day whether you let me or not," I declared. I looked her dead in the eyes without blinking so she knew I meant business.

"You're a pain in the arse," Trudi grumbled. She watched me eat a few bites of omelet. She had a plate of untouched white toast in front of her.

"What's going on between you and my doctor?"

"Nothing," I said.

———

For the first time in the six years I'd operated my gallery, I wasn't attending Art Basel. I'd never submitted an application for my gallery to participate in the fair; I just couldn't see the panel of distinguished jurists letting in the Paige Realist Gallery. Besides, it was a six-figure investment to participate, which was a lot for my small but worthy enterprise. But I had always attended, listening to the latest gossip and enticing the serious collectors to my gallery. That wasn't poaching because all was fair in love and art.

That year there was just too much else going on for me, with Alex in Brookton and Trudi in chemo and the suit against George. I was reluctant to spend the money for a plane ticket when I still had that giant tuition payment on my credit card. Moreover, there was another payment due. I talked to the registrar at Brookton, explained the circumstances, and begged for an extension. They were unenthusiastic but polite enough to accommodate me. I could hear the clock ticking in the background. I'd have to pony up more money soon.

Marty said the suit to recover the cost of Alex's therapeutic school was proceeding and he expected to have George's lawyer's response any day. He didn't say what we both knew: that George's papers would be, as always, full of abject scorn for me and for everything I did.

In the past, he was the one suing me. He lost, though he didn't seem to care. I couldn't bring myself to think that I "won" even though the judge had found in my favor. After all, what was "winning" in the face of a colossal black hole that sucked in money, time, and energy better spent elsewhere, that left bad feelings in its wake, and that enriched only the attorneys?

Only this time, because Alex needed specialized help and I couldn't afford Brookton, I had initiated the legal proceedings. But it was still his game because that was how he liked to relate to me. He manipulated the situation until I found myself with little choice other than to turn to the legal system to help me pay for what Alex needed. Nor did Marty's services, as much as I appreciated them, come cheap. George had to reimburse me for legal expenses, according to the terms of our settlement contract, but it somehow was never a complete reimbursement and there were still always additional expenses.

So no Art Basel. But there I was in Sag Harbor, on Main Street, stepping off the jitney in front of the municipal building. It was about eleven on Saturday morning and Carl waved to me from down the street. He stood by his car, a well-appointed, sublimely understated Mercedes. His driver sat in the front.

I skipped down the sidewalk. He jogged toward me, grabbed me, and hugged me fiercely.

I had to take my happiness where I found it.

Carl's driver got out of the car and came around to open the trunk.

I remembered his name. "Andrei, hello."

Andrei, who sported a gold tooth on the left side of his mouth and a closely shaved head, smiled broadly. "Nice to see you, Miss Sarah."

Carl put my leather duffel bag in the trunk; Andrei closed it and then opened the passenger door. Carl held out his hand to help me in, which I didn't need but took anyway because it gave me an opportunity to smile at him. He slid in after me.

We drove through town and took a winding road toward the water. Carl kept up a running patter about the town and its various landmarks. I wondered if nervousness was making him loquacious, or if he was just being a congenial host.

We curved around a quiet lane into a private enclave and arrived at his place. It was a sprawling, white beachfront house with about two acres of pristinely landscaped grassy lawn. It had sweeping western views across Shelter Island Sound. The vista alone was worth many millions of dollars.

"I've got a fixed, deep water boat dock," Carl said.

"Carl, your apartment in the city is beautiful but this is beyond belief!"

He smiled and took my leather duffel bag from Andrei.

"Come on inside, let me show you the place."

We walked around tall lilac bushes and red maples to the door and stepped up onto the porch. I noted the patio that wrapped around to the beachfront side of the house.

Carl said, "You can't see them from here, but there are some chairs on the patio. I like to sit outside in the evening and watch the sun go down over the Sound."

"You are reading my mind, Carl," I murmured.

He led me indoors into the living room, which was all smoothly sanded white hardwood floors, white walls and airy white furniture on which were scattered bright red and blue throw pillows. Long plate glass windows let in the light falling down from the heavens and dancing off the water.

"This way to the kitchen," he said. The chef's kitchen echoed the light and airy theme with white wooden cabinetry, River White granite countertops and matching hand-marbleized white tiles. The center island was also topped with River White granite. The appliances were all Wolf.

The dining room was off the living room on the waterfront side of the house with its exquisite views.

"Bedrooms are upstairs," Carl said.

He stepped up onto the landing and gestured for me to follow him. We arrived at a long hall with several rooms off it. He paused, not looking at me, and pointed. "Here's the guest room."

*Time to take the bull by the horns.*

I took my leather bag from his grasp and set it on the floor. Then I stepped to within a few inches of Carl so that our noses almost touched.

"I'm not welcome in your bedroom?"

Carl flushed.

"Well, ah, yes, of course. I didn't want to presume."

I put my arms around him and kissed him.

He seemed surprised at first and then he was eager. His mouth opened and he thrust his tongue in my mouth. He tasted like black coffee and orange juice. He pressed his body against me and I found myself enjoying his warmth and the sturdiness of his frame.

I liked the general direction things were headed so I softened into the moment.

Carl kept kissing me and then he maneuvered me into one of the rooms off the hall. We stumbled into it and he closed the door behind us.

"This is my room," he said, his voice hoarse.

There was a big bed with a white sateen duvet. The headboard was upholstered in the same white fabric, which was not a good sign. Beds for couples should always have either slats or posts for tying each other up. I figured Carl and I could make do if we ever came to that point.

"Lovely," I said and went back to kissing him, because he felt solid and good in my arms and because I liked and appreciated him.

Carl made a soft whuffling sound deep in his chest and he pulled at the neckline of my shirt. I raised my arms and let him slip it off. I was wearing a pale peach La Perla bra. The Tanga panties matched, which he would find out in a minute or two. I unbuttoned his shirt and it fell to the floor, and I ran my hands over his shoulders and chest. His was a well-kept, mature body, freckled and hardened in places and slack in others. There was some softness about his gut; even so, it was clear that he worked out regularly. His chest was furred with curly salt-and-pepper hair.

Carl was kissing my throat and collarbones, and he slid his fingers inside the waistband of my skirt. I reached around, unzipped and stepped out of the skirt. I unbuckled his belt and he stepped out of his pants. We stood looking each other over for a moment. His face was rapt with appreciation and he said, in his husky voice, "You're so beautiful!"

I felt beautiful in that moment. The sixteen or eighteen years between us tipped in my favor, and I forgot about the physical frailties that neither yoga nor careful eating could erase, frailties that always felt so glaring when I stood beside Scott.

I said, "You are, too."

He kissed me some more and stroked me in all the right places, and we did that specific and awkward waltz toward his bed. I dropped down onto it with a smile and pulled him down next to me.

"I haven't done this in the middle of the day in years," Carl remarked with a grin.

"Is there a time of day you prefer?" I asked. I curled my hand around him, thinking that he was well-endowed in a way that fit his barrel-chested body, even when he was flying at half-mast.

Carl looked at my hand.

He said, "Beta blockers …"

His voice trailed away. He kissed my mouth.

"I can take a pill."

"If you want, sure." I scooted closer to him and kissed him and stroked him.

His breath hitched in his chest.

He asked, "What do you want?" He put his arms around me and quickly unhooked my bra.

"So you're good with your hands?"

Carl nodded, his blue eyes flashing.

"Then we're in business."

Turns out, he was an expert with his hands, and by the time my climax proved that to both of us he wanted his pill. I got a condom from my bag and put it on him. It made for an enjoyable midday.

# CHAPTER TWENTY

SUNDAY MORNING I WOKE early, which often happened when I slept away from my own bed. I held my breath as I rolled out from under Carl's arm and slipped out of his bed. I tiptoed to my leather duffel and pulled out my yoga pants, top, and travel mat. It was so beautiful outside by the water that the temptation to practice yoga out on the dock was simply too great to resist.

I dressed in the bathroom and padded quietly downstairs. I paused for a glass of water in the kitchen and then I let myself out the sliding glass door from the living room. I walked down the porch steps and across the lawn, which sparkled with golden dew in the early sun, and made my way to the dock. I laid out the mat on its gray slats and stood at the front in samasthiti, coming to my breath in my body. The air that inhabited my breath was sweet with red oak and white pine trees and bright with sunlight and salty from the sea. Seagulls shrieked overhead.

Long ago, I had choreographed a yoga practice for myself for those times I could not go to class or access an online class. I knew my routine well; sun salutations flowing from one into another, standing warriors growing ever more challenging, triangles, twisting triangles and bound extended side angles, balance poses that situated me squarely in the present with no possibility of my monkey mind wandering off lest I'd fall off the dock into the water. I did arm balances and hip openers and backbends, both camel pose and full wheel because it felt so delicious to curl up into the morning, like a bud blossoming. I finished with seated poses, twists, Janu Sirsasana and a straddle facing the side of the dock. I came back to a cross-legged seat and centered myself. I didn't let myself go into a trance but simply stayed aware: the lapping of water, the distant hum of a lawnmower, the barely audible rising and falling drone of traffic, the warm, yellow light falling on my scalp and shoulders, my loose, warm hamstrings and the ache in my triceps, my heart beating.

I grew aware of myself as the congealing of the breath, that is, I was the breath and the flesh was the condensation from myself. I was perfectly balanced like a pendulum hanging in space, full of potential movement. That equipoise was the primary reason I had committed to a practice of yoga. A flexible, lithe body was, of course, a prime mover, but what really drew me back to my mat day after day was that sense of peace.

After some space of time, I found myself staring at the water, which sparkled an invitation. I rose and slipped off my yoga pants and walked to the end of the dock. I slid down into the cool, buoyant water and dog paddled out until I could float on my back. I floated facing up to the mirroring sky, paddling sporadically with my feet, until the cold seeped through my muscles into my bones and I remembered I was hungry.

My teeth were chattering as I climbed up onto the dock. I pulled on my yoga pants hurriedly and went back to the house. Carl met me at the door with a fluffy towel, a mug of coffee, and a crooked smile. He wore a lush navy blue robe belted over a pair of tighty-whities. "There's the mermaid."

"It was so beautiful, I couldn't resist." I huddled into the towel and accepted the coffee gratefully. I was pretty sure my lips were blue.

"It's early in the season, the water must be chilly."

"It is. This coffee is perfect—almond milk and stevia powder. How'd you know how I like it?"

He raised his eyebrows.

"Trudi!" I exclaimed. "What else did she tell you?"

"Not to put cheese in your omelet."

He gestured for me to come inside.

"I don't want to track water in," I demurred. "I should dry off out here."

"Don't worry about it, these floors have withstood my grandchildren's sandy feet."

I went indoors behind him.

Carl said, "I'm just starting the omelet. You have time for a quick rinse."

I sped through my shower and when I came back down he was flipping the omelet onto a plate.

"That looks delish," I said. "Is there more coffee?"

I seated myself at the breakfast nook.

Carl came over with a pot of coffee and refilled my mug then set the coffee pot on a trivet on the table. He went back to the counter and returned with two plates, each with half an omelet and a fruit salad consisting of strawberries, blueberries, and curled orange slices. Around the rim of the plate curled an attractive parsley garnish.

"Wow, fancy," I said, in admiration. "Is that artichoke and fines herbes in the omelet?"

"Nancy did all the cooking but after she died I knew I had to feed myself. I went to a cooking class with a girlfriend." Carl looked up sharply. "Not a serious girlfriend. Just someone I was spending time with. I don't see her anymore."

"I didn't think you were a virgin before you met me, Carl."

That made him chuckle. He made another trip to the counter and came back with a mug of coffee for himself and a copy of the *New York Times* that he held up inquiringly.

"The arts section, please," I said.

"That leaves business for me," he said with some satisfaction. He separated the paper into sections and handed me the one I'd requested.

We ate and read in silence. The omelet tasted even better than it looked; it was perfectly salted and peppered and the balance of sour artichoke against sweet tomatoes was sumptuous. I wasn't surprised that Carl was an excellent cook. He was one of those people who did everything well and made it look effortless.

"This is nice," Carl remarked when he put down the business section and picked up the sports section.

"Yes, it is," I smiled.

I reached over and touched his hand.

"I could get used to this," he said.

I paused in the midst of an article about the celebrities and assorted honchos descending on Art Basel. There were already pieces being sold; the wealthiest and most titled art patrons wouldn't wait for an art show. They expected to be shown the best pieces early and privately, and they were obliged. Everyone knew that only the preview days mattered. I wondered who bought the realist pieces; there was work in my gallery they'd love. I'd have to call my friends in the business next week to get the scoop.

I told Carl, "Never ask me to cook. Or babysit."

"Don't worry about the babysitting. But no cooking, ever?"

"I hate cooking."

"What'd you do when your children were young?"

"Take-out from the market, rotisserie chicken, oatmeal, and Chinese food delivery," I recited. "I order in brilliantly. I make a great bowl of granola. If all else fails almond butter out of the jar. You're welcome to share whatever I've got."

"No cooking. I can live with that."

He poured himself another cup of coffee before cutting his eyes at me. "Are we mutually exclusive?"

"No."

I went back to the article.

"No?"

"No."

"Why not?"

"Too soon. We're not at that stage yet."

He breathed noisily which he did when he was absorbed in his thoughts.

I got to the end of the article and looked up.

Carl was leveling his laser-gaze at me.

"What stage are we at?"

I suppressed the words "the booty call stage" which naturally rose to my lips. Carl was not going to get my sense of humor. Then I thought, *What the hell? Am I supposed to hide myself from this man when I'm sharing his bed?*

"The booty call stage."

"Certainly not. I do not do booty calls!"

"Why not? They're fun."

"Because I am a gentleman of substance."

"You weren't that gentlemanly yesterday afternoon," I pointed out.

He sat very erect and said stiffly, "You didn't want me to be gentlemanly."

"True. Thanks for that, by the way." I smiled at him. As I'd suspected, he knew exactly what to do in the sack.

"You thanked me yesterday," he growled. "It wasn't necessary then and isn't now."

"I'm grateful to be well laid."

Carl tapped his fork alongside the green garnish in his otherwise empty plate.

"The booty call stage. Hah. At my age."

———⌒———

Carl took us to Shelter Island in his boat. We ate a picnic lunch on a rocky yellow beach there. As we were stepping into his boat to go back, my cell phone rang. The call originated from the Brookton Academy.

"It's about my daughter, I have to take this," I told Carl, apologetically.

Carl nodded.

I walked down the beach and answered the call.

Lindsay, Alex's therapist, was on the line.

"There's no easy way to say this, Sarah. Alex is flouting the school's rules. We're worried she's going to get pregnant."

"What are you telling me?" I asked. "What's the next step here?"

"We recommend sending her to wilderness camp," she said grimly. Over the next twenty minutes, she outlined what that would entail: a middle of the night transport out of Brookton by people who knew how to do interventions. She would be checked for drugs and weapons, then transported to a wilderness camp where everything was stripped down to the basics. Trekking through the mountains, cooking over a fire, sleeping in a tent. She would wear mostly unisex, heavy outdoor gear so personal vanity was discarded. The leaders of the program were experienced counselors and at night, around a campfire, the kids would be guided to talk honestly. They could make some real shifts.

Best of all, Alex would be stringently separated from boys so she wouldn't get herself in trouble.

"Give me some time to think about this and to run it past her therapist at home," I said, before hanging up.

Carl glanced at my face and we didn't speak on the trip back to his dock. I rode in the front of the boat with my eyes turned to catch the wind so the tears would be blown away.

While he tied up his boat, I sat on the dock and explained the latest turn of events.

Carl shook his head.

"It's so heart-breaking that Alex has brought herself to this point," I said. "I'm already embroiled in a legal battle—yet again—with George. He'll probably start a new suit over this, just because he's such a jerk."

"I've run into the Calhouns," Carl said, his voice dry with distaste. "If George had come from another family he'd have picked up a gun. Since he's a Calhoun, he's firing his lawyers at you."

"Good times," I murmured, aiming at a levity I could not attain in that moment.

Carl finished with his boat and sat beside me. He sat close enough that I could feel the warm, solid outline of his body. He didn't speak at all; he didn't say any of those stupid things that people with perfect children say, or any of the false reassurances and fake palliatives that just reinforced the sadness and helplessness of watching your kid spin wildly out of control. So we sat in the afternoon sun and let the June breeze flow over us.

# CHAPTER TWENTY-ONE

I SPENT THE NEXT day crying, speaking with Bailey, conferring with Marty, and drafting an email—a terribly polite and thoughtful missive—to George. It was Monday and the gallery was closed. I usually went in anyway but that day I stayed home and tended to Alex's business. I walked Groucho through Central Park until he lay down near the reservoir and put his head on his paws. That was his sign that his feet were hurting. I rubbed his swollen paws and ankles and poured water from my bottle into his mouth until he shook himself and rose, and then we walked home. I realized guiltily that I couldn't drag poor Groucho on long walks that were meant to soothe me. He was just too old for it. We stopped at a pet store on Amsterdam Avenue and I bought him a big bag of his favorite chew treats.

George emailed me back, telling me to go screw myself. There was not a word about Alex and her troubles.

Over the next few days I filled out forms for the wilderness experience. It turned out that there was a lot of paperwork to send my flailing, troubled teen to an outdoors program designed to turn her around. I cashed in a small gift-to-minor account I was keeping for Alex and used the funds to pay for the intervention, her transport, and the wilderness therapy.

I thought about calling Dani. I wondered what distorted, phantasmagorical tale she was hearing about Alex and me from her father and his wife. I got so far as to dial her cell phone number on my home phone. But she would only snarl at me, if she picked up at all. That's what the last year had taught me. I just couldn't bear her cruelty right then, I felt too vulnerable. I hung up the phone before it rang and dug out a picture of

Dani and me in Paris, standing in front of the beautiful carved facade of Notre Dame. That hadn't been so long ago—two years. How had it gotten so bad with her, so fast?

Had her alienation from me been brewing since the day I left her father? Or were some of my unwise actions, like changing her email password to "Spoiled Brat," truly so abhorrent that she was justified in despising me? What had happened to the elasticity of our bond? What had happened to the tolerance that people in close familial bonds extended to one another? Despite everything, I loved and missed Dani.

By the middle of the week, I was thoroughly depressed. I came home from the gallery in a funk, not having sold a single item. I changed into yoga gear and did an hour-long online class with enough chaturangas to make my arms quake. I felt better. I supposed I could eat dinner. I went to the fridge and held the door open and stared at the empty shelves and burst into a fresh round of tears.

I could not indulge myself in my despair.

I splashed water on my face and slathered on some liquid complexion, just enough to hide the redness and swelling around my eyes. I applied rose-colored lipstick. I stuck my debit card in the pocket of my yoga jacket and headed out the door for the market.

It was about seven and still light outside, that periwinkle blue luminosity that seeped through the warm afternoons in June, one of the months that Manhattan was at its best. Usually, there's not too much rain in June and the summer heat hadn't made the streets smell like garbage and piss, as was the case by August.

I ended up at Fairway at 73rd Street and Broadway. I stood in front of the pre-washed, pre-cut veggie packages, wondering if I had the personal wherewithal to sauté zucchini for myself.

*No, I do not. That is way too much effort. God, I hate to cook.*

I turned with every intention of patronizing the take-out counter—Fairway made a delectable rotisserie chicken—and a tall form blocked my path.

"Sarah!" Scott sang. "You've been out of touch! I called but you didn't get back to me. What's going on?" He looked genuinely delighted to see me and he threw his arm around me and kissed my mouth. He was dressed casually, in jeans and a dark green T-shirt; somehow he must have gotten home from the office at a reasonable hour.

"Just, you know. Stuff."

"You're food shopping? Good idea. Janey said your refrigerator was bare. All you had were eggs, a cucumber, and a box of Mac n' cheese."

I rolled my eyes because I didn't have a snappy comeback. I felt as if all the snap had been beaten out of me by Alex's continual, all-consuming problems.

"I have an idea," Scott said, his deep voice deepening most mellifluously. He stepped closer and leaned in toward my ear. "Come over for chocolate. To my place. Right now. We can shop another time."

"I'm not in the mood," I said mournfully.

"You're always in the mood," Scott said, with a confused look on his face.

"No, I'm not."

"Yes, you are."

All at once, chocolate seemed like exactly the right nutritional meal, with a healthful complement of vitamins and protein.

"Yes, I am," I said.

He took my basket and nested it inside his, replacing the baskets neatly into the stack and then dragged me out of the Fairway. He pinioned my arm between his arm and chest, as if he were worried I'd dart away, and he stroked my hand.

"I'm saving Friday for dinner with you. No matter what."

"Bullshit. If one of your patients needs you, I'm chopped liver."

I said it more vehemently than I intended and found myself taken aback by the energy.

*Do I have feelings about Scott's frequent unavailability?*

"I'm a good and caring doctor," he said, indignantly. He squeezed my hand until I withdrew it with a hard jerk.

"You're a good and caring lay, too. But you'd make a lousy boyfriend."

"Good thing we're just at the booty call stage," he retorted. His cheekbones reddened and he didn't say anything else until we stood in his elevator. He pressed the button to his floor and swung around on me. "It's not like you want more with me. Every time I bring it up, you shoot me down."

"Scott, my life is falling apart. Just about everything's going south on me. I'm like a feather floating down. Nearly weightless, but gravity is winning. I don't have room inside myself for one more person whose feelings I have to care about." Maybe it wouldn't always be true, but it was true right then and it was one of the most honest things I'd ever said to anyone in my life.

"I'm not just one more person. We have a real connection. I matter."

"Of course you do." I took a deep breath and sighed. I laid my hand on Scott's arm. "I don't want to argue with you."

"You don't know what you want. You fuck me like some wild thing and then tell me I can't bring a toothbrush over. Half the time, you don't answer my calls. I called you today to invite you over but you didn't return my call and if I hadn't run into you at Fairway we wouldn't be here now!" He was working himself into a lather.

I let him simmer and the elevator door opened on his floor.

He put his keys into the lock on his door.

"You almost never share anything about yourself. I've told you about myself. Hell, you met my kids. And my ex-wife."

"Thanks for that," I interjected and I realized I was feeling better, even with Scott nagging me, because some of my old irony had bubbled up to the surface.

*Maybe it's just that I always feel good when I'm with him.*

"All I know about you is that you own a gallery and have two daughters. Do you know that I researched you online to find out more about you? The bio on your gallery website has been more forthcoming than you have. You went to Princeton, you got your master's in London, you worked at some prestigious art galleries, you write articles for art journals—apparently you know a lot about Renaissance art—but you never talk about any of this."

"And, yet, I still don't want to argue with you."

He pushed open the door, dragged me in and pushed me up against the wall. He kissed me hard, driving his tongue into my mouth. His hands worked my yoga pants down my hips.

I was not expecting the onslaught and was paralyzed for a moment.

He got my pants down to my knees. With one hand he held my wrists together above my head; he ran his other hand down the rise of my pubis, cupped me for a second, and then thrust his fingers up inside me.

I was swept by a wave of the most delicious consuming warmth. I was wet and getting wetter as he pressed his fingers harder into me and then pulsed them back and forth. I pressed my hips up into him.

He released my wrists and withdrew his hand from me, eliciting a moan.

"Don't stop," I begged softly.

"Take off your pants," he ordered. He was unzipping his jeans in between kissing me, and I kicked off my yoga leggings obediently.

He jerked me into his chest and bit my neck hard. Then he threw me back against the wall so that I faced it. He grabbed my hips and stuck his knee between my thighs and pressed up a little, lifting me, and then he stooped down to position himself, and then he was pounding inside me. Another time I might have had to use my hand on myself because the rear entry provided so little direct stimulation. This time, however, it was so steamy; his desire was so intense and my surrender so profound that I climaxed quickly, shuddering back against him.

He made a sound and shook, and then he pulled out of me. He cradled my weight back into his body and wrapped his arms around me. I could feel his chest rising and falling against my shoulder blades.

"Thank you," I said.

He rested his cheek against the back of my head.

*I'll be wearing a scarf around my neck for a week.*

"We didn't use a condom," I realized.

"So whatever you've got, I'll have," he said, in a matter-of-fact tone. "I'll run some tests."

"You don't have much to worry about. I married just about everyone I slept with."

"So did I."

By tacit agreement we ended up in his bed, undressed, and entwined. We didn't speak; we just stroked each other.

After a while, Scott said in a determined voice, "I'll come to your gallery and buy a painting."

"Didn't Lisa get all your money?"

I ran my hand lightly along his belly, enjoying the warmth and texture of his skin.

"I'm a successful physician. I can afford to buy a painting."

"I sell really beautiful paintings. They're expensive."

"Maybe a small painting; I could afford that. You can pick it out for me. There's plenty of wall space in this apartment."

"Even a small painting at Paige Realist Art is pricey," I told him. "But I appreciate your support of the cause."

He shrugged. "I'll invest less in the kids' college accounts for a few months."

That made me smile. I touched his face.

"No, you won't."

"Probably not. I went to college on a scholarship, work-study, and student loans. I don't want my children to have that pressure."

Scott's dark eyes focused inward and the angles of his face sharpened. "My dad had a rug business in Cleveland. He was a drinker and a gambler and he never saved any money. Then one day he left. My mom taught school and did a lot of tutoring to make ends meet."

"That sucks. I'm sorry."

"What about your parents?"

"They're dead."

"How did they die?"

"Car crash. A kid in a pickup truck was leaning down to change the cassette. His truck jumped the divider and hit their car head-on." I said it with the old weariness that descended through me, like the extra gravities at the bottom of the ocean, whenever I recited the story.

"How old were you?"

"Twenty-two."

Scott shook his head solemnly. "So young. That's awful."

"That was a long time ago for me, Scott," I said with a smile.

"It was a long time ago when I was twenty-two," he said with a flash of exasperation. He pushed himself up on one elbow to glare better at me. "I'm not a boy, even though you imply that I am."

I giggled and smoothed my finger across his soft mouth.

"You're a good boy. A *very* good boy. I bet you send money home to your mother."

He nipped my fingers playfully with his teeth then caught my hand in his.

"What's wrong with that? She made a lot of sacrifices for me and my sister and brother."

"I wish my kids were as thoughtful and appreciative as you."

———

Alex's intervention went off without a hitch. I didn't sleep the night it happened but received reports. The next morning I felt wrung-out, fatigued, and fragile as I sat in my kitchen and phoned contacts from the art world to get the inside details about Art Basel.

Harold, my friend from Sotheby's, got on the phone and gossiped wickedly. He shared my taste in representational art and he was more than willing to dish about the art fair in all its glittery corruption. He gave me the dirt on which billionaires bought what, who slept with which celebrity at what party, and what the word on the street was about the state of the market. After ten minutes of viciously dissing Damien Hirst, Jeff Koons, and the rubes who bought their balloon animals and formaldehyde junk, I finally felt a little better about my life. It was a bright spot in an otherwise uninspiring day. I could always count on art to regenerate me, at least partly.

Two other colleagues asked about the well-to-do silver fox who was squiring me around. When I remonstrated, I was reminded that, "There are no secrets in the art world, only lies."

# CHAPTER TWENTY-TWO

"LOOK AT US. THIS is like a real date," Scott said, with a boyish lilt I'd not heard before in his voice.

"It is a real date," I agreed.

For our long postponed date we left the Upper West Side and traveled to the Flatiron District. We sat at a table in the prix-fix room of Gramercy Tavern. The fare was wonderful and the chic, rustic, elegant ambiance made guests feel pampered in a cozy way. George had brought me there once or twice but I hadn't been back in years. Clif always looked to me when the bill came at a restaurant, and I invested every dime I didn't spend on the girls into the gallery. Fancy restaurants were the first things I cut from my lifestyle.

"You look beautiful," Scott said.

He stretched his long arm across the table, took my hand, and beamed at me.

"Thank you, Scott," I said with some amusement, because he'd complimented me at least six times. I guess he was used to seeing me in yoga garb or my ratty nighties. I did look pretty good; I could admit that to myself. I wore the quintessential little black dress, a vintage-inspired crepe sheathe with a sheer mesh yoke and sheer mesh sleeves. The seams on the front whittled my figure most curvaceously. I wore my hair down princess style and curled under at the ends. I figured—hoped—I looked at least five years younger than my actual age.

I said, "You look good, too."

He was freshly shaven and wore a well-cut Zegna suit and a Brioni tie. They fit his tall, toned body to sleek perfection. They seemed more elegant than his usual sartorial standards, although he always looked good in his office in a suit or sport coat.

I asked idly, "Lisa pick out that suit for you?"

He touched the tie. "I am more than capable of buying myself a decent suit."

I looked at him.

"Yes, she chose it."

He would have said more but the waitress came with our menus.

She was a sprightly, red-headed lass in her late twenties, well put together as all restaurateur Danny Meyer's service personnel were. She was probably an actress who supported herself between gigs by waiting tables. Like Rosa, she had the look of a woman containing her glamour for her day job. She cut her eyes at tall, good-looking Scott as she handed him the wine list.

*I probably shouldn't jump up and slap her.*

Scott seemed oblivious.

"Do you like red or white wine?"

"Red."

Scott stared at me with a serious, critical scowl, as if we were deliberating over a patient's chemotherapy treatment.

"Maybe we should start with a cocktail?"

"I'm good with wine. I drink white, too."

I smiled at him and wondered if we were still, by some incomprehensible fluke of fate, together in ten years when I was fifty-eight and he was my age, if he would still be immune to the glances of pretty girls?

"Would you send the sommelier over?" Scott asked the girl.

She gave a deferential nod that was almost, but not quite, a bow.

I watched her go.

"What?" Scott asked.

I tilted my head inquisitively.

"What's wrong with our waitress?"

"Nothing."

"You don't like her," Scott persisted. "Why not?"

"I like her just fine."

"No, you don't."

I played with the stem of my water glass.

"Because she likes you."

Scott crinkled his nose and gave me a look as if I'd recently been sprung from an insane asylum. "What are you talking about?"

"The way she looked at you," I started, but the words withered under Scott's incredulous gaze.

"Do you think I care about any woman in this restaurant other than you?" he demanded. "Do you think I care about any other woman in this state other than you?"

I picked up my menu.

Scott plucked it from my hands.

"Sarah, look at me. I'm serious."

"Nice to meet you, Serious. I'm Hungry."

He grinned with half his mouth.

"I know you're in fine form when you start making lame jokes—you're like a bottle of ginger ale and that's the sign that your fizz is back."

"I've never been compared to soda before," I said. "But I was recently painted as Hera."

Scott chuckled once.

"My mother had a series of West Highland White Terriers. I read about them. The AKC standard said, 'West Highland White Terriers are possessed with no small amount of self-esteem.' That's you."

"I am not like a Westie," I objected, with some heat. "Those are little yappy dogs. I'm regal and stately, the queen of the goddesses."

"No, you're not. You're lively and smart and spunky and bold. You think you're bigger than you are. Perfect Westie."

"I am not bold!"

"We got together because you asked me to take my pants off. That's the definition of bold."

"If I'm a Westie then you're a German Shepherd. Those are very serious dogs. Intelligent. Serious. I bet they're workaholics. A very attractive species. Did I mention they're serious?"

He was going to reply but a slender, knowledgeable-looking chap appeared at our table.

"I'm Martin, the sommelier. May I help you with the wine selection?"

Scott nodded. "We want a good, dry red wine. And could you see that we get a male waiter?"

---

I had read about a new gelateria near Union Square that was supposed to be particularly Italianate. I had a fetish for gelato ever since I'd spent a college semester in Florence so I asked Scott if we could get our dessert there. He agreed and we strolled out hand-in-hand.

It was a beautiful June evening, warm and soft; the night sky was filled with as many stars as Manhattanites would ever see through the haze of light pollution. The streets pulsed with people hurrying to their evening events.

A couple with a young daughter walked by and I thought of Janey.

"You never said how Janey's birthday party was."

"Good." Scott paused. "I got into a fight with Rick."

"You didn't tell me that!"

"We didn't see each other that week."

He hesitated.

"Mrs. Waterston didn't mention the black eye?"

I shook my head.

"How did Rick fare?" I asked mirthfully.

"Worse than me," Scott said in tone that was both satisfied and uneven. "He had it coming. For a long time."

"I'm sure. Did you use a cross? Or a hook? My dad used to watch boxing matches on TV. Good thing you're not a surgeon. Surgeons have to protect their hands."

"Rick said he wanted the kids to call him 'Daddy.' I turned around and hit him. I didn't even think about it—I just punched him."

I giggled.

"Did you feel the skin and bone crunch beneath your fist?"

"Yes, I felt the cartilage of his nose crunch. I will never do that again. I am not that man. I sure as hell don't want to model that behavior for my children. Later, Janey suggested they call him 'Poppy,' so that's what it will be." He dropped my hand and pulled me against him and kissed me thoroughly. "I think that's perfect for him. It's like a grandpa. Or a girl."

I felt breathless and weak-kneed but I attributed that to the wine we had with dinner.

I put my arms around his neck and kissed him for real with some tongue. His warm, soft, mobile mouth emptied my brain. I was happy to be distracted from everything going on in my life, including the latest from Alex. As part of her wilderness experience therapy, she had sent letters home owning her misdeeds. While I was encouraged to see her starting to take personal responsibility, it had been hard to read her list: swim practices and meets she'd cut to meet her friends for drugs; a gold bracelet inherited from George's grandmother that she'd sold to finance a secret party. I sometimes wondered how much more pain I could take.

More kissing.

I got marron glacé gelato and Scott got strawberry, and we strolled through boisterous Union Square park.

Street bands were playing hip-hop music and a guy with a saxophone was playing some wonderfully eccentric blues song. Packs of kids were laughing too loud, and a zillion passersby in every conceivable flavor of humanity flowed around us. All of it receded into the background.

Scott and I were the only two people in the world.

"If you're a Westie and I'm a German Shepherd, we'd make very strange looking puppies," he mused.

I shook my head.

"I'm past that, Scott. Can I taste your gelato?"

He held the cone toward me.

"Oh, I know. That's why I didn't worry about pregnancy when we didn't use a condom. You're in perimenopause."

I would have gasped except for the creamy cold strawberry ice cream filling my mouth. I swallowed.

"What?"

"Your age puts you in menopause transition. Your ovaries are producing less estrogen," he explained.

"You are not talking about menopause right now!" I exclaimed, horrified.

"It's a natural cycle of life. It usually begins in a woman's forties but can begin in her thirties. It lasts until menopause when the ovaries stop releasing eggs."

"I still get my period every month!"

"I haven't seen that," he said.

I was mad.

"You are *not* talking about me going into menopause!"

"Just because you're sensitive about being older than me doesn't mean we should avoid discussing your physiology. We're both reasonable adults."

"Oh my god!" I snapped.

Just like that, I shoved his hand so his ice cream cone slammed onto his tie, leaving a sticky blotch of pink goo on the brilliant Brioni fabric.

"Hey, my kids got me this tie!"

He tried to scrape off the ice cream with his free hand.

"Not your kids, Lisa," I hissed. I swiped my marron glacé over his tie, adding a brown splotch to the pink. "I don't like Lisa."

"Hey!" he said again. "Stop that this instant, Sarah!"

But that was like waving a red flag at me, so I deliberately stroked the top of my gelato across his jacket, from one shoulder to the other.

Scott stabbed his ice cream into my chest and drew a pink line down to my navel.

"You're paying for the dry cleaning," I said.

"You're paying for my dry cleaning!"

He looked mad as a hornet.

I went to tag him again but realized I didn't want to waste the gelato, so I stopped it just short of actually landing on him and brought it back to my mouth. It really was too good to waste. Even with the fuzzies from Scott's suit it was light and fresh while still being creamy and rich—the most authentic gelato I'd had outside of Italy. I could taste the candied chestnuts. I'd be back for more; it was worth the trip downtown.

Scott gaped as he watched me eat.

"It's too good to waste," I explained over a buttery, sweet, nutty mouthful.

Scott broke out into peals of laughter.

I realized how ridiculous we were and I laughed too.

Scott pushed on my wrist to move the cone away from my mouth. He pulled me in close, our squishy ice-cream fronts gluing together, and he kissed me and kissed me.

I forgot about the gelato and kissed him back. I forgot about everything while we were kissing.

After a while, Scott lifted his head.

"You're still paying for the cleaning. This is my nicest suit."

"It looks really good on you," I told him. "How about we get back to my apartment quick, so I can get you out of it?"

# CHAPTER TWENTY-THREE

I HELP UP A blue lace cocktail dress. "Should I wear this?"

"No. He's already seen you in that dress," Marcia said. Her beautiful blonde head was bent over her iPhone. She was in town for about thirty-six hours and had dropped by to help me get dressed. She finished texting her next appointment and laid her phone on a stool. Gently she shouldered me out of my closet so she could peer in.

"For the co-hostess of a Fourth of July eve cocktail party with Mr. Successful I think you can go showier. What about this red silk tea-length? I love the deep scarlet with your hair and the neckline couldn't be more flattering. You look very precocious in this dress!" She held out the dress with a flourish.

"This is New York, not LA," I said. "This is a party on the Upper East Side. I'll be judged. Like, the women there are all going to judge me for having last year's purse."

Marcia shrugged and replaced the dress in the closet. "I'll get someone to comp you a bag."

"That's not the point," I said. "If I had this year's purse, they'd judge me for having last year's shoes, or the wrong shoes. Or for living on the Upper West Side. Or for having bangs."

"Women on the Upper East Side understand bangs. Trust me, they do." She smiled and flickered her fingers through my bangs before turning back to the closet.

"Then they'll judge me for running a gallery. The point is that precocious is not the look I'm going for with these freakishly judgmental women who are shallow and soulless and have nothing better to do with themselves than dress up and spend their husband's money."

"Do they shag the pool boys? If they do, then they could be Beverly Hills wives," Marcia rejoined. "Of course, I've shagged a few scrumptious pool boys, so who am I to judge?"

We both giggled. "I'm shagging a pool boy myself these days," I confessed.

"Are we referring to the hot young doc? Does he know we refer to him by that particular term of endearment?"

"He knows I objectify him and expect him to service my needs," I replied, and we both giggled again.

"Have him wear a bathing suit, carry a towel, and speak with a Spanish accent. It will add a touch of spice," she advised in her naughtiest naughty-girl voice. Nobody did a naughty girl voice like Marcia Mensdorff.

"Oh, I like that. You know, I always loved that scene in *Risky Business* where Tom Cruise and Rebecca De Mornay do it on the train. Maybe I could get the pool boy to put on a black shirt and jacket and I'll put on a blouse and skirt and a blonde wig and we could play the Phil Collins song and act it out in my living room."

"That is a hot scene," Marcia said in a tone of commingled reverence and approval. We both breathed and contemplated the scene.

I might have been panting.

"The thing about the hot pool boy is that he's younger than me," I said.

"So?" Marcia asked. "Younger men are more flexible and more emotionally available. That makes them more accepting of who you are."

Then she got serious about directing my wardrobe, deciding on a green silk dress and advising me to put my hair up. Before she set off for her appointment, Marcia said, "A word to the wise, from someone who has juggled men. Keep them separate."

"Of course I wouldn't mix them, do you think I'm stupid?" I protested, air-kissing her cheek at the front door. "I wish you were coming to the party. I can't wait for you to meet Carl."

"Me too, darling!" She looked at me very directly. "I think you're naive sometimes when it comes to men. If they ever come in contact with one another, you'll have to choose."

"I hadn't planned on mixing the two of them," I assured her.

———~———

Carl gestured at Clif's paintings. "Aren't they gorgeous? I am so very pleased to have Clifton Perini, the artist, here with us this evening." He put his hand on Clif's shoulder. "I've seen your work in various places, Clif, and I'm delighted to have your river nymphs gracing my home."

Clif nodded respectfully, "Thank you, Carl."

Carl spoke for a few more moments in front of the forty-some people assembled in the dining room of his apartment, saying how fortunate he was to have dropped by my gallery so I could suggest Clif's paintings to him. He asked Clif to say a few words.

His guests clapped as he stepped back to let Clif occupy the space beside his paintings.

Clif naturally emanated unpretentious approachability. He knew how to hold a room spellbound. His friend Nicole, who had greeted me without meeting my eyes, watched from the crowd.

Carl made his way to where I stood beside the door to the kitchen. He threw his arm around my waist and kissed me.

"How was I?"

"Brilliant," I said sotto voce. "You know you were. I'll be shocked if half these people don't turn up in my gallery."

He chuckled softly and pulled me out of the way of a caterer with a platter of hors d'oeuvres. I snagged two of the little fig and manchego cheese crostini as she passed by.

"These are delicious," I said.

"I'll make sure they leave some behind for you to take home." He paused, his blue eyes twinkling. He put his hands on my waist. "Will you come out to Sag Harbor this weekend?"

*Scott will be in Boston and Trudi's son Peter is coming into town. Why not? It's an alternative to working in the gallery and hiking.*

I nodded. "I'd love to. Thanks for inviting me. I'll come in Saturday morning so I can be at the gallery Friday night." I watched Clif make an open-hearted gesture that his audience adored.

"You know," Carl started, his pebbly voice awkward.

I focused on him, tuning out Clif. Clif was talking about his process as an artist, a theme I had heard in billions and billions of variations. I could probably recite all the versions by myself.

"Yes?"

"I could rent a storefront in town and you could open a pop-up gallery for the summer." He was fixing his gaze on me, watching me very carefully. "You'd get plenty of foot traffic and some new clients."

I shook my head. "Carl, you're being generous and I adore you for it. But if I'm going to open a pop-up shop I will research the market and the location and rent it myself."

"It's so easy for me to do, I know everyone in town. I could have it done in a few days, and we could spend a lot of time together at the house. You'd bring back a whole new set of contacts for the fall."

"Oh, you're good," I said, with admiration. "But we don't have to go to Sag Harbor to spend time together."

"We don't?"

"No. That's what makes a booty call so much fun. You call late at night for express, nefarious purposes."

He chuckled again. "I should call you at nine or ten in the evening and have only one thing on my mind?"

I nodded.

"Where were you when I was twenty years old?" he joked.

*Still in diapers*, I thought, before I could help myself. Impulsively I leaned forward and kissed his cheek.

He drew me back in and kissed my mouth. "Think about the pop-up shop. It would be fun."

Clif was finishing his speech and Carl's guests applauded thunderously. Carl winked and moved off. He went to talk to his friends, Joe and Regan and I followed him, intending to eavesdrop.

Three couturier-dressed, slim, attractive women moved in front of me. Two were Originals and one was a Trophy. The Originals were older than me and the Trophy was younger. They were all thinner and in much better shape than me. They were also better dressed, wearing posh jewelry and next year's shoes.

I opted to think of them as potential clients instead of the judgment committee.

"Ladies, I hope you enjoyed Clif's talk," I said, cheerily.

Deborah, the queen bee Original and the wife of Carl's oldest friend, cut right to the chase.

"Clif Perini is a talented artist, a wonderful speaker, and an attractive man. Your ex-husband, isn't he? Is the divorce final? No chance of reconciliation?"

I smiled. "It's amicable, but there's no chance of reconciliation. We're better working together than living together. It's not quite final but that's a function of the legal process in the state of New York."

Deborah nodded and continued, "Carl is quite smitten with you."

"I am taken with him. He's a wonderful man." I glanced over to where he stood, his arm around Joe's shoulder and his other hand waving expansively at Clif's paintings.

*He's selling paintings for me. This must stop.*

Deborah said, "He hasn't thrown a party since Nancy died."

*She wants to know my intentions toward her friend.*

I looked her square in her elegant, youthful face.

"Nancy's death was a great tragedy. No one could ever replace her but it is good to see Carl enjoying himself." I figured that would satisfy that group, at least for the moment. They'd have more questions. I couldn't escape them forever, not if I kept seeing Carl. I said, "It's so nice to chat with you. Would you please excuse me?"

I smiled and waved and moved off to stand near Carl. As expected, he was extolling the praises of Clif's work and my gallery. I let my energy presence thicken so he'd take notice.

"Ah, here she is, the proprietress herself, Sarah," Carl said in a jovial voice. He turned and put his arm around my shoulders to draw me into the circle.

"Regan, Joe," I smiled.

We chatted for a moment; Regan was a bombshell, obviously a Trophy, but also well-spoken. She said a few smart things about Clif's paintings and then they drifted away, promising to drop by my gallery.

I raised my eyebrows at Carl. "You're amazing at promoting my gallery. Masterful."

Carl's chest expanded. "Watch and learn, Grasshopper." He swaggered off toward Deborah and her husband Stephen.

I took a deep breath. I loved seeing the spring in Carl's step, but I could not let it stand. I marched over and tapped him on the shoulder. He swung around with a big grin and I said, "Carl, stop."

"What?" he gripped my arm from underneath, his craggy face furrowing in concern.

"I'm not your Grasshopper. I'm a competent gallery owner. I can sell my art. I don't need you to do it for me."

"I didn't mean—"

"You mean to be generous and helpful. It's coming out as patronizing and condescending."

He recoiled slightly. "That was never my intention."

"I know," I shrugged.

———~———

By late in the evening the last partiers were lingering in the sumptuous living room. There the judgment committee accosted me again. Deborah wanted to know if I'd met Carl's children yet.

I glanced around for Carl, hoping he'd rescue me from his friends' wives' clutches. No sign of him. Where was he?

"They are terrific! Nancy was a perfect mother," Deborah said.

The other women murmured their assent.

"And an ideal wife for Carl," Deborah continued. "Anyone who dates Carl seriously would have to understand the legacy."

*I will never be perfect*, all of my selves chorused. I murmured, "I'm sure Carl will explain it to me."

I scurried away into the dining room where I caught Carl and three of his comrades smoking cigars, drinking scotch, and cackling with bonhomie, like finely feathered old hens.

"What are you doing smoking in here?" I demanded. "Do you know what tobacco smoke does to fine paintings? You're going to ruin these masterpieces. Take those nasty things into another room by a window. Or better yet, upstairs and outdoors on the patio."

The four men stared at me in bemusement. Stephen, who had attended Andover and Yale with Carl, recovered first, bless his soul.

"Boys, we'd better listen to the Boss. Come on! We'll take this outdoors." He slapped Carl on the back and they moved off past me, cigars in their mouths and glasses in hand.

Carl kissed my cheek and then squeezed my ass as he passed, eliciting some ribaldry from his friends.

I figured I'd toss him a well-deserved bone, and I didn't call him on it.

It was close to midnight when the last guests left, and I meandered back to the kitchen to assist in the clean up by eating the leftovers. The caterers had actually finished cleaning and packing their accouterments and were filing out, murmuring polite farewells. As directed by Carl, they'd left a few trays of hors d'oeuvres behind, neatly covered with plastic wrap. I hopped up atop the counter and pulled a platter into my lap, tore off the plastic, and helped myself.

Carl bustled in.

"There you are."

My mouth was full of crostini, so I waved.

"I think that went well," Carl said, in a pleased tone.

I nodded.

"Everyone loved Clif's paintings."

I swallowed.

"If I was a dog, what species would you say I was?"

Carl gave me a stolid look.

"Never mind," I said. "You know who wasn't here? Trudi. I thought she was coming."

"Oh," Carl came over and leaned into me. He smelled of scotch, stogie smoke and Deborah's perfume from her last proprietary hug. He put his hands on my hips.

"Trudi called just before you arrived. She wasn't feeling well. She was having a bad night. Of course I told her to take care of herself and we'd see her as soon as she felt up to it."

"She could have called me!" I cried, hurt.

"I think she didn't want to upset you right before the party."

"Like I'm that fragile?"

Carl reached into the tray on my lap for a crostini. He chewed it and swallowed and said slyly, "My friends liked you."

I wagged my head. "The men, sure. How about their wives?"

"I heard only good reports."

"Let's see what comes in tomorrow," I said dryly.

"Nonsense. You're terrific, and you look smashing in that green silk dress. What are you, a size four? Six?"

"Either. Six, but I'm pretending I'm a four." I was eating a crostini but I spoke with my mouth full. "Don't send me any dresses, Carl."

"You've got to let me do a few things for you."

"Why, so I can be perfect according to some standard of yours?" The words were severe but my tone was soft.

Carl crinkled his face and gave me a hurt, confused look.

I sighed. "Carl, I know how wonderfully generous you are. The thing is, I married rich the first time around. I soon regretted it. The disparity in wealth between George and me meant that he looked down on me. I was never his equal; I was his servant and his possession. I bitterly resented it. I swore I'd never again put myself in that position."

"Why'd you go and marry a Calhoun?" Carl asked with a moue of distaste. "I told you, I've had some dealings with them in the business world. It's not like they respect women."

"Interesting that you say that. I remember that Dani got sick when she was a freshman. The campus medical center couldn't track down the cause so she came into the city and I sent her to a doctor I know who does integrative medicine. That doctor was board certified in two specialties, mind you, but she was a woman and she was Indian. George carried on like I had sent our daughter to a witch doctor. Dani actually told her father that she wasn't a witch doctor. But I always wondered if he felt the need to be derogatory about that doctor and her tests because she was a woman or because she was Indian."

Carl shook his head. "Both, but the crux of the matter is that you recommended her."

"Probably," I said, picking up another crostini. "I've asked myself a million times why I ever married George Calhoun. My best answer: I was young and stupid."

"You'd have had to be."

I held up my finger. "Wait just a second. To be fair to myself, when I met him, George had some excellent qualities. He was smart and funny and generous. He was excellent company. I never lacked for anything and I had everything I wanted when I was with him."

I sighed and thought back through the intervening years to my decades with George Calhoun. I remembered George's happy face when he proposed to me. He had handed me an engagement ring with a large, sparkling diamond. Really, it was a lavish ring. "In the future, if you ever need a car, you could sell this and buy one," he said proudly. He was so delighted to be generous to me. I was so thrilled and grateful—and awed —to be with him.

I would never have guessed, in the early years when I was a student at Princeton or a new mother in my late twenties, that George and I would come to this pass. I thought my children would have everything they ever needed, and that if they lost me the way I lost my parents, they'd still have the Calhoun tribe. I didn't know they'd push me away so they'd have only the Calhoun tribe.

"I guess it was an honest mistake." Carl's voice sounded skeptical.

I shrugged and returned to the present, to the warm and solid man standing so close to me. "All I had to do was accept being a third class citizen; accept their condescension. Listen to George continually telling me that I was crazy and incompetent and a rage monster and that no one else but him would ever want me."

"You didn't get out of that marriage soon enough," Carl observed, his blue eyes scanning my face. "It does explain a few things. To be clear, Sarah, I'm nothing like the Calhouns."

I smiled and touched his face. "I know that, Carl. You're absolutely lovely. Trudi calls you a 'jolly good bloke.' That's high praise from her. The only other person she called that was a soccer player from Manchester."

He took the tray from my lap and scooted my thighs apart so he could position himself between them. He circled me with his arms. "How about a booty call? Or do the rules preclude me from inviting you if you're already here?"

Now he was speaking my language. I draped my arms around Carl's shoulders and smiled. "There are no rules for booty calls. You make them up as you go along. I'd be happy for a booty call right now."

"Stay the night?" he asked. He kissed me. His breath had the stench of cigar on it.

I held him at bay. "Ugh, yes, if you brush your teeth. That cigar taste is dreadful."

"Deal." He smiled and pushed off. "I'll take care of that immediately. Come up to the bedroom when you're done pigging out?"

"I didn't eat dinner, and I was busy mingling so I didn't get many of these during the party," I said.

He got to the door and turned around. "A poodle."

"Huh?"

"The kind of dog you'd be. A poodle."

I shook my head.

"I had one when I was growing up," he explained. "They're proud. Exceptionally intelligent. They have an elegant appearance and a great deal of personality."

"What would you be?"

"The owner," he quipped.

I gave him a withering glance.

Carl laughed. "I'm playing with you. A bulldog, of course."

"A Yale bulldog."

"Yes. Like a bulldog, I'm tenacious. I find something good and I don't let go. I hold on."

I picked up a crostini with shrimp and pesto sauce.

*I should brush my teeth, too.*

"Carl."

"Yes?"

"Hold lightly."

He tipped his head to me, his blue eyes full of sparkle and vim, and slapped the lintel on his way out.

# CHAPTER TWENTY-FOUR

AT THE END OF July, I sent Dani a birthday card. I was torn because she hadn't sent a birthday card or Mother's Day card to me, but I was trying to be the bigger person. After all, I was her parent, her mother. I missed her every second of every day. I wanted to demonstrate generosity of heart to her, the way I was supposed to demonstrate maturity to Alex. I was still hurt by Dani's nastiness toward me and still bewildered that she didn't care about my feelings, but I didn't want to be vengeful.

Dani did not reach out to me on her special day. I supposed she thought she'd sprung whole and adult from her father's forehead without the help of a nurturing womb and decades of tender care.

The day of my eldest daughter's birth passed quietly, if with heartache, and the next day Brigit and I drove far upstate to collect Alex from the wilderness camp. The plan was that she would spend the weekend at home with me then I'd drive her back to Brookton where she'd finish out the trimester. At that point, which would be around Labor Day, I'd bring her home and enroll her back at Devon Town School for her junior year. That was an arrangement that Bailey had effected, mediating between George and me. It seemed fast, like we were rushing Alex through a healing process that needed to unfold in its own way but, if she was going to return to her former private school in the city, then that was the timing. Mr. Villanova had agreed to accept her summer work at Brookton toward the completion of her sophomore year if she could start the new school year on time. She would be on probation for the entire year, but if she passed her junior year without incident, she would be a senior in good standing at Devon Town. I still hoped she'd graduate with her class there.

Our conversation was desultory on the ride home. I drove too fast in a work zone on the New York Thruway and was pulled over by a cop. Meekly, I submitted to the ticket. I glanced at Alex and hoped I wasn't proving too terrible a role model. I wanted to smack my head but didn't. At least I didn't fight the consequences but accepted them with grace. Maybe that would be enough, for now.

We finally got back on our way.

"Did you eat OK?" I asked Alex. "Did you sleep OK? Were you warm enough?"

"I had a urinary tract infection," she said, shrugging. "We were given specific times to pee, and we had to go in a group of girls. We couldn't go off on our own. I tried to hold it too often."

"That sounds painful," I said with a pang.

"They got me medicine. We hiked a lot and cooked our food out. Usually, we slept in these little cabins, but on a long hike we'd bring our sleeping bags and tents and camp out."

"How was the hiking? Did you like it?"

"It was kind of a pain in the beginning," she said. "Then I saw how beautiful the stars are at night. The trees are so tall but where there's a clearing you can look up and see the Milky Way. I don't think I ever saw it the same way. And I could feel my heart beat. Everything slowed down. Nothing mattered anymore, none of the stupid stuff that I always care so much about."

*If only this feeling could last for her,* I wished, with a lump in my throat. I said, "If we get back to the city in time, we'll stop by Trudi's, she was going to have dinner waiting for us. I'll have to make sure she's up for it since we won't be in until late."

"It'll be good to see Aunt Trudi," Alex murmured. "Is she better now?"

I shook my head. "She's in a clinical trial but I don't know how well it's going. Just so you know, she looks pretty bad."

"Aunt Trudi always looks well put together."

*You haven't seen her bald and scrawny.*

I went on, "I rented a place in Fire Island for the weekend. I thought you and I could walk on the beach and talk."

"I want to talk with you, mom, that would be nice," Alex said. Then her face lit up. "Can I bring my guitar? I've really missed it. When I couldn't sleep, I'd lie in my sleeping bag and try to remember chord progressions and fingering."

"Of course, I'd love to hear you play," I said. It had been a long time since Alex reached for her guitar. I hoped it meant she was turning herself around.

---

We reached Trudi's apartment after nine but she and Robert were still waiting for us. Alex walked into their third-floor apartment behind me and I saw her flinch when she circled around me to hug Trudi.

Trudi had lost weight and most of her hair. Her face was drawn and sallow, her cheeks sagged inward, and her baldish head wasn't smooth and pink but grayish with a few limp gray tufts. She wasn't wearing a covering over her head, although she wore a hat when she went out. I thought about getting her a wig and wished I could be one of those friends who shaved her head in support of the person undergoing chemo, but that wasn't me. I just wasn't that selfless. I'd have to show my support and love for Trudi in other ways.

Alex and Trudi hugged for a few seconds longer than usual. Then Alex stepped back with the sweetest smile I'd seen on her face in forever, and I remembered how soft and loving she could be. How soft and loving she once was, once upon a time, before drugs and boys and her father's disregard for her reckless behavior. She said, "Aunt Trudi, how are you feeling?"

"It's not my worst day," Trudi said, in her arch way. "Don't be fooled by my appearance. It's been three and a half months since I was diagnosed and I'm still here. I beat the odds. One could say I'm on the road to recovery."

"So am I," Alex said.

"I certainly hope so, young lady. You've worried us all," Trudi said.

"I didn't mean to worry everyone," Alex said. "I just didn't think about anyone but myself. It's like I couldn't stop myself from what I was doing, you know, like a snowball rolling down the hill. I just had to do everything. It swept me away."

"Maybe it's time to make a snow-woman out of the snowball. I've got a carrot for the nose in my refrigerator," Trudi responded with her old, lovable mix of asperity and warmth.

Alex grinned and shrugged. "I'm just trying to get through one day at a time."

Trudi said, "I kept the lasagna warm for you and your mum."

"Lasagna?" Alex cried. "That sounds wonderful!" She hugged Robert who stood there grinning sheepishly.

"So how was the great outdoors?" Trudi asked, gesturing for us to follow her into the dining room.

"Big," Alex said with a sigh. "A lot bigger than me. Bigger than the city. I just gave up trying to outdo it. I stopped trying to control everything. And the food wasn't very good."

I thought it was one of the most real conversations she'd had with anyone in years.

———∼———

Alex and I had a quiet weekend. We took the ferry to Fire Island and didn't really talk; we just sat beside each other and watched the boat shrugging away from land into the waves. Groucho scooted under our legs and slept. When we reached the Island, I got a hand cart and pushed our luggage while Alex carried her guitar slung across her shoulder. We had some distance to walk and Groucho whimpered a bit. I'd rented a tiny cottage in Fair Harbor, a few houses from the beach via an online service, and I wasn't expecting much. All I wanted was to get Alex away from the city before it got its hooks back into her.

The cottage was as rudimentary as I expected, but we ate dinner out and brought back baked goods and granola for our breakfast that we ate out on the porch. Alex downloaded a ringtone app onto my phone and assigned the song *Here Comes the Sun* to her own number. We laid out on the beach. When we weren't tanning by the water, I read and Alex played the guitar and sang, her strong alto reaching for its old highs. Her strumming and her voice were rusty from her time in the woods but she persisted and, by the time we were ready to go home on Sunday afternoon, she'd regained some of her old fluency.

On the ferry back to Manhattan, I put my arm around her shoulders and drew her toward me so that she rested against my heart. There's nothing as fulfilling for a mother as putting your arms around your child, whether she was six months old, six years old, or sixteen years old. It replenished that bottomless reservoir of love that a parent feels for her baby. I'd feel the same way when Alex was sixty and I was in my nineties. I wondered when I'd get to hold Dani again, if ever, and prayed that it would be soon. Alex and I cuddled like that until the boat docked in Bay Shore. We got steaming, milky, salty, potato-laden clam chowder to-go from the restaurant near the ferry terminal, and I bought Groucho a hamburger for his forbearance.

Once home, Alex disappeared into her room and I had some shaky moments wondering if I'd found all of her concealed drugs. I'd hired my cleaning lady to come for an extra session and she and I had scoured the room together. Analyn was a tiny, phlegmatic lady from the Philippines who didn't seem to judge but just gathered the paraphernalia together and disposed of it for me. I took cell phone pictures in case I ever needed to show a judge the lengths to which Alex had gone to keep herself stolidly incapacitated by substances. I hated that I had to think that way and that I couldn't just clean Alex's room and move forward with hope and faith. But discretion being the better part of valor, I had to keep George's litigiousness in mind. Our suit about payment for Brookton still wasn't settled.

# CHAPTER TWENTY-FIVE

"IT'S MY BIRTHDAY ON Friday. I'm bringing the kids into Manhattan on Thursday night. I'm taking the day off. I'm taking the weekend off," Scott was saying. I had come out of an early morning class at a yoga studio on the Upper West Side and run into Scott on his way to the crosstown bus.

"You're taking three whole days off? For real?" I wiped the sweat off of my face. August had arrived in Manhattan in all its broiling, odoriferous glory. Even at that hour, just past seven in the morning, the streets sweltered.

"Starting Friday," he affirmed. "I was going to call to invite you; I'm glad I ran into you. Spend the day with us. We'll take the kids to the Met then we'll go out for lunch. We'll have dinner at my apartment."

"The Met?" I was intrigued.

He was smiling; he had me sniffing the bait on his hook and he knew it.

"Yes. It'll be fun. You can teach Janey and Max about art. There's an exhibit opening that features Renaissance artist Domenico Ghirlandaio. Isn't that your time period?"

Ghirlandaio was a contemporary of Botticelli, and I loved the Flemish influence in Ghirlandaio's work.

*Ghirlandaio was Michelangelo's teacher.*

Suddenly I was salivating to see the exhibit. "OK, I'll get Rosa to cover the gallery."

"Who's Rosa?"

"My assistant in the gallery."

*You never, ever need to meet her, pool boy.*

Which reminded me. I said slyly, "Since it's your birthday, I'll have to think of a special present to give you."

"Chocolate?" His deep voice roughened. He leaned close and said solemnly, "Not with my kids around."

*God forbid.*

"I'm in enough trouble because of the red peignoir set. I would like to see that again. That would be a great birthday present on a night my children are not here."

"Sure. Um, did you ever see *Risky Business*?"

"Of course. That's a great, classic movie." He smiled a little.

"There's this hot scene ... on the train."

He was quiet and I could hear his thousand gigabyte brain with its hundred million gigahertz processor whirring as it searched its files.

"Tom Cruise ushers a homeless guy off the train and then does Rebecca DeMornay. You know, people used to say I looked like Tom Cruise."

*I wouldn't go that far.*

"Yeah, I can see that, absolutely," I said. "Remember that train scene? I was thinking I could get a blond wig and a blouse and a skirt like Rebecca DeMornay's, and you could get a black shirt and a blazer, and we could recreate it."

He was quiet for a few beats and then turned and frowned at me while clasping my elbow. "The New York subway is not a turn on."

*And yet, despite all that brainpower, you're dense.*

"In my living room. Or yours. When your kids aren't around. Playing the Phil Collins music."

"Oh." It was a quiet word but teeming with interest.

"Are you interested, pool boy?"

"I'm not a 'pool boy.' I'm a respected medical doctor. Also, last time she was in, Mrs. Waterston asked me what was going on between us."

I felt my heart leap to my throat. "What did you say?"

"That we were having a torrid affair and I was fucking your brains out every chance I got."

I held my breath.

He giggled. That was the word for it: giggling. It was not dignified. It did not befit a respected medical doctor. He smirked at me. "I changed the subject. Why don't you want her to know?"

"It's complicated."

Trudi never said so, but after all those years of friendship, I knew what she thought: that Carl would take care of me.

"Maybe once we move past the booty call stage, we can be open with her," Scott said. "It's going to be hard for me to concentrate on my patients today with the image of you in a blond wig and red peignoir in my head."

"That I do not believe for one second," I said.

———⌒———

Friday morning, Scott, Janey, Max and I arrived at the museum without Max managing to defenestrate himself through the taxi window. I was a member so I claimed them as my family and got our admissions stickers. I handed one to Scott and one to Janey even though, technically, she didn't need one. I requested one for her because I knew she'd like having it. She watched me closely as I peeled off the sticker and attached it to my shirt. Then she did the same.

"Hold him so I can do my sticker, will you?" Scott asked. He thrust Max at me.

Little Max was as solid and stout as an elephant leg but writhing like an octopus undergoing electrocution. He was also heavier than he looked. He couldn't have been cuter, with those incandescent, mischievous dark eyes turned up toward me.

The next thing I knew he was out of my arms and sprinting toward the information desk, which he scaled as nimbly as a monkey.

"Damn!" Scott exclaimed. He darted off after Max.

"Is he always like that?" I asked Janey.

She nodded. "But not when he's sleeping."

Scott thought Max was squirming in a way that meant he had an urgent need for the bathroom, so our first stop was the bathroom just past the European Sculpture court.

Janey and I waited by the dramatic marble *Ugolino* by Carpeaux. She eyed the sculpture skeptically.

"I don't like that sculpture."

"I don't think you're supposed to," I told her. "The artist, Jean-Baptiste Carpeaux, meant for it to make you feel unsettled and anxious. See that man biting his fingers? That's Count Ugolino. He's thinking about eating his sons. Those are his sons around his legs."

"Ew!" Janey said, her face contorted with fascinated repulsion. "That's gross. Why is he going to eat his sons?"

"He and his sons were thrown in prison in Florence for trying to overthrow the government, and they were all left to starve to death. His sons begged him to eat their bodies so he wouldn't die. They told him to do it."

"Ew!" Janey repeated. She stepped closer and really looked at the piece. "Is the little boy by his foot already dead?"

"The littler ones died first. One by one, they all died."

"Is he really going to eat them?" she gasped.

"It's all written about in a wonderful, amazing, beautiful book called Dante's *Inferno*," I told her. "Dante says, 'His hunger was more powerful than his grief.'"

"Gross," she said, in total fascination. "So he ate them?"

"Yes. He's called the 'cannibal count.'"

"Ew. Is Dante's *Inferno* like Harry Potter?"

"Oh, it's even better," I assured her. "Dante wrote about Satan the devil having three faces. And about how hell isn't fire, at its worst it's ice. It's so unbelievably freezing cold."

She tilted her head as she walked around the *Ugolino*.

"I don't like to be cold."

"Me, neither. I get cold too easily."

Scott and Max joined us. Max sat on Scott's hip and pointed.

"Pee pee!" he shouted, pointing at the penis of one of Ugolino's sons. "PEE PEE!"

Janey clapped her hand over her mouth.

A crowd gathered around us.

I said, "Yes, Max, that is his pee pee."

Scott interjected, "I don't think this conversation is appropriate for my children."

"Pee pee!" Max shrieked at the top of his lungs.

The assembling onlookers giggled.

"You know this is high art, right?" I asked Scott.

"Of course I do! I just think he's too immature to handle it," Scott said.

"Ugh, Americans are so weirdly puritanical about the nude male form," I said. "Should we ask the Met to attach fig leaves?"

"I didn't say that," Scott returned.

"Sarah, why does Jean-Baptiste Carpeaux make them naked?" Janey asked. Her dark eyes were fiercely fixed on the sculpture. "Why aren't they wearing clothes? Even in prison, they would have been wearing clothes?"

"It's something the very greatest artists do: they show the human form nude."

"Why?" Janey asked.

"Lots of reasons. What do you and I and Max and your dad all have in common? I'll give you a hint: it's not our age, our gender, or our hair color."

"Your hair is reddish brown and Dad's is brown. Me and Max have black hair," Janey said. She studied my face. "We all have brown eyes."

"True, but what else do we all have in common?" I asked. I held up my hands and wiggled my fingers and then tapped the top of my head and then patted my elbow.

"We all have hands and heads and elbows," Janey said.

"That's right," I said. "The human body is universal. It represents the human being. However we may look different on the outside, we still have the same basic shape. And implied in that shape is what's on the inside, what we need to live: our hearts, our brains, our stomachs." I looked at Scott. "Our pancreas."

Janey and Scott both nodded. Scott's lips tugged into a smile.

"When an artist paints or sculpts a naked human form, he's suggesting all of that, all of our commonality and all of what makes us human. Because there are no clothes to disguise that or to distract the viewer from facing our humanity."

"We need our bodies to be alive," Janey said.

"Exactly!" I exclaimed. "In fact, I knew an art teacher who said that the sculpture of the human body is a metaphor for the human desire to live forever. Because, you know, when you die, you aren't in your body anymore. The soul goes away."

"I think the two little boys are dead," Janey said, pointing to the two younger sons. "And I think the big son knows he's dying soon and he's scared."

I nodded. "Why do you think that?"

"Because of the way their faces look," she answered. "That boy's face looks really scared."

"So that's another thing that a nude sculpture shows: feelings. It's something else we all have in common, our feelings. We love our families and friends, we want to be happy, we hope for good things, we're sad when something or someone hurts us, and we get scared.

"How do we feel our feelings? In our bodies. Your tummy gets fluttery when you're anxious. Your heart beats faster when you're excited. When you're happy, you get a light feeling in your chest and your lips smile. Ugolino here is so upset that he's chewing his own fingers. His son's eyes are widened in fear and horror. But he's also wrapping his arms around his father, pleading with his father to eat him so his father won't die—he's willing to sacrifice himself for his dad!

"But when an artist shows a nude body, he's talking about more than feelings. Look—" I took her hand and dragged her down the hall to Canova's glorious *Perseus with the head of Medusa*. Scott and Max trailed us, as did the group that was listening. "This is Perseus, who was the son of the king of the gods, Zeus, and a human princess named Danae. Perseus grew up to become a great hero.

"On one of his adventures, he cut off the head of Medusa. Medusa was a terrible monster who had snakes growing out of her head. Anyone who looked into her eyes was turned into stone.

"Even if you don't know the story, you know that this is a hero on an adventure. Perseus's body is so perfect and he's so graceful. You can tell just by looking that he's someone special, like Batman or Superman, a being like us but of a higher order than us.

"Canova sculpted Perseus naked, especially so that you'd notice his body, his gracefulness, and balance. This ideal body houses courage and inner strength, that's why Perseus looks directly at Medusa: he has defeated her utterly; she can't turn him into stone. He was willing to face fear, which can freeze us into stone, and he won.

"You know all that just by looking. You get lifted up. You feel it inside your own being.

"Because Canova looked at a model in his studio, and his amazing skill at looking at the human body allowed him to translate what he was seeing into a piece of art. He designed *Perseus* to give a specific impression. It isn't just that Perseus is a hero; it's also that Canova was a master artist who could say something important about courage and strength.

"So you see, Janey, the art of the human body is the most profound, most expressive, and most difficult art an artist can make!" I finished.

Applause broke out. Janey clapped enthusiastically.

Scott situated Max in his arms so he could join in.

I felt myself blushing but I made a graceful bow with my hands in Namaste.

"How do you know so much about art?" a lady asked eagerly. "Are you a professor?"

"I'm a gallery owner, let me give you my card."

---

Afterward, we headed to a Szechuan place on Second Avenue that I recommended. Scott and Janey were hesitant, however, deliberating over the gluten and MSG issues, but Max decided the issue by pounding on his father's chest and hollering, "Hungry!" So we filed in and were seated. Max crawled out of his highchair and sat on the table banging two sets of chopsticks together and knocking over our water glasses. Janey, Scott, and I chatted around the ruckus and pretended not to notice the dirty looks from the other patrons.

When the food came, Max slithered back into his seat and devoured handfuls of shredded beef with Asian celery.

We opted to walk home through Central Park because Max needed a bath and we didn't want to get into a taxi with him, and also because he needed to run around and burn off some energy. The air was hot and muggy and still, and I was gooey with sweat and enervated, but the humidity didn't bother Max. He ran in circles around us, often darting off only to be retrieved by Scott, usually as he was on the verge of climbing something: a fence, a tree, a pole, a dog, another child's stroller.

"That child has a lot of energy," I noted after Scott pulled him off a picnic table near the pull-up bars.

"He's not hyperactive," Scott replied, wiping sweat from his forehead.

"I didn't say he was."

"You implied it. You're used to girls. Boys are different."

"I didn't imply anything. There goes your not-hyperactive son again," I pointed as Max tore off at an angle. Scott leapt after him.

We were emerging onto Central Park West when Scott's cell phone rang. He looked at the caller ID and frowned. He picked Max up and plunked him into my arms, then walked off a few yards to take the call.

I felt a fearful flash of premonition.

"No," I said firmly when Scott got off the phone. "Absolutely not. I'm not babysitting right now."

"It's just for an hour. I have to deal with this; it's urgent," Scott said earnestly. "A patient confused his appointment date. I'd reschedule him but he's come in all the way from Massachusetts. He's a very sick man; I don't want to force him to travel unnecessarily. I'll grab a taxi there, handle the situation, and taxi back. Less than an hour."

"Scott, no. No way," I said.

"It'll be easy. By the time you reach your apartment, Max will have worn himself out. He'll be good and tired. He'll sit and look at a book—Janey said you have picture books. He may even nap."

"Oh my god, *no!*" I exclaimed. "What part of that do you not understand, the 'n' or the 'o'?"

"I'll help Sarah," Janey piped up.

"What a good girl, helping Daddy and Sarah," Scott enthused. He bent down to kiss the top of her head. Then he looked into the road. He spied a taxi and hailed it. He ruffled Max's hair, then grabbed me by the shoulders—around Max's squirming body—and kissed me on my forehead. "I owe you, Sarah. Thank you. I love you."

He got into the taxi and motored off.

I stood there with sweat soaking the armpits of my shirt, overheated damp air frizzing my hair, and a wriggling two-and-a-half-year-old not-hyperactive boy in my arms.

*What am I supposed to do with Scott's last comment? Did he mean that or did it just pop out of him in the moment?*

I asked, "Max, do you like cough syrup?"

"Max is allergic to—" Janey started.

"I'm not going to give him any medication to make him sleep," I grumbled.

Somehow I got them both to my apartment in one piece. And by 'somehow' I meant that I locked Max against my chest, despite the fact that we were both radiating heat like a furnace. I carried him into the bathroom and plunked him on the floor and ran a cool bath.

Max saw the water and knew what it was for. Showing the first inkling of the Bauer intelligence, he stripped himself naked and launched himself over the porcelain and into the tub.

Janey and I stood and watched him splash and gurgle happily.

Groucho came in to gulp water from the tub, causing Max to giggle and shriek and splash the dog.

"Do you want to get in with Max?" I asked Janey.

She shook her head. "He poops in the bath tub."

"Oh, great."

Eventually, I got him out of the tub, dried him off and wrangled him back into his undies. Then I fished his droppings out of the tub and flushed them, emptied the water, and sprayed the tub with antiseptic cleaner. By that point, I wanted to change my shirt so I sat him on the sofa beside Janey, who had found the Harry Potter book from her previous visit. I handed Max *Goodnight Moon*.

"Sit here, and stay here!" I ordered fiercely, shaking my finger at him.

I ran to my bedroom and sloughed off the sweaty, stained shirt and found a replacement in my drawer.

*Crash.*

I raced back to the living room, donning the shirt on the go.

Max had thrown some books off of the bottom shelf of the bookcase and then scaled the first two shelves. He clung precariously to the third shelf up.

The bookcase was starting to lean away from the wall.

A vision of him flattened beneath the heavy wooden bookcase flashed through my head. Despite my heart stopping, I was on him even faster than Scott could have been. I peeled Max off the bookcase and shouldered it upright.

"That's it!" I yelled. "You're going to kill yourself!" He was flailing in my arms but I marched him into the kitchen.

Janey followed us.

"Sit here and do not move," I told Max, placing him in a chair. Of course I knew he'd move. "Janey, hold him down for a second. See that he doesn't leave this chair."

"How?"

"Sit on him."

Obediently she parked her bottom on top of him. Though she was tall, she was slender and appeared birdlike with hollow bones; Max, who was built like a fireplug, probably outweighed her. Still, she managed to keep him in the chair.

I watched his arms and legs wave around under and behind her and then I got into the cabinet beside the pantry where I kept useful odds and ends—like tape.

Masking tape, no. Clear packing tape, no. Unfortunately, I had no duct tape, which was what I really needed. Then I saw a fat spool of black vinyl electrical tape.

I grabbed the tape and dove on Max, who was starting to dislodge his sister. "Great job, Janey. You can get up."

She leapt up. Her big eyes were twice their normal size.

I ripped open the tape and affixed Max to the chair, winding the tape around his torso, mummy-fashion. He was writhing and squirming but didn't yell. Thirty or forty circles around and he was firmly secured to the chair. He wasn't going anywhere. He pulled at the tape; it stretched but didn't give.

"I'll say one thing for your brother, he doesn't cry and yell much," I murmured.

Max stared at me in utter bafflement.

"Don't worry, I'll get you something to play with," I promised him. "Watch him for a second please, Janey."

I ran to a hall closet where I kept art supplies, dug out some old Sculpey Bake & Bend kids clay and some modeling tools, and ran back to the kitchen.

"Here you go," I said, panting. I tore off a chunk of bright purple Sculpey and handed it to Max. "If you make something, I'll bake it and you can take it home with you." I seated myself beside him with a sigh of relief. "I'll show you how. Janey, would you like to join us?"

"My daddy is going to kill you," Janey said, sitting in the chair across from me.

"I'll give you a dollar not to tell him." I handed her a piece of blue clay.

She kneaded it with a thoughtful expression.

I took a ball of yellow Sculpey and showed it to Max, who was crunching the clay in both fists. "We'll make a doggy. First, you have to tear off a smaller piece."

"Seventeen dollars and ninety-nine cents," Janey announced.

"What?"

"You said you'd give me a dollar not to tell my dad. But I need seventeen dollars and ninety-nine cents to buy the next Harry Potter book."

"I don't have change. I only have some twenties." I tore off some other small pieces of clay and showed Max.

Janey screwed up her face. "I don't have two dollars and one penny."

"That's amazing! How did you figure that out?" I gasped.

"Seventeen and ninety-nine cents is almost eighteen. Twenty take away eighteen is two. Then there's the penny to make seventeen ninety-nine into eighteen."

"Wow. Do people tell you all the time how smart you are?"

"Yes," she said in a matter-of-fact tone.

"Tell you what, if you fetch my purse out of the bathroom, I'll give you a twenty and you can keep the two dollars and one penny."

She grinned broadly, slid down, and skipped out of the kitchen.

I showed Max how to roll a small piece of clay into a tube shape.

Janey returned with my purse. I dug a twenty from my wallet and handed it to her.

"What about my mommy?" Janey asked, with an innocent but determined air. "Do you want me not to tell her?"

I made a face but dug out another twenty.

"Uncle Rick?"

"Your dad said you call him 'poppy.'"

"Only when I talk to him." She stretched out her hand.

I gave her a look of high suspicion and laid another twenty in her palm. "You have a talent for obtaining money. I respect that. You would be successful in the art world. However, you and I are not going to have a relationship that is solely pecuniary."

Janey's face lit up. "What's that mean, pecuniary?"

"I'll tell you this time, but next time, you can look it up in a dictionary. It means 'of or relating to money.'"

"Pecuniary," Janey repeated. "Mommy lets me look words up on her iPad."

"I thought your parents don't like you on screens."

"Mommy lets me play with her iPad when daddy's not around." She stuck the three twenties in the pocket of her dress and climbed back up into the chair. She saw what I was doing with the clay and tried to emulate me.

I smothered a smile. "Why do you need all this money? Don't your parents buy you books?"

"They do," Janey nodded vigorously. "They buy lots of books since daddy moved here. All I have to do is tell mommy that I miss daddy or tell daddy that I miss him, and they buy me lots of stuff."

I laughed, I couldn't help it. "Seriously, kid, you have a future in the art business. Let me know if you ever need a job, I'll put you right to work in my gallery."

"That sounds fun. What's your gallery like?" she asked.

"My gallery is a magical place filled with beautiful paintings and a few sculptures," I smiled.

"Like *Perseus* and *Ugolino*?"

"Well, not as nice as those," I admitted. "But someday, that's the plan."

# CHAPTER TWENTY-SIX

MAX AND I EVOLVED a strategy whereby I rolled clay tubes of various colors and he squished them together to make things.

"Excellent work, this is really great, Max," I said, holding up a tubiferous creation in red, orange, and blue. It had a central torso and tubes extruding in various directions, and Max had jammed other tubes onto those. It resembled an antenna giving birth to other antennae.

*Impressive*, I thought.

"What's that?" Janey wrinkled her nose. "That's nothing. It doesn't make sense."

She was making perfect little clay dogs, ears, tail and all, exactly as I'd shown her.

"It's an objet d'art," I chirped. "In the abstract market, it would sell for, like, twenty thousand dollars."

"Doggy!" Max said, giggling.

But he wasn't pointing at the objet d'art he had made, he was pointing at Groucho, who had sprawled out on the floor and peed all over.

"Oh, no, Groucho," I scolded him, jumping up. But of course, it was my fault because I hadn't walked him.

Groucho whuffled and looked tired and rolled over onto his back with his feet in the air, begging to have his tummy scratched. I mopped up the floor around him with one hand and scratched his belly with the other. His hind leg made windshield wiper motions in the air.

"No, Max!" Janey cried.

I rose up on my knees to see Max reaching for two of Janey's doggy creations. The devilish look on his face signaled his intention to mash them together.

I moved his hands away. "No, Maxwell, is that your name? Maximilian?"

"That's not his name," Janey said and she smacked his chubby grabby hand that reached under mine.

"He makes a lot of trouble but he doesn't say much. That's not all bad in a man."

"Mommy is worried because he doesn't talk but daddy says it's normal in boys," Janey said. "Daddy has a friend who's a physicist at Stanford and he didn't talk until he was four. Daddy says it's not correlated with intelligence."

I looked away so Janey wouldn't see me rolling my eyes at her vocabulary. "What does your mommy call Max when she's mad at him for misbehaving?" I hoped to get his full name so I could reprimand him properly.

"Damn kid."

I laughed out loud. Both kids looked at me.

I chortled, "I'm starting to like your mom."

"She doesn't like you," Janey confided. "She doesn't like your red pajamas. But I told her that you look really pretty in them and she should like you because daddy likes you a lot."

I laughed again as I sat there on the floor, wiping up my aging dog's urine beside a two-and-a-half-year-old hellion whom I'd taped to a chair and a six-year-old who had a better vocabulary than I did. I laughed for real, those big gut-busting peals that start in your toes and pulse in a growing helix throughout your whole being.

The buzzer rang for the front door downstairs.

"Oh crap, that's your dad," I jumped up. "We can't let him see Max like this! Janey, you go to the door and stall him."

"What does that mean?" she asked, a quizzical expression on her face.

"Don't let him in! Make excuses! Buy me some time to get Max out of this and dressed!" I got the kitchen shears and cut through the electrical tape at the back of the chair. I took a damp rag and wiped it on his little brown gut hoping to loosen the adhesive. That didn't seem to be working so I poured a glass of water down his front and then I tore the whole wad of tape off of him.

Max made a weird mewling sound and his face took on an agonized expression but he didn't cry.

I pulled him out of his chair and kissed his cheek. I stroked his belly, which was red and speckled with gray adhesive but was otherwise fine.

*Thank god electrical tape adhesive doesn't harden like cement. Next time I tape a kid into a chair, I'll remember to put a shirt on him first.*

I crooned, "You're amazing, Max. You're the best little boy ever. I'll buy you candy and treats. Don't cry."

He wriggled and then sagged into my chest, letting his warm cheek rest against me. Was it possible that he was getting tired? I hoped it was that and not that his belly hurt.

I jogged past Janey, who was chatting with her dad through the door.

Janey gave me a palms-up, 'what now?' gesture.

"One more minute," I whispered. I dove into the bathroom, squirted a handful of shea butter lotion onto my hand, and rubbed it into Max's belly that wasn't as red as before, thank goodness. I found his dirty shirt and slid it over his head. He was slimy and sticky, but then he always was. He'd pass.

I came back out and gestured for Janey to let her dad in.

Janey threw open the door.

"Sweetheart!" Scott leaned down and kissed his daughter. He straightened and rushed to me and kissed me on the lips. "You must want to kill me, Sarah. I'm so sorry."

"I knew it would be more than an hour. Have you ever read *The Ransom of Red Chief?*" I passed Max to him. Then for the first time, I looked at the clock atop one of my bookcases. It was after six o'clock.

"I had no idea this would happen, that it would take this long," Scott continued in a penitent voice. He nuzzled Max. "Max seems happy. Clearly, he wasn't as bad as the boy in the O. Henry story."

"Hmmm," I said.

"I got this for us." Scott held a loaded-to-the brim Citarella market bag toward me.

"What's this?"

"My birthday meal. I stopped at home and retrieved it. I thought it would be easier if you just cooked it here since you and the kids are already here." His angular face wore a pleased expression.

"Huh?" I took a wrapped package out of the bag. "Salmon?"

"Yes. Would you put it in the oven? I got broccoli rabe from the deli counter and a pre-made salad, but I figured that it wouldn't be too hard for you to bake fresh salmon."

I looked at Scott in frank disbelief.

"You expect me to cook for you? After babysitting?"

"Just put the salmon in the oven to bake."

"I don't cook. I hate to cook. I own a gallery. I sell great art. I barely even cooked for my own kids."

"My mother worked all day teaching class and worked in the evenings tutoring, and she made us a good dinner every night," Scott said in an accusatory tone.

"Your mother is a saint. I'm not."

He made a face.

"It's your kitchen, and it's my birthday. Just put it in the oven. It's not that hard to bake salmon. It's not real cooking."

I gave him a skeptical look without answering. I was tired of being steamrolled by him. First babysitting, now cooking. I had to let him know I wasn't a pushover. I had enough of being expected to be a servile caretaker for some grown man. I didn't get out of two marriages to knuckle under now to any man, no matter how hot.

*Time to set some boundaries.*

"You can put salmon in the oven on my birthday, can't you?" he demanded.

"OK," I said. "OK."

I headed toward the kitchen.

"There's wine and a birthday cake in the bag, too," Scott called.

"OK."

I unpacked the bag and set everything out on the counter. First things first. I uncorked the wine, a decent Cabernet Sauvignon from Australia, and poured myself a generous glass. I guzzled half the glass and then refilled it. I turned the oven on "broil" and retrieved a broiling pan from the bottom cabinet. I laid out the salmon; it really was a beautiful fillet of fish, just the right orangey-red and streaked with white squiggles of fat. I arranged the broccoli rabe and salad alongside the salmon and put the broiling pan into the oven. I took another wine glass from the cabinet and poured a glass of wine for Scott.

"Forty-five minutes," I said blithely, carrying the wine to Scott.

Scott sat on the couch with Max on his lap. His not-hyperactive child was calmly leafing through *Goodnight Moon* as if he never tried to pull down my bookcase. Janey sat beside them, absorbed in her Harry Potter book.

Scott accepted the wine glass with a smile.

"Don't you think that will dry out the fish? Are you cooking it at a very low temperature?"

"Who's robbing this train, Jesse? You or me?"

He shrugged and sipped the wine. "This is pretty good. Do you like it?"

"Very much," I said. "I've certainly earned it."

I curled myself into my leather easy chair with a sigh and took another long swig. It was a very decent cab, and it got better the more I drank.

"Come on, it couldn't have been that bad," Scott said.

"It wasn't," I admitted. "Janey was a pleasure and very helpful. Max eventually settled down and made some rather provocative abstract sculptures. He's got a bright future in the Venice Biennale. Although he's already surpassed most of the other artists in skill."

Scott smiled. "Janey said you guys played with clay."

"We didn't play," I corrected him. "We *created*."

"Groucho peed on the floor," Janey volunteered.

"Oh, that's right, I need to take him for a walk."

I withdrew my legs from the traumatized cocoon into which I'd curled myself.

"Max and I will do it, won't we, Big Guy?" Scott said, jumping up.

Max said, "Doggy!"

"Really? That's so nice," I exclaimed.

"The least I can do, since you babysat and you're cooking," Scott said. "Where are Max's pants and shoes?"

"In the bathroom, I'll get them," Janey said. "Max pooped in the tub."

Scott winced. "Sorry about that."

"The leash and some plastic bags are on the secretary by the door," I said, pointing. "No rush. It's going to be another forty-two minutes."

Later, Scott and Max banged open the front door. Groucho limped in as usual but otherwise seemed none the worse for the wear. Scott said, "I can smell the fish from the hallway. What'd you put on it?"

"Secret recipe," I said. "How was Groucho?"

"How old is he?" Scott asked. He laid the leash on the secretary.

Max bolted over to me, climbed up into my lap and bounced.

I exclaimed and set the wine on an end table before it overturned, then I situated Max until he and I were both semi-comfortable. Max fingered my earring but I firmly moved his chubby little hands to clasp each other.

"Groucho isn't young. I guess he's twelve. No, wait, oh gosh. He's getting close to fifteen."

"Has he been to the vet recently?" Scott asked. He sniffed the air. "Sarah, I can smell that fish. Should we check it?"

"No, *we* should not. *We* should wait another twelve minutes," I said. "I've got this. You assigned it to me, so I'm handling it."

Scott headed for the couch and then changed his mind.

"Sarah, I'm checking that fish."

"No, you're not, I'm cooking," I said indignantly.

Scott was already disappearing into the kitchen. I rose and chased him, bouncing Max on my hip. Scott found the oven mitts and pulled the broiling pan out of the oven.

"What the hell is this?" He stared in disbelief at the blackened mass of fish and vegetables. He swiveled around on his heels and stared at me.

"I do not cook. And I'm not your mother."

Scott stood as unmoving as *Perseus* but without the gracefulness. His upraised hands were sheathed in oven mitts and, although symmetrical, did not lend any elegance to the pose. He stared at me in abject disbelief.

I stared back.

After a few beats, he took off the mitts and turned off the oven.

"Janey, Max, we're going out for dinner."

---

We sat at a trattoria located not far from me; it was probably the best Italian restaurant in the neighborhood. The Upper West Side was notorious for mediocre, overpriced food but that place was the exception, and I loved their tasty lamb chops.

I wasn't sure how Scott had gotten us into the trattoria, especially with Max's state of grunge. Max sat, peaceably for him, in a high chair beside Scott, gnawing a breadstick. Janey sat in a chair between us, her nose buried in her Harry Potter book.

I stared at the menu, wondering if I was hungry enough to order a primi. Maybe I could get Scott to split the pasta con funghi with me.

"You can get salmon here if you're really in the mood for salmon," I noted.

Scott shot me a furious look.

"I understand that you were trying to make a point, Sarah. But did you have to destroy a perfectly good piece of fish? It wasn't cheap, you know."

"That really was a beautiful piece of fish," I agreed. "The color was a rich, deep coral and it was marbled with fat in just the right way, like something out of a still life. Caravaggio could have painted it, it was that beautiful."

Scott threw down his menu and glared at me.

"So explain to me why you had to destroy it? Why didn't you just tell me to cook? I am a competent cook. Did it occur to you that I could put it in the oven?"

"I wouldn't order you to cook, that wouldn't be kind."

"So it's kinder to destroy the fish that I bought? Why didn't you just tell me you wouldn't cook?"

"I did. You didn't listen."

"It wasn't cooking, it was just putting a piece of salmon into the oven. Who could call that cooking? And you didn't say, 'I won't cook.' You said, and I quote, 'I don't cook. I hate to cook. I own a gallery. I sell beautiful art.' End quote. 'I don't cook' and 'I won't cook' are two separate statements that mean different things."

"What are you, a lawyer?" I retorted. "You're good at arguing but don't give up your day job of blowing people off to go see patients."

Scott went on as if I hadn't spoken.

"At no time did you say, 'I won't cook and if you make me I'll burn the goddamn salmon alongside the goddamn salad and goddamn vegetables.'"

"I did so. You're just dense."

"No, you didn't. I'm not dense. I went to Harvard."

I chortled, "Oh ho, I know plenty of people who went to Harvard who are totally dense."

Janey said, in a quavering voice, "You two are fighting? Please don't fight on my daddy's birthday! I don't get to see my daddy all the time."

Scott immediately looked stricken but I had that kid's number. I dug in my purse for my wallet and pulled out my last twenty-dollar bill. I pushed it across the table to Janey. Magically her tears dried.

Scott said, "What is going on?"

His head swung from Janey to me and back again, like a German Shepherd guard dog.

"Nothing," Janey and I chorused.

Scott's jaw set and an unholy glint, like an evil extraterrestrial growing inside him, took over his eyes. He stuck his hand in front of Janey and waggled his fingers, *gimme.*

Janey was no fool. She handed over the twenty.

Scott said, "Janey, you do not take money from strangers."

"Sarah's not a stranger, she's your girlfriend."

"I'm not your dad's girlfriend," I objected. I wanted to say I was his booty call but restrained myself as it wasn't appropriate in front of his kids. Besides, Scott looked like the top of his head was about to pop off.

"I'm not a stranger either."

The glint in Scott's eye got steelier and he continued to look back and forth between Janey and me. He dropped the twenty in front of me.

I wasn't sure who he wanted to spank more—Janey or me.

Janey folded her hands atop the table and said, "Sarah and I do not have a relationship that is solely pecuniary."

Scott said softly, "Jane Josephine Bauer, you do not take money from Sarah."

"Yes, Daddy."

"Sarah Paige," he continued, his deep voice icy, "you do not give money to my children."

"Lighten up, will you? It's your birthday."

Scott gave me a disgusted look.

"Is that how you raised your children? Is that why your daughter turned into a stoner tramp?"

I gasped. "That's just mean! It's … it's dirty pool!"

I threw the menu on the table and jumped up to leave.

Scott's fingers clamped over my wrist. "You're right. That was mean. I'm sorry. I'm just really mad that you burnt that beautiful piece of salmon and gave my daughter money. That's not your place. And I was really looking forward to that salmon."

I was mad. My face was red and hot tears struggled to escape my eyelids.

"I did my best raising my children and I guess my best sucked all the time. That's what my oldest daughter would tell you. Like her dad, she has exactly nothing good to say about me because in her mind I am the epicenter of evil and not a human being. And you're right; my youngest daughter is a stoner tramp. I have tried everything humanly possible to pull her out of that and get her back on track, and everything I attempt to do fails because her stupid father is on a blood vendetta to thwart my every effort!"

Scott held up his free hand in a gesture of peace while keeping a firm hold of my wrist. "Sarah, I'm sorry. I had no right to say that. Come on; sit down. Please. I apologize. I'll forgive you for the damn salmon if you forgive me for my nasty comment. It was out of line."

His dark eyes searched mine.

"Come on," he murmured. "Lisa's getting the kids Sunday morning and we can have lots of chocolate. All afternoon. All evening."

"You're not buying me off that easily," I said. I dashed the back of my hand across my eyes.

"Yes, I am," Scott said, gazing directly through my eyes into my soul.

"Not this time." I gave him a watery smile. I waved to Janey and Max and turned to walk out of the restaurant.

Janey jumped up and ran over to grab me. "No, Sarah, please don't go! Daddy, say something! Don't let her go!"

Scott rose, looking hesitant.

"Daddy, Sarah is really nice to me and Max. She burned your salmon, so don't make her cook anymore," Janey said. "But we have a lot of fun playing, and she's going to hire me for her gallery."

She took my hand with both of hers, pulled me next to her and grinned up at me.

I looked down into her sweet face and my heart melted. My entire chest pulsed with warmth. I could not remember a single instance over the last twenty years where either Dani or Alex had stood up for me. The Calhoun family's culture of contempt for me, their own mother, prohibited that. It was one of the reasons I'd cut myself loose from George.

Janey said, "Come on, Daddy!"

Scott said, "Sarah, sit down. We're having dinner together."

He stepped closer and touched my cheek. "Forget about the stupid salmon. I'm sorry I asked you to cook."

I looked at him.

*This was what it must be like to be in a regular family where every member is valued. People apologize to each other. People stand up for each other.*

I said, softly, "I'm sorry about your salmon."

"It was a little over the top," Scott said, dryly.

"Sometimes I'm a bit over the top," I admitted.

He grinned and his face softened. Unmitigated acceptance washed over it—an acceptance of me and my quirks that I had not seen before, even from my parents who could not grasp that I didn't want to be like them, religious in one way or another.

Scott said, "I'll manage." He drew me back to the table and held out the chair for me and I seated myself.

Janey clapped and sat back down. "You have to be here for the cake, Sarah. The waiter will bring out a cake with a candle on it and we'll sing Happy Birthday to daddy."

I looked around the table at Janey and Max—who was covered in goo—and at Scott, who was giving me a warm, lopsided grin.

I said, "Not cake that's brown or red."

I was suddenly, deeply happy about the birthday present I'd chosen for Scott. It was a small painting, not from the gallery but one I'd bought for myself years ago in Paris at the foot of Sacre Coeur on the Boulevard de Clichy. A runty, bedraggled Romanian guy had set up a stand on a street corner apart from the usual swarm of artists, claiming his wife was the artist. He had six small, exquisite, Surrealist panels depicting tarot card images, each about four inches wide by about six inches high. That's all he was selling on a TV tray table covered with green canvas. I told him they looked like Victor Brauner's handiwork and he got squirrelly and started packing up his table. Hastily, I said I was joking and coaxed him into selling all six to me for a lot less than they were worth, but for a lot more than I was worth at the time.

I was giving Scott the King of Swords.

# CHAPTER TWENTY-SEVEN

THE COURT DATE FOR my legal suit with George over the payment for Brookton was set for mid-August. I put on my most conservative navy blue suit and sat for a few hours in the Superior Court of New York with Marty at my side. George was surrounded by his latest team of attorneys. Every time he lost one of these battles he hired a more aggressive, more expensive team for the next time. I couldn't imagine the hourly rate he was paying for that batch. I wondered for the nth time why he insisted on throwing his money away in court? The Calhouns had buckets and buckets of money but surely they had better things to do with it. And I couldn't imagine why Katherine was so foolish as to let her husband's legal crusade against me continue. Didn't she realize that it just kept his attention focused on me? Why wouldn't she put an end to it and keep her husband's mind on her? Of course, knowing George I knew it was possible that she didn't want him focused on her.

Maybe focusing on me kept them from having to deal with whatever mishegas was between the two of them.

Nothing was decided in court. George's papers included a copy of my blitheringly nasty email to him and a statement that I'd walked out of the therapy session with Alex. Both were construed to prove that I was a terrible person as well as a terrible mother and, therefore, he shouldn't have to pay for Brookton. Despite that, the judge sent word a few days later that George should pay.

I felt the same as I always did after one of those legal events: exhausted, relieved it was over, and frustrated that George had chosen the legal system as a means of communication. Of course, if I'd been willing to let him browbeat me into doing whatever he wanted according to his caprice of the moment, the legal system wouldn't have been necessary. It was only my ridiculous intransigence that my responsible parenting be treated with respect that had left him with no alternative.

A day or so later, I boxed up the last few months' worth of Dani's mail that had been delivered to my apartment. I sent it to her Princeton P.O. box along with two gifts: a leather-bound notebook and a loose peasant blouse in an Indian print that would look beautiful on her. I was making peaceful overtures toward Dani and taking a leadership role in our reconciliation. Dr. Maitra had advised me to be a leader with my children, despite George's constant attempts to thwart me.

A few days after that, I was en route to the post office in Chelsea, lugging a canvas bag of postcards advertising the gallery talks. The first one was scheduled for the end of September. I found that a combination of direct mail and email was the most effective was to advertise an event. The snippy editor from *American Artist* agreed to give the first talk and to discuss Alessio Abbate's work. He had thawed toward me; some time closer to his talk I'd ask him about publishing my article.

My cell phone rang and Dani's name appeared on-screen. My heart nearly exploded.

"Dani? Are you OK?" I dropped the canvas sack onto the ground.

"I got the gifts. I wanted to talk about the problems I have with you," she said, her voice accusatory.

"Oh," I said. "You mean why you won't talk to me or tell me when you come into the city? Why you hang up on me when I call you? Why you ignore me on my birthday and Mother's Day?"

"Dad doesn't make me feel so bad. You changed my email password to 'Spoiled Brat'!"

"Sometimes you are a spoiled brat," I said. "We all have better and worse selves."

"It's unbelievable that you can shame, blame, and literally destroy the self-esteem of everyone around you but expect to be treated delicately in return!" Dani screamed. She launched into a profanity-laden rant about how toxic I was and she snarled names at me.

"Wait a minute, Danielle," I said, shocked. I took a breath. "Who do you think you're talking to in that tone of voice? I'm your mother. You have to respect me. You've been treating me contemptuously for the last year, and that's not OK."

"You have to respect me!" she screamed.

"That's not the deal," I said slowly. "My responsibility is to take care of you, and I've always done that. I continue to do that. Your responsibility is to be respectful toward me."

She accused me of various horrible behaviors. Then she snarled, "What do you want?"

"I want a loving and respectful daughter."

Dani screamed some more.

It took me a few moments—as I was operating from a state of shock —but eventually, I heard her father's voice speaking through her: I was crazy. I was a rage monster. I was a terrible person. It was George's shtick repackaged for Dani's use. It didn't matter that she was the one shrieking obscenities at me or that she was the one who had unilaterally ended our relationship or that she was well compensated by her rich father for every new act of meanness toward me.

I was trembling when I cut in.

"Danielle, that is enough. I am not interested in your contemptuous treatment. I have my own life."

*I have to stop her because spewing venom at her mother isn't good for* her, *even if she doesn't know it—even if she enjoys it.*

I added, "You call me when you're ready to be a loving and respectful daughter. I'll welcome you back."

I hung up on her.

I stood there on the street corner and breathed while the world whirled around me, unscathed and unaware. A crushing sense of sorrow and loss descended through me. I knew how stubborn Dani was and how crucial it was to her to always be right. Dani was never one to own her wrongdoings and apologize; a trait she'd buttressed by getting all A's, winning at tennis, and going to Princeton. I was also clear about how little my feelings meant to her.

I managed to pick up the canvas bag and resumed my errand to the post office.

———

I took a trip to Los Angeles for a much-needed break. Carl was away with his family; they'd gone to Forte dei Marmi, Italy, and Scott was in Cape Cod with his children. Both men had invited me to join them but I'd declined. I didn't know how Scott would manage with Janey and Max and no help, but he didn't seem concerned. Carl, I knew, would have a splendid time with his kids and grandkids. Trudi and Robert stayed in the city; Trudi was resting at home in-between cycles of treatment. Her son Peter, a photojournalist in London, was still in town so I figured she was well enough taken care of that I could sneak away for a few days.

I flew into Burbank airport and rented a cheap, tiny Ford that didn't have nearly the personality of my Brigit. My first stop was at a Staples for tape and bubble wrap. Then I got on the Pacific Coast Highway to Santa Barbara. I passed Montecito and drove into a neighborhood near the Douglas Family Preserve where I followed a winding road for too far, got lost, and had to turn around. I was looking carefully for a hidden cul de sac. It took a half hour of driving back and forth before the street made itself visible to me, and I followed it to the home of the painter, Chloe Kennedy.

Chloe lived in a small two-bedroom ranch with a detached guest cottage that she'd turned into her studio. I pulled into her driveway and got out of the car. Chloe peeked out the screen door and then descended her steps to greet me.

I greeted her warmly. Chloe was diminutive in form but large and soft of spirit. She was in her sixties, with a round moon face and black and white hair that fell to her shoulder blades. She was three-quarters Native American Indian/First Nations and one-quarter Scotch-Irish; her ancestry was Mi'kmaq and Cherokee. I hadn't chosen her for her Cherokee background, which of course appealed to me, but because she was an exceptional painter. She had the hand of Thomas Moran but her work was informed with the feminine sensibility of Georgia O'Keefe. I adored her paintings and would have filled my own home with them if I didn't need to sell them to feed myself and my decrepit dog.

Chloe was my own particular find, too. Four years ago Marcia and I had driven to Montecito to visit one of Marcia's ritzy friends. The friend owned one of Chloe's paintings, bought at a local art fair. I was Chloe's first gallery.

"Come in for tea?" Chloe asked in her quiet way.

"I'd love some," I accepted gratefully. I had barely eaten on the plane and I stank like airport and bad coffee. I said, "I didn't have time to wash or change. Sorry about my smell."

Chloe smiled over her shoulder and led the way into her home. I followed her into her living room, where she'd set out a plate of cookies, crackers, figs, and cheese.

"What kind of tea would you like?" she asked.

"Anything with caffeine," I said. It felt like an endless day in some kind of Twilight Zone-esque travel loop. It was frying my brain, and did I mention I smelled bad?

Chloe disappeared into her kitchen and I exhaled loudly, stretched up high, bent over and touched my toes, and then sat down on her white couch. I helped myself to a few tasty dried figs.

She reappeared with a teapot. "Earl Grey?"

"Perfect!" I looked around her walls. "Chloe, I see at least ten new paintings you've hung in here. Which ones can I have? Can I have them all?"

She smiled. "You don't waste time, do you?" She seated herself in a wooden rocker across from me and eyed me quizzically. She looked at me as if she were really *looking* at me, the same way I looked at art. I wasn't used to that from other people.

"I love your work; you're amazing."

She tilted her head. "How are you, Sarah?"

*So many things suck.*

But I was in a business setting and said blithely, "Great. How are you?"

She looked at me.

*She doesn't buy my upbeat facade. I'm as bad as Scott is for showing my feelings.*

I admitted, "I have a lot going on in my personal life. But I don't want you to worry. I love your art and I can sell it. There's only one painting remaining of the last batch you gave me."

She leaned forward and poured us each a cup of tea. "So what's going on?"

*Not going to mention the gallery.*

"Problems with my kids. Problems with my ex-husband. Dating two men. It is what it is."

"What kind of problems with your kids?" she asked. She handed me fragrant, steaming tea in a violet-adorned cup sitting on a matching chipped saucer.

"My oldest daughter doesn't talk to me. She blames me for everything wrong in the world. She claims I was a terrible mother."

"Were you?"

"I wasn't a perfect mother, that's a fact. I did a hundred things wrong but I sure as hell wasn't the abusive horror she claims." I dumped several teaspoons of sugar into the tea and then unloaded the whole story—from Dani's announcement that everyone at Princeton had a perfect life except for her, to her screaming phone call, to Alex's drug use and sexual risk-taking, to my legal battles with George.

I didn't really know why I did so, except that Chloe's clear gaze demanded honesty,

Tears rose to my eyes.

"Dealing with Dani, Alex, or their father is like living down in Alice's rabbit hole. Right is wrong and down is up. When I tell Alex to do her homework her father says, 'Do whatever you want. Your mom and her values don't matter.'

"When I tell her to go to class her father says, 'Do whatever you want, your mom's rules don't apply.' Dani functions very well but she's also heard some version of: 'Treat your mother however you want. She doesn't matter. Her feelings don't matter.' If I say, 'My feelings matter,' then George says, 'See? Your mother is abusive.' It's surreal. How am I supposed to mother my children in the face of that?

"The truth is, I've made plenty of mistakes as a mother. A hundred mistakes; maybe a thousand. But I deeply and profoundly love my children, I've taken care of them to the best of my ability, and I've always been there for them. Yet there's no give in the system for a normal relationship where people are just people connecting with each other throughout their various foibles."

Chloe sat back in her chair and stared at me for a long time. We both sipped our tea. Finally, she said, "There's no perfect, ideal mother. There's no perfect, ideal system. But under basically healthy conditions—when real abuse isn't present—children don't reject their parents. When that happens, you're witnessing an inauthentic attachment system. You're seeing a case of parental alienation."

"What do you mean? That's a real thing?" I felt an instant recognition and understanding of the term she'd used.

Chloe nodded. "What happened to you wasn't an accident."

For a split second, I was breathless with shock and anger, then I said, "Through all the years that I was with George I heard him say over and over again that if anyone pissed him off he was going to 'squash them like a bug.' That's what he wants to do to me! Why didn't my shrink explain it that way?"

"Not all therapists understand parental alienation properly. This idea of a child refusing to have a relationship with a parent, without a good reason in a divorce scenario, is a concept that's still making its way into the literature."

She looked at me piercingly. "Children are motivated to bond with their parents. Even in a conflictual relationship, children are still motivated that way. In parental alienation, something else happens. There's detachment behavior, not attachment behavior. The child doesn't just have a conflictual relationship with the parent, they detach. They don't feel grief about the separation. They treat the alienated parent badly and they feel no remorse about that."

"It's true," I said. "Dani never expresses love, affection, or appreciation. She doesn't send Mother's Day or birthday cards. Dani doesn't miss me at all. Alex is a mess but sometimes she seems sorry that she's hurt me, and once in a while she'll tell me that she loves me.

"Other times, she acts like I'm supposed to be a wooden puppet and tell her that she's wonderful all the time, no matter what disaster and catastrophe she's wrought, or what the consequences are for her or for those around her. The two of them act like I was a heroin-addict prostitute who left them to raise themselves while I was shooting up and servicing johns. They show no recognition that I'm a decent, loving person and a loving, concerned parent—they don't show any ambivalence at all about their nasty treatment of me. It's shocking."

Chloe nodded. "I'd guess that your ex-husband didn't feel normal grief when you left him. He felt a wound to his ego. That manifested as anger and rejection of you. He made you bad, all bad, in order to preserve his shiny image of himself. One of the favorite tactics of an alienating parent is exactly what you mentioned: rejecting the target parent's authority and parenting decisions. 'Your mom's rules don't apply' is a classic, textbook example."

"George didn't want to collaborate with me for our children's best interests," I said. "Maybe he did in the beginning but it soon became about him resisting everything and anything I suggested."

"The emotional part goes along with that and those tactics are even trickier to negotiate," Chloe said. "Subtly or not, he implied to your children that *you* were the reason for their pain. You're the bad parent. It's your fault. At the same time, he insisted that you didn't matter, that your feelings didn't matter, and that your values were unimportant. Your children internalized his anger and resentment toward you and that, along with the seductive 'do whatever you want' message, led them to reject you."

"That sounds like what I've experienced. It's so awful, and I don't know what to do about it."

Chloe said, "The thing is, Sarah, when they're with you painful emotions *do* come up. Your kids need and want to bond with you but they're conflicted. They bought into the theory that you're bad. So when they're with you they feel difficult feelings: alienation, sadness—the normal grief response.

"But as normal and healthy as it is to feel grief in this situation, it's not pleasant and it actually reinforces your husband's position. When they're with him, they don't feel bad; when they're with you, they do. They don't realize that the bad feeling is their own grief, the normal grief response. They're interpreting the feeling to mean that you're abusive."

I said hoarsely, "I wouldn't wish this on my worst enemy."

"Your children cannot escape the knowledge that you're part of them," Chloe continued. "They will probably suffer from self-contempt, depression, and anxiety. I'm not surprised to hear about the drug abuse."

"Is there any way to heal this?"

"You'd need a therapist who's very skilled and perceptive and who can see through the bullshit. Too many therapists accept the favored parent's and the child's misrepresentations and take them completely at face value. You'd need someone who's dealt with this pattern before and can see it for what it is. It requires reorienting a child to their authentic self and helping her reattach to the nurturing, non-narcissistic parent. The child has to be re-taught how to bond with that parent."

Grief quaked my shoulders. I struggled to quell it and to take hold of myself. Finally, I rasped, "I don't see how that will happen."

She shrugged. "Stay open to a shift but don't count on it. Your daughters will have to go into the belly of the whale to heal this, and it doesn't sound as if they want to do that. So take care of yourself. Don't allow them to be cruel to you."

"You know a lot about psychology for an artist." I almost couldn't take in everything Chloe had said. I wanted to change the subject.

"I wasn't always an artist. I had another life before this."

I grinned with half my mouth.

"Chloe, you've been painting a long time. I see the mastery in your technique, in your brushwork. They reveal decades of experience."

She nodded. "I've painted since I was a young girl. I studied painting in Venice. But once upon a time, I had a husband and a son and I was a psychologist in private practice."

"I didn't know that," I said in a wondering tone. I looked at the beautiful landscapes hanging on her walls.

*Shouldn't I have known?*

There was an intense emotional atmosphere in her work. She depicted not just trees and ponds and hills and flowers, but their individual psyches —and yes, looking at Chloe Kennedy's paintings the viewer believed that each tree and every stone had its own personal story.

"What happened to your family?"

"They died in a fire. I got out, they didn't."

My heart opened for her and I stared at her, wondering how she had survived such a loss. "I'm sorry."

"Me too." She poured more tea for herself.

"Chloe, how did you survive that?" I had to know.

"Who says I did?" she asked with a small smile.

"I do. You've made a lovely home for yourself, you've accomplished a great deal in your painting and achieved a rare mastery in your art. You have wonderful friends. You have a life. You've survived."

"Saint Teresa of Avila said, 'When we accept what happens to us and make the best of it, we are praising God.' I came to understand that eventually. Maybe five years after I lost everything. At first, I couldn't do anything. I was frozen. And then I started to paint, and I realized that to be human is to be vulnerable. Everything had fallen to pieces so I stayed with the pieces. Until I was ready to start picking up the pieces, one by one."

I didn't know what to say that wouldn't be shallow, so I stayed silent with my heart open.

Chloe said, "The paintings ... they're me picking up the pieces, one at a time, in my own way."

———～———

In the end, she allowed me to take eight paintings, which I promptly swathed in bubble wrap before she could change her mind.

"More paintings would be better," I told her while ripping and affixing masking tape.

"Some of the new ones I still need around me," she said, twisting her fingers in front of her chest.

"Chloe, I'm giving you a show. In December," I decided

spontaneously.

*I'll have to bump Andrew Xaffey to January. He'll bitch and moan but I want Chloe's paintings to get the holiday sales blitz.*

"Let's say your show will open December 5?"

"Do I have to come to the opening?" she asked, doubtfully.

"Yes. The gallery will send you a plane ticket and put you up in a hotel."

"I have friends I can stay with but you know I don't fly. We've discussed that in the past."

"How about a train ticket? Or what if I can hire someone to drive you cross-country? Will you come then?"

"Maybe," she said while shaking her head. "Who could you get to drive me?"

"My assistant Rosa is an actress with a ton of actor friends who always need money. I can find someone."

"I don't know."

"Chloe, come on. You need to be at your opening. It'll be fun. You'll enjoy yourself."

"I'll think about it," Chloe muttered. She helped me wrap her paintings and load the car.

When I pulled out of her driveway, she stood on her porch and waved.

# CHAPTER TWENTY-EIGHT

SCOTT ROLLED OFF OF me and picked up the PDF he had been reading from the nightstand. He hadn't even taken his glasses off for our tryst.

I stood up from his bed and pulled on my skirt.

"That was twelve seconds of bliss."

"Excuse me?" Scott mumbled without removing his eyes from his reading material.

I slipped on my bra and hooked it and then turned it around on my torso to face the correct way. "Twelve. Seconds. Of. Bliss."

That got his attention. He turned quizzical dark eyes toward me. "You had a good time."

"I always have a good time. It's something I promised myself after my last marriage ended."

"You could have done more."

"I did *everything*!" I said, a bit exasperated. "You showed up with a boner."

"I have a lot on my mind. I'm looking over the data from my trial because it's going to be reviewed. This is important. Does it have to be earth-shattering between us every time?" he snapped.

"Of course not," I snapped back.

I pulled my shirt over my head. "But it doesn't have to be perfunctory."

I walked into his living room and found my jacket lying neatly over the arm of his sofa. I slipped it on, even though the September evening was bright and warm. My skirt zipper wasn't lying straight—side zippers are a form of purgatory on Earth—so I unzipped it, twisted the skirt around and then re-zipped.

"It wasn't perfunctory," Scott stated. He stepped into his jeans.

"Look, Scott." I went to him and cupped his face with both hands.

I sighed.

"Sweetie, you didn't even take off your glasses. If, by some impossible chance, we're still together in fifteen years, then that might be acceptable. But we've been doing this for about five months. I just don't think it should be so complaisant after five months."

"It's almost six months, and why wouldn't we be together in fifteen years?" He followed me to his front door.

"Why would we be?"

I opened his door and then turned and faced him.

"Your patients and your work come first. That's fine; it's your life. But I want so much more than that. I didn't end two marriages to be last on some man's list of priorities."

I shrugged.

"I want attention and appreciation and lots of affection. Quality affection that lasts longer than twelve seconds. You need to find a woman who can accept the way you want to live. I'm not that woman. I guess that's why we haven't moved past the booty call stage."

I moved out into the hallway and pressed the elevator button but Scott came fast on my heels. He grabbed my arm.

"Don't go. Let's do it again. I can do better. I *will* do better. You're right; I was distracted. It wasn't my best work."

"Damn it, Scott, it had better never be work or why do it at all?"

I stretched up on my toes and kissed his mouth.

"Not tonight. I've got a million things to do before the gallery talk."

The elevator arrived, I stepped in, and waved goodbye.

He stood there in his jeans, barefoot, shirtless. Tall, toned, a shadow on his jaw line, totally gorgeous. His dark hair was perfectly combed.

*That's on me; maybe it wasn't my best work, either.*

For a moment I wished I could stay and give him his do-over, but I really did have a plethora of details to resolve before the gallery talk.

I decided to walk home. It was only eleven blocks and the evening was a superb example of September in New York City—clear with a refreshing breeze. People were walking with a bounce in their step and a lilt to their voice as the new social season and school year commenced. September in New York wields some vivacity.

My phone rang; the ring tone played the Brandenburg Concerto.

"Carl."

"Hey, beautiful," he said, his throaty voice happy. "This is a booty call."

*Not tonight. No way. No matter how lackadaisical it was with Scott.*

I had made an ironclad rule for myself that I wouldn't sleep with both men on the same day—my psyche just couldn't handle that.

"Oh, Carl, tonight won't work. I've got a ton of work to do in preparation for the gallery talk and I'm headed home to do more. Rain check?"

"Of course," he said. "How about dinner after the talk? I checked with Trudi and she's feeling some improvement. She and Robert could join us."

*Would you please stop acting as a go-between between my best friend and me?*

But it wasn't fair of me to be annoyed. Carl genuinely liked Trudi and wished the best for her and Trudi liked him. She took comfort in his experience with pancreatic cancer, even if his wife's outcome had been sad. I pushed away my annoyed self and reached for gratitude.

"That would be lovely. But it may run late for me. I'll be talking to clients and so forth."

"Understood. I was thinking of a quiet place in Tribeca. We can get a private room; that might make Trudi feel more comfortable about her appearance. I can tell she's having a hard time with it."

"She's usually well put together in nice pant suits, with her hair done just so and good jewelry," I murmured. "You're right, this is probably hard on her."

I shouldn't have needed Carl to remind me of that. Between Alex's shuttling between my apartment and her dad's, the impending gallery talks, the need to make some sales, and my juggling of Scott and Carl, I had not been the most observant friend in the whole world.

In fact, I was remiss.

I mentally kicked myself about a dozen times.

*I'll take Trudi out for lunch tomorrow; sit with her and really listen, even if she's throwing up.*

There was a lot of that lately, despite the anti-nausea medication she took.

"I wish she was getting better results from the trial. She's hanging in there, but I would have liked to hear more positive news," Carl said quietly.

"I thought she was getting good results. She told me she was on the road to recovery."

"That's a stretch. Her results aren't nearly as good as we'd hoped," Carl said. "I'd heard that this trial yields markedly mixed results. I may make more inquiries. You know I endowed a chair for research into pancreatic cancer at Columbia-Presbyterian."

"I did not know that, Carl," I said, surprised.

"The Nancy L. Hopkins Professorship of Pancreatic Cancer Research. Pancreatic cancer research is woefully underfunded by the NIH. Trudi and I discussed it; I thought she'd tell you. Maybe we should move her to a doctor at Columbia. She'll receive special consideration if I make the call."

"I think that has to be Trudi's decision, don't you? She's a grown up and quite expert at research. Besides, I think she's getting special consideration."

"I heard good things about her doctor," Carl admitted. "She's just not coming along."

———

The next day I brought Thai take-out to Trudi's place for lunch. She usually enjoyed pad thai but barely touched it.

"Come on, Trudi," I cajoled. "You have to eat more than that. Is your appetite completely gone?"

"Last night we ordered in shrimp scampi and I ate the whole dish. I can still taste the garlic. It's coming right back up on my tongue." Trudi used a single chopstick to swirl the rice noodles into a nest.

"When is your next treatment? And how is your CA 19-9? Is it still elevated?"

"Next Monday and just fine."

She looked up at me with a cheery smile that was meant to distract me from how pasty her complexion was and how gaunt her frame had grown. She ran her hand over her scalp, which she'd finally shaved bare. Her hand shook with a slight tremor.

"How are the preparations for the gallery talk?"

"Fine, good." I took a deep breath. "Carl said your results aren't as good as we'd hoped."

"Oh, pish," she snorted. "He worries like an old woman. He gossips like one, too. My results are modest but definite."

"Modest but definite in what way?" I challenged her. "I want specifics."

"My CA 19-9 marker is slightly elevated, but we think that's because of inflammation of the pancreas not related to the cancer."

"How elevated is slightly elevated? Is it over a thousand?" It had been four hundred when she began Scott's trial. Why was it coming back up? My heart plummeted into my stomach and I decided I'd collar Scott for a discussion.

*He'll talk to me, his medical ethics be damned.*

"What's the number?"

She shook her head. "I'll call my doorman to escort you from my apartment if you keep this up. What's your head count for the talk?"

"Thirty-five for sure, but we could get a hundred," I murmured. I perused her face with its scholarly aspect, so familiar even when distorted with cancer and chemotherapy. She had become very dear to me over the last twenty-six years; she was part of my family. It was unthinkable that she might not be around for the next twenty-six.

My voice softened.

"Trudi, I know you don't want to upset me, but I'm your friend and I love you. I'm worried about you. I feel like you're not being honest with me." I meant to keep going but Trudi cut me off.

"You haven't been honest with me about Dr. Bauer, now, have you?" she asked tartly.

I looked away. I didn't mean to, but somehow my hands put down my chopsticks.

"Hmm," she said.

"We've been sleeping together. Casually."

Trudi snorted.

"Since when is sex casual for you? You marry everyone you sleep with."

"That's a bad habit that I'm breaking. It will save me a fortune in legal fees when it's time to get a divorce."

"Did that happen before or after he became my doctor?" She tilted her head. "Before, I presume, because I vaguely remember some questions about dating younger men, and then he almost fell over when you walked in with me the first time."

I flushed.

"We had a, uh, fling before your first office visit. We met at a candy store and I offered him some chocolate. One thing led to another."

"A fling? And you didn't tell me?" She looked intrigued. "You've broken the best friend code. After all the times I commiserated when you complained about bad sex with Clif. From now on, if you have a fling, whether or not a candy store is involved, I expect the postmortem immediately. With full details." Then she giggled. "Postmortem, and I'm six months post-diagnosis of stage three pancreatic cancer, so I'm probably facing imminent death. That's funny."

"That's not funny, that's your sick British humor talking. Besides, didn't you just say that you had definite results?"

She looked away.

After a moment, she asked slyly, "How is my good-looking oncologist between the sheets?"

"Pretty awesome, usually," I admitted.

"What's the 'usually'?"

I sighed.

"It means he's better at work than at relationships."

"Remarked the pot to the kettle," Trudi murmured.

I flinched.

"Fair enough; I am twice divorced. But in my defense, I will say that I choose badly when it comes to men so I pour myself into my gallery to compensate for my feelings of inadequacy. It's different with Scott. He just doesn't get it that relationships require work."

Trudi snorted again.

"You, feelings of inadequacy?"

"Yes," I exclaimed.

How could my best friend think I was immune to feelings of inadequacy? I enjoyed a moment of self-righteous indignation even though I do, as a rule, consider self-righteous indignation to be a masturbatory pleasure, best enjoyed privately.

Then I confided, "I feel bad about myself because of the failed marriages. Amongst many other things."

"Oh, please. You're someone who thinks she has feelings of inferiority but doesn't really." Trudi wrinkled her forehead at me. "So is Scottie the hottie a top or a bottom?"

"That's as many details as you're getting," I said crisply. "A top."

"Is 'I am not a narcissist' tattooed on his chest? Because I know that

Carl is anything but a narcissist. He's one of the most thoughtful, generous men I've ever met."

"Scott's lovely. Just young and preoccupied with work. Also, he has two little kids and, Trudi, I just don't know if I want to go there again. I don't know if I can."

"So where does that leave Carl? He hasn't said anything but I know you slept over in Sag Harbor and sometimes you do in the city. Is he a good shag? I should think he would be."

"Carl knows what he's doing, for sure. Let's just say he's an expert in that department."

"He's expert in many departments," said Trudi. "He's also kind. He'll be as good to you as you'll let him. Can you say that about Scott?"

"I'm not saying much about either man," I said firmly. "I'm keeping it casual with both of them. There's too much going on in my life to get serious with anyone right now. No commitments and they both know that. I'm not misleading anyone into thinking it's mutually exclusive."

We sat quietly together for a few beats, and that was one of the sweetest things about friendship with Trudi: she knew how to sit quietly and receptively so you could just breathe and feel yourself and her at the same time. She understood about stillness.

After a while, she said, "From the celibate spell with Clif to frolicking with two men. That's one way to balance things."

"I don't frolic with them on the same day," I said, making a wry face. "I guess it never rains but it pours."

"Nick used to say things like that to me. I've been thinking about him lately."

Trudi's face softened with the memory of her brother.

"For the longest time, I couldn't remember his voice nor the fine details of his face; it's like he'd become an impressionist painting. A bad one, where everything is saccharine and cloying and hazy and without any purpose other than the fuzziness itself, what Renoir was sometimes accused of even by people who should know better. But lately, Nick's come back into focus. The lines of his jaw and his nose and his cheeks are sharply delineated, photorealistic. His blond eyebrows. His voice in its full timbre is in my ear."

I asked, "What is your CA 19-9 marker, exactly?"

"I feel better than I did, I'm coming along," she insisted.

I didn't believe her. I wanted to call her on it but could I, if that's what she wanted to believe, and if it made her happier to do so?

————~————

I returned to the gallery to put the last touches on the final announcements for the gallery talk: social media alerts and reminders, a blog post for the gallery site, a YouTube video that Rosa and I made in iMovie with video footage of my gallery that I recorded on my iPhone. Rosa emailed reminders and a fresh round of invitations. And just when I despaired of receiving the shipment of Abbate's paintings from Italy, they showed up at the front door. I decided not to hang them until after the first talk but to instead reveal them from under a sheet—a dramatic flourish to whet potential collectors' appetite. There were only two more days until the event.

My cell phone rang; it was Alex.

"You're home from school?"

"Just got in."

"Did you come directly home?" That was our agreement. Had she adhered to it?

"Yes, Mom, I came directly home! Would you listen to me? I think something's wrong with Groucho. He's lying on the kitchen floor and kind of moaning. He had diarrhea all over the kitchen. I tried to get him to stand up so I could clean the floor, but I can't get him to. He can't get up."

*Alex tried to clean up?*

It was still a shock that she could be considerate that way; I was cautiously hopeful that she was finally turning things around. It was only mid-September but as far as I knew, she hadn't skipped a single class at school.

Yet.

"Hang tight. I'm coming home. Call the vet on 79th Street and say it's an emergency and we'll be bringing Groucho in as soon as I get home."

I hung up and turned to Rosa.

"Your dog?" she asked, her blue eyes clouding.

I nodded.

"I'm sorry, I've got to go deal with this."

Rosa said, "I've got everything in hand. Go."

————~————

Alex knelt beside Groucho, stroking his head. She had done her best to wipe up around him but there was still a gooey slick of wet diarrhea alongside his body. He lay flat out on his side and bleated.

"Poor guy," I crooned, stroking him.

"Is he going to be all right, Mom?"

"I don't know." I looked around, wondering how we were going to transport him to the vet. I jumped up and ran to the linen closet and yanked out a big sheet. I figured we'd roll him onto it and each of us would hold an end while we carried him the few blocks to the vet's office. But the process required two sheets, one to wrap around Groucho and another for carrying him. In the process of maneuvering him, Alex and I both got splattered with muck. Alex didn't say a word of complaint.

Ordinarily, Groucho weighed about sixty-five pounds; I realized now that he'd lost weight and was down to fifty-some pounds, which was still heavy enough to make moving him laborious.

*Why hadn't I noticed that Groucho was losing weight? Scott asked me when he'd been to the vet. I'm the world's worst pet owner.*

But beating up on myself would have to wait until later. Besides, I hadn't seen him eat less. He still scoured his bowl clean and asked for more twice a day.

Moving carefully, Alex and I got him out the door and into the elevator, while Groucho kept bleating. Luckily, it was a gorgeous day, sunny and warm. We made slow headway, carrying him over to Broadway and then down to 79th Street. Hardened New Yorkers saw the sick dog and stopped to offer words of encouragement. A teenage girl, two young guys, a take-out delivery guy on a bicycle, and an older, Orthodox Jewish man with a cane all offered to help us carry him. A mom with a baby offered to take the little girl into her arms and let us use her stroller to push Groucho.

"We've got it," Alex said every time. "Thank you."

To the concerned mom, I added, "You're very kind. But we don't want to slime up your stroller."

By that time, Groucho was vomiting, and he still had the runs.

We finally got him to the veterinary office and a lady with a cat in a carrier held the door open for us. The assistant glanced at Groucho and immediately ushered us into an exam room in the back. I felt bad placing him on the metal table, both because it would be cold for Groucho and because he was going to leave filth all over it.

Dr. Lee, a young Asian woman who had studied veterinary medicine in Italy and who gave every impression of being devoted to animals heart, body, and soul, came running. In better times, she and I had enjoyed rapturous conversations about the food in Bologna. Now she patted and murmured to Groucho without seeming to care about how dirty he was. Then she washed her hands and pulled on latex gloves and somehow, in that moment, I knew the prognosis wasn't good.

Groucho had kidney disease.

Dr. Lee wanted to keep him overnight on an IV. We would be able to take him home with medication and prescription dog food the next day.

She said, "Chronic renal failure is progressive and irreversible. Given his age and the severity of his renal failure, we're going to give him medication to alleviate his symptoms and to make him more comfortable. He should have fresh water available at all times. I'd like to see him at least once a week to monitor him."

"How long does he have?" I asked, my throat dry and sore.

We were standing in the exam room without Groucho, who had been taken to the back by the vet tech.

Dr. Lee shrugged. "Maybe a few months, at most."

"Oh no," Alex exclaimed. "He's going to die?"

Pale tears spilled down her face in a straight line. Groucho had come into our family when she was still a baby, one year old, and just barely walking. She'd grown up with him. When she was four, she'd insisted that he was her brother and her pre-school drawings reflected that. She still let him sleep on her bed when she was home.

I put my arm around Alex's shoulders, knowing I wouldn't be able to comfort her because I was crying, too.

"I'm sorry," Dr. Lee said. "I'm surprised his appetite has been so little affected. There'll probably be a time when he doesn't want to eat and you can't get his pills down. You may have the feeling that his quality of life has irretrievably deteriorated, that he is suffering. That will be the time to consider euthanasia."

"Oh my god, how am I supposed to make that decision?" I cried, as Alex wailed. "How will I know when the time is right?"

Dr. Lee wasn't more than thirty years old and she had to visibly steel herself against our grief.

"For one, he has to be ready. We know there's no way to cure him and we don't want to see him suffering endlessly. Two, you have to be ready to let go. But be reasonable. You don't want Groucho to suffer for weeks or months because you're not ready."

I looked at her and just shook my head.

"Follow your heart," she said. She sighed and blotted her eyes. "You'll know in your heart."

# CHAPTER TWENTY-NINE

THE FIRST GALLERY TALK went off without a hitch and was immensely enjoyed by everyone in attendance; the wine and cheese and the witty, erudite words of the magazine editor were completely consumed. After the talk, the guests mingled in good convivial spirit, gushing about Alessio Abbate's talent; we ran out of price lists, business cards and postcards for the upcoming shows, including Chloe's.

I sold not a single painting.

Everyone had something else more important to pay for that precluded buying art. The richest ones were fretting about market volatility. I'm no economist, but I'd come to believe in the trickle down theory only because, as the proprietor of a small gallery, I'd seen it in action. It goes like this: when the super wealthy—the two percent—felt confident about the market and their money, they bought art. When they bought art I paid my rent and utility and internet bills. I also paid the artist, the shipping company, the grocer from whom I obtained the hors d'oeuvres, the liquor store where I bought cheap but passable wine to entertain my customers, and I paid the salaries of my assistant and myself. The artist bought art supplies; sculptors who used clay as a medium paid a foundry to cast their works in bronze. Rosa bought acting lessons. I paid for my daughters, the vet, and my younger boyfriend's daughter's silence. Money trickled down and flowed in ever-widening circles. I'd seen it in action.

It is not a theory, mind you—I'd experienced it first hand. Economists who leaned toward the right patted me on the shoulder and smarmily congratulated themselves for their perspicacity in delineating complex economic structures. Left-leaning economists told me I was wrong, that I didn't experience that and they knew why. Then because they were the Left and, in the way of the great pendulum at the heart of public discourse, the Left was the new thought police and repository of all truth and goodness—like the McCarthyists and the Holy Roman Inquisition before them—they insisted that believing in trickle-down economics meant I was a *bad person who needed re-education*. That's why I eschewed both sides and kept my eyes firmly fixed on the prize: operating a thriving gallery of beautiful art.

However, nothing was trickling down after the first gallery talk. I was holding a second talk in three weeks led by Clif, with commentary from a sympathetic art critic. Clif was going to talk about the burgeoning atelier network that was teaching realism and the figure to eager young artists. They couldn't find that information in the college and university system, which was too often institutionally focused on abstract expressionism and digital manipulation. That was a shame and shortsighted on the colleges' part, because art-crazy kids really did want to learn how to draw like a Renaissance master. The first set of announcements for Clif's talk specifically invited young artists, not because they had the money to buy the works for sale in the Paige Realist Gallery, but because Clif had tens of thousands of these kids from all over the world following him on social media, and they had relatives and friends with that kind of money and an interest in spreading it around.

Hopefully.

I was pondering the urgency of the need to make a big sale as I walked home a few days later. It was a gorgeous balmy day and Rosa was working until closing time, so I left the gallery just after five o'clock and walked in a smooth, fast gait up the bike path along the Hudson River beside the West Side Highway. It felt so good to get the exercise that I promised myself I'd take myself to the Gunks over the weekend.

*But only if Alex can stay with Groucho.*

We were trying to be with him as much as possible. I'd hired Mrs. Zlotowitz, an elderly lady in my building, to come into my apartment and check on him twice a day while I was at work and Alex was at school. She had my cell number and the number of the gallery and strict instructions to reach me ASAP if Groucho took a turn for the worse.

I emerged from Riverside Park at 72nd Street, remembering that I needed a few items from the Fairway market. I walked past a newish Italian restaurant and glimpsed Alex's long hair as her tall form entered through the door. She didn't see me. I paused and remembered that she was meeting her father and his family for dinner.

I spun around and looked in the window, spying a big group of Calhouns congregating around some tables. Rather, two groups. One group consisted of the younger generation of cousins, and my heart sank because in their midst stood Alex's first cousin Harrison. He was an artist of sorts, whose mediocre talent didn't keep him from daubing ghastly neo-Warholian canvases in fulfillment of George's older brother's unlived-out counter-culture fantasies. Harrison was also the one who brought drugs to the family gatherings.

The cousins, including Alex, laughed and jostled each other as their circle tightened around Harrison. I hoped Alex wouldn't be tempted by Harrison's pot—or whatever his trust fund allowed him to provide for the shindig—but that she would stay clean. Crossed my fingers and toes and prayed that she'd know better after everything she'd been through so she wouldn't slide once again down that slippery slope.

The other group included the usual suspects: George, Katherine, his brothers and their wives, his parents, his uncles, his aunts, a few cousins. They were a jolly crew, greeting each other with handshakes and hugs. They were, in fact, an iconic American family with roots all the way back to the Mayflower. George was one of five brothers; all were successful. Three of them, including George, were attorneys, all of whom had clerked with federal judges. The fourth brother was an investment banker; the fifth, George's little brother Jed, ran the family's charitable foundation.

I didn't miss a single one of them. I remembered the first time I met one of George's sisters-in-law, and she looked down her nose at me and said, "George will never marry someone of your class. He's just playing around with you."

That was the high point of that relationship. It wasn't much better with any of the other Calhouns. George's mother didn't even look me in the eyes for the first two years that I dated him. George didn't care because his real allegiance was always to them, not to me, and that never changed. I didn't know if I'd ever totally shaken off the sting of that.

To be fair, his mother had made a valiant effort to connect with lower-class me when I produced grandchildren. Truthfully, I didn't dislike her or even the snotty sister-in-law. I didn't dislike any of them. I just didn't like them. It was different with George's grandparents. I loved them. All four of them, and they were all very different people. Too bad they were no longer alive because they would have been good role models for my daughters. They were always generous and respectful to me, especially when my parents died. Even with their wealth, they were humble people without airs or pretensions, for whom privilege meant service, not the entitlement that Alex's generation insisted on. George's grandparents embodied good old Yankee Calvinist values of modesty, hard work, thrift, deferred gratification, obligation to their community and, indeed, obligation to something larger than themselves. They talked about what they could give, what their responsibilities were, and how they could contribute.

I wondered what they would think if they could see the dissolution and lack of a moral center in their line.

With the desire to be my better self came the belated desire, however weak, not to judge those people who were my daughters' relatives. After all, the Calhouns were generous to a fault. They donated to all the best social and educational causes, and their branch of the family had moved North after the War of 1812, so they were on the correct side of the Civil War. They were not the slave-owning Calhouns, as I'd heard many times over the Easter ham. They were the Calhouns who had participated in the underground railroad and helped slaves escape.

Dani wasn't amongst them; perhaps she was coming, but with the semester in full tilt at Princeton, I doubted it. She'd be studying and playing tennis. I hoped she was winning because it made her so happy to do so.

It would only make Alex uncomfortable if she spied me outside on the sidewalk, looking in. And I certainly didn't want to deal with any negative energy wafting out toward me from George or his hateful wife. I hurried onward.

———⌣———

It was my week, but Alex spent the night at her dad's apartment. I hoped that wasn't because she was stoned and didn't want to face me. But she was back the next day, Friday, after school as she was supposed to be. I couldn't tell if she was hiding anything from me or not. She was reading a book at the kitchen table and eating a bowl of cereal, Groucho sprawled out over her feet, when I came in from work at about five thirty. Rosa was covering the late shift again and I wanted to spend some time with Alex.

"Hi Sweetie," I said, ruffling her soft hair. A flower scent tinged the air, indicating that she'd showered and shampooed recently.

She grunted.

"How was school?"

"Good."

"What're you reading?" I asked, pouring myself a bowl of granola.

She mentioned a popular novel.

"Is that homework? Don't you have homework?"

She rolled her eyes. "Mom, stop."

"Alex, you know you have to be a model student this year, and that means doing your homework."

"Mom, I said, stop. I'll do my homework, Jesus, I'm just reading," she snarled. "Can't you ever leave me alone?"

I looked at her through narrowed eyes.

She pretended to ignore me.

The doorbell rang and I rose to answer it. "Are you expecting anyone?"

"No," she said, through a mouthful of cereal and milk.

I went to the door. "Hello?"

"It's me," said Scott.

My heart lifted. Unexpectedly buoyant, I threw open the door, glad to see Scott. I grabbed him, kissed him swiftly and let go just as quickly. "How do you always get up here without me buzzing you in?"

"Someone always lets me in. It must be my good karma." He thrust a paper shopping bag at me. "This is for you."

Alex came in from the kitchen and stood behind me with her arms folded over her chest. "Who's that?"

"Alex, this is Scott Bauer. Scott, this is my daughter, Alexandra Calhoun," I introduced them with a wave.

"Good to meet you, Alex," Scott said, urbanely. He reached out his hand and shook hers.

"I've seen you before," she replied, withdrawing her hand. Her voice was suspicious, but I was pleased that she shook Scott's hand and looked him in the eyes when she did so. I wanted her to have good manners and graceful social deportment. I cared if Alex presented herself well. It mattered in the world.

"Since you were somewhat altered at the time, the less said about that the better," Scott said in the same authoritative, no-nonsense voice I'd heard him use in his office with Trudi when she was being recalcitrant.

"Oh, yeah," Alex murmured, unembarrassed. "What's your deal? Are you dating my mom?"

"Yes," Scott assented.

"No," I murmured, peeking into the bag. Something yellow and hairy … a stuffed animal? I reached in and poked it. A blonde wig! I whooped with laughter and quickly closed the bag. I looked up and met Scott's gaze, still laughing. His dark eyes effervesced back. I noticed then what he was wearing: a black T-shirt under a sports coat that rather resembled Tom Cruise's jacket in *Risky Business*.

"You like?" Scott asked, quirking one eyebrow

"Yes, oh yes, very much," I said. "But, um, not today?" I tilted my head toward Alex.

"Ugh, disgusting," Alex muttered, with a sneer. She stood there eying us with nearly complete repugnance, the virulent kind that only a teenager can muster and that she reserved for people over the age of thirty doing the kinds of things she believed were the sole province of people under the age of thirty.

Scott eyed her back impassively.

"Ah, would you like to come in, Scott?" I asked awkwardly, hoping to break into their staring contest. "We were just having dinner."

"Take out?" Scott asked. "I know you don't cook."

"Mom cooked once," Alex interjected. "Believe me, you don't ever want her to do that again."

"She cooked for me once. It was an unmitigated disaster that will never be repeated," Scott told her.

They both looked at me.

"Granola," I said gaily. "Or we could order in."

"How about I take you both out for dinner?" Scott offered.

Alex brightened before she could restrain herself with her usual irritated ennui. "What about Groucho?"

I said, "I'll call Mrs. Zlotowitz."

"Fine." She stomped off.

"Is that what I have to look forward to?" Scott asked, as he put his arms around me and pulled me into him. "Yikes."

"I don't think it'll be quite as bad for you, but it might be," I said, in a low voice. "Wow, I love, um, what you're wearing and what's in the bag! Wow!"

"I have the music on my iPad. When can we play it?" he asked, breathing in my ear before kissing my neck. "I left work early today, hoping to spend some time with you."

"Soon," I promised.

"You guys, ugh," Alex said, marching past us. She threw open the door. "Are we going out or what?"

———∽———

We arrived at the trattoria and sat one table over from where we sat on his birthday. Scott glanced over his menu at me and said wryly, "I hear the salmon is good here. They don't bake it into a charcoal briquette."

I grinned ruefully and covered my face with my menu.

Alex, with her keen instinct for needling me, saw the exchange and pounced. "Uh oh, what'd you do this time, Mom?" It was the sneering voice her father employed when talking to or about me.

I winced and started to speak, but Scott spoke first. In a quiet, firm tone, he said, "Nothing she wasn't entitled to do, and shouldn't you speak to your mother more politely?"

She flushed and sat straighter in her chair and studied her menu as if it were a novel that she was reading for fun.

I thought she'd never before heard anyone defend me. There was a first time for everything.

The waiter came and took our orders. Scott turned to Alex. "How's school going, Alex?"

"OK, I guess," she said, with a demoralized half shrug.

From behind his glasses, Scott's dark eyes perused her. "You're not happy?"

Alex made a face. "It's OK. Everyone's weird because I got kicked out last year. They look at me funny and say things when they think I can't hear them."

"It's early in the academic year," Scott said. "People have short memories. If you keep your head down, they'll forget and move on to the next thing."

I looked at Scott in surprise, not having expected such wisdom from him. I realized I was witnessing a remarkable conversation. Alex was being forthcoming, not defensive.

"Move on?" Alex's whole person lit up with hope. "You think so? I'm so tired of being the dumbass freak who got herself kicked out!"

Scott was nodding. "Head down. Work hard. Contain yourself and it will pass."

"Huh," she said, staring at him as if she wanted to believe him but wasn't sure she could.

"You might get a nickname or get teased," Scott continued. "Laugh it off. Don't respond. They'll get bored with trying to yank your chain."

Alex softened and scrunched down in her chair. She suddenly looked woebegone and younger than her sixteen years. "That's the problem, I guess. I'm not good at laughing it off. They come at me and I want to come back at them. I have to."

"You have some fire in your belly," Scott said and his tone expressed approval. "That's good in the long run. You just have to control it and not let it control you."

"I guess," Alex said. "But I just don't know if I can."

# CHAPTER THIRTY

I CALLED TWO OF my best collectors," Clif said. It was a breezy October day and he sat in my office on the edge of my desk. A week ago, we had signed the papers that ended our marriage and inaugurated our friendship. We were always good at working together but now there was a new ease between us and I was glad for it.

"Are they coming by the gallery to see your work?"

Clif shifted around.

"They both want to come to my studio and buy directly from me."

"I see," I said, softly.

Clif put his hand on my shoulder.

"Sarah, no. I won't do that. I won't exclude you from any sales. They both want a bargain but I won't give it. I'll charge the gallery price and give you your cut."

I sighed and rubbed my eyes. Things were getting bad enough that I had to make some hard decisions. Like making Rosa a part-time employee, or perhaps taking her off the payroll altogether and paying her in cash when I needed her. I was at that point.

"Clif, if you make a sale out of your studio, what am I going to say? Am I going to demand a piece of it?"

"What about Carl? Won't he buy more pieces?"

I leaned my head back onto my chair.

"Yes, he would. I just don't want to go there. I just can't. It'll make things weird for me. I don't want to feel obligated to him."

"So give him a really good deal," Clif suggested. "He loves the nymphs. He has more than one place, he told me about a beach house in the Hamptons. Have him buy a painting for the beach house."

I shook my head and rose and paced around the small office.

"Clif, no. I just can't. It'll put me in a compromised position. End of story."

Clif shrugged. "The gallery will be packed for my talk. I've had over a hundred RSVP's. Maybe some of the guests will be customers."

"Yeah, Rosa says we'll be full to the brim. That's encouraging. But they're mostly kids. Art students. Art students can't even feed themselves, let alone buy art."

"Nicole's inviting some of her friends. They have the means to buy art."

"Good for Nicole," I said crisply. "Tell her I'll cut her in for ten percent of any sales that come out of her friends."

"I don't think she's in it for the money," Clif murmured, avoiding my gaze.

The front door jangled open and someone walked through. I motioned that I'd be right back.

"Sarah Paige, this a fine show you've got up," boomed a hearty voice. It was James Harte, patron of the arts and chairman of the executive committee of the New Britain Art Museum.

"Jim Harte, good to see you," I exclaimed, delighted. I went over and hugged him.

Jim was a towering, robust African-American man with an impeccable taste in art. He'd started his career at Howard, double majoring in art history and business, and then he obtained a J.D. from Columbia. He worked for a law firm for a while and then went on to run an insurance conglomerate. He retired in his fifties with more money than God and the seemingly unquenchable desire to do good in the world, which included funding and overseeing various arts institutions. He seemed equally delighted to see me and squeezed me hard.

"How's it going, Sarah? I hear you and Clif have split up but it's all amicable?"

"It is friendly and he's in the office now. He's been helping me strategize some things for the gallery. We're a much better team now that we're not married. How's Alfie, as wonderful as ever?"

"You know Alfie, she keeps busy saving the world. She's also trying to save me from my high blood pressure. She's got me doing yoga with her, do you believe? Can you see big ole me in downward facing dog?" A giant smile wreathed his face and he shook his head.

"Can only help, yoga's good for everything," I said, laughing. Jim was often funny in a charming, self-deprecating way.

He patted my arm. "So how's business here?"

"Why, what have you heard?" I asked, trying to keep my voice restrained.

He raised his eyebrows. "I heard that you didn't go to Art Basel."

I eyed him. "You've heard more than that, Jim."

"I heard that your last show didn't sell out. Also, you're two months behind on your rent, and four months means your lease is compromised."

"Damn, you have good sources." I rubbed my chin.

*Are the vultures circling already?*

My gallery was completely dependent on the unbelievably fortuitous fifteen-year lease I'd signed with the owner, who was a childhood friend of my mom's. He still felt tenderly toward her and so the lease gave me the space for about twenty-five percent of what it was really worth. As long as I kept current on my rent, the monthly nut stayed low and I could renew at an advantageous rate.

*But I'm not current…*

I said, "Every business goes through tough spots."

"Indeed," Jim said. He strolled around the gallery with me at his heels. He paused in front of Chloe's last painting from the previous batch, not one of the new ones, which weren't out yet. "Chloe Kennedy, my God, Sarah, you have some eye. What a find!"

"Are you acquiring for New Britain?" I asked with a hopeful lilt. "I can give you a good deal!"

"I wish," he said. "We're deaccessioning, in fact." He turned his whole barrel-chest to look at me square on. "That's not why I'm here."

He was giving me an opening. Did I want to take it?

I said, "OK. I'll bite. Why are you here, Jim? I can't believe you want my gallery to sell the museum's paintings for you. You've got Sotheby's for that."

"We've got Sotheby's for that," he agreed. "I'm here because Mel is retiring in February. He and his husband want to tour the world."

"Wow, I hadn't heard that!" I said, astonished. Melvin Prentiss had run the New Britain Art Museum for the last twenty-five years, and he'd done a brilliant job of it. The museum had always been respected, but under his leadership it had grown into a dynamic and influential establishment. I couldn't believe he was retiring; I always thought he'd run the place until he keeled over from old age. Which he would probably do in front of some wildly popular new exhibition he'd masterminded, finagled, or otherwise maneuvered to get installed within his small but worthy Connecticut museum.

"No one knows; it's very hush-hush. I'm telling you first."

"Why are you telling me?" I asked. Then it struck me, the proverbial light bulb going on over my clueless head. "Jim, you can't be, you're not…?"

"I am indeed, Sarah. I'm offering you the position. I'd like to nominate you to the board and offer you very favorable terms," he said.

"Could anyone replace Mel Prentiss?" I asked bemused.

Jim grinned and clapped my shoulder.

"No, and that wouldn't be what's best for the museum. We need someone new to come in and take charge and come up with fresh ideas. Put her own original stamp on the place. Keep it evolving." He stood and pointed across the gallery at one of Alessio Abbate's paintings. "Someone who has the ingenuity to find and introduce worthy new artists."

"Will I be the only nominee?"

"There will be a few others. You've got longer odds," he admitted. "Email me your C.V., OK? And if you have a letter of reference from your stint at Sotheby's, attach that."

"The other candidates will be better qualified than I am." I shook my head. "You know I never finished my dissertation."

"I know everything," Jim said, lowering his voice theatrically. Then his affect got serious, and I got to see why he'd been so successful in the business world. It was a treat, albeit a scary one. He recited a bibliography comprised of my last several published articles, referred to several times I'd spoken publicly, listed a dozen recent sales, and finally named the three artists I was most proud of having discovered: painters Chloe Kennedy and Andrew Xaffey, and sculptor Rhonda Fadela. He mentioned the gallery talk around Abbate's work. He concluded with, "You were supposed to have an article in *American Artist* but it wasn't in the issue. Did it get bumped?"

"You do your homework," I said, nonplussed. I took a deep breath. A job offer was the last thing I expected. "I was late with the article but it'll come out next month."

"I look forward to it. I love your rants against postmodernism, they're highly entertaining and very well written," Jim said. "Tell me you'll consider the offer?"

"Hey, Jim," Clif called, as he emerged from my office. He smiled and stuck his hand out to shake Jim's.

"Clif Perini, good to see you," Jim bellowed. He pumped Clif's hand. "Your paintings got some good placements recently. Glad to hear it, you're a talented painter. One of the best."

"Sarah does a great job with my work," Clif said.

Knowing Jim was referring to Carl's purchase of the river nymphs, I asked, "Jim, where *do* you get your information?"

Jim winked at me. He asked Clif, "What are you working on these days?"

"An Orpheus and Eurydice piece, a study of the full spectrum of shadow and luminosity. Usually, I focus on a sliver of the available scale, a slice of the pie, but in this painting I want to explore the fullness of light and shadow, the whole reach of the ancient myth."

"Sounds ambitious," Jim noted.

"The artist must seek challenge, always. But I'm still in the early stages," Clif said. "You were asking Sarah if she'd consider something?"

"Attending a cocktail party. Alfie and I are hosting a party at the New Britain Art Museum," Jim said. He squeezed my arm slightly. "Why don't you come, too, Clif? Everyone says it's amicable between you two. Feel free to bring a date. You too, Sarah. I always wanted to meet Carl Hopkins. He's got quite the reputation on Wall Street."

I gave Jim a mock-glowering, highly skeptical look.

"Where do you get your intel? Do you have my gallery bugged?"

Jim laughed as he hugged me goodbye.

"Middle of November, the Friday before Thanksgiving," he said. "Tell me you'll be there. Both of you. Otherwise, Alfie will be very disappointed."

"Like I'm cruel enough to disappoint the saintly Alfie Harte?" I murmured. "Not I."

"I'll be there," Clif added.

"Great, consider yourselves RSVPed," Jim said. "More details to follow. Sarah, the board will be there, so wear something spiffy; Clif, you're an artist, you can wear whatever the hell you want." He bade us farewell and went out of the gallery, waving cheerfully.

"That was interesting," Clif said. "A cocktail party. Is he interested in my work, do you think?"

"The New Britain Art Museum should be interested in your work," I said quietly.

"I'd love to get a show there," Clif said.

Just then my cell phone rang its generic ring tone.

I answered, "Sarah Paige."

"Sarah, it's Mr. Villanova from Devon Town."

"Mr. Villanova," I said breathlessly.

He cut me off. "I realize that your dog's illness is truly very sad, but is that an excuse for Alex to miss school?"

"Ah, uh," I stuttered, taken aback.

"I accepted her back here on the condition that she demonstrate a vast improvement over her past behavior. And while she has completed many of her assignments, she hasn't completed them all. Now your allowing her to stay home to take care of a sick pet certainly doesn't support her in her academic career."

"Mr. Villanova—"

"Please consider this a last, final, friendly warning. Alexandra must be in class every day unless she is very sick and has a doctor's note. Her dog's renal failure doesn't serve as sufficient excuse for an absence." He hung up.

---

I went home to look for Alex. Instead, I found Mrs. Zlotowitz in her silky floral print dress kneeling on the floor beside Groucho, who was clearly in agony. The old lady looked up and struggled to rise to her feet. I rushed over to lend her an arm.

"I was going to call you. I'm sorry, Sarah, I don't think there's anything I can do," she said sadly, leaning into me.

I released her arm and sat beside Groucho. I peered into his cloudy eyes and stroked his head. I could feel a dreadful ebbing within him, an emptying out. He moaned and his ears shifted around. I glanced over at his dog bowl and noted that it was, indeed, still full.

*This is it.*

I took a firm hold of myself, making my voice as strong as I could. It still broke. "You can go, Mrs. Zlotowitz. I'll take care of him."

She hesitated for a moment, pursing her lips and trembling with empathy. Finally, she said, "I'm so sorry." She closed my front door quietly on her way out.

I kept stroking Groucho as I pulled my cell phone from my coat pocket. I tried to call Alex but got her voicemail. I said, "Call me. It's Groucho." I pulled Groucho onto my lap. The motion made him whimper. I called Scott, got his voicemail. I said, "It's an emergency. I know you're at work, but can you call me?"

Groucho's tongue lolled and I scratched behind his ears. I called the veterinary office.

"Hi, it's Sarah Paige."

"Oh, Mrs. Paige, how's Groucho?" asked the desk clerk.

"Not good," I said, aching. "This is it. He's in too much pain. I'm bringing him in."

She didn't say anything but clucked sympathetically.

I hung up and sat there, remembering Groucho as a fluffy puppy fresh from the Long Island shelter where George and I found him. Dani and Alex were little and we'd brought them out to the shelter with us. Groucho was one of three remaining pups in a litter of eight from a pregnant mutt that was abandoned on the very doorsteps of the shelter. There was something about the way he'd eyed us, one ear cocked, that drew us to him.

We rode back to the city with him lying across my lap so he wouldn't shed in George's pristine BMW. Groucho kept hopping up to peer over my shoulder into the back seat at Dani and Alex, which the girls thought was wonderful. I could still hear Alex, who was a toddler, laughing and clapping her hands. Dani at five was already heartbreakingly beautiful, precocious, and athletic; she'd chosen the name 'Groucho.'

The phone rang and the ringtone told me it was Scott.

"Hey," I said softly.

"Sarah, I'm at work," Scott's voice was brusque. "Is this a real emergency? I'm not talking about scratching your horny itch."

I kept silent for a moment.

"Screw you."

I hung up and pressed Carl's number.

He picked up immediately.

"Sarah? Is everything OK?"

"It's my dog," I said, in a hoarse voice. "I have to put him down."

Carl hesitated. Then he said, "I'll be there in about forty minutes. I have to finish something up but then I can come right over. Can you hang on until I get there?"

———~———

Carl was good for his word. Forty minutes later he walked into my apartment and found me crying on the floor, cradling Groucho in my lap. Turned out I didn't have to go through the horror of watching Dr. Lee stick a lethal injection into him because Groucho died a few minutes before Carl arrived. I wouldn't let Carl or Andrei handle the body. I carried it myself down to Carl's car. Carl asked if I wanted to take him to the vet or bury him out in Sag Harbor, and suddenly Sag Harbor seemed like the perfect place for Groucho to rest.

We drove out to Carl's house in Sag Harbor. I huddled into Carl with Groucho still in my lap. When we arrived at the house, Carl opened the door and I climbed out and stood with Groucho in my arms. Carl tilted his head at Andrei, who nodded once and trudged off toward the garage.

The afternoon sun cast long, slanting shadows. The glassy autumnal light combined with my heightened state of grief to open a window of vision in my mind, and I could see the ley lines glowing across the gently sloping land. They were a grid of juicy, electromagnetic ribbons that slipped across and through the ground all the way into the water. Some were thicker and more prominent, pulsing with a current that alluded to wind and water; others were narrow and delicate, fine etchings into the planet. There was a juncture of crossing lines that overlay a deep well—I could see the fresh light of liquid bubbling up at that point. I wondered if Carl knew about the water.

Carl put his arm around my shoulders. "What do you think about behind the lilac tree?" He pointed toward a big lilac tree situated near the house between some round red maples. I imagined Groucho sniffing the tree. When he was young, he would have gamboled across Carl's yard, enjoying the expanse of open space and the salty ocean scent in the air.

"It's perfect."

Andrei trudged back with a wooden-handled steel shovel in hand. Carl nodded toward the lilac tree and Andrei went to it. He paused with the round point of the shovel poised above a spot about a foot and a half from the bole. He had chosen, perhaps coincidentally but more probably with that innate sense with which humans feel energy, a place where two slender, coppery ley lines crossed.

I nodded.

Andrei dug a hole in the ground, piling the dirt beside it. Carl pressed me closer into his side. We watched Andrei dig. Finally Andrei stepped back.

I walked toward the hole, dropped to my knees awkwardly, and then placed Groucho into the earth. I patted his head. I'd had enough time with his empty body in my arms that I felt complete. I stood and stepped back.

Carl said, "Oh God, whose mercies cannot be numbered, accept our prayers on behalf of this beloved dog. Grant him entrance into the land of light and joy, in the fellowship of thy saints."

I stared across Carl's yard down toward his dock. I imagined Groucho bounding across a field of light and being greeted by my parents. It was not a vision, mind you, it was my heart's desire. My parents had loved dogs, my Dad especially. We had a terrier mutt named Topsy when I was growing up. Standing on Carl's property with Andrei throwing soil over Groucho, I realized that Topsy did not go to live on a farm when I was away on a teen tour after my freshman year of high school; he must have died. I wiped my sleeve across my face, drying it.

Carl said, "We pray for the dead because we still hold them in our love and because we trust that in God's presence those who have chosen to serve Him will grow in His love until they see Him as He is." Tears glistened on his lower eyelashes and I knew he was thinking about the wife he had loved and lost. I put my arm around him, feeling for him.

Carl asked, without looking at me, "Anything you'd like to add?"

I said, surprising myself, "Exalted and hallowed be God's great name in the world which God created according to plan. May God's majesty be revealed in the days of our lifetime. Blessed be God's great name to all eternity. Amen." It felt good to speak these solemn words; it was the first time I'd ever been grateful for the copious religious instruction I'd received as a child.

"Amen," Carl said, his pebbly voice even rougher than usual.

Andrei patted down the Earth with his shovel, then bent his head and muttered something in Russian.

We all stood there for a moment, reflecting. Carl broke the spell. "Stay out here tonight?"

"I have to go back to the city," I said. "Something's up with my daughter."

# CHAPTER THIRTY-ONE

IT WAS LATE WHEN I got back from Sag Harbor. Alex's bedroom door was closed and when I peeked in, she was sprawled across her bed, snoring, her face turned away from the wedge of hallway light falling across her.

The next morning I overslept and Alex was gone by the time I stumbled to the kitchen for my morning coffee. I hoped she was at school. She'd left a note by my Bialetti brewer: *Mom, sorry about not calling yesterday, I got busy with some friends doing a school project. Is Groucho at the vet's? I'll go see him after school.*

A school project was almost believable but then, Alex was clever. Still, a school project wouldn't keep her from picking up when I called, or from calling me back when she heard it was about Groucho. Only being too high to talk rationally kept her from speaking with me.

Rosa had opened the gallery when I arrived. She took one look at my drawn face and said, "Oh, Sarah, I'm so sorry! He was such a great dog!"

I wanted to cry but I bit the inside of my cheek to avoid that. I had to tackle a task that was almost, in its way, as formidable as burying Groucho. I had to let Rosa go.

I accepted her hug and murmured thanks and went to get some coffee.

Rosa sat down in the chair across from my desk. Her dark hair swung down around her shoulders and her beautiful, exotic face grew very serious. "Do you want to talk about it, Sarah?"

I took my cappuccino to my desk and seated myself. "Carl drove me out to Sag Harbor and we buried him there."

"Not that," Rosa said. "The other thing."

I took a sip from my mug and thought, wistfully, how hard it would be not to see Rosa all the time. I valued her work, especially her skill with clients and her creative approach to promotion. More than that, I enjoyed her company. I loved having her at my side over the last few years. She was a stellar aide de camp for my foray into the trenches of art sales.

She continued, "I saw the email from your accountant. We haven't made a single sale since Carl bought Clif's paintings. I know what's going on."

"Please don't be kind and empathic, Rosa, it only makes it harder," I begged. I took a deep breath. "My lease is in jeopardy."

She said, wistfully, "I'll have more time for auditions."

"I'm so sorry. I just can't pay you a salary right now. I have to let you go." It was both easier and harder to say those words than I had imagined. Easier because the words rolled right out as I thought about the sales I hadn't made. Harder because I had to acknowledge the possible failure of my wonderful, magical art gallery, which I loved and believed in and had fought for.

Rosa was nodding.

There were words I'd practiced in my head as I rode the subway that morning, so I recited them. "I'll give you the best reference in the history of employment. I'll write a letter that shows how you're Superwoman, only better. If you have the time and inclination, I'd like to hire you on a cash basis for special events. I wouldn't have lasted this long in the gallery business without your help, and I'm truly grateful. You have a sterling character. If you ever need me as a friend, I'm there."

Rosa smiled crookedly even though her eyes filled up with tears. "You've been an amazing boss, Sarah."

I didn't feel like an amazing boss. I felt like a failure.

Rosa said, "Maybe the next few talks will turn things around. Or Chloe Kennedy's show."

"Maybe," I agreed. But I didn't believe it. Maybe it was just that it was a day of despair. Or maybe the months of struggling—with and for my daughters, for Trudi, for Groucho, for the gallery—had finally caught up with me. I asked, "Are you going to be all right, Rosa?"

"I sort of knew this was coming for a while," she answered somberly. "I've got an introduction to some people on the Upper East Side who need a part-time nanny. They're willing to be flexible around my auditions."

It was a small comfort, but these days, all my comforts were small.

I was demoralized so I stopped by Trudi's on my way home. I wasn't going to tell her about Groucho dying or about letting Rosa go; I just wanted to be around Trudi. In the old days, before she had cancer, Trudi always knew how to comfort me. Now her presence—the mere fact that she was still alive—was solace in itself.

The doorman to her building said she was home, but she didn't answer when I knocked. I figured the doorman was wrong. I was about to give up when my intuition pinged and I knew that she was inside. Long ago she had given me a set of keys to her apartment, as I had given her keys to mine, and I used the keys to let myself in her place.

"Trudi?" I called, walking in. My heart pounded.

*What if she's lying somewhere, dying or dead?*

"Trudi!" I spied a still form on a hassock in the living room and I ran to her.

She sat, unmoving, surrounded by a colorful sea of hats, all kinds of hats: bonnets, cloches, bowlers, fedoras, berets, boaters, casques, pillboxes, toques, bucket caps, cocktail hats, fascinators. They had wide brims and short brims and no brims, veils and feathers and leaves and bows and beads and flowers, they were made of felt and straw and fabric and fur. There had to be more than a hundred strewn around her.

I cleared a path and knelt beside her.

"Trudi, are you OK?"

She looked at me with a distracted air. Her face was gaunt and introspective, and her eyes were hazy, as if she were drunk or drugged.

"Sarah? What are you doing here?"

"You didn't answer your door so I let myself in," I said. Gently, I laid a hand on her arm.

Trudi blinked at my hand and then jerked away. She leapt up off the hassock and stomped off, treading heavily on several hats, flattening them.

"Trudi?"

"I hate my hats," she said. "Bloody things. I despise them all."

"Some are so beautiful," I said in a cajoling voice. I picked up a brimless scarlet porkpie hat with a modest bow. "This one is gorgeous. The color, the simplicity. Isn't it one of your favorites?"

"I hate the bloody thing."

"No, you don't. You wore it when Dani was baptized; remember? George's mother complimented you. Here's one you wore when you came hiking with me. You're probably the only person who's ever worn a cocktail hat with peacock feathers to Lost City."

With my other hand, I picked up the royal blue hat with fluffy, curling turquoise feathers. I stepped carefully through the headgear mess to stand beside her. I smiled encouragement into her cancer-ravaged face and held aloft both hats. "See? They're beautiful."

"It was cold that day in Lost City," Trudi murmured.

"Cold and windy! How did you keep it on? Does it have an elastic?"

"A comb," she said. "The other one has an elastic."

"Oh, right." I pulled the elastic out of the red hat, carefully placed the hat atop her head, and then gently pulled the elastic down to go under her chin. "It looks wonderful on you."

"Sarah, no!" Trudi flung off her hat. Her eyes came into brilliant focus as she glared at me. "No, damn it. The elastic is worn in back, under the hair."

"I'm sorry," I said.

"No!" shouted Trudi, who never, ever raised her voice. "No! No more bloody hats! I don't have any hair to go over the elastic. All I have is a big, bald, lumpy, ugly skull. That's all that's left. And I'll never grow any hair back, never! Because I'm not beating this thing. I'm not. The treatments aren't working."

"Give them some time," I said warily. "You're going to pull through this, Trudi. You will."

Trudi's fists thrashed in the air.

"Time. I don't have time to give them!" Her face turned red and her eyes seethed with molten fire. "Damn it, Sarah Paige. Get your head out of your arse and understand what is happening. I'm dying. Don't you understand? What's wrong with you?"

I stood with my brain stuttering. I didn't know what to say. I was grasping for something, anything, that would soothe her.

*Trudi hates sappy sentiment.*

I said the first lame thing that popped into my head. "You have a big skull because you have a big brain."

"Big brain? My brain has cancer in it." She stood there breathing heavily, squinching up her face, willing herself not to cry.

I put my arms around her.

Trudi pushed me away.

"No. No, you don't get to feel better by comforting me. No. No. You don't get to feel better. I don't get to feel better."

I didn't have any words. I didn't have any stupid jokes. I couldn't hold her bodily because she didn't want me to. So I stood beside her in silence and watched her battle herself.

---

I was a mess when I arrived home. Alex sat at the kitchen table, eating granola and reading a book.

She said, "What's the deal with Groucho? And why don't you ever have anything in the cupboard other than cereal? When I'm at Dad's, Katherine always makes something delicious. Shouldn't you take better care of me?"

"I don't have the leisure to shop. I work," I said. "Sometimes seven days a week. I take care of you and I miss your sister and I have to deal with your father's constant aggression." I compressed my lips before I said anything more about George. I walked to my bedroom.

She caught up with me in the hallway and roughly grabbed my shoulder.

"Mom! Where's Groucho?"

I turned and faced her.

"Why didn't you call me yesterday?"

Alex, one of the world's most accomplished liars, didn't bat an eyelash.

"I told you. I was doing a school project with my friends. It's a really hard project and I was too busy to call you."

"You have a phone specifically so you can phone me," I snapped.

"Yeah, well, *Dad* got me this phone, so technically, I only have to call *him*," she sneered.

I stepped closer to her.

"What project was this, Alexandra? For which class?"

She squirmed a little, a tiny wiggle, barely discernible. "Uh, history. It was a history project."

I started to get mad. Really mad. It had been a shitty few days. My patience was cracked and eroded like a layer of varnish on an old painting. I said, "What exactly were you doing with your friends for this project? Whose house were you at?"

"My friend Caitlin's," she snarled, and the air between us thickened as her rage came up. She screamed, "What the fuck? I don't deserve to be interrogated like this! Why can't you be like dad, he never asks any questions! He's a better parent than you'll ever be."

I was boiling but, with some effort, reined myself in. I said, harshly, "Tell me everything you did on that project, but tell me *backwards*. I want to hear it all in reverse order. What was the last thing you and your friends did on the project when you were at Caitlin's?"

"Leave me alone!" she screamed. "Leave me alone, you fucking bitch!"

"How dare you!" I screamed back, stepping closer to her so that I was right in her face and we stood nose to nose. "Who do you think you're talking to, calling me those names? You were stoned again! I know you've been cutting class, Mr. Villanova called me!"

Her fist swung out and she punched me in the face.

My cheekbone gonged like a giant brass bell. It hurt. Both my hands thrust out before I had a moment to think. It was instinctive. I slammed my hands hard with my body weight behind them, into Alex's two shoulders and knocked her down.

She lay on the floor screaming and cursing, spewing the ugliest words in her vocabulary at me.

I stood there, panting, shaking, shocked. I was shocked at Alex for hitting me. I was shocked at myself for knocking her down. I was shocked that such a moment had arisen in my life. I forced myself to take a few moments to breathe while Alex kept screaming and crying. I tuned her out as best I could and focused on inhaling, exhaling, inhaling, exhaling.

When I had attained an infinitesimal modicum of inner balance, I said, "I won't have this in my home. Pack your bags. You can live with your father until you're willing to meet some minimum requirements. One is that you go back to drug rehab. Another is that you don't cut a single class at school until you graduate."

"You knocked me down, you bitch," she screamed. She rolled upright and stood. She was weeping and her face was swollen and red.

"Groucho is dead."

I turned and went to my bedroom and closed the door. I leaned backward against it, crying silently.

Alex packed a duffel bag and went to her father's house.

# CHAPTER THIRTY-TWO

THE NEXT FEW DAYS unfolded in slow motion. I had some sober discussions with my accountant about the gallery and its future. I completed some paperwork so Rosa could file for unemployment benefits. I conferred with Marty about Alex hitting me. I let him know that I'd kicked her out and that if she wanted to live with me, there were conditions. I finished preparations at the gallery for Clif's talk.

I checked StatCounter for the gallery website and found an IP address with a hostname that, when I googled it, belonged to a law firm led by a slithering snake of a divorce attorney. That reptile was all about ripping the faces off of his opponents. Unlike Marty, he didn't believe in peaceful, win-win solutions. He was a scorched earth, take-no-prisoners, nuclear holocaust divorce attorney who charged over a thousand dollars an hour, and he was the logical next step for George, who would never forgive me for leaving him. I copied the information and pasted it into an email to Marty.

Marty responded, "No way. Al Fish wouldn't step down as Calhoun's attorney without telling me. That firm must be interested in the art you're selling. Maybe they're redecorating their office."

But I knew better. I knew George. And I knew that the wound to George's pride was such that he wanted to destroy me and would spare no expense to do so.

———— ～ ————

The day of the gallery talk arrived. After setting out the wine and cheese, I went into the gallery bathroom for some personal reconstruction. I washed my face, reapplied my makeup, and then changed into a shapely black silk noil dress I'd bought in Milan a decade ago and one of my favorite go-to little black dresses. I stepped out from the bathroom and found Trudi, Robert, and Carl clustered together at the front door. They were early and bore bottles of wine as gifts for me.

"Welcome!" I said, throwing open my arms and feeling suddenly happier to see them than I'd felt in days.

Trudi, gaunter and paler than ever and wearing a turquoise turban with a feather in it, submitted to a hug and kiss on the cheek. "I'm sorry about Groucho, Sarah."

"Me too," I said.

In a low voice, she said, "I'm sorry about the other day. Yelling at you."

"Don't apologize, you have a free pass. You get to yell. It shows you're human like the rest of us. Thank God!" I grinned at her. Then I leaned close and whispered, "Are you up for tonight?"

"Wouldn't miss it," she said. "Is Clif here? I can't believe you didn't ask me to give one of these gallery talks. I'm offended."

"In the new year," I promised her, more breezily than I felt. I didn't know if either Trudi or the gallery would be around in the new year. Trudi probably wouldn't be if the cancer had metastasized to her brain.

Robert was practically curled around Trudi to support her but he unpeeled himself to buss my cheek warmly.

"Sarah, you look lovely," Carl said, kissing me and squeezing my upper arm.

I touched his cheek. "Thank you for coming."

He took my hand in his and kissed my fingertips so sweetly that I nearly dissolved.

Trudi was looking around. "Where's Rosa? I'd love to hear how her acting career is proceeding."

"Oh, she'll drop in later," I said. "Is this beautiful wine for me?"

"Isn't she working?" Trudi asked sharply.

I shook my head. "Why don't I put your coats in my office?"

"And the champagne in the refrigerator," Carl said. He handed me a bottle and then swept off his coat and gave that to me as well.

Robert was helping Trudi with her coat. Trudi shook slightly as it slid down her arms, which were pretzel-thin inside her sleeves. She wore a silky twill peplum top that hung on her as if on a wire coat hanger. Did she weigh more than ninety pounds? I doubted it. She asked, "Why isn't Rosa working today?"

"She's on reduced hours," I said blithely. "I love that turban, Trudi. It's very stylish."

Clif came in behind them at that moment, and their greetings gave me an excuse to slip off to my office with the coats and wine. I hung the coats on the coat rack and then opened the refrigerator to find space for the bottles.

"Did you let your assistant go?" It was Carl standing at the threshold of my office.

"I cut her hours."

*To almost nothing.*

It wasn't exactly a lie; Rosa had agreed to work for cash when I needed her if she wasn't busy.

"Is your gallery struggling?" Carl asked, his gravelly voice thoughtful.

I smiled. "Don't worry about it, Carl. I can manage." Gently I placed my hand on his shoulder and leaned close to smile into his eyes.

He smiled back and circled me with his arms.

Trudi appeared at the door but she backed away.

"Come in," I told her, stepping away from Carl.

"I'm sorry to intrude," she murmured. "There's a flock of young people at the door. They resemble my Barnard students, but they're rather more odiferous. And badly dressed and poorly groomed. They seem terribly excited."

"Those would be art students," I said. "Stinky, sweaty, and broke, with eyes shining from the love of their field. Poor suckers."

"Art students can't afford art," Carl said, narrowing his eyes. "Certainly not the quality of art in your gallery."

"No, but they have parents and friends who might be able to," I said. I held up my hands to show Carl that my fingers were crossed with hope. "I'm getting creative here."

---

The gallery was filled with a sea of people, mostly energetic, and yes not-entirely-hygienic, young folks. I stepped back to watch the ebb and flow and to enjoy the liveliness in my gallery.

Clif was getting ready to speak at the podium on a small dais that I'd acquired for the talks.

I was near the door and felt a waft of cold air as it opened. I turned and Scott stood at the threshold. He wore a black wool coat over his suit and carried a bouquet of red roses in one gloved hand. His head was cocked as his eyes swept the gallery.

He was looking for me.

Trudi trotted over to him to say hello.

Scott kissed her on the cheek and beamed at her. Then he straightened and looked directly at me. Behind his glasses, his dark eyes fixed on my face. His expression blanked out and he did that frozen sculpture thing where he was totally immobilized.

I was a little immobilized myself. I couldn't tear my gaze from Scott's.

"Who's that?" asked Carl, who suddenly stood at my shoulder.

"Trudi's doctor, Scott Bauer," I murmured.

Carl stiffened. "Bauer's the non-exclusive part of our arrangement?" The tone of his voice indicated that it wasn't really a question; it was a statement to which he already knew the answer.

I nodded.

Carl said, with pure authority, "Get rid of him."

I turned toward Carl but he didn't look at me. Then I understood: he was forcing a choice, and he didn't want to be watching if the decision went against him. Despite his authority, he didn't want to get hurt. He was vulnerable.

I said softly, "OK."

I walked over to Scott.

"Sarah," he exclaimed, released from the freeze. He reached for me but I held up my hand and stopped him.

"Trudi, would you give us a moment?" I asked quietly.

Trudi melted back into the crowd.

"Scott, you have to go," I said.

"Why?"

"Because I'm here with someone."

Scott looked across the gallery at Carl, who stood in profile to us, talking to Robert. "That guy talking to Mr. Waterston?"

"His name is Carl." I pushed open the door and went out into the chilly night of Chelsea. A group of art students stood in a semi-circle nearby, smoking cigarettes and talking in loud voices about Clif's paintings. I walked up the avenue to get away from them and give us some privacy.

Scott followed. "Why that guy?"

"Scott, this thing between us is never going to work out. Not in the long run."

Scott said, "Is it because he's rich? He looks rich."

That pissed me off. Carl was not taking care of me. "Because he'll never ask me to babysit for him."

"In ten years, you'll be babysitting him!" Scott responded, hotly.

I felt myself get soft and small and still in the crisp October evening. My voice sounded subdued. "Is that what you think about me because I'm older than you? That in ten years you'll be babysitting me?"

"You're not seventy years old, Sarah," he snapped. "Don't make this about our age difference."

"OK. I'll make this about the way you prioritize work over everything. Or your inability to be available to me for anything real."

"You never wanted anything real."

"Yes and no. It's true I enjoyed the fantasy. That was a lot of fun. But, also, I didn't want to get into more than that with you, because you couldn't. You're already married to your work. I guess I'm like Lisa—I don't want to be the mistress in your life.

"And yes, whether or not you want to face it, the age difference matters. I look older than you and that makes me feel awkward when we're standing together. It makes me feel unsafe." He started to protest but I talked over him. "But also, I'm old enough to know what I want and what I don't want. And I don't want to babysit your small kids when you traipse off to work at a moment's notice, no matter how lovely they are. And Scott, they are lovely. But it's not what I want out of life now."

Scott stood, quiet but galvanized, like a vortex bursting at its seams. He didn't speak. He gave me an impenetrable look and then swung around and stalked off.

I watched him throw his bouquet into a garbage can at the corner of the street. With an ache, I returned to my gallery to listen to Clif give one of his riveting, mesmerizing talks, and to hope that the art students would prevail upon their parents to buy some art.

―――――

Alex sent a carefully worded email to me, stating that she wanted to live with me but didn't feel it was fair for me to impose conditions, especially since her father was paying me financial support on her behalf. It didn't reflect her usual casual—even sloppy—diction. With one of those flashes of heart-rending clarity that struck me from time to time, I knew it was composed in conjunction with her father and his new attorney. They were trying to back me into something that they could use against me in court so that Alex could do whatever she wanted, whether she lived with me or with her father.

So that was how it was going to go: Alex would join forces with her father and use the legal system to beat me up to do her will.

I forwarded the email to Marty. Then I texted Dr. Maitra that I needed to speak with him and called his secretary to schedule an appointment.

But I wasn't waiting for Dr. Maitra to decide my course of action. Alex was my daughter, even if, as Chloe said, George meant to erase me from her life. If Alex wanted to live with me, there were nonnegotiable conditions. She had to attend school without skipping a single class. She had to go back to drug rehab. She had to obey reasonable curfews. And it was about time she got a job. Obviously, at sixteen years of age she was qualified only for something basic. But she could start to inculcate some personal responsibility through holding down a job, even if it was only a regular babysitting gig. I was going to set forth those conditions clearly.

I should have established them earlier when Dr. Maitra first told me to teach my daughter. But I had thought the therapeutic school and wilderness intervention would impress on Alex the need for her to contain herself.

The spirit of foreknowing weighed on me like all the gravities at the bottom of the deepest part of the ocean, and I knew that the conditions would not be accepted. They were in Alex's best interest and would help pull Alex out of the hole she insisted on throwing herself into, but that's not how they would be interpreted. Alex, her father, and the new attorney would spin my requirements into proof that I was a bad mother. George would have a new stick to hit me with. There would be litigation. Someone would have a Pyrrhic victory—Pyrrhic because no matter what the verdict was, Alex was going to damage, perhaps irretrievably, her relationship with her mother who loved her and was trying to help her.

# CHAPTER THIRTY-THREE

I HELD THE LINE on my list of requirements that Alex had to meet in order to live with me. If I couldn't teach Alex anything else, as Dr. Maitra suggested I should, at least I could demonstrate for her what integrity meant: sticking to your principles even when it was hard. Especially when it was hard. On Dr. Maitra's advice, when a new psychiatrist hired by George refused to let me know what medications Alex was currently taking, I added another requirement: she had to sign a consent form to give me access to her medical records.

One Friday evening early in November, Rosa called me at the gallery as I was getting dressed to meet Carl for dinner. I was changing in the bathroom into something more elegant, something suitable for the upscale restaurant at which Carl had made reservations. At first, I was delighted to hear Rosa's voice but she said, in a serious voice and with no preamble, "Sarah, are you friends with Alex on her social network?"

*Hah. As if.*

"No." I winced as I remembered losing that battle. "I tried to make it a rule that I should be, but Alex insisted that she was entitled to her privacy from me, and her father and her shrink backed her up on that."

"I *am* friends with her online. I'm sorry to be the bearer of bad news, but she's posted an outrageous announcement about a party or should I say a drug-filled orgy? It's happening tonight at her Dad's. I'll send you a screenshot."

I sat down at my desk with one eye mascaraed and the other eye bare. I opened my email. I felt sick to my stomach as I opened Rosa's message. There it was: a breezy announcement by Alex for a booze, sex, and drug-filled rumpus at her dad's place.

*Where is George? Why won't he be home?*

I had to let him know. I emailed and texted him, then finally even phoned him: no answer.

In desperation, I called his parents. They explained that George was on vacation in Cabo.

I said, "You'd better find out if he gave permission to Alex to have a party in his home. Tell him that this party will be filled with underage kids drinking alcohol. If anything happens to any of those kids, he's liable because it's his apartment."

I knew the legal aspect would reach a Calhoun the way a moral obligation wouldn't.

George's mother got back to me explaining that no, George had not given permission for said party.

In the end, my evening was ruined, as so many of them were, by Alex's self-destructive choices. I cancelled with Carl and went to George's apartment instead. The doorman wouldn't let me up. I told him that was OK, but I was calling the police to report underage drinking in the penthouse. Perhaps he could let my daughter know so she could clear out her friends before the police arrived?

Then, standing in front of the doorman, I proceeded to make the phone call to the police.

The doorman looked sweaty and green as he called up to George's apartment.

While I waited for the police to arrive, I called George's parents again, asking what George wanted me to do with Alex, who could not stay at my home until she agreed to my terms. They suggested taking her to her uncle's place. Jed had been alerted and he was expecting her.

Herds of kids streamed out of the elevator and shambled through the lobby.

After the kids cleared out, Alex showed up. She was wearing scads of black eye makeup that was smeared around her eyes, and a tube top, hoop earrings, a pleather miniskirt, fishnets, and the highest stilettos I had ever seen.

I wondered if she'd set up a pole in George's living room.

She walked unsteadily ahead of me several paces as I accompanied her to Jed's place, which was also on Central Park West.

The next day, George sent a one-word email: "Thanks." That was the extent of his gratitude for my efforts at averting a potential lawsuit because some drunk, stoned kid got hurt in his apartment while he was in Cabo.

The following week, his new attorney filed suit against me to give George sole custody of Alex and deprive me of all parental rights. He let Marty know that Alex, who was a plaintiff along with George, had her own attorney.

---

The doorbell was buzzing and I didn't want to get up. I had awakened early, around five a.m., as I'd done ever since kicking out Alex. Now it was Sunday and I lay in bed and felt how bruised I was in the deepest part of my essence by the way my children treated me.

I missed Groucho. I missed Scott. I missed Dani. I even missed Alex, despite how much pain and trouble she'd caused me.

The doorbell refused to stop ringing. I sat up in bed, blinking, and then shrugged on my robe. I had no plans except to see Trudi later in the day. Carl was away on a business trip.

I made it to the door and heard weird little scratching noises. I glanced out the peephole but no one was there. I threw open the door.

A curly-haired black puppy stood there, making a puddle underneath herself. I bent down and lifted her. She had the silkiest, densest coat I'd ever felt on a dog. Around her neck was a red ribbon; hanging from the ribbon was a hand-written sign that begged, "Love me."

The puppy softened like a noodle in my grasp. She gazed at me out of clear, shiny eyes and I felt myself softening in reciprocity.

"You like her?" called Carl, who had slipped out from behind a bend in the hallway.

"She's adorable but I don't know, Carl, a puppy's a big responsibility," I said, cuddling the warm little thing into my cheek. "I don't think I can handle the responsibility right now."

Carl came over and gave me a kiss on my other cheek. "How are you doing?" he asked, his voice lowering in concern.

"Do I look that bad?" I positioned the dog in front of my face and she licked my nose eagerly. I had to giggle.

"That's the first time you've smiled in days," Carl said, with relief in his voice.

"Well, you know," I said, grimacing.

*Well, you know, when your self-destructive kid that you love fiercely and that you've been trying desperately to help sues you, it's devastating.*

But I didn't say it aloud.

He put his arm around my shoulders. "I know." He furrowed his brow and frowned. After a moment, he shook off the heaviness. "This is a miniature poodle puppy from the best breeder on the East Coast. She is exactly eleven weeks old and she has had her shots. Her sire and dam were both champions."

"That gives her a better pedigree than mine. I'm one hundred percent mutt."

"That's what makes you so beautiful," Carl said, soothingly, as if to a disturbed child. "The car is loaded with accoutrements, a crate, a bed, food, food bowls. A collar and leashes. If you want to keep her."

"I don't know, Carl. A puppy? Puppies are a lot of work." I held the dog up and looked into her sweet little face.

*Damn you, Carl. This is dirty pool.*

"You know I work long hours. I won't be able to bring her to the gallery every day. And she needs to be potty trained."

"I'll hire a dog walker and a trainer for you. I have a list of great ones in this neighborhood. Why don't you try her for a week, see how you get on? If it doesn't work out, I'll bring her back to the breeder."

"In a week I'll be totally in love with her and I won't be able to give her up."

Carl smiled slightly. "I'll have Andrei take care of her when we go to the cocktail party in Connecticut this Friday."

"That's right, that's this week," I murmured. The days were blurring together. I pulled the dog against my chest and hugged her. Warm and soft, she wriggled against me and licked my neck. Of my own initiative, I wouldn't have gone out and acquired a dog. I didn't know how I was going to cope with the demands of a puppy when my life was falling into shards around me.

But how could I refuse her? She was there, appealing and cuddle-able as puppies are. She was a gift from a man I cared about, and who cared about me.

She was also a sign of my own passivity, and I had promised myself, after leaving George, that I would never allow a man to control me. If I had been able to roust myself from my despondency, and if I had been able to establish better boundaries with Carl, I would not be holding her in my arms. Adorable as she was, she represented my failings. I said somberly, "Carl, I love you for your generosity, but you've got to stop trying to take care of me."

"I hate to see you so sad," he said softly.

"It makes me feel like you don't believe I can take care of myself," I said. "Like you think I'm incompetent."

"That's not it at all!" he exclaimed. "I just want to help you because I care about you. Why don't you let me take you away this weekend? We can drive to the airport on the way back from the cocktail party. We can go to the Caribbean, catch some sun, come back Monday night."

"I don't know about getting a flight on such short notice," I objected. "Besides, I have a new puppy. I can't travel."

"My company uses a service to charter private jets," he said. "We can bring the puppy with us. What are you going to name her?"

"Beatrice," I said spontaneously.

His blue eyes glimmered approval. "From Dante."

*From the Inferno, because this time in my life, despite your companionship and generosity, is hell.*

"Let me think about the trip, Carl. It's a lovely idea, but it means I'll have to close the gallery on Saturday, and that's when I get the most foot traffic. Tourists like to walk around Chelsea and tour the galleries. Even jaded New Yorkers enjoy gallery hopping. I have to be open for that. If the weather is good, I would lose business from closing."

"Have your assistant come in," he suggested, studying my face.

I shook my head.

He said, "I'll pay her—"

"No!" I exclaimed, loudly enough to startle the wiggly puppy into stillness. She whined anxiously. I tried to soothe her and said, "Carl, do *not* do that. Do not."

He said, "Sarah, it's such a small thing for me."

"But not for me. It's a big thing for me. I learned the hard way what happens when a wealthy man takes care of you."

"I'm nothing like your first husband," Carl said with a grimace. "Don't put me in the same category. It's offensive."

I didn't mean to offend Carl. I just wanted to hold on to myself before my daughters' betrayal, my gallery's failure, and my best friend's illness eroded it.

# CHAPTER THIRTY-FOUR

I INSISTED ON DRIVING us to New Britain, despite Carl's well-reasoned arguments for Andrei and the Mercedes. But I was sick of letting him maneuver me into his idea of the way things should be, even if his way was superior. He was right; I would be less tired for the party if Andrei drove us. Stubbornly, I insisted on driving anyway. I needed to do it for my self-respect, which was at an all-time low. The frustration, anger, and pain of Alex joining forces with her father to bring legal suit against me, and the sorrow around the loss of my relationship with Dani, left me feeling empty, low, and adrift.

I also missed Scott more than I'd expected. I had enjoyed our lovemaking. I had enjoyed our conversations. I had enjoyed Scott. I wondered how his kids were doing, if Janey had finished reading the Harry Potter series, if Max ever got another opportunity to play with clay or if he was still a Tasmanian devil wearing a little boy's body. It was better for me to have chosen one man and Carl was, all things considered, the wiser choice. But, still.

My life had a surreal quality to it, as if it weren't really happening to me but was instead a bad dream happening around me. Despite everything I attempted, I found myself on a path of affliction and uncertainty. I felt like I'd been sucker-punched and couldn't get air into my chest. It was surprising that I could put on a pinstriped skirt suit and silk blouse and forge onward and that I had the wherewithal to meet the board of a museum where I might be offered a job.

But something in me, something muffled and distant, didn't let me give up on my life. Perhaps it was my parents' love for me and mine for them, the love that continued despite their passing that prompted me to model something better than quitting for my daughters. Even if my daughters hated me right then. Even though they treated me with contempt.

As I often did, because great art haunts us, I thought of Frida Kahlo's painting, "*Las Dos Fridas;*" the Two Fridas; the double self-portrait. The loved Frida and the unloved Frida. The unloved Frida's heart was broken, with a vein from her heart emptying blood onto her white skirt. That vein circled around and connected the two Fridas.

It was the most graphic representation of the loss of contact that is despair that I had ever seen and the painting sat in my heart, connecting me back into myself.

When I idled Brigit in front of Carl's building on Park Avenue, he slid in and eyeballed her with thinly veiled disdain.

"Quick, drive away," he said, "before my neighbors see me in a car like this."

"Carl, meet Brigit; Brigit, this is Carl. She's a Volvo; these are classic cars. You have nothing to be ashamed of, Carl."

"Drive away before my doorman thinks I'm being kidnapped for ransom and he calls the police," he said dryly. When I pulled away from the curb, he asked, "Does this vehicle have shocks and struts? Or was the suspension system not invented when she came off the assembly line?"

"You get used to the bounce," I said. "It makes a road trip adventurous, like a ride at an amusement park."

"This is going to be a long two hours," he grumbled.

"I'll play the music very loud to distract you. How do you feel about pop rock from the eighties and nineties?"

"Now you're being sadistic, Sarah," he said grimly. "Let's find a station we can both agree on." He looked over his shoulder into the back seat. "You left Beatrice at home?"

"I asked my neighbor Mrs. Zlotowitz to watch her."

*Thanks for the dog, Carl, she wakes me up twice a night, every night, to go out.*

But I held my tongue because, after all, I had accepted the gift of the puppy and that meant I accepted the consequences of that gift. I thought about banging my head on the steering wheel, but if I gave in to that urge, Carl would insist on using his car and driver.

It turned out we both liked classical Spanish guitar music. He agreed that turning it up loud served as a distraction from the somewhat less-than-smooth ride. He was rolling his eyes as he said so but I pretended not to notice.

When we arrived at the New Britain Art Museum, Carl clambered out and shook himself. "I believe your second former husband and his lady friend have arrived." He was adjusting his tie and he nodded toward the other end of the parking lot.

I got out and stretched and hoped my makeup hadn't wilted in the car ride. I had road fatigue behind my eyes and I was slightly dehydrated. "Yes, that's Clif with Nicole."

"She has a nice little Audi," he noted, his gravelly voice pitched higher with approval. "That would make a good car for you, Sarah. Much safer than this hunk of junk you're attached to."

"Don't you dare, Carl," I warned him. "Yes, I am attached to this hunk of junk, so please refrain from disparaging her."

Carl stayed at my side as we went into the New Britain Art Museum. A girl at the admissions desk was checking names on a list and she waved us through when I told her mine.

We went into the main gallery, where a bar was set up and hors d'oeuvres were being passed. People were already congregating to chat and examine the paintings. Alfie and Jim stood near the door talking to a group of people. Jim caught my eye and beckoned us over. He was delighted to meet Carl, who was equally happy to meet him; the two men had intersecting circles. They played "which muckety-mucks do you know, what boards do you sit on?" and otherwise compared bank accounts and penis sizes while Alfie glanced over my dress and scrutinized my face.

Alfie was a buxom woman of medium height. She was rounded and full, with dreadlocks coiled into a bun on her head and a sweet, warm face. She kissed my cheek and said, "You look beautiful as always, Sarah." Then she whispered, "Go into the bathroom and touch up your lipstick, straighten your skirt. You're Jim's horse in this race."

I smiled and excused myself and went to tidy my skirt and lipstick.

When I returned, the group around Alfie and Jim had enlarged and included Clif and Nicole. Carl drew me in beside him. Jim introduced me to swanky-looking Heather and Oliver who were not married but were both board members. At the other end of the group, Paula Clarke, head of Post-War and Contemporary Art at Christie's, started talking about the future of the museum.

"The museum's mission and vision are clearly defined," Paula remarked, sounding rehearsed. "It's dedicated to serving all people and to being one of the most welcoming, most educational art museums. Mel has created a strategy that perfectly promotes that mission and vision. He's put it in place and it will stand for the next decade, keeping this museum on course in its public service role and allowing it to thrive."

She was an expertly-groomed brunette wearing over-sized gold jewelry and a navy blue Roberto Cavalli sheath dress; she was just as swanky-looking and suavely Connecticut-ish as Heather and Oliver. She was fit and taut like someone who attended daily spin classes, and I knew she had a PhD in Art History. She probably slept in full-dress makeup in case she had to meet a client at three a.m., and her abs were way tighter than mine. She was in every way the perfect choice to run the museum. She had clearly prepared that speech. She said, "Mel has also created close relationships with the best galleries and most prestigious museums around the world, and those relationships are the envy of other museums. They're money in the bank for New Britain."

That was the party line, of course: maintain the status quo. Most of the board members would be happy to hear Paula toeing it. But Jim was gazing at me with a half-grin that lifted one side of his mouth. He wanted me to make a response. He wanted me to make *my* response.

What the hell, why not?

I was the black sheep, the wild card candidate with soft abs and well-defined triceps because that's what yoga produced. I had earned my PhD with sweat and tears from the school of Selling Beautiful Art. I might as well give Paula a run for the money.

Someone inside me reared her uncomely head and I saw her face clearly for the first time, though she had always been present. She was my survivor self, the ornery self who kept me going despite my circumstances. She had succored me when my parents died. She would sustain me through my children's awfulness. I had certainly inherited her along with the Cherokee and Jewish blood, and I knew in my bones that she had kept one set of my forebears alive when they were marched down the Trail of Tears, barefoot in the snow, and she had kept my other set of forebears going when their families were burned up in pogroms. She took control of my mouth now because I simply would not concede to Perfect Paula without a fight.

"I think about it differently," I said with some zest. "Probably because

I come from the gallery side. Do you realize that only five blue chip galleries account for one-third of the solo shows in American museums? Gallery representation at the right gallery has become a path to a major museum show. In fact, it's just about the only path, and it's become a closed and incestuous game of mutual back-scratching. We could even call it corrupt. Because museums rely on gallery funding to foist shows. And galleries rely on museums to validate artists—to promote them, essentially—so that their artists can command substantial prices. So there is no longer any separation between the market and the museum.

"I can travel around the world, visiting the top galleries and museums in New York, LA, London, Zurich, Dubai, and I'll see the same fifty or sixty artists. There's seldom, if ever, any real, true curatorial initiative put into finding new artists, unheard-of artists, who display originality. Inventiveness that's skill-based rather than shock-value-based. Museum curators play it safe by looking at who's playing well in the Art Fairs. Therefore museums and galleries both show the same, familiar artists."

I walked over to a wall and pointed to a painting by one of those regulars. "Is a painting by this guy, for sale in a gallery, a safe investment for a collector? Sure it is, and partly because the New Britain Art Museum collects his works. But is that really what public art museums should be about? Is that really what *art* is about—the safe investment for consumers of the Marlborough Gallery?"

"I think the Marlborough Gallery shows artists who are among the best alive today," said an unassuming tenor voice. It was Mel Prentiss in the flesh, standing at the entrance to the room. He was a tall, slim man with graying hair, a smoothly-shaven face, and a red bowtie that matched his red suspenders. He was looking at me with a quizzical gleam in his eyes and a curious arch of one brow.

"Mel, you're a super genius, but I'm going to disagree with you. Partly. Marlborough shows the well-known artists, yes. But in my experience, the most original artists today are working outside the airless top gallery system."

I waved toward Clif: case in point. Mel, along with just about everyone else in the room, looked at Clif and then back to me. Clif, who was never one to miss a cue, straightened and managed to look even more handsome and charismatic than ever.

I said, "My question is, does that system, which has been called the 'toxic art market trade'—"

"By you, in print," Mel interjected, with a sly grin.

"Not by me alone," I insisted. "Does this bell jar art system really serve *the people*? Does it really effectively educate them about art? Does it expose the public to the diversity and richness of art and artists working today? Or does it just exacerbate the erosion of the distinction between curating art and selling art, so that only the most familiar painters are ever shown in either galleries or museums?"

"What would you do," Paula asked, in a tone verging toward scoffery and disbelief, "Hang a bunch of total unknowns on the walls here? Who'd come to the museum then? What press would cover it?"

I took a breath, my mind racing to figure out how to answer her. Finally, as I usually did, I opted for the straight up, in-your-face response. "Yes. I would hang a bunch of totally unknown artists on the walls. Along with the established artists, or in rotation with them." I walked to another wall and pointed. "I love Marsden Hartley. This is a great painting. But you know, Regionalism didn't end with him. Or Grant Wood. Or Alexandre Hogue. But the museum's collection might lead a person, a bona fide member of *the people*, to believe it did, however unintentionally, which is to the detriment of educating the people and to the detriment of the field of art as a whole and, ultimately, to the detriment of this museum. I'm showing an artist now, Chloe Kennedy, who puts me in mind of Georgia O'Keefe, and who holds her own."

"Holds her own with Georgia O'Keefe?" Paula was now openly scoffing. "That's a big claim."

"Yes, it is," I agreed. I felt my legs under me and it gave me strength. One thing I believed in was the merit of Chloe Kennedy's painting. "Peruse her work and I think you'll agree with me. Mind you, Kennedy isn't derivative of O'Keefe. Kennedy has her own distinct voice. But there's a beautiful resonance. Simply gorgeous. I'd like to show a few paintings by Kennedy alongside some of O'Keefe's. Seeing the two painters side-by-side educates the public about the history, influence, and evolution of art, and it also fixes it in everyone's mind that art is a living, breathing field. It's happening right now. Great artists are doing great art *this very second.*

"For this reason, I'd also like to show Clif's work, perhaps alongside Thomas Hart Benton and Walter Kuhn. Get in some of Donald De Lue's sculptures as three-dimensional counterpoints," I said. "Let's take a look at the figure in American Art, in the history and the present of American

Art. That would be real curating and I don't need Marlborough's permission to do it."

"I can recommend some of my pieces for such an exhibit," Clif offered with a smile and a lilt that elicited chuckles around the now attentive room. But I knew that he was serious. He and I exchanged a glance.

"You asked what press would cover it?" I took a deep breath. "That depends partly on how the exhibits are presented to them. If we pre-digest the information about the exhibit for them and make the shows relevant there'll be press coverage. But I wouldn't just rely on the usual suspects for promotion. I'd heartily engage social media."

"We have a vigorous online presence in all the major social media venues," Mel said, crossing the room to stand beside me.

"I'd push the envelope. Hire some twenty-somethings to do live, streaming videos of openings. Oh, and hold selfie contests. The best selfie of the opening, or of the week if there's no opening, wins free admission for the winner and three friends. Feature those videos and pictures on the museum website. The gallery website should be fluid and dynamic, not static," I said, gesturing with both hands for emphasis.

"Museum," Carl standing at my shoulder corrected, sotto voce.

"The museum website should be fluid and dynamic," I said. "That's part of the strength and appeal of the internet. It will engage the community, too. People like contests and they like to see themselves as part of something larger than themselves. Your visitors will like seeing themselves on the museum website. It will keep them invested in the museum."

Mel was looking at me with a gleam of both mirth and respect, I thought.

He said, "Sarah, I should pay more attention to your articles. You've made some interesting points."

"I feel like I should applaud," Jim called and clapped a few times. "Bravo, Sarah, that was some brainstorming you did on the future of the museum! What great, original ideas!"

Swanky Heather stepped up to talk to me and I turned my attention to her, but not before Alfie caught my eye and nodded once.

---

"That was some speech you gave," Carl said en route back to the city. He was driving. He insisted and I meekly allowed him to take the wheel. In exchange, he had to promise not to insult Brigit for her lack of pep. "You were as fiery as an old-time gospel preacher."

"Thank you." I laughed. "I just went for it, I guess. I have nothing left to lose, so why hold back?"

Carl was quiet for a few beats. His hands gripped the steering wheel in the textbook ten o'clock and two o'clock position as he expertly maneuvered Brigit around slower cars. It was dark and passing streetlights threw transient wisps of light onto his craggy, patrician face.

"Thanks a lot," he said.

"Excuse me?"

"Nothing left to lose; that includes me? I'm part of nothing?"

"What are you talking about?"

"I've been in business a long time, Sarah. Long enough to know a beauty contest when I see one. That was a beauty contest. You're being considered for a job there. Why didn't you tell me?"

"Mel is retiring and Jim approached me about the directorship," I said quietly. "But I'm a long shot. I really don't have the credentials."

"You're Jim's choice, that's obvious."

"I went to the cocktail party today mostly out of curiosity. The museum board may have been intrigued by my speech but in the end, they'll go with Paula, who's got the perfect resume, and who won't rock the boat. Or with Reggie Vargas, who's Mel's protégé and has the experience."

"Not if Jim Harte has anything to say about it." Carl set his jaw, looked in the mirror and changed lanes. "Why are you even considering a job at this museum in the boonies of Connecticut? How badly is your gallery doing?"

"Jim wanted to meet you; that's another reason I went," I murmured. "Isn't he lovely?"

Carl shot me a quick glance. "So if you're offered the position, are you going to take it? Move up there and run that museum?"

"Carl, I really hadn't thought that far ahead because I don't have a snowball's chance in Lucifer's backyard of getting that job."

"You'd better start considering it," he said, in an ominous tone. "Where does that leave us if you move up here?"

"Carl, please. You're getting way ahead of yourself."

"Did you even think about the impact of a move like that on us?"

"No, because I'm not moving," I said with some exasperation.

"I suppose you could telecommute part of the time," he said slowly. "You wouldn't have to be there every single day."

"Carl! I'm a gallerist, not a museum curator! That board is never going to offer me the directorship," I said with a derisive and distinctly unladylike snort. "For Pete's sake."

He pursed his lips. I figured the conversation was over and I turned up the Spanish guitar. *Rodrigo y Gabriela* came on and I sat back to enjoy their sumptuous sound.

Carl turned the music down. "What about us?"

"What about us?"

"You said you had nothing left to lose. Am I really not even a consideration?"

"Of course you're a consideration!"

"As much a consideration as Bauer?"

"I'm not seeing him anymore. Only you." I laid my hand softly on his thigh. "What's going on, Carl?"

"I like having you around the city," he said. He dropped one hand to squeeze mine. "I don't want you to move out, even part-time. I want you close by."

"Do you think I'm going anywhere with Trudi the way she is?" I asked softly.

He drew my hand up to his heart. "Is that what this is about? Fleeing the city because Trudi is dying?"

*There's that sucker punch again.*

Carl didn't mean it that way but that's the way it felt.

"Alex is in the city. There's a chance she'll come around, see that I'm trying to help her, and agree to my terms. Maybe she'll come to her senses and this legal battle will fade away."

Carl shook his head. "I'm sure her father is encouraging it. I can't believe his behavior. Even for a Calhoun. Did you remember my friend Joe from the party?"

"He's married to Regan. She's quite the bombshell," I remembered.

*She was one of the Trophies.*

"She's his second wife," Carl said.

"I figured as much," I said dryly.

He flashed me a grin. "Tut, tut, glass houses, darling."

"I'm closer in age to you than she is to him."

"Not by much," he said, his voice chagrinned. "The point is Joe's first wife, Sandra, was an alcoholic. Also addicted to pain pills. A real mess. He divorced her when she relapsed after her third stint in rehab but the whole time his kids were little he never said one negative word about Sandra to them. Never once. When they complained to him, he told them they had to respect her because she was their mother. Even when he had to take care of them because she was high as a kite he insisted that they respect her."

"He's a class act," I acknowledged.

"That he is," Carl nodded.

"How are the kids now?"

"Great," Carl said. "Lovely, well-adjusted. His oldest daughter is married with two little girls. His younger daughter is getting her MBA. His son is getting married in June; he works for me, one of the best hires I ever made. And Sandra got her act together when Lucy got pregnant. She's clean now and has good relationships with all the kids."

"Sandra was lucky," I said. "Me, not so much."

# CHAPTER THIRTY-FIVE

CARL WANTED ME TO spend Thanksgiving with him and his family, but I demurred. Trudi had already invited me to her place. When the day arrived neither their son Peter nor I could eat much. We sat at the table staring at Trudi who didn't eat at all. It took a lot of work not to comment on Trudi's appearance. She was barely a skeleton inside her clothes; she was like a flattened, shrunken cardboard cutout of herself.

Robert roasted a turkey and baked corn bread stuffing, Peter made squash and green beans and a salad, and I brought a cake and a pie from Zabars and a bottle of Pinot Grigio from the wine store on Broadway. We had a quiet early dinner, a late lunch really, and then most of the food got wrapped and put away. Peter and I killed the wine. Peter extracted a second bottle from his parent's wine cabinet but I stopped drinking, mostly because I wasn't all that good at holding my liquor. Peter finished the bottle himself while trying not to look at his mother. He was a photojournalist and it was one of the few times I'd seen him without a camera in his hands.

Earlier in the day, I texted "Happy Thanksgiving" to both my daughters. I missed them terribly. I hoped they were having a happy holiday feast with their father and his family. I also wished litigious George would go die in a hole but that wish probably wasn't going to be granted any time soon and, anyway, it wasn't in keeping with the spirit of the season.

I believed in gratitude and I loved Thanksgiving because I made time to reflect on my many blessings. This year the list seemed shorter. My appetite for giving thanks was dulled. Still, I had to make the effort. I reminded my depressed self not to wish bad things on anyone, no matter how much they deserved it, on Thanksgiving; it just reinforced my own low feelings.

Alex texted back, "Happy Thanksgiving to u mom."

Dani didn't respond.

I was supposed to leave Trudi's around six to have dessert at Carl's and to meet his son and daughter, but the strain of false cheerfulness drained me. I cast about for an excuse to leave Trudi's early. Luckily, the new puppy wasn't housebroken. I was suddenly and profoundly grateful for Beatrice, which struck me as ironic considering all the accidents I'd wiped up and all the curses I'd sent hurling through the ethers at Carl for bestowing a puppy upon me.

I departed for home and Beatrice. I left early from there for Carl's and brought her along, much to the delight of his grandchildren—who were, naturally, quite adorable. His daughter Jennifer and his son Alan and their spouses couldn't have been lovelier. They made me feel welcomed and included and made much of the Zabars pie, bottles of wine, and flowers I brought. They praised Clif's paintings and asked a hundred questions about my gallery. Carl sat there like a happy king in his gorgeous dining room, beaming and holding my hand under the table.

It gladdened my heart to see Carl so happy. Still, I envied him. Rather, I envied his warm, close bonds with his children. He had paid a steep price in losing the wife he thought he'd grow old and die with but he had emerged on the other side of affliction with these tender relationships. His children obviously adored and respected him, and he valued and appreciated them. He was fortunate. They all were.

I didn't know when—or if—things would ever improve with my children, my errant, fiercely loved, much-missed children. Not knowing made me feel lonelier. It made me feel deficient. I chided myself for the selfishness of my self-pity in the face of the pronounced grace of the hospitality I was receiving. But I was still in the midst of it, in the thick of anguish and obstacle. I could not help the way I felt. I could witness my emotions but I couldn't sway them. I stood in the thunderous midst of dark and painful things while Carl had come through to the other side.

———～———

It was around nine when Andrei dropped Beatrice and me off on Amsterdam Avenue by a deli where I could buy almond milk for my morning coffee. I tucked Beatrice under my arm as I made my purchase. The deli clerk was kind enough to ignore her because puppies weren't allowed in food stores, by law. I slid a dollar bill over the counter at him and mouthed "Thank you." I went outside and tried to extricate Beatrice's leash from the house keys in my coat pocket but I wasn't quick enough and she let loose a stream of urine all over my coat.

"Beatrice!" I exclaimed. I knelt and put her down on the pavement. "Bad girl," I scolded. "Go on the ground. Not on my coat."

A couple was walking past. The man stopped and turned toward me. A deep voice asked wonderingly, "Sarah?"

I swiveled around, tangling my heels into the leash, and fell flat on the sidewalk. I scrambled to rise to my hands and knees, tearing a hole in the knee of my pantyhose.

"Scott?"

He reached his hand to grip my arm and help me stand.

"You have a new puppy?"

"Yes, this is Beatrice," I said. Then I dove on her as she was trying to eat something gnarly off the ground. "Drop it!" I whispered to her. I picked her up and held her in my arms, pretending the front of my coat wasn't covered in puppy pee. "She can't eat stuff she finds on the street, she'll get sick."

"Cute puppy, is it a poodle?" enthused the girl. She was tall and slim like Scott, though very milky-skinned and blonde. She had a face of jutting angles and strong lines; she was striking in a sharp-featured way. She wore a camel-colored cashmere coat, a bright blue scarf around her long neck, and she carried a sleek Prada purse. She was maybe all of thirty-two or thirty-three. She scratched Beatrice's head and grinned at her.

"Sarah, this is Kelly," Scott said.

"Kylie," the girl said. She looked up from Beatrice and smiled.

"Sarah," I responded.

*I bet she's an investment banker; she* looks *like an investment banker.*

Although I approved of investment bankers when they bought paintings in my gallery, investment banker was code for a heartless, money-grubber on Wall Street who took advantage of Main Street. But that was my snarky, jealous self, and given the crappy totality of my life, I resolved not to give any of my worse selves a warm reception. I pushed my jealousy away.

Kylie was looking me over with genial, unperturbed interest. I wasn't a threat to her—she was a young and beautiful investment banker on a date with a hot doctor. And by investment banker, I meant cold, ruthless Scrooge-ish manager of money whose unbridled greed nearly destroyed our financial institutions a few years ago.

*So it'll take more than a few words of reproach to get rid of my jealous self.*

"When did you get a puppy? What happened to Groucho?" Scott asked.

"Groucho died."

"When?" Scott asked.

"October. About seven weeks ago."

His eyes narrowed in calculation and his face did that cool Scott Bauer trick of exactly mirroring the progression of his thoughts. I hoped the investment banker girlfriend wasn't adept at reading him because Scott was putting the date of Groucho's death together with my midday phone call to him and his snide return call and he didn't like how the equation came out.

"Well, good to run into you. I don't want to keep you on Thanksgiving," I said. "Hope it was a good one."

"You're not keeping us, I was just walking her ..." Scott started.

Kylie and I both looked at him. Kylie raised her eyebrows.

"Good to see you," Scott said. He took her arm and they glided off, a perfectly matched pair of tall, beautiful beings, the doctor and the investment banker, and by investment banker, I meant a younger, prettier woman who was far more financially successful than I was and probably ever would be. Plus she had Scott on her arm.

———～———

Back home I settled Beatrice into her crate. She curled up on her foam doggy bed and immediately fell asleep, looking all too cute, just like a Norman Rockwell icon of canine innocence. I wasn't fooled. I knew she'd be up at one in the morning, whining to go out. I changed into my nightgown and drew on a robe, got a glass of water, and stood at the kitchen sink drinking. It wasn't late but it had been an emotional day.

*Ohmigod, Trudi ...*

I was looking forward to curling up in bed. I'd bought a new book about Fra Angelico and the Florentine market. *The New York Times* gave it a glowing review, and I was salivating to dig into it. In my opinion, Fra Angelico, whom the Italians called Beato Angelico, had been somewhat ignored by art historians of late. The new book would stir up well-deserved interest in his ravishingly beautiful paintings. Devoted Fra Angelico, who wept when his brush touched the canvas to paint his Savior, had reached a height of spiritual grandeur seldom seen in art before or since his lifetime.

Maybe I could write a review of the new tome for *American Artist* magazine?

I grabbed the book off the table and checked my cell phone one last time to see if Dani had responded. Nope. I took another peek at Alex's response: "Happy thanksgiving to u mom." It was a connection of sorts, small but appreciated; even a molecule of connection staved off the despair. Then I turned off my cell phone, left it on the kitchen counter, and padded back toward my bedroom.

The buzzer rang at the front door. For a split-second I wondered, *Scott?* But it was surely Mrs. Zlotowitz with a toy or treat of Beatrice's that had been left upstairs in her apartment last time she babysat. I was always leaving something.

"Mrs. Z, what'd I forget this time?" I asked, throwing open the door.

Scott stood there.

I was struck dumb. I didn't know what to say. He didn't make a move toward me.

He just looked at me and for once, his angular face was enigmatic.

I reached out and grabbed the lapel of his coat and pulled him inside.

That must have been the invitation Scott was waiting for because he put his arms around me and kissed me. I had forgotten how delicious it was when he did that, and I dissolved like sugar in hot tea. He didn't say anything—our mouths were busy so that was to be expected—but he maneuvered me backward into my living room and pushed me back down onto my sofa. He pulled off his glasses and set them carefully on the end table and then leaned down and kissed me again.

His mouth tasted like turkey and trimmings and faintly of wine.

My hands got busy unbuttoning his wool coat. He wore a blue, button-front chambray shirt with the posh hand of Italian fabric; it was more upscale than his usual T-shirt, and my fingers tripped on the mother-of-pearl buttons.

*He went all out for his date with that girl.*

My robe was no obstruction, and he untied it and pulled it off quickly. He grinned when he saw my derelict nightie.

I unbuttoned his shirt. He got my panties off and he pushed my nightie up around my neck, put his hand between my legs and pushed his fingers inside me.

I moaned and writhed and then stood up on my knees and kissed his mouth, letting my tongue taste deep into his mouth and inviting his inside me. I pushed my breasts into his bare chest and then unbuckled his pants, which he took over because he was quicker at working them off. Finally, he was naked and pushing me back down onto the sofa while lowering himself on top of me. I was soft and wet and open and so hungry for him.

"Wait," I said, rearing up. "Condom?"

"Better than that," he said. He reached down for his coat on the floor, dug into the pocket, and brought out a yellow box. "Plastic baggies!" Then he was struck by a thought and his dark eyes narrowed. "I didn't bring a rubber band."

I giggled and Scott leaned forward to kiss me and then I ruined it all. My giggles turned to tears and instead of fucking me like my whole body craved, Scott pulled me into his lap and let me sob into his warm, bare flesh.

That was what my soul wanted.

We sat in silence when I was finally done weeping. I rubbed the snot off my face. I said hoarsely, "I might move to New Britain, Connecticut."

"Why?" he asked. He stroked my hair off my shoulders and neck.

"I might get a job offer there."

He kept smoothing my hair back and running his hands along my shoulders and arms.

"At the New Britain Art Museum," I clarified.

"What about Alex?"

"Alex is suing me, with her father. She hit me and she's doing drugs again and cutting class. I kicked her out and told her she had to go back to drug rehab, get a job and never cut class again if she wanted to live with me. Those were the conditions; so she and her father are suing me." The words tumbled out in one long run-on sentence. I took a deep breath and exhaled forcefully.

"She *hit* you?" Scott said, in a serious voice. His hands tightened around my upper arms.

I nodded.

"I'm glad you kicked her out." He put his hands alongside my face and tilted my head so my eyes met his. He looked faintly cross-eyed from his near-sightedness, as he always did from that distance, about eight inches. "You did the right thing."

"I feel like such a failure. Everything is crashing. My gallery is foundering and my kid is suing me." It was a relief to say it openly that way. I peered into Scott's eyes. "Trudi is dying."

Scott's lips tightened and he cuddled me into his chest.

"I've extended her treatment far beyond what the protocol calls for. I don't know what else to do. I'm sorry. Some people don't respond. Some of my results are so good, but not hers."

"It's not your fault."

"I know, but I take it personally." A tightly-held emotion clenched his body. Then he asked, "Why didn't you tell me that your dog was dying? I wouldn't have been such a jerk. It wasn't fair."

"Life isn't always fair," I murmured. I slid off his lap and sat beside him. I pulled down my nightie to cover myself and twined my fingers into his. Beatrice yelped in her sleep. I asked, "How are Janey and Max?"

"Janey loves her new school. They've advanced her a grade, which they never do, but she was so far ahead of the other kids in reading and math that they ended up doing that." Scott sounded proud.

"She is absolutely that smart," I agreed with a smile.

"They ask about you. Weirdest thing. They were over at my apartment last weekend. Max found a roll of tape and brought it to me. He said, 'This is for Sarah.' I couldn't figure out what he meant. Janey giggled and wouldn't say anything. Do you know what that was about?"

"Max is talking?"

He scooted around so he sat facing me; one of his long legs crooked for his ankle to rest on his other knee. "Yes, he speaks sometimes in full sentences. You never know when. His pediatrician doesn't seem concerned. Of course, Lisa took him to a pediatric neurologist, who isn't concerned either. So what is the deal with you and electrical tape?"

I did not want to get into a discussion with Scott about taping his son to a chair. I asked, "Do you ever give him clay to play with? He's so tactile, he really enjoyed that."

"I'll get some for my apartment," Scott said.

"I recommend Sculpey. And get sculpting tools, too."

He reached out and smoothed my bangs down. "It won't work, you know."

"What won't work?"

"Running away. That's what I did when Lisa dumped me for Rick. I ran away. I called Ron Gelder, who taught me at Harvard, and asked if there could possibly be a place for me at Mount Sinai. He jumped at it. So I came here and then Lisa and Rick decided that moving to New York was what they wanted, too. We were all starting over in the same city. I realized that I could leave Boston but my problems were going to come with me wherever I went because my problems were inside me." He grinned in a rueful, half-hearted way. "I couldn't run away from myself."

"Being the director of the New Britain Art Museum would be a good career move for me, a real coup, since my gallery isn't going to make it," I argued.

Scott shrugged. "If that's what you want, sure, you can go be the director of the New Britain Art Museum. But, Sarah, you're bringing yourself with you. All the hell that's in your life will ride on your shoulders to Connecticut. So be sure that moving to be the director of that art museum is what you really want."

"I am not my problems," I objected. "I've done everything I can to the best of my ability to solve them and still this shit is raining down on my head!"

Scott ran his index finger under the yoke of my nightgown and along my collarbone. "I didn't articulate it very well. I didn't leave Lisa; she left me. All I got to choose was how to respond to what she did. So I ran away and nursed my bad feelings. Then, when I met someone wonderful," he ran his hand up my neck to cup my cheek, "someone lively and beautiful and odd—"

"Hey!"

"Odd in a good way," he qualified. "Odd like she'll screw you if you have a plastic baggy and no condom. Odd like she'll smear ice cream on your best suit."

"Gelato."

He smiled. "Delightful odd. The thing is, I fell back on my old habits. I treated her the same way that I had treated Lisa. I ignored her except for when it was convenient for me. I made her feel less important than my work. I put up barriers."

"I didn't cause my children to hate me! I was a good-enough mother!" I felt myself succumbing to self-pity and I tried but failed to quash it. I said, "I don't deserve for Dani to hate me or for Alex to sue me or for George to have a blood vendetta against me. I don't deserve to have my gallery fail or my dog die or my best friend suffer from incurable cancer. It's so unfair!"

"Life is not always fair. *You* would tell me that." Scott shrugged.

"I did tell you that."

"I'm not implying causality. I don't think you caused all these things, Sarah. Maybe some of them, I don't really know. I'm still not saying it correctly." He tilted his head and his face shuttered. Finally, he looked back at me with a vulnerable expression. "There is a great mystery at the heart of life; I see it every day with my patients. All these things cross your path, sometimes violently. Events, catastrophes. Terminal cancer. Abandonment, rejection, loss. They upset everything and change the course of your life. Sometimes for better, sometimes for worse. All you can do is see them as an opportunity for yourself. For you to wake up and grow. There's a kind of divinity in seeing the opportunity that's offered for you to wake up, for you to keep your heart open. To love again.

"After Lisa left, it took me a while to see that I still had a decision to make, and that was to say 'yes' to what happened. To be open to what came next. That's why I said 'yes' to you that day in the candy store."

I wanted to argue that he was the one who propositioned me, but déjà vu descended. I had the same feeling that I'd experienced in Santa Barbara when Chloe was talking to me: that I should be still and listen with an open heart.

Scott grinned and shook his head. "From that moment, there's been this thing ... this loose and erotic connection between us. I prefer orderliness. I wanted to control it. I wanted it to look like what I've known before. But it's a mistake for me to try to control it, this thing with you. Because when I go with it, I feel hopeful. Despite the hurt and betrayal— my dad leaving when I was a kid, Lisa dumping me for Rick, watching good people die every day at work—I feel open and hopeful. I feel undefended. It's an amazing feeling. Scary but worthwhile." He stood and picked through the clothes on the floor for his underwear and then his pants.

I watched him dress. Finally, I said softly, "Stay. Don't go. Spend the night."

He was buttoning his shirt. "I always wanted you to invite me to sleep over."

"So?"

"So, no. You have to figure some things out." He grinned lopsidedly. "I may be younger than you but I'm old enough to know what I want.

Also what I don't want and that's to share a woman with another man. That doesn't work for me. That's me saying 'yes' to who I am."

"Do you want me?" I asked, plaintively.

"Sarah, you know the answer to that." He ruffled my hair. "To be clear, I don't want a mistress. I'm looking for a partner."

"Do you know the difference?" I said with kindness, not confrontation.

I was so attuned to him that I could feel him thinking "fair question." I loved that he was willing to acknowledge that. "I think so. I'm willing to learn."

"Will you keep seeing that girl?"

Scott studied my face. "Yes. Kelly's great. She sure beats the hell out of sitting alone in my apartment on nights I don't have the kids."

"Kylie," I corrected.

Scott grimaced. "I met her a few weeks ago. She had Thanksgiving dinner with friends and invited me to join them. It's not my year with the kids and I didn't want to travel back to Cleveland because of work, so I went with her."

"Uh huh. What does she do? Is she an investment banker?"

He nodded, picked up his glasses from the end table, and positioned them on his face. "She works at Morgan Stanley."

*I knew she was an investment banker! And by 'investment banker' I mean soulless lucre obsessed ...*

Scott was watching me and grinning widely.

"What?"

"You do this thing," he said, his affect and his voice softening like melted caramel, "this amazing thing. You express all your thoughts on your face. You don't like investment bankers. Or Kylie."

"I like them when they buy paintings at my gallery," I muttered. "At least you got her name right. If you're going to keep dating her, you'd better remember her name."

"Are you going to keep seeing that rich guy?"

"Technically, I'm in a mutually exclusive relationship with Carl. I shouldn't have slept with you ... well, we didn't. But almost. I would have ..."

Scott shrugged on his coat. "You have a problem with fidelity. You should work on that. It's not your best self." He pulled on his gloves. "I won't put up with it. I won't ever again get into a serious relationship with a woman who won't commit exclusively to me."

He walked to the door and turned and faced me. "Sarah, I'm ten years younger than you, and I have two young children and I get called in to work even on my birthday. If you're with me you're going to be babysitting."

He turned away and opened the door.

*Not cooking.*

"God no, not cooking," he said, without turning around. "So you see, the question isn't, do I want you, it's do you want me?"

# CHAPTER THIRTY-SIX

IT WOULD BE INACCURATE to say that I suddenly got a grip on my life. Everything still sucked. In fact, it got worse.

Carl's birthday in early December coincided with Chloe's opening. I went to his apartment for a celebratory dinner the night before. Sergei took me up in the elevator. He said, "Your friend is here."

"My friend?"

"The English lady who is very sick," he clarified, in his thick Russian accent.

"Trudi is here?"

*What's she doing at Carl's?*

We had spoken earlier in the day on the phone and she hadn't mentioned anything to me about coming for dinner.

"With her husband," Sergei said, nodding. "I take them up two minutes ago."

The elevator doors opened and Carl came into the foyer. His craggy face wore a curious expression but brightened when he saw me. "Sarah, sweetheart." He kissed me.

I handed him his birthday gift. "Happy Birthday, Carl. This is for you. Trudi's here?"

He nodded and took my coat. "Trudi and Robert are in the dining room." He smiled at the parcel, which I'd wrapped in glossy paper and tied with a gold bow. "Thank you for this!"

"Happy birthday," I repeated. Then I skipped into the dining room to find out what Trudi was doing there.

She looked slightly less ghastly than she had at Thanksgiving. She hadn't gained back an ounce of the weight she'd lost but a bit of color enlivened her cheeks. She looked up and smiled at me, and it was a sincere smile. She looked peaceful and composed.

*Is there good news? Is she turning the corner finally?*

I felt a cautious burst of hope. I hugged her and then Robert. I sat down at the table, which was set for two, not for four. I folded my hands atop the table and gazed expectantly at Trudi.

Carl hurried into the dining room. "Can I get you anything, Trudi? Robert?"

"We're fine, Carl," Trudi said, gesturing for him to sit down. When he took the seat beside me, she said, "We don't want to disturb your elegant dinner."

"Nonsense, I cooked plenty, there's enough for four; why don't I set two more places?" Carl said in that tone he used when it really wasn't a question but a command that he was phrasing politely. "Then you can join us for cake."

"Maybe some cake; sweets are about all I can eat these days. In a moment. Robert and I have something to tell you two."

"You're pregnant," I offered, trying for levity.

Carl laid his hand on mine.

"I do so enjoy American humor," Trudi said and gave me one of her mordant looks that meant she loved me. "I will miss it. Robert and I are going home."

"Home? Your home is in the West Village," I puzzled, then I got it. "Wait, no, you're going back to London?"

"Dartmouth, Devon," Trudi said, nodding. "My grandparents' cottage. My cousins live there. You visited years ago, Sarah. That's where I spent summers when I was a child. Peter will join us."

I vaguely remembered a large English period residence with five or six bedrooms, with river and countryside views and a conservatory. "Why are you going to Dartmouth?"

Carl squeezed my hand.

Trudi perused my face. After a few beats, she said, "There will be no more chemotherapy treatments. I'm going back home to live out the remainder of my time. That's what I want."

"Trudi," I whispered.

She nodded slowly. "After all these years, you're a sister to me, Sarah. The sister I never had. I am sorry to leave you. I know it will be hard for you. I know you'll want to come be with me, but I don't want that. It will get worse before the end and I want you to remember me with my dignity intact."

"A lot of people have good results. Maybe if you do a few more treatments the protocol will start working," I suggested.

She shook her head.

I said, "Wait, Carl endowed a chair at Columbia-Presbyterian for pancreatic cancer research. Why don't you try one of the doctors there? Scott won't mind. He'll be happy to see you trying another option—"

"There are no more options for me," Trudi stated.

I took a deep breath. "There are always options!"

"Only for the living," she said softly. "I am not among the living. Look at me."

I looked across the table and met her eyes, so hollowed in her face that it now looked like the afterthought of features pasted onto a skull, she was that attenuated. She was also placid and set. I said, "If that's what you're going to do, I'm coming. I'll close the gallery; it's failing anyway. There were a lot of bedrooms in that cottage; there'll be one for me."

Trudi looked steadily at me. "Sarah, I don't want you to come. I love you, but no."

She had voiced aloud that she loved me—something she never did as a matter of ingrained British self-restraint. I grasped the finality of her departure to England. My breath rasped and tears dripped down my face. Trudi hated overt displays of emotion, and I didn't want to make her uncomfortable but I couldn't stop the tears.

Trudi fidgeted. She said, "About that cake, Carl? I think we could all use a piece right now. Which bakery is it from?"

Robert put his arm around her. "Trudi, you are doing what is right and good for you. I support you and I will be with you. We understand that we have to let go of you. You must understand how hard that will be for us. I am losing my other half, the greater part of my life. Sarah is losing her closest friend, a sister. You have the harder passage but our lives will never be the same."

"I am terrified," Trudi said in a low voice. She leaned into him and pressed her face into his shoulder. Her shoulders shook slightly.

Carl covered his eyes with one hand.

I knew Carl was weeping and that he had been triggered into re-experiencing his own loss, but I couldn't reach out to comfort him at that moment. I could only sit in his sumptuous dining room with Clif's river nymphs staring down at me like the guardians of a gate to another world and remember my time with Trudi. I remembered when we celebrated her PhD with pints in a London pub. Was there better beer anywhere than sour ale in a London pub? I remembered her job offer in New York. She was the matron of honor at my wedding to George and she refused to wear the dress I chose and instead showed up in a simple dark blue skirt suit and matching hat.

She was there for me to cry on through my first divorce.

I remembered her telling me tartly, "Please rethink this impending disaster," when I told her I was marrying Clif. But she insisted on coming with us to City Hall anyway and she and Robert bought us dinner afterward.

She had commiserated with me when the relationship with Clif flat-lined—and she never once said, "I told you so."

She used to drive to New Paltz with me and hike and then drink cheap wine in the local climber's hangout and argue about Pop Art or Neue Sachlichkeit or Impressionism, all of which she liked more than I did.

These many years, I had shared everything with Trudi.

---

Afterward, I would always wonder about that time when we were all simply present in the flow of feeling; there was no sense of the past leading to the present that gives way to the future. Carl, Robert, Trudi, and I sat together in a higher knowing than I had ever before experienced: a knowing of deaths and ends. A knowing that everything was meant to be let go of so that our souls could stand naked in the void.

It shattered me and it was the most sacred moment of my life.

And then ... and then ... the planet started whirling again. Clocks chimed. My nose itched. Trudi took a shuddering inhalation and Robert coughed. Carl's stomach rumbled.

Carl rose from the table and brought out his birthday cake, a yellow buttercream confection with chocolate frosting. He used a butcher knife to cut off uneven chunks. We ate without napkins or silverware, licking our fingers, and that struck us all as perfect and then silly. We giggled, even Trudi who managed to eat a few bites.

"Open your present, Carl," Trudi said, pushing my gift toward him.

"Oh, all right," he said, lighting up like a little boy. He slid his finger through the tape on the bottom, then his blue eyes sparkled mischievously and he tore open the wrapping paper.

"The Emperor," Trudi said. She gave me a sharp look and I hoped her piquancy wouldn't leave her until she took her last breath. The world would be poorer without it.

"This looks like ...Victor Brauner," Carl said, his gravelly voice impressed. He held the painting close to his face and studied it. "Didn't he do a tarot card series?"

"He did, but I don't know if he painted this," I admitted. "It's not signed and I've never taken it to be authenticated. I bought it years ago in Paris. A Romanian guy was selling it on the street and he claimed his wife painted it."

"Sarah, I'm touched. It's absolutely beautiful," Carl said. He leaned toward me and took my head in both hands and kissed my mouth.

I cared deeply for this man, and I had just shared something inexpressibly compelling with him, but I couldn't help but think of my response when Scott kissed me.

*Is it just chemical with Scott? Or is there more, because there's something real here with Carl.*

A while later, Trudi and Robert took their leave. We didn't hug because we didn't need to. We were bound together in a way that couldn't be broken—though I knew that Trudi's passing would challenge that.

Then I knew I had to hug her anyway.

I rang for the elevator. Sergei brought me down to the lobby and I ran down Park Avenue coatless. I caught up with Trudi, grabbed her, and squeezed and squeezed and hung on.

Trudi hugged me back, her tiny frame like a wisp of smoke in my arms. Finally, she said, "So it's the Emperor now? Not the King of Swords? Are you sure?"

I released her enough to look at her. My teeth chattered in the freezing December night.

"Scott has it in his office, behind his desk," she said. "I saw it this fall. I noticed it again today when I informed him that I was leaving."

"I thought you wanted me with Carl," I said, shivering.

She smiled. "I want you to be happy. And healthy. Now run along inside before you catch a cold. I'll call you from Dartmouth."

---

The next day was Chloe's opening and who appeared at the gallery in the early morning but Chloe Kennedy herself, shepherded off the red-eye by the irrepressible Marcia Mensdorff. Marcia, with her extraordinary skills of persuasion, had managed to get Chloe on an airplane. They had six paintings with them. It was an unexpected boon.

Carl showed up at lunch time with his secretary Karen, whom he said was going to be my assistant for the day—as if I couldn't handle the details of my own show in my own gallery. It left me in an awkward position. I didn't want the woman around, but how could I refuse Carl's thoughtfulness?

He insisted on taking Chloe and Marcia out for a good meal. I stayed behind in the gallery, scrambling to rearrange the paintings that were already hanging on the wall so as to include the additional works. It was a hassle and time was short. Karen stood there, wringing her hands and wanting to help, and I felt pressured.

Still, I was thrilled to have the extra paintings. The show was full and powerful, a poetic powerhouse that focused on Chloe's mastery of form, line, and color; her landscapes were mystical and intimate while also being objective, elusive, and mythic. I was proud of the show. I was proud of Chloe for her work and even more proud of her for boarding an airplane to attend.

Karen was typing up the last of the new labels under my rather strenuous supervision when my cell phone rang: *Holiday* by Madonna. It was Scott.

"You're having an event at your gallery today. Good luck."

"Thank you," I said, smiling. It was good to hear his voice. I walked out of the gallery into the street. "How's Kelly?"

"Kylie," he said. "Mrs. Waterston is flying to England this afternoon. Are you OK with that?"

"No, but it's not my decision. Are *you* OK with it?" I asked. He had tried his utmost to save Trudi and failing was sure to be painful for him. Scott cared about his patients.

"Not really, but it's not my decision, either," he said, his deep voice suddenly ragged. After a few beats, he said, "Enjoy your opening."

He wanted to go but I had a question for him. "Scott, you understand that in ten years I'll be nearly sixty, right?"

"And I'll be nearly fifty."

"You can do the math."

"Yes, I got a perfect score on the math SAT. I got an A in every math class I ever took."

I interrupted him. "I'm not talking about computation. I'm talking about the irrational human calculation of time. When you're almost fifty and I'm almost sixty, you'll be gorgeous and distinguished looking. That's the way you'll age. And I'm going to look my age. I'll fight it—I will fight it tooth and nail, ungracefully and ferociously—but that's a battle I will lose. I'm afraid I'll look like I'm your mother."

"I see what you mean by irrational," he said dryly.

"Irrational doesn't mean unreal."

There was that warm and silent thrum of a massive brain in gear. When Scott spoke, he was subdued. "It doesn't mean unreal, but it does mean I have to think about it before I respond. I'm better with computations. I'm not good with irrational. It challenges me. I hope your opening goes well," he said. "I hope you sell a hundred paintings and you don't have to move to Connecticut."

In the end, seven of Chloe's gorgeous paintings sold—one to Katsu, who didn't try to bargain but who gratefully accepted the ten percent neighborhood discount I offered him. With the proceeds, I paid my mom's old friend the rent that was due, and I paid the tax bill and a few other bills.

I was at zero. And desperately grateful to be there.

# CHAPTER THIRTY-SEVEN

MARCIA AND CHLOE STAYED three days, during which Chloe was often at the gallery, receiving the acclaim she deserved. I put her up in a small and decent, if not lavish, hotel on the Upper West Side. Marcia stayed at the Four Seasons, as usual.

I made some phone calls and got Chloe some interviews with the art press. I invited the *American Artist* editor to lunch with Chloe and me and he was charmed by her quiet demeanor and outrageous talent.

I contacted Vimal Mercer, a Brooklyn arts blogger whose site got upwards of ten thousand hits every month, and arranged for him to have tea with Chloe. Afterward, he walked around the gallery with Chloe and live-streamed their conversation about her paintings on social media. I captured the stream so I could upload the video into YouTube. Vimal left raving about Chloe's work, and I knew we'd have a glowing review seen by all Vimal's loyal followers.

I took Chloe to the Frick and to Sotheby's and introduced her to the folks I still knew in those places, just so the art world would be talking about Chloe Kennedy and her extraordinary landscapes.

If I took the job in New Britain—if it was offered to me—I was going to miss bringing the work of worthy new artists to the public's attention; miss seeing them buying those works, bringing them home, loving them and being uplifted by them. It was my way of tendering a blessing to the world.

Maybe in my next life I could be an artist myself; I was sure that Frida Kahlo and I were soul sisters and that our souls grew together in the same soul group like grapes in a single cluster. But in this life, I had the joy and privilege of finding and showing great artists.

Chloe's presence meant that Marcia and I couldn't get ourselves into trouble, as was our wont. So we promised to meet again soon for merry mischief. Marcia texted confirmation of said nefarious plans from the airport as she accompanied Chloe back to the West Coast.

Sitting at my desk in my gallery, I read her text with a smile. I texted back that she would have my full cooperation. The gallery door opened and Carl's friends, Joe and Regan, walked in. I jumped up and went to greet them with kisses and handshakes all around.

"We're here to buy paintings," sang the bombshell Regan with a flourish. She wore a female-skin, full-length, fully-let-out mink coat whose sheen brought out her own feminine silkiness.

"Paintings, plural?" I lit up.

*Ka-chink, ka-chink* went the mercenary cockles of my soul.

"Where will you put them?"

"New York," Joe said.

"Palm Beach," Regan said at the same time.

They looked at each other.

"New York," Regan said.

"Palm Beach," Joe said over her.

I got a bad feeling.

"You're interested in Chloe Kennedy's work?"

"Yes, we're interested in Chloe Kennedy," Regan said. She looked around. "Which ones are hers? Any of these?"

"She painted all these landscapes, aren't they beautiful?" I enthused. I led them around the gallery.

Joe inquired about the price of every painting. After we circumnavigated the gallery, Joe and Regan put their heads together and whispered. I excused myself, ostensibly to check my email, but really to give them some privacy.

Marcia texted back an appallingly ribald outline for an evening of unmitigated revelry, complete with fountains of champagne, dancing boys, and monkeys playing guitar. I had to giggle. It felt good to let in some levity. It felt good to laugh. Frida Kahlo said, "Nothing is worth more than laughter. It is strength to laugh and to abandon oneself, to be light."

It was a light that co-existed with shadow. Nothing in my life was solved; the court appearance for Alex and George's suit against me was scheduled for next week, I still had to worry about the gallery rent for January, Dani still wasn't talking to me, and Trudi had called from her family place in England sounding weak and tired. But I was starting to say 'yes' to my life. I was accepting my life without resistance or clinging to an ideal of how things should be. It wasn't resignation or submission; it was surrender to the moment. In some mysterious way I couldn't parse, by surrendering to how much everything sucked came the possibility for laughter as well as tears.

Regan and Joe appeared at the door to my office.

"We know what we want," Regan said. She named the two priciest of Chloe's paintings—her two largest works.

"Yes, we want those," Joe echoed, beaming.

"You're looking for large canvases?" I asked. "Those aren't really representative of her work; typically, she works on a medium-sized canvas. Do you have the wall space for them?"

"Yes, we want large pieces," Regan exclaimed.

"They're beautiful," Joe exclaimed. "We'll put them in Palm Beach."

At the same time, Regan said, "They'll be perfect in New York."

They exchanged a sly and humorous glance then stood holding hands, smiling at me and looking very pleased with themselves.

I felt sorry about bursting their happy balloon but I knew what I had to do.

"I'm sorry. Those paintings aren't for sale."

Regan and Joe looked dumbfounded. She tucked a lock of her glossy hair behind one ear and asked, "They're not?"

"We'll buy two others," Joe said, with an expansive gesture. "What are two of Chloe Kennedy's best paintings?"

"None of my paintings are for sale."

I stood up from behind my desk. "Carl is lucky to have you guys."

"Ah, uh," Joe muttered with a pained look on his face.

"Is he reimbursing you for the paintings, or are you buying them outright because he asked you to?"

"Oh, no," Joe said.

Regan didn't bother to obfuscate. "Sarah, Carl is worried about your gallery. He's only trying to help."

"I love him for it, but I don't need his help." I walked through the door and gestured for them to follow me. "I appreciate you coming in."

"Come on, Sarah," Regan coaxed. "We love art and we want to patronize your gallery. That's why Carl asked us to come by."

"Really? What other artists do you collect?" I asked. "Name one."

They didn't have an answer. I held the door to the gallery open.

"Don't be mad at Carl," Joe mumbled, kissing me goodbye.

"Don't worry, I'm not mad at Carl," I promised. But something in me crystallized and by that, I meant it had become clear like a crystal refracting light, as well as manifest into something solid. I went back to my desk and picked up the phone without thinking it all through, except in some subterranean, subconscious way. That's the thing about losing everything: you have nothing left to lose so you can go for broke, go all out, go after a truly big dream that doesn't have a prayer of coming true.

I called Jim Harte.

"Sarah! The board is meeting once more this weekend, but I think we'll have good news for you," Jim boomed, in his hearty voice. "There's been a lot of discussion but the board is impressed by your creative approach."

"Jim, I have a request," I said. "It's a big one. I'd like you to put up a show about modern classicism that includes Clif Perini's works."

Jim was quiet for a few moments. "You aren't taking the job, are you?"

*That is a very intuitive man.*

"No."

"Why not?"

*Because I have to go after my 'yes'.*

"My gallery is foundering, Jim. You knew that. I made enough at Chloe Kennedy's opening to squeak through but it's no way to run a business. I'm going to close up shop and look for a position here in the city."

"I'm sorry to hear that, Sarah."

"Me, too," I admitted. There was a deep ache in my chest just below my breastbone, but there was also relief. It was a keen and cutting consolation to voice aloud the very path I had tried so mightily to avoid.

"I suppose it's understandable that you want to stay in the city."

"Yes."

"So you're not going to take the job, but you're asking me to put up a show of Clif's work? This is irregular. What's in it for the New Britain Art Museum?"

"Free work, Jim. I'll do this for you for free. Plus you wanted something fresh. This will be fresh," I said. "Come on, Jim. It'll stir things up at New Britain while you guys have your interim period, and make some excitement. It'll be a beautiful show and it will make New Britain look good."

"It costs money to foist a show," he objected.

"I'll get some donations into the museum for the purpose of the show."

*I'll hit up Skinny Mrs. Banker, tell her it will be good karma for the new baby.*

It was a stretch but I could make it work. If not, I'd find someone else to shake down.

"You're going to leave me with Paula Clarke as director and that broad spends too much time at spin class," Jim grumbled.

I giggled. "Great minds think alike. What do you say about the show?"

"You expect me to tell the board that you won't replace Mel and despite that we should do a show of Clif's work that you will curate and fund on a volunteer basis?" Jim clarified.

"Maybe spin it as a show about modern classicism rather than specifically mentioning Clif," I advised.

"You're telling me how to spin a pitch?" Jim laughed. "Come on, Sarah. Take the damn job. You'd enjoy it and I'd enjoy working with you."

"If the museum was fifty miles closer to Manhattan, I would," I said. "But I'm here, now."

Jim rumbled, "I'll think about it," which meant 'yes.' I could feel it. He hung up.

Instead of phoning Carl, I texted him, asking him to meet me that night for a drink at the bar in Chelsea we liked.

---

I sat down at a wooden table in the bar and felt my tummy explode with moths and fireflies. It was going to be hard. I had arrived before Carl and I ordered myself a glass of red wine. Maybe it would calm my nerves. Was I making the biggest mistake of my life? Did I understand what I was giving up?

Carl came in a few minutes later. He came to the table and seated himself and his laser blue eyes scanned me. "I hope you're not offended about Joe and Regan."

"I understand that you were only trying to help."

I perused his craggy, aristocratic face and solid form and thought how much I was going to miss him. He was dear to me. My heart wrung out.

"Because I care about you, Sarah," he said.

"I care about you, Carl."

A waiter came over to take his drink order. Carl ordered a scotch. When the waiter left he asked in a huskier voice than usual, "Why are you breaking up with me? What did I do wrong?"

"Nothing. You've done everything right," I said. I took in a big gulp of wine.

"Is this about Trudi going home to England to die?" he asked softly. "You're bound to be in turmoil over that. It brings up a lot of feelings for me, and I haven't been her closest friend for more than twenty years."

I shook my head. "That's some kind of transition for me but I don't know what. It's not that."

"Is this about Bauer?"

I paused to consider the question because it deserved an honest answer. "No. It's not about him."

His blue eyes were glued to my face. "Explain it to me then, because I thought we had something good, something real, something that would endure."

"So did I," I said sadly. I tried to explain to him what was going on inside me. "There are things in my life I can't change. Painful things. I've been flailing around, not knowing what to do about anything. Not knowing what couldn't be changed and what could. I've been like a beach ball on the ocean during a hurricane. Passively acted on by the storm."

Carl nodded.

"To cope, I put up barriers to what I was feeling. I don't know if that makes sense."

Carl smiled a tiny wisp of a smile. "It makes perfect sense. That's how I got through Nancy's death and the year after it."

"You've been an incredible support; someone for me to turn to but there's something you don't understand about me, Carl. That's this: I don't want to be taken care of the way you need to take care of someone. It makes me feel inadequate and incompetent. Even when you're right about what I need, which you usually are. Always, damn it, you're *always* right, OK? But it feels closed and unyielding to me, like another barrier, and I already have so many. But I'm finally waking up inside of my life. It's kind of a nightmare, but I want to find my way in it, whether it's a nightmare or a fantasy, without barriers. I want to find where I feel open.

That's all I have, my feelings. So I want to give myself that gift of finding the openings. I want to explore that self who doesn't defend herself from what is. The self who is 'yes.'"

Carl sat and sipped his scotch. After a while, he said, "I can restrain myself."

"No, you can't. Then you aren't being who you are—you aren't saying 'yes' to your own self. You're just naturally generous and encompassing. It's a wonderful, amazing quality. Don't ever change." I felt tears well up in my eyes but I held them back—it wouldn't be fair to Carl for me to cry.

"I really have enjoyed being with you, Sarah," he said. "I'm really going to miss you."

# CHAPTER THIRTY-EIGHT

I WAS HOME DECORATING a three-foot Christmas tree while listening to pop rock from the eighties and nineties. I decided to celebrate Christmas—and Hanukkah—whether or not my prodigal daughters celebrated with me. When I was a kid, my mom and dad had observed both holidays. I received both gelt from Mom and toys from Santa, aka Dad. It was one of the few times through the year that my parents' onerous dual observance worked in my favor.

I strung the lights around the tree. It was the Sunday night before the Monday of the court date for George and Alex's suit against me. The lurking, suffocating numbness returned. I wondered how I could have been stupid enough to break up with Carl, whose loving, supportive company would have bolstered me right about then.

*What kind of nonsense was that stuff about barriers and finding 'yes'? What's wrong with having someone who cares about me give me what I need?*

I could have slapped my forehead. Instead I picked up an old ornament, a sparkling glass reindeer, from the box of ornaments and hooked it on the tree. Dani had always loved that reindeer; it had been 'hers' to hang. I remembered various times when Dani, Alex, and I had decorated a tree; then I pushed away the memories. I was already lonely; there was no point in torturing myself.

I picked up another ornament, a glass caroling mouse. I pushed Beatrice down from the box so she didn't grab anything fragile and shatter it inside her mouth.

Suddenly a lightness, an exultation, swept up my body.

I was shaken with surprise. I stood and turned around slowly in my living room, looking for a physical explanation for what I was feeling.

Just then, Trudi stood before me in the center of the living room. She was smiling and whole, of normal weight, her blonde hair thick and shoulder-length, styled in her trademark pageboy. She wore her favorite gray pantsuit, a yellow scarf around her neck, and a cerulean blue silk crescent hat with poms and a veil.

Beatrice yipped.

I blinked and Trudi was gone. I was filled with a radiant equanimity. *Trudi is dead.*

I retrieved my cell phone and the house phone, put them on the sofa, and sat next to them. Robert would be calling. I felt Trudi. I didn't see her, but I felt her. It was like she hung over my head, but she wasn't quiescent; she was downloading into me. What was she downloading? I couldn't say. Something luminous and unfathomable.

I should have been shattered. I should have been mourning. Those would come. For the moment, I was exalted.

Twenty minutes later, the phone rang. It was Robert.

"She's gone, Sarah."

"I know," I said.

He was weeping. "She was heavily doped up for the last few days. A few hours ago, she came awake. She told Peter and me that she loved us. She told us to tell you that she loved you. Then she drifted off. And then she was gone."

"It was about twenty minutes ago," I murmured, tears on my face. "I'm sorry, Robert."

---

The next morning, I met Marty O'Shea at the courthouse. The venue was family court, not superior court, where all of George's other suits against me had been heard. Carl theorized that George's new lawyer moved the venue because George kept losing at superior court so perhaps the judges there disliked him. I thought it had something to do with Alex joining him. Marty hadn't commented on the change of venue.

Marty was well dressed in a good suit. He was focused and intense, as he always was in preparation for his presentation to the judge. I could feel him gathering himself into a laser line of intention.

I was quiet and shaky. I wanted to collapse and run away. I woke at four and wanted to phone Trudi to get her support for the travail I had to face, but Trudi was dead. I came unglued in the pre-dawn hour as I realized what that meant. I shouldn't have had to be reminded, of course, given the loss of my parents, and the way I'd grappled with the awful finality of that. But right then I was glad they were gone so they weren't around to see me sued by my own daughter.

Marty led the way through the security check and into the courthouse. We took seats in the waiting room alongside the drug dealers and hookers who wanted to see more of their children and were seeking to alter custody arrangements.

The judge's clerk, a young, well-put-together Spanish man, came looking for us. He beckoned us to a private meeting room. He and Marty talked in quiet voices. I sat there, nodding and listening, occasionally adding a detail.

"Unfortunately, despite all my client's efforts to help her, Alexandra has been completely off the rails," Marty said. He turned to me. "Show him the pictures, Sarah."

I felt a hand on my shoulder. I literally looked over my shoulder to see who stood behind me.

The space was vacant.

The hand grew firmer. I smelled Trudi's favorite perfume, a sweet but earthy Penhaligon scent that always evoked English rain. My fingers trembled as I took out the printed pages I had gathered. I showed the clerk the social media images of Alex pole-dancing unclothed. I showed him the screenshot Rosa had sent of Alex's party invitation. I told him about calling the police to come break up a party filled with underage kids drinking and taking drugs.

His face tightened very slightly but was otherwise neutral.

I mentioned that Alex hit me and that she used my email account to excuse her absences from school. I showed the photographs of the hidden paraphernalia and substances in her bedroom. I explained the reasons for my conditions for her to live with me. Most of that was in our court documents, of course, except for the graphic images of Alex.

After a while, the clerk left.

As Marty led me out of the conference room, Alex was being led into a different conference room by her attorney, a pear-shaped older woman with curly gray hair and a soft face. The woman looked warm, matronly, and compassionate—the exact opposite of George's super slick atomic bomb attorney. I was glad to see that; for all her bravado and rage, Alex had an innate tenderness that needed protecting.

"Mom!" Alex exclaimed. She'd been crying. Her face was red and swollen and her voice was hoarse.

"Alex," I cried, and I barreled over to her and wrapped my arms around her.

We clung to each other fiercely for a long moment. Then Alex's attorney gently called for Alex.

———~———

We waited a long time before coming before the judge. At every moment, I wanted to give up. I felt sick to my stomach. I worked hard to suppress the waves of nausea that contorted my gut. Just when it became more than I could bear, the invisible hand would settle on my shoulder.

George made several appearances, crisscrossing the waiting area and conference rooms with his officious pack of attorneys, chief among them being the Genghis Khan/Attila the Hun guy whose hostname had been on my gallery website.

George was twitchy with nerves. He studiously avoided looking at me, except for one time when our gazes crossed. His lip curled and he turned cherry red from his collar to the widow's peak in his fair hair. I figured his blood pressure had shot up and wondered if he was on medication yet for hypertension.

I didn't care if he knew I was watching him so I continued to do so. George looked as he always did, like the Upper Crust Yankee he was, the spitting image of his Upper Crust Yankee father. All five brothers bore a striking resemblance to their dad and to each other; it was a much-commented-upon, frequently-jested-over Calhoun trademark.

At fifty-one, George looked worn. He had heavy bags under his eyes and deep lines engraved into his cheeks and forehead. He wasn't wearing his age like Carl did, with casual ease and a kind of offhand elegance. George just looked like an angry guy getting on in his fifties.

What was George doing with this eternal vendetta against me? Didn't he have better things to do with his time and money and energy? Life was too precious to waste in a quest for vengeance. What was George thinking, that 'Here lies George Daniel Calhoun who sued his first wife five times' would be engraved on his tombstone?

Obviously, the suit was partly about money, because George hated paying child support. It seemed to be both insult and injury to him. If he took away all my parental rights along with our custody arrangements then he wouldn't have to pay any more. But still, the Calhouns were loaded, and George himself was successful. The lawsuit had to be costing him nearly a year's worth of child support. Money was symbolic of something else.

All at once, I felt sorry for George. I didn't know how it happened except that it was a completely unearned and unexpected grace. I felt sorry for the empty man seeking to fill himself with aggression toward his first wife. His hate kept him locked into me. Even though he was married and I was twice divorced; even though he had seduced our children to his side with his money and his privileged, self-congratulatory family; even though my gallery was failing and he was still a rich lawyer from an uber-rich family with a beach compound in the exclusive, old money part of Rhode Island, I still felt sorry for him, because I had moved on in my life. I was finding 'yes,' as painful as it was—and it was excruciating. George, however, was stuck in a tantrum of 'no.'

Dr. Maitra always insisted that contempt masked fear. George treated me with a superabundance of contempt, a continuous, never-ending tsunami of the stuff. If my cherished shrink was right, and he usually was, then George was dog paddling in a sea of fear as big as the Pacific Ocean.

Fear I understood. Fear haunted me, too. Fear of Alex getting hurt, or worse, on one of her drug binges kept me up at night. Fear of Dani feeling abandoned and psychologically hurt, even though she had been the one to sever our bond, worried me in my dreams. Fear of not selling enough paintings kept me scrambling in my gallery. That fear, in fact, was prompting me to close my gallery and seek another position with a steadier income. Next week, when the dreadful court date was over, I was starting in that direction. It was a bend in the path I had planned for myself. But life did not always go as planned, and somehow I had evolved enough to heed life's changes despite my fear, to trust in the cycles of life, and to adapt.

I knew that my pity for George belonged to me alone. No magical thinking fooled me into thinking that my pity would soften him. No matter how sorry I felt for George, he was going to pursue his own agenda of hate and aggression as long as it suited him.

———～———

We sat there all day and finally marched in to see the judge shortly before the courthouse was due to close, which it had to do on time, due to budgetary constraints. George strode in with his pack of attorneys, Marty and I went in, and Alex's attorney came in. Alex was a minor so she did not enter the courtroom.

Marty spoke in his usual measured and persuasive way, while George's attorney attacked my character with great bluster and force. He called me "willful" and "impetuous" and all sorts of other terms designed to make me out to be a mentally deficient child of about seven-years-old.

The judge sent us out at precisely four o'clock, wondering aloud why we couldn't come to an agreement among ourselves for the benefit of the child.

# CHAPTER THIRTY-NINE

I GOT UP ON Christmas Day and saw the single box under my shabby little tree, and resolved not to burst into tears.

The box was from Trudi and Robert. It was not wrapped; it was just a plain brown parcel that contained authentic English candy: Jelly Babies, Flakes, and Double Deckers. I loved them so Trudi always sent them to me when she travelled to England. Robert had addressed the package and mailed it, but there was no question about its contents.

There were no gifts from my children under the tree. Last year, Dani had snubbed me but Alex had celebrated with me and given me a basket of lotions and scents from L'Occitane while Santa Claus—meaning me—had left several presents under the tree for her.

This year, a few days ago, I had dropped off gifts for them at their father's building, giving each of them a colorful cashmere sweater and a basket of high-end skin-care products. Neither daughter bothered to remember me.

It was about seven in the morning and Beatrice, who had mysteriously taken to sleeping in bed with me, wanted to go out. I put Beatrice in her crate, brushed my teeth and washed my face, threw on warm clothes, and took her down to do her business. We came back and I made coffee and fed her and then ate my bowl of granola. I took the box from Trudi, tucked Beatrice under my arm, and went to get Brigit.

Only a few cars dotted the New York Thruway on that chilly Christmas morning. I made it to the Shawangunk Ridge in record time. Beatrice managed not to pee in the car and she let loose in the Warwarsing parking lot. I put her on her leash and we walked up onto the carriage trail. I brought the box with me.

It wasn't quite nine yet and no one was out, not even the extreme climbers. The temperature was slightly above freezing, but not windy. It was cold enough to outline the trees in a thin band of blue-white radiance, but not so frigid as to be unbearable. There hadn't yet been snow that winter so the ground wasn't wet or icy, though white mist threaded around the scree.

For a tiny dog, Beatrice was nimble and game. She was happy to be outdoors. She frisked around my feet until I took off the leash and let her race around in circles. She kept close and followed when I turned off the main carriage path onto a narrower trail. She climbed right alongside me as I scrambled up onto a large flat boulder abutting a sycamore tree with smooth, whitish bark. I drew my knees up against my chest to stay warm and Beatrice lay down beside me.

The sun, shedding a milky light, rose higher, and despite its pallor burned off some of the fog. Tree branches were stark and bare, the sky was pearlescent dove gray, and my breath made billows of white in the air. I was glad to be wearing my thickest warm stocking hat, a leftover from the days I was married to George and had the money to ski. Beatrice scooted closer to me, wedging her body under the crook of my knees between my feet and my bottom.

I thought wistfully of Dani and Alex and I sent them my love from the deepest, truest part of my heart.

After a while, I opened the parcel and took out the Jelly Babies. They tasted like elderberry jam and sugar. Beatrice put her front paws up on my knee and begged. I gave her one, but only one, because even if Jelly Babies weren't as dangerous for dogs as chocolate, they certainly couldn't be good for her.

Beatrice chewed and chewed and then coughed it up.

I wondered what Scott was doing. Was he with his children? How did they celebrate the holiday? Or was it Lisa's day with the kids and Scott was spending time with that girl, the investment banker?

I dug into a bag of licorice allsorts and picked out the nonpareils to eat.

A trio of scrawny deer tiptoed past the boulder. They flicked their ears at Beatrice, who watched them in fascination, her black eyes glittering. Turkey vultures and hawks winged overhead and a couple of crows cawed as they settled into a nearby tree. It was a peaceful moment. Some tears drained out from my eyes and down my face.

In that space of woods and creatures, I was free to disassemble myself into component parts. Sad self, scared self, angry self, sarcastic self. Reactive self. Nasty-letter-writing self. Rejected self. Projected-upon self. Resolute self. Survivor self. Happy self, peaceful self, creative self. Business self. Friendship self. Frisky self. Over the last year, I had seen more faces of my self than I had imagined possible. I understood that to be a gift that felt like something else, something far less beneficent.

The freedom of rocks and trees and animals seeped into the selves. All of them, the parts of me and the parts of nature, floated together like flotsam and jetsam on an ocean whose name I couldn't speak. It was all just an inclusive expanse that made my heart pump warmly. It was all love. This was the gift my life had given me: the opportunity to love all of it. All of myself. Even what hurt.

After a while, my fingers and toes felt numb. I stood up, clapped my gloved hands and stamped my feet, feeling light-headed from eating sugar on an empty stomach. Beatrice jumped straight upward, boinging like a spring, eager to be on our way. I laughed and decided to drive to the deli at the foot of the mountain.

---

During the week between Christmas and New Year's Day, Jim Harte phoned me at mid-day at the gallery. He said the show was on and the opening date was March 1. He made it clear that his neck was on the line and that I'd better deliver the most fabulous, popular show in the history of the New Britain art museum, or he'd hunt me down and make me pay.

I told him not to worry and reminded him that I was doing it for free.

"Free? Hah! You're doing it purely as self-promotion," Jim returned, a bit grumpily. "This show is to demonstrate what you can do, so someone will hire your sorry ass when your gallery closes. It also escalates the price value of your ex-husband's paintings. This isn't something you're doing for charity, out of the goodness of your heart. This is pure calculation. Gotta say, I like it."

"Jim," I said, giggling, "Have I told you that you're a super genius?"

"Not today," he replied. "I'm willing to hear it. You should just come work for me at the museum. Then you can flatter me all the time."

"No, but I'll put up an amazing show," I promised.

I was about to call Clif and share the most excellent news when my cell phone played "Love is a Battlefield." Marty was calling.

"Marty!" I exclaimed.

"Sarah, Happy New Year," he started.

"Marty, just tell me. Is there news?"

"The judge dismissed their case. Without prejudice, whatever that means."

"Dismissed it?" I gasped. I sat there trembling.

"Yes, dismissed it. I know this isn't the time," Marty said, "so I'll call you after the holidays and tell you a really good joke I heard. Be well, Sarah. I hope you can relax and enjoy yourself."

He hung up.

I sat there with the phone in my hand, considering my next move. There would be no contrition from Alex, no apology, no agreement to meet my conditions. I knew that as surely as I knew my own name because I knew my daughter. Alex loved me but she was too steeped in her father's contempt toward me and his need to devalue me and everything I believed in to surrender to my terms. She would not be coming home. I closed the gallery and went home immediately, not caring about the possibility of lost foot traffic.

Sure enough, an hour later, a text came in from Alex: "I need my stuff."

I packed up everything in Alex's room and took it downstairs to the lobby of my building. Then I texted her back: "Your belongings are waiting for you in my lobby."

By then it was dark and cold. I was about to order in Thai food but remembered I still hadn't told Clif the news about the show at the New Britain Art Museum. He was so over-the-moon ecstatic that he invited me out for dinner and drinks—Nicole's treat.

I stumbled back home at nearly ten at night and tossed off my coat onto the floor. Mrs. Zlotowitz knocked on my door as soon as it was closed behind me. I opened it, weaving on my feet. Nicole was generous with the champagne. I was happy for Clif that he'd found a rich woman to take care of him—a rich and generous woman. I was happy that I finally had some things to celebrate.

I said, "Yes, Mrs. Z? Everything OK?"

"I just wanted to tell you I saw your daughter earlier today. She was with her father," Mrs. Z said.

I wiped a hand over my face and summoned all the sobriety I could. "She was picking up her stuff?"

Mrs. Zlotowitz nodded. "She kept saying, 'I can't believe mom is doing this, I can't believe mom is kicking me out.' She said it over and over." The old lady shrugged and backed away from my door. "But I saw all those times she was smoking outside on the sidewalk. I saw all those times she came home and she was messed up. A few times during the day when she should have been in school, I saw her in the park with her friends, doing things they shouldn't have been doing. I think you did the right thing, Sarah. You're going to walk Beatrice, right? I stopped in earlier to take her down but I'm sure she has to go again." She left waving.

I groaned and picked up my coat, because even drunk, I fulfilled my responsibilities.

———

Toward the end of January, a colleague of Trudi's at Barnard called to invite me to their memorial service for Trudi, which was happening the following week. She said that Trudi's husband was invited, but he was still in England. She asked if I wanted to speak. Of course I did. She relayed the information regarding the service.

It had been three weeks since Marty had called with the news of the judge's dismissal. I hadn't heard a peep out of Alex. Or George. Or Dani, of course, but that I expected. I waited until the day before the service and then texted the details to Alex. "In case u want to say goodbye to ur godmother," I concluded. I didn't bother to copy the text to Dani because Alex had told me a while ago that Dani disliked Trudi; it was part of Dani's rejection of me. If I contacted Dani with the information she would just ignore it and I would be hurt both because Dani didn't respond and because she was shunning Trudi and dismissing her death. It wasn't worth the pain of extending myself to Dani; I felt Trudi's loss too keenly.

In the middle of the night, the phone rang. Beatrice, asleep on my neck, jumped up and whined. I shuffled her to the side and picked up the phone groggily.

It was Alex, sobbing.

"Shhh, Alex, please," I murmured. "Are you OK? What's going on?"

"I can't believe Aunt Trudi died," she said. She was weeping and incoherent. She let loose a steady stream of words, some that made sense, others that were just a stream of random babble.

*What have you been taking?* I wondered. I did my best to soothe her. I told her that Trudi had loved her and believed in her.

Finally, apropos of nothing in our conversation, she said, "Do you know why I sued you?"

I was sitting upright by this time. I gripped the phone harder. "No. Why?"

"You have to promise you won't tell anyone, Mom," she sobbed. "Promise. I'm not supposed to tell you."

"Out with it, Alex," I said. "Just tell me."

"Dad told me he'd get me my own apartment in New York if I did," she wept. "Dani got a car. I was going to get my own apartment."

*OK*, I thought.

*OK. Of course.*

For a moment I could barely breathe. The complete venality of George bribing Alex with an apartment, and of Alex's accepting, left me shocked and airless. I could hear in my head Chloe saying, *"What happened to you wasn't an accident."*

Struggling for composure, I said hoarsely, "Alex, come home. Go back to drug rehab and sign the medical consent form. Attend all your classes without skipping any. Get a job. Come home and do these things, they will help you. I will help you."

She sniffled as if she was considering it but I didn't think she really was. Alex was going to follow the path of least resistance. It was her father telling her to do whatever she wanted. She said, "No" and hung up.

# CHAPTER FORTY

IT WAS THE FIRST of February and the day of the memorial for Trudi. I put on a charcoal skirt suit and a black silk knit top and topped it off with a hat that Trudi had given me—a purple straw side sweep festooned with silk organza and a velvet flower. It had a deep amethyst hue and sported a wide, saucy brim. I wouldn't say it was a hat noticeable from the International Space Station but neither was it a hat that could be overlooked. Trudi would approve.

I jotted notes on index cards that I tucked into my purse and set off for Barnard College.

The memorial was being held in Lehman Auditorium in Altschul Hall. Students were already milling about in the lobby when I arrived; I went past them into the auditorium, which was a well-appointed lecture and screening room with graduated seating. A group of professors stood around the lectern. A young woman, who was probably an assistant professor, unpacked a stack of programs with Trudi's name and photograph printed on the cover. I shook hands with Trudi's co-workers whom I recognized and introduced myself to those I didn't. There were plentiful hugs and murmured words of condolence, not just given to me, but given by me to tearful professors young and old, male and female, who missed our dear colleague and friend. Trudi had been at Barnard for more than twenty years. She was a beloved fixture at the school.

The service was scheduled for four o'clock and the doors opened at a quarter to four. Students streamed in. I stood down by the lectern behind a cluster of people reminiscing about Trudi in solemn tones.

A tall dark-haired man came in with the tide of students. It was Scott, wearing a crimson knit beanie hat. As he took a seat near the front, I saw that the hat was emblazoned with a pair of oars and the letter "H."

He looked well and he looked good, and my heart sang to see him. He was a sphere of light in the solemn dusk of the auditorium. He shrugged off his wool overcoat without seeming to notice the admiring glances of the girls around him.

I wondered how I had gone a single day without talking to him. Without holding him. *What was I thinking?*

I got out my cell phone and thought for a moment, then texted, "Hey Harvard, at 38, u r too old to say what u got on ur SAT's."

He was putting his cell phone into his jacket pocket as he seated himself, but took it back out and glanced at the screen. He smiled and tilted his head for a moment, thinking.

I couldn't quite read his expression or his thoughts from that distance. I stepped behind the group to make myself less visible so he couldn't read mine and waited for his text to come in.

My phone chimed.

"E and pi" read the text.

*What the hell?*

I looked up and saw Scott standing and looking around the room. I stepped out but his glance passed by me—the purple hat was *so* not Sarah —then returned to me. I held up my hand in greeting.

Scott nodded, the antennae standing straight up on his head.

It was four o'clock and a lit theory professor gestured for me to take a seat in one of the chairs set up on one side of the lectern. On the other side, a chamber music quartet was set up; the cellist and the violinist were tuning their instruments.

I sat alongside a host of professors and several students who were slated to speak. The service was going to be a lengthy affair, as befitted Trudi's standing and popularity.

Scott was watching me and I gave him a subdued smile and a small shrug. He set his cell phone on his lap—a downward slope from his knees to his thighs, because of the length of his legs—and texted something.

The text read, "Are you ok?"

I texted back, "I miss her. U ok?"

He looked up, met my eyes and nodded, then focused on his phone.

My phone chimed. "Nice hat. Very purple."

I replied, "E and pi??"

"Irrational numbers. Necessary for computation."

I looked up, rolled my eyes, and he grinned widely, pleased with himself.

I typed, "Ur a math nerd. I m in love with a math nerd. Dear god."

Scott dropped his phone.

It made me smile in a way that was altogether inappropriate for a memorial service, except that I knew that Trudi, wherever she was in the ever-changing matrix of the ethers, or in the Elysian Fields, or in the world to come, would be happy if I were happy. I could be happy with Scott. I could even be happy babysitting his children. Sometimes, not as a regular job.

My phone chimed. "Don't play with me."

I replied, "Purple hat comes with sometime babysitter, if ur still interested."

Trudi had been the chair of the art history department, and her successor rose and held up her hands calling the service to order. The Barnard chaplain stood beside her, waiting to lead a prayer.

Scott was leaning forward, texting intensely.

My phone chimed. "Sometime babysitter, full time partner???"

I texted back, "Yes." Then I turned off my ringer and made a small show of bending down to place my cell phone in my purse, which was tucked beneath my chair.

The Barnard chaplain invoked his God with palpable reverence. There was a moment during the prayer when a piercing, sweet sobriety descended on the audience. It enveloped and united us all. It reminded me of the fullness that I had felt in the woods, except that it wasn't about nature and me and all my selves.

It was about Trudi and about everyone in the auditorium and about our shared love for her and our shared grief over her loss. It was a powerful support for me.

For the first time, I understood that it was exactly what my bi-religious parents had wanted for me when they pressured me to choose a religion. It was never about controlling me. It was never about not accepting me. It was about the consolation of community and access to spirit. Psychological work in session would never be enough. There was another dimension that was crucial for wholeness, and I found it in the chaplain's prayer. I wept for Trudi and I thanked my parents.

Shortly before the end of the program, Scott slipped out of the auditorium. As soon as the art history chair concluded the service, I grabbed my purse and yanked my cell phone out. I didn't care about the reception with wine and cheese and hors d'oeuvres. I wanted to know what Scott wrote back.

"Work called," Scott had texted. "TBD."

I stayed at the reception far longer than I expected. Trudi's students wanted to talk to me; I was the stand-in for her family because Robert and Peter remained in England. The students and faculty loved my speech, which I began by introducing the purple hat independently, as an entity in its own right. I explained that it was Trudi's gift to me, eliciting chuckles because Trudi was known around campus for her hats. I recounted an argument with Trudi about Constructivist art that I had lost; an argument about marrying an artist that I had lost, because that marriage had, as Trudi foretold, not survived; and an argument about her staying in New York for more rounds of chemo that I had lost. I related that I had recently felt her with me and even smelled her perfume when I found myself in the scorching center of a personal crucible. The gist of my speech was that Trudi had a unique and precious distinctness that would stay with those of us who loved her.

I enjoyed their reminiscences. Her students told me how she had always listened to them; how she had advised them, often pithily, on their studies, their relationships, and their future careers. Her colleagues told me of Trudi's support during family crises and personal misfortunes. There were a lot of hugs. I finally escaped.

I got home and walked Beatrice, then went back upstairs and fed her before even removing my hat as she was whining and panting for her dinner.

The buzzer rang for the front door.

*Mrs. Zlotowitz or Scott?*

My heart sped up and thumped loudly, hoping it was Scott. I rushed to the door and peeked through the hole. At first, I couldn't see anything except a peachy blur. Then it centered and was still, and I discerned the written words: "I ... am ... not ... a ... narcissist."

I opened the door in bemusement.

Scott stood there with his coat and jacket slung across his arm. His shirt was unbuttoned and hanging open. The words were scrawled in thick black lettering across his chest, just below his nipples where his chest hair was sparser. I couldn't figure out how he positioned that area in front of the peephole.

Scott said, his voice unsteady, "Did you mean it? Did you mean what you said? About my kids? About me?"

I shrugged helplessly. "I like your kids, Scott. I can be there for them. Not every day, OK? But yes. Yes to you and to your kids."

He laid his hands on both sides of my face and kissed me. Then he released me and strode through my door.

Staring at his chest, I exclaimed, "Tell me that's not a tattoo!"

"Sharpie," Scott said. He reached into his jacket pocket and held up a black marker.

"Did Trudi put you up to that?" I reached for him but he grabbed my hands.

He said firmly, "We have to talk."

"Not that again," I said ominously, then I giggled because it felt so dizzyingly good to have Scott in my apartment.

Even if he insisted on talking.

"I tried to drown my sorrows, but the bastards learned how to swim, and now I am overwhelmed by this decent and good feeling," Frida Kahlo said. I understood her words in a new way, with the twist of my own life. My sorrows were still present, *and* they were swimming in the good feeling. It was a both/and phenomenon.

Scott touched his chest and made a thoughtful face. He trotted into my kitchen and called, "You can jump me later."

"I'm not going to jump you."

"Yes, you are, but I'm going to clean this off first. And we have to talk." He put the marker down on the table, set down his coat and jacket, and then slipped off his shirt and hung it over the back of a chair. Making himself at home in my kitchen, he wet a paper towel, squirted dish soap on it, and scrubbed at his chest. "About a week before she died, Mrs. Waterston called me from England. She claimed that you would commit only to a man who had this written on his chest."

I thought of a thousand things to say to him, but Scott had his own agenda about the conversation. I could give that to him. I picked up the Sharpie and examined it. "Scott, this is a permanent marker. It won't come off with dish soap."

Scott scrubbed harder and the paper towel frayed on his chest hair. "I thought I'd hear from you before today."

I plucked a dish towel out of my drawer and dampened it, then took a bottle of rubbing alcohol out from underneath the sink. I poured some alcohol onto the towel. "Try this."

He threw the paper towel pieces into the sink and took the towel from me.

I said, "I wanted to talk to you every day."

"So?"

"So there was a process ... Trudi dying. I was in court because of Alex. I'm not taking the job at the New Britain Art Museum but I'm curating a show for them. And I'm asking around about a job in the city and making preparations to close the gallery."

"How did the court appearance go?" He was perusing my face carefully.

"The judge dismissed their case." I leaned close to his chest; the word 'am' was slightly, but definitely, lightened. "I think the alcohol is working. Maybe nail polish remover would work better. I have acetone."

"I don't want you to feel unsafe with me, so I came up with a ten-point plan for us to deal with the age gap," Scott informed me. "But only if you're serious about being with me. Did you break up with that guy?"

"Carl. Yes, we ended things before Christmas."

He stared at me and froze the way he did sometimes and asked breathlessly, "And my kids? You can deal with them?"

"I already said yes."

He leaned down and kissed me swiftly and hard on my lips.

I wanted to pull him back into me but I laid my hand on his arm and asked, "What about Kelly?"

"That ended right around Christmas," Scott admitted. He rubbed the 'not a.' "She didn't have much of a sense of humor."

*What do you expect from an investment banker, pool boy?*

"Acetone, definitely," I said. I turned to go to my bedroom and fetch it. Scott followed me. I said, "I have chemicals I use when I'm cleaning or repairing a painting, but I think those will be too harsh on your skin."

"I like that hat on you," Scott said. "Purple. Wow."

"Oh right," I murmured. I unpinned the hat from my hair and tossed it onto my dresser. I went into my bathroom and got the acetone from the cabinet. I handed Scott a fresh washcloth. "Here. Wash yourself with water before you put on the acetone."

"That was a beautiful speech you gave for Mrs. Waterston," he said softly, holding to the washcloth under the faucet. "She would have liked it."

"Yeah," I said. I slumped down for a moment.

*Trudi.*

My heart hurt. I took a deep breath to release it then I tugged playfully at his belt. "The ink will come off faster if you take off your pants."

"You have to hear my ten point plan first. Then you can take off my pants."

"If you insist." I kicked off my good pumps so I could stand comfortably. "Shoot."

"One, I let myself go, and you don't." Scott poured acetone on the washcloth and started scrubbing.

"Don't do that, pool boy, I love your body," I said, in a frankly admiring tone. I leaned forward and put my hand on his taut belly.

Scott smiled. "It wasn't my favorite strategy. Two, you keep taking care of yourself, doing yoga and whatever else you do to work out, you can even run with me, and you stop being neurotic and caring about the age difference. This stings." He held the washcloth away from his chest.

"Probably because you mixed the rubbing alcohol and the acetone and dish soap," I said. "Number two isn't going to work because my neurotic self has staked out some prime real estate in my soul and isn't going to vacate the premises. Not entirely."

"Can't you just get some psychotherapy so you're not so nutty about it?"

I laughed and groaned and my eyes welled up with tears. "Don't you think I'm working on myself? Am I really so unacceptable as I am?"

"No, Sarah, damn it," Scott knelt in front of me. "I accept you exactly as you are! I'm just screwing this up. Don't you see? I'm going to screw this up." He threw down the washcloth and pried my hands off my face so he could peer into my eyes. He held on to my wrists and gripped them tightly, but not so hard it hurt. His dark eyes crossed slightly; we were at that distance from each other. The acetone was smearing the ink on his chest but the words were still legible.

I wanted to laugh and I wanted to cry and he was serious and present and vulnerable.

He knelt before me with an open heart. He said, "You have to stick, anyway. I'm going to screw this up, *and* you have to stick. That's the deal."

*That's the best offer I've had in forever.*

I slipped my wrists out of his grasp and put my arms around him. "I'm going to screw this up, too."

Scott picked me up and carried me into my bedroom and laid me on the bed. He stretched out alongside me. For a moment we lay side by side, facing each other, caressing and stroking.

"I can help you with your daughters. Alex and your older daughter," he said. "Mrs. Waterston was upset about their relationships with you. She asked me to help you."

"Dani and Alex," I murmured. "You can't help with them."

"I can talk to them," he said. "We can do family counseling."

"I love that you want to. But only Dani can help Dani, and only Alex can help Alex. They have to want to have a good relationship with me. That's on them." There was an ache in my chest as I heard myself surrender to knowing that: I could only love them. I couldn't choose for them to be in a relationship with me, even though they were my children, my precious, beloved children whom I had borne and raised. They had to choose for themselves. I hoped they would. With every angstrom of my being, I prayed that they would come back to me. I wasn't going to stop living my life while I waited for them to do so.

"We'll see," he said. He was bare-chested and he unbuttoned my shirt. "I'm spending the night. I want a drawer. Or two."

"Yes," I said. "Yes."

"Janey and Max are with Lisa this weekend. I want us to spend it together. We could go out of town. I'll be a lot less available for work if we do that. I can be present for you."

"Let me take you upstate," I suggested. "I go hiking in the Shawangunk Ridge. I'd like to share that with you." I had a flash of Scott sitting beside me on the big gray boulder beside the sycamore tree. I sensed that he would enjoy the place and tap into its magic.

"Hiking. Sounds good," he said. He rolled closer to me and put his arms around me so his hands could unzip my skirt. "I'll bring chocolate."

"Just bring yourself," I said. "All of you."

# THE END

# Acknowledgements

I am grateful to all those who have encouraged and supported me along the way.

Many thanks to Susan Dalsimer for the expert help.

Many thanks to Brandi Doan McCann for the gorgeous cover.

Thank you to Roxanne Rhoads for the book blog tour.

Thank you to Gerda and Mark Swearengen, Michelle Czernin, Ying Li and Weidong Huang, Stuart Gartner, Mark Weaver and Fred Nadler, Linda Hillebrand, Komilla Sutton, Marc Tsavaris, Tom Farina and George Frost, Debra Jaliman, and Dr. Bill Chambers.

I am grateful to my early readers who gave thoughtful feedback: Ashley Perkins, Paul Brothe, Megan Gibson, and Melissa Cain.

Thank you and I love you to Madeleine Howard, Julia Howard, and Jessica Hendel.

Thank you most of all to Sabin, to whom I say: Yes! Always.

# Books by Traci L. Slatton

*Immortal*

*Broken*

*Fallen*

*Cold Light*

*Far Shore*

*Blood Sky*

*The Love of My (Other) Life*

*Dancing in the Tabernacle* (poetry)

*Piercing Time & Space*

*The Art of Life* (with Sabin Howard)

*The Botticelli Affair*

*El Inmortal*

*Caido*

*How to Write, Publish and Market Your Book, Yourself Independently*

*El amor de mi (otra) vida*

# About the author

Traci L. Slatton is a graduate of Yale and Columbia. She lives in Manhattan, and her love for Renaissance Italy inspired her historical novel *Immortal* (BantamDell). *Broken* is a historical novel set in Occupied Paris from 1939-1942. Also the author of novels *The Botticelli Affair, Fallen, Cold Light, Far Shore, Blood Sky,* and *The Love of My (Other) Life,* Slatton has published *The Art of Life,* a photo essay about figurative sculpture; *Dancing in the Tabernacle,* a book of poetry; and *Piercing Time & Space,* a non-fiction title on science and spirituality.

See www.tracilslatton.com for news and updates.

www.ingramcontent.com/pod-product-compliance
Lightning Source LLC
Chambersburg PA
CBHW060945030726
47503CB00003B/740